The Vanishing Angle

Books by Linda Ladd

Claire Morgan Homicide Thrillers

Head to Head
Dark Places
Die Smiling
Enter Evil
Remember Murder
Mostly Murder
Bad Bones

Claire Morgan Investigations Series

Devil Dead
Gone Black
Fatal Game

Will Novak Novels

Bad Road to Nowhere
Say Your Goodbyes
Witness Betrayed
The Devil's Work
The Vanishing Angle

The Vanishing Angle

A Will Novak Novel

Linda Ladd

LYRICAL UNDERGROUND
Kensington Publishing Corp.
www.kensingtonbooks.com

LYRICAL UNDERGROUND BOOKS are published by

Kensington Publishing Corp.
119 West 40th Street
New York, NY 10018

All Kensington titles, imprints, and distributed lines are available at special quantity discounts for bulk purchases for sales promotion, premiums, fund-raising, educational, or institutional use.

Special book excerpts or customized printings can also be created to fit specific needs. For details, write or phone the office of the Kensington Sales Manager: Kensington Publishing Corp., 119 West 40th Street, New York, NY 10018. Attn. Sales Department. Phone: 1-800-221-2647.

First Electronic Edition: December 2019
ISBN-13: 978-1-5161- 0741-4(ebook)
ISBN-10: 1-5161-0741-1 (ebook)

First Print Edition: December 2019
ISBN-13: 978-1-5161-0744-5
ISBN-10: 1-5161-0744-6

Printed in the United States of America

Chapter 1

One late afternoon on the ides of October, Will Novak tied up the *Sweet Sarah*, the forty-foot Jeanneau Sun Odyssey sailboat that he had ordered custom-made several years back. Novak was a big man at six feet six inches and two hundred and forty pounds, and needed everything aboard to accommodate his size, at least as much as could be done in the confines of a sailboat. He'd made sure he got a bunk long enough for his legs, which had been his main objective.

Novak had put in earlier that morning at the big marina on the Potomac River several miles south of Washington, D.C. He'd spent a couple of hours scrubbing the salty brine from the blue-and-white hull and battening things down nice and tight before he showered and dressed for his dinner date with Lori Garner. They'd been together for a while now, but she had recently taken a job with the Department of Defense, so he had sailed east to spend some time with her.

Securing the cover of the hatch, he shivered from the chill wind sweeping in off the river. He pulled on a black windbreaker over his blue dress shirt, not yet used to East Coast autumn weather. The temperature had been in the seventies when he'd sailed down the wide and sluggish Bayou Bonne that edged the back of the old Louisiana plantation house he'd inherited from his mother on the day he was born. He had sailed the deep royal blue waters of the Gulf of Mexico in sight of the white beaches before he'd turned and entered the Intracoastal Waterway to Norfolk, Virginia, and then out into the magnificent Chesapeake Bay. Motoring up the Potomac took forever, but it was a beautiful experience with mile after mile of wooded shores, the dark scarlet of giant oaks, and the golden splendor of maples, all glorious to behold, a vivid patchwork quilt that glowed brilliant under the bright sun.

Zipping his jacket, he looked up at the buildings above him, now lit up in the growing darkness and bustling with tourists. He was in National Harbor, Maryland, just south of Washington, a favorite spot for tourists to stay outside the crazy traffic and expensive hotels inside the Beltway. He glanced around the boat, giving it one last visual check. It was battened down tight, all his homemade alarm systems in place, a habit he'd found necessary after he'd become a private investigator and made some enemies that harbored long memories. Novak walked across the dock, glad to be back on solid ground again. They were to meet at a steakhouse he'd suggested to her, one not too far away in northern Virginia. He'd found it when he had spent some time working at the Navy Yard in D.C. That was before he'd joined his SEAL team and been deployed to the Middle East. The Back Alley Grill would take about an hour's drive, but it would be worth it. They served the biggest and best T-bone steaks that he'd ever eaten in that little hole-in-the-wall restaurant. He and Lori had met not long ago on a case where they'd worked to put a crooked Galveston judge in prison. They had liked each other instantly, becoming friends and then lovers.

Lori Garner was a veteran like him, having worked as an MP in battle zones and later as a sniper because of her skill with a rifle. But it was her experience and training in IT work that was most in demand. After she'd opted out, she and Novak had worked some cases together while his PI partner, Claire Morgan, was off on maternity leave. A few months ago, she had given birth to the most beautiful little girl whom she and her husband, Nicholas, had christened Olivia Rachel Black. He'd spent the last few months there with them at Lake of the Ozarks in Missouri while recuperating from a gunshot blast to his side that had nearly killed him. Lori had stayed in a cabin with him on that beautiful quiet cove, nursing him back to health and putting up with his foul moods at being confined so long. She had taken this new job almost a month ago.

Now as he climbed the path to the street, he realized how excited he was to spend time with her. The job at the Pentagon had been unexpected. Her training and expertise with computers and programming had made her invaluable to her former Commander. When he had been promoted to a one star and assigned to the Pentagon, he'd immediately requested her to re-opt and work for him, if only temporarily while he got acclimated to his new position. She had agreed to help him set up a new office, but only planned to stay until things evened out.

Novak hoped that was still her plan, but wasn't so sure it would be. She loved the new work. Her voice was always eager and excited when she told him about her day. Novak was fairly certain she would stay on. That decision was good for her career, but bad for Novak. His gut told him that she would hit him with that news tonight. He couldn't and wouldn't stand in her way. She was good at what she did, and she was a woman who knew her own mind. That's what he liked most about her.

Novak passed lots of tourists, mostly families with young children running out ahead of them. Everyone seemed to be having a great time. He was ready to do the same. The street was lined with bustling restaurants and pricey boutiques. There were several condominiums up on the hill above the river. On his left, a giant Ferris wheel was silhouetted against the darkening dusk, flashing red and blue and green geometric patterns against the night sky. He could hear distant screams from those in the swinging cars stopped up top. They could probably see the Washington Monument from that high, maybe even the Capitol dome.

Novak did not plan on going into the city while there, no way. He'd had enough of the traffic in that place to last him a lifetime. He hoped Lori had picked out a nice quiet Bed and Breakfast somewhere out in Virginia near the steakhouse. Two weeks out there with Lori all to himself sounded damn good.

The Uber driver was waiting inside a black Cadillac at the next intersection. The woman was an African-American who looked about forty but was probably older. When he tapped on her window, she climbed out in a hurry and greeted him in a friendly but professional manner. She identified herself as Mrs. Betsy McClelland. She asked him about luggage, but he held up the black nylon backpack that he always carried with him in case of emergencies. It had his clothes for the weekend, as well as burner phones, water, energy bars, GPS vehicle trackers, and medical supplies. He'd learned to always be prepared while with the SEALs and later as a PI. That little precaution had saved his life more than once. He never left home without it. He climbed into the front passenger seat and placed his bag on the floor at his feet.

McClelland asked for his destination and read it into her vehicle's GPS. Novak waited, rubbing absently at the thick scar tissue across the left side of his waist. The wound was practically healed now but still ached some. The cooler temperature didn't help. Briefly he relived that existential moment in the Guatemalan jungle when the man he'd tracked there had pulled the trigger on a .357 magnum. The slug had knocked Novak off his feet, and he hadn't remembered much after that until he'd regained consciousness in a hospital bed in Guatemala City. He'd been lucky. A few inches higher and the bullet would have exploded his chest cavity. Yep, Novak was lucky to be alive. That kind of near-death experience made a man consider his life choices. The recovery had been a long, hellish ordeal, but he was better now, almost back to his old self.

Novak didn't encourage conversation on the drive, and the lady didn't force any. She did tell him that the Back Alley Grill was the best place around and their T-bone steaks melted in your mouth like butter. He told her that he already knew that, and then asked her about the six little kids in the photograph on the dash. She said they were her grandchildren—a seventh was on the way. He told her she looked too young for grandchildren, to which she scoffed and then laughed. She asked no questions about his life, and the rest of the drive was silent. He liked her immensely.

The Back Alley Grill was in a nondescript huddle of buildings not far past White Oak, Virginia. The rural highway where they ended up was practically deserted, all the work-weary commuters on the Interstates headed out of D.C. Lori had texted on the drive with news that she'd booked them into a private cottage at a B&B south of Fredericksburg so it would be an easy drive after dinner. Apparently, Betsy McClelland knew the route by heart, and in no time the little cluster of red-bricked buildings around the famous restaurant appeared seemingly out of nowhere. It was an old center that had catered to farmers in the old days. The street was lined by those ancient two-storied buildings that looked to be from the Civil War era, with raised wood sidewalks and tattered awnings and big plate-glass front windows. It appeared most shops were now empty. He hoped the steakhouse was still in operation.

Last time he'd visited, the same street had been bustling with people eating ice cream and playing video games in the arcades. Now it looked like a ghost town. They passed little traffic and no pedestrians until Betsy turned into the narrow alley that led to the restaurant. That's where the excitement began. Five vehicles were lined up between the brick buildings. People were walking up from the parking lot down at the far end of the alleyway. A group of diners crowded under the canopied entrance while others formed a line against one wall.

An attendant stood at the door, no doubt shooing away disappointed people without reservations. He was a big guy, maybe six feet and one or two inches, stocky and muscular but with a pudgy belly where anybody fighting him would punch him first. He was dressed like a trendy nightclub bouncer, wearing a black leather jacket with lots of unnecessary zippers and tight black jeans with leather boots. He was blond and used a lot of gel to make his hair stand up straight in a widow's peak. He was God in that alley, with his own red velvet rope suspended between metal posts to reinforce his power to choose.

Betsy braked and inched along with the other cars until they reached the doorman under his canopy. Novak thanked her, grabbed his backpack, and exited the car, and Betsy drove away, job well done and with a sizable tip. The minute he got out, his olfactory senses were hit with a smell that could only be described as heaven-sent. After weeks on the water enjoying his own cooking, his stomach reacted violently to the aroma of perfectly seasoned grilled beef. He'd had nothing to eat since that morning, and that was a bowl of cornflakes. His mouth watered.

Unlucky people who thought they could get a table without reservations stood subdued and patiently waiting, probably owing to the size of the bouncer. He eyed Novak and frowned. Tough guys gave Novak attitude because he was usually bigger and stronger than they were. This guy acted as if he were manning an official White House gala for important dignitaries. Novak ignored him and glanced around for famous faces out of the Beltway. He'd never eaten here without at least one or two politicians, lobbyists, or news anchors at nearby tables. He didn't see anybody of note. All Novak wanted was to get a table and order his steak.

The bouncer had to look up to Novak. He didn't like that, either. His plastic nameplate said Jack Casinger. Jack had broad shoulders and bulging arms that he kept folded across his chest. He looked Novak up and down as if gauging whether Novak was going to start a brawl. Novak hoped he didn't try to search him, as he was carrying concealed, a Kimber .45, just like he always did. Novak waited politely, then gave the guy the name on the reservation. Lori had been given permission to use her new boss's influence, which appeared to have significant pull with this guy. He acted suitably impressed and quickly swung open the door, standing back for Novak to enter.

The restaurant interior was more impressive than the alley outside. It was old-fashioned, a shabby-chic decor. It looked like an old tintype of some elegant restaurant where Abraham Lincoln would court Mary Todd at dinner. The lighting was subdued with replicas of gas-flamed chandeliers. Maroon-flocked wallpaper that looked soft to the touch festooned the walls behind booths covered with worn black leather. About twenty tables were positioned in the main room, each covered with pristine white linen and a flickering oil lamp. Most were full of customers, and the people looked happy. Two rooms opened off on each side, and could be glimpsed through velvet-curtained arches. The long mahogany bar at the back was crowded.

Behind the bar, murals made of beautiful stained glass depicted scenes inside a turn-of-the-century New York saloon. It didn't take long for an effusive, eager-to-please, but tired young hostess to come running, vellum menus in hand. At his request, she led him to a quiet table for two sitting inside a shallow alcove near the front door. Novak took the chair that placed his back to the wall and gave him a clear view of the room and front door. Old habits died hard, but they'd also kept him alive despite a few close calls. As he watched the other diners, an incoming text vibrated inside his pocket. He pulled out his cellphone. It was Lori, apprising him that she'd been delayed by a meeting lasting longer than expected. She told him to go ahead and order without her; she'd get there within the hour. Novak was hungry enough to go ahead, so he scanned the red-tasseled menu and ordered the biggest T-bone they had, medium rare and topped with the delectable butter-sautéed onions he remembered so well. The girl scribbled it all down in a hurry and smiled at him, as if she'd known what he wanted before he opened his mouth. Novak spent the wait studying the patrons sitting around him. He saw no familiar faces, but lots of couples and family units. Nobody paid attention to him, so he watched the outside door for Lori, his eagerness to see her embarrassing him somewhat.

The giant steak came out, covered with those onions and still sizzling on a hot metal serving dish, along with a second text from Lori telling him to go ahead and eat. She was about thirty minutes away. The place was still loud and busy with new groups continually being seated. Each time the front door opened, he looked up, expecting to see Lori.

This time it wasn't his date standing at the entrance. It was a young woman, quite young, probably not yet twenty. She had bleached her hair to a bizarre stark white shade with maybe four inches of jet-black roots showing. Her hair boasted the kinky, coiled-up kind of curls, like Shirley Temple's. It fell around her shoulders in a big bushy, unkempt mass. She was impossibly skinny, which of course was the fashion of the day, and she wore a pair of white jeans so tight that nothing was left to the imagination. She had either bought them ripped apart at the knees, or attacked them with scissors herself. Novak often wondered about the intelligence of the youth.

She had black tights underneath her jeans and brown fuzzy boots he vaguely recalled as "Uggs." Lori had a pair, or he wouldn't have had a clue. The woman's red-and-black, buffalo-plaid flannel shirt was unbuttoned, hanging open over a white T-shirt. More noticeably, she was absolutely strung out on some kind of illegal drug. It looked to Novak as if she were in the last stages of opioid withdrawal. Her eyes looked teary and tired and bloodshot, and she kept wiping her runny nose on the back of her shirtsleeve. She kept shivering and holding her stomach as if she had cramps. Her movements were jerky, and she looked ready to come apart at the seams. Novak put down his knife and fork, watching her for whatever was going to happen next, because something was definitely going to. Her eyes darted around nervously. She came off as frantic. He felt that if she didn't get a fix soon, she would start screaming and overturning tables.

There were two men with her, both also clad in flannel, one in green plaid, the other in blue plaid. They looked a bit older than her. They hemmed her in tight on both sides and looked like twin lumberjacks in a Paul Bunyan tale. Neither was tall, maybe around five feet nine or ten. Their brown hair was shaggy and uncut on their back of their necks, and they looked as if they were trying to grow beards, but without much luck. Their faces were tanned brown, and they both wore *I'll-slit-your-throat* expressions. He had a feeling they were well-acquainted with bar brawls and drunk tanks. They were either guarding her or controlling her—it was hard to tell.

Novak decided fairly quickly that it was the latter. He would also bet both those guys had concealed weapons, probably handguns in belt holsters tucked under all that worn flannel. The three young guests looked out of place beside the other patrons of the elegant eatery, in dress, demeanor, and state of mind. No one around seemed to notice the trio except for Novak, all continuing to eat and talk and sip wine. Novak wondered why the bouncer had let them in. She was obviously in bad shape and about to lose it. Novak's instincts for impending danger flamed up bigtime. These three young people were not there for a cut of steak. They were trouble waiting to happen.

Novak had been an NYPD detective for a couple of years before he'd joined the military. Now he had gone private. Those experiences made him savvy to the street. Something bad was about to happen. The young woman was in trouble. She looked ready to collapse as she scanned the tables, obviously looking for someone. Those big watery eyes were heavily blackened with eyeliner and eye shadow, reminiscent of the stark Cleopatra look. They darted from table to table, definitely searching for someone or something.

Novak pushed back his chair and got ready. Something would happen in the next few minutes. When her drug-addled eyes fixed on him, he met her stare and watched all manner of emotions flit across her face. There was fear behind that look, and what else? Shame? He lifted his glass and took a sip of beer without breaking eye contact. The other diners sat and ate, blithely unaware. The hostess was nowhere in sight; maybe she knew something about those three kids that Novak didn't. A lifetime of facing felons and criminals told him to be poised to act. Then the kinky-haired blonde junkie lifted her arm and pointed a forefinger directly at Novak. Novak put down his glass and waited. The two men approached him. The girl remained standing beside the door, looking terrified. That wasn't good, either. The Paul Bunyan clones stopped on either side of Novak's chair in a play to intimidate him. They kept their backs turned to the other customers. Two pairs of big brown eyes pinned him to the chair. Their pupils looked normal. They were not using drugs, at least not at the moment. The guy on his left carried a SIG M17. The other man had his hand resting on the butt of a Glock 19. Both weapons were outfitted with small silencers that looked homemade, yet another bad sign. Hick bullies and rednecks did not use silencers. They reveled in loud bangs.

"You don't have to get hurt or play the hero," the guy in green plaid finally said. He sported some patchy black scruff on his cheeks. His eyes, the color and size of black marbles, riveted on Novak's face. "Just come along outside with us, nice and quiet-like. Nobody gets hurt."

Novak sat unmoving. He felt it highly unlikely they would shoot him down inside a steakhouse in front of fifty witnesses, but they looked quite stupid, so they might. "Why don't you give me a good reason why I shouldn't finish my steak? What's your problem? I don't know you and I don't want to."

Novak's calm reply annoyed the second guy, the one with no facial scruff and a black knit watch cap pulled down over his ears. It looked out of place inside. His voice was low and gravelly, like Louis Armstrong's. "You stay in that chair, mister? Somebody's gonna get hurt bad."

"And that would be you two."

His remark appeared to startle them. They hazarded nervous glances at each other. Watch Cap tried to look tough. "See that pretty little girl standing over there by the door? Her life just might depend on what you do right now. Put that in your pipe, mister."

Novak shifted his attention to the strung-out teenager in the tight white pants. She was watching them, fingers fidgeting together, eyes darting everywhere as if expecting all hell to break loose. She needed a hit in the worst way. He didn't know her, was certain that he'd never laid eyes on her before. But she was in trouble, he knew that much.

Novak weighed his options. There weren't many. Things could go bad fast inside a crowded dining room, could escalate and explode in gunfire and collateral damage that might include small children. These young men were not mental giants, but they could bolster each other's courage and cause major injuries at the surrounding tables. "Okay, fellas, I'll bite. What's this all about?"

Scruff said, "Get up and walk outside with us. We don't want to hurt anybody."

Novak didn't really believe that. His own wellbeing was definitely in no man's land. Still, they were being civil, and he could take them both on any day of the week, especially if they didn't want to shoot up the place. They couldn't disarm him, anyway. He could disarm them both before they blinked. That's how green they were. He clicked off a mental list of possible outcomes. At the best, their altercation would escalate into a two-against-one knockdown-drag-out with overturned tables and broken bottles. He was used to odds like that. It would be really nice if Lori showed up about now. She carried, too, and she knew how to use her weapon and fight better than most men. This had to be a case of mistaken identity. He didn't know them or the girl. Maybe they could work out a peaceful solution to the misunderstanding without anybody getting hurt or ending up dead.

Still, he was irritated because he didn't finish the T-bone. He rose and dropped enough cash on the table to cover his meal and a tip. The flannel twins stepped back in tandem like two well-trained footmen, but showed a bit of surprise when he stood taller and had about eighty pounds on them. They motioned him to precede them, still in polite fashion. He did so. At the door, the stricken young woman stared up at him. She was a tiny little thing, five feet, maybe less. She looked so terrible and even younger than he'd thought, maybe not more than sixteen or seventeen.

"I'm really, really sorry, mister," she whispered. Her voice was as shaky as the rest of her.

Then she turned away from him, pulled open the front door, and went out fast. Once in the alley, it was evident that he'd been wrong. She was not the one in trouble with the two thugs. They ignored her. When Novak stepped out, they moved up close on both sides. There was nobody left waiting in line now, no cars dropping off customers, the alley completely deserted. Unfortunately, there was no sign of Lori Garner, either.

Two vehicles were waiting for them, their motors still running. The first car was a brand-new white BMW convertible; the second was a nondescript black Volkswagen van with dark-smoked windows. That would be his ride. On the ground to his right, Mr. Casinger, the burly security guard lay face down on the bricks. The back of his head was a bloody mess.

"Get your hands up," Watch Cap growled.

Novak obliged him by punching him in the face as hard as he could. He went down on top of the bouncer, blood spewing out of his nose and mouth. Novak got the other kid by one arm, swung him around and jabbed him in the ear with a doubled fist. He staggered sideways and fell drunkenly against the van. That's when two other guys, older and better trained, jumped out of the black van. Both had weapons pointed at him. Novak raised his hands. These men looked like professionals. They were dressed in camouflage, and their holsters were strapped low on their thighs beside their Ka-Bar knives.

"Get down on the ground. Now!"

Novak obliged. The guy held his weapon on the back of Novak's head and placed his knee in the small of his back. He frisked him, quickly and expertly, and pulled out Novak's Kimber 1911 .45 caliber. He took it, put it inside Novak's backpack, and threw it into the van.

"Okay, you got me. What's this all about?"

One of the camo guys barked orders. "Get up, you two losers, and get back in the van. Irina, you're riding in that Beamer." Then he stood back and held the gun on Novak's face. "Okay, get up. Don't try anything stupid."

The little blonde junkie hurried over to the white car and got into the back seat. The BMW drove away while Novak was muscled toward the van. Even with his side nearly healed, he wasn't sure he could take down all four of these guys at once. Not when they all had pistols trained on him. Now he was curious. He wanted to stall to give Lori time to show up and save the day, but she didn't appear. He hated it when she was late.

Novak considered things for a moment. If these guys had wanted him dead, this dark, deserted alley wouldn't be a bad place to put him down. Scruff opened the door for him, Mr. Polite, all of a sudden. Nobody said anything. They pushed Novak inside. He was not bound, which was their first big mistake. They were still asking for cooperation instead of pistol-whipping him. But the moment he was inside, they jerked a black hood over his head, and he felt the jab of a needle in the side of his neck. He felt the burn of whatever had been injected, having about three seconds to get angry before the drug hit his conscious mind like a weighted baseball bat.

Chapter 2

Novak tried to force open his eyelids, instantly felt dizzy, and shut them. His mind was spinning thoughts like a spider on crack. He couldn't remember much. There had been a black hood over his head, he thought he remembered, but it was gone. That made him anxious. He knew he was disarmed and outnumbered and shot full of some drug. The girl, she'd had that kinky blond hair. She'd gotten him into this thing. He stayed still and tried to clear up the blurry recollections. The men had worn flannel shirts, different colors.

When he realized he was inside a car, he sat up and felt people close beside him. He opened his eyes and saw them clearly. The one on his right smelled like blood, and had a tissue stuffed up his nostrils. The other guy kept rubbing his ear. Two more men rode in the front seat. They were the bad ones. The van was quiet. Nobody said anything. He could hear the tires on the pavement, echoing a little hum.

The van was moving fast, the driver clearly in a hurry to get somewhere. Novak's captors all stared straight ahead. He knew he was in a bad spot, but he didn't feel he was in immediate danger. That would probably come at the end of this road. Ahead of them, in the bright spears of illumination thrown by the van's headlights, he could see the white BMW that the girl had gotten into, also driving fast. He couldn't tell if she was still inside. Maybe she was dead by now, shot and left somewhere on the side of the road. Maybe he would be next unless he did something. He had no idea how long he'd been unconscious or how far they'd driven, but he didn't think it had been long. He decided to make some waves.

"Okay, guys. I'm awake now. I'm fine, really. Don't worry about me having dangerous aftereffects from that knock-out drug." He looked at the guy on his right. "So tell me. Where the hell are we headed so fast?" Nobody thought he was funny. Dead silence prevailed. He felt invisible. No use wasting words on these guys—they weren't going to bite. He considered how things had gone down back at the steakhouse for a time and wished he'd gotten to his gun and put them all down when he'd had the chance. He would've if he'd known they were going to shoot him up with a drug. There weren't any ill effects right now, but that might come later. Maybe the front-seat duo belonged to some paramilitary unit; that's how they came off, and that's how they dressed. Maybe there was a wilderness camp where they shot at pictures of terrorists. That didn't fit well with the two flannel boys, but it did with the other two.

The girl had chosen him, on purpose, a complete stranger, for reasons unknown, but she was sorry. Whatever crime or misdeed she was accusing him of, he was damn sure he hadn't done it. He was no angel and never had been, but he didn't mess with teenagers. She hadn't chosen him on a whim. That meant she had a reason to point him out.

Chances were they weren't going to kill him, or they would have already done so. That was a given, and a point in his favor, but the only good one at the moment. He had questions he needed to ask, but he wasn't going to get answers out of any of these guys. He watched the road ahead, looking for identifying signs. He wanted to know where he was. There was any number of states they could be traveling through right now. He was going to have to bide his time, and find the right time and place to get away. Hopefully, he could do that without ending up dead. This thing needed to play out on Novak's terms. He figured the young girl was the key. Her actions seemed to be forced upon her. She could be another victim. Or she could be calling the shots—stranger things had happened. They treated her with kid gloves, sort of, except for the fact that she was about as strung out as a spool of yarn dragged off by a rabid cat.

The highway stretched out ahead, undulating over gently rolling hills like a satin ribbon tossed on ocean ripples. They had started out in Virginia, which is where this looked to be. It was dark and rural and forested, with some little farms here and there. He was proven correct when he saw a sign that said Fredericksburg and an arrow pointing right. The number of miles until the destination was not listed. They bypassed that road without stopping. That meant he hadn't been out long and they were still in Virginia. The rural road did not look familiar, but he hadn't been down that way in a long time. There were a few closed gas stations but no fast food joints. No traffic to speak of. A speed limit sign whizzed by reading 35 MPH. They were going double that, maybe more. They were out in the middle of the sticks, alright.

Everybody inside that van knew he was conscious, but they weren't threatening him or pulling out weapons or sticking hypodermic needles in his arms. He was still unbound and free as a bird to commit havoc when the time was right. All of which pointed to him possibly coming out of this thing alive, but that was still a big maybe. Novak settled back, relaxed his tense muscles, and watched miles of wooded road fly by. Nothing else he could do, not until they stopped the car. Sure, he could wrestle a weapon from one of the young punks in the back, no problem. He could have one in a matter of seconds. Disarming three more inside a speeding car might be iffy. He'd have to wait until they stopped and then make a break for it. His guards were way too relaxed—one appeared to have fallen asleep. What the hell? They had just kidnapped him; they should have been more alert. Drugs seemed to be a component in their circle. The one they'd injected into him had been fast-acting but not long-lasting, he didn't think. He felt no side effects, but experienced moments of lightheadedness a couple of times.

Maybe they were small-potatoes drug dealers from some dead little podunk town around there. Maybe the girl had thought he was someone else. That probably wasn't the case. Novak didn't look like most other people. He was too big, too tall, too heavy, and looked too rough to mistake for any average Joe. His curiosity was definitely piqued regarding what he'd find at the end of this road. If that tiny girl was in trouble—and he was pretty sure this was all about her—maybe he could help somehow. Maybe that's why she'd chosen him out of all the people in that restaurant. She'd seemed unafraid of the baby lumberjacks, but the camo guys ordered her around like they owned her.

Then his thoughts returned to Lori Garner. She would have shown up at that steakhouse by now, probably not long after they'd taken him. She would question the staff and other customers, and she wouldn't like what she heard. She would know full well that he hadn't up and left her high and dry with no explanation, especially with the bleeding bouncer outside. She was going to flash around her Pentagon badge and ask a ton of questions, maybe even get the law involved. As a former MP, Lori was good at asking questions and getting in people's faces, so sooner or later, she would find out what happened to him. Then she'd call on her personal resources and great instincts. One of his favorite things about her was that she never gave up, not on anything, not ever. She had ways to track him, but they had taken his weapon, cellphone, wallet, and pocket knife off him. They had the backpack in the floor of the back seat. He was glad to see it. It had a GPS tracker in it, so Lori would know exactly where he was. He hoped she remembered it. They were in a business where they had to be careful. Stuff like this was expected now and again. He hoped she was hot on his trail, weapon in hand, and getting closer by the mile. More time passed in silence. This was like riding with a quartet of armed L.L. Bean mannequins. He got bored first, and then he got angry. He wondered where they were headed. Richmond wasn't too far to the south. He saw no stars out the back window. It was cloudy and starting to sprinkle rain. After a while, he leaned his head back and shut his eyes.

Minutes later, the car started to slow. They had entered a small town that looked as if it had come straight out of a Hallmark Channel Christmas movie. He'd only seen one of those movies when Lori had forced him to watch it while he'd been a captive patient in bed without a remote. It had been cutesy and sappy, and it had the same kind of old-fashioned, curlicue-decorated gazebo sitting out in the middle of the town square. The couple holding hands and watching snow drift down while townsfolk sang Christmas carols was missing, and so was any vestige of human life. He spotted no one anywhere along the dark streets.

Again, Novak briefly considered forcing a showdown, but controlled the urge because they were following the white BMW around the cute gazebo and then down a deserted blacktopped road with dark woods closing in on both shoulders. Not long after, the driver turned on his right blinker, which was absolutely unnecessary under the circumstances, and hung a turn onto a narrow road that turned out to be an entry drive. They eventually emerged from the woods into long, grassy fields enclosed with miles of neat white fences. The driver proceeded up a little rise where an enormous country home came into sight. This and the big stables over to the side looked like the fabled horse farms of Virginia that he'd heard about. The car slowed to a stop in front of a flight of red brick steps leading up to a wide front veranda. There were rockers lined up down the front with pots of bronze mums between them.

"Time to meet the boss," said his new tough-guy friend in the front seat. He was the one who'd ordered the girl around.

"And who would that be?"

"You'll find out. He likes to introduce himself."

"Could've fooled me."

"Get out. Don't try anything stupid."

Novak was glad to get out of that stifling van. He stood and looked up at the house, stretching out his cramped neck and shoulders, gauging which guy he should hit first. The men inside the BMW all climbed out in a hurry, four more armed bullies in camo. Two of them roughly pulled the girl out of the back seat. She resisted and started cursing in some very blue language as they half-dragged, half-carried her up the front steps. They were using more force than was actually needed. She probably weighed ninety pounds, tops, if that much. Still, she was resisting and freaking out and digging in her heels and calling them names that he'd last heard at a Marine bar fight in San Diego. Under normal circumstances, Novak would have stepped in and made sure those guys knew how to treat a woman. At the moment, however, Novak could not dredge up a whole lot of sympathy for the kid. She'd gotten him into this mess. He didn't owe her anything.

Prodded at gunpoint, he mounted the steps, walking in front of his guards. He crossed the porch, and entered the house. The foyer was long and beautifully decorated, but the furnishings looked like they would be more appropriate in a mansion on the Cliff Walk of Newport. The room was wide and had portraits of lots of equestrians wearing tan jodhpurs and black jackets and riding helmets while sitting atop beautiful thoroughbred Arabian horses. Greek statues were placed here and there, the kind that looked legit and two thousand years old. Whoever lived here had an exemplary and wonderful cash flow. He followed the girl and her rowdy guards past a gigantic mahogany staircase to some closed double doors. When the guard knocked, a deep voice bade them to enter. The girl and Novak were encouraged to go inside with a hard shove to their backs. Only two of the men followed them inside. The door closed quietly behind them.

The instant Novak saw the guy calling the shots, he recognized him. In the second instant, he knew his trouble had moved from fourth degree annoyance to first degree red alert. The great leonine head of white hair was a thing network legends were made of, as well as the man's handsome, craggy darkly tanned features and clean-shaven square jaw. The Honorable Charles Edward Blackwood Esquire himself sat there before them in his big brown leather club chair, like the Emperor of Rome—Caligula, to hold the analogy. At one time, this guy had been a mega-famous nightly news anchor, but he had turned senator and served many decades in the hallowed halls of Congress. He was also the most crooked son of a bitch who ever walked up the Capitol steps, a man who had only escaped jail time by paying off many, many young female accusers. This guy was the epitome of scum of the earth, and Novak had always loathed the sight of him. During Blackwood's television career, he had repeated insults about the military and its men, endlessly maligning them with snide falsehoods.

He was a bombastic, despicable hypocrite well known for holier-than-thou speeches and a fortune in the billions, most of it garnered illegally. Blackwood said nothing, just stared at them. The fireplace beside him was roaring like a dragon's mouth, hickory logs snapping and crackling and helping to provide the picture of the Victorian English lord in his library, which was what the former Senator wanted. To top off the effect, he wore a green velvet smoking jacket and held his trademark ivory meerschaum pipe cradled in one palm. Yes, the Charles Dickens Christmas card images just kept coming.

"Ah, there you are, sweetheart," he said to the drug-dazed, angry teenager. "You look rather exhausted, my dear. Please, Irina, ask your Mr. Novak to sit down."

'Your' Mr. Novak, Novak thought. *What in the bloody hell is he talking about?*

Irina scowled furiously at her father, as all teenage daughters were apt to do, then crossed her arms and put a pretty effective pout on her mouth. Despite her surly attitude, she looked so far gone that her pupils were nonexistent. She kept twisting a big gold senior class ring that she wore on her left hand. The big fake ruby glittered in the fire's glow. She looked briefly at Novak and jerked a thumb at a tufted dark green velvet loveseat across from her father's chair. She sat down atop the raised hearth and crossed her legs, trying to look bored. It didn't come off. She needed a drug fix in the worst way. Novak took a seat where she indicated.

So now things were getting interesting. He'd never met Senator Blackwood in person, but he knew the man had a big horse farm somewhere in Virginia where he raised prize-winning Arabians, probably the ones in those foyer portraits. He knew Blackwood ran with the big dogs in Washington politics as well as the smoking cigars in the news media. Blackwood regularly attended every dinner party on Embassy Row and even visited the White House. Having strangers kidnapped out of popular steakhouses did not fit the picture of the regal law-abiding citizen that he presented in public.

"Thank you for coming," Blackwood said to Novak. He spoke in that famous slow-as-dripping-sorghum southern drawl for which he was so well known. He was retired now, Novak thought he remembered, but wasn't sure. Novak tried to recall more about the guy. He had been elected first as the junior Senator from the Commonwealth of Virginia. During that campaign, he'd claimed direct kinship to George Washington, which was a baldfaced lie that had come out after the election. It was a safe bet that

Novak was now on the property of Blackwood's fabled farm. He called the place Arabian Nights, if Novak remembered correctly.

"I had little choice but to come, Mr. Blackwood. As you well know."

"So you recognize me?" The old man actually sounded pleased. Novak tried to calculate his age. Blackwood had to be nearing eighty, if not already an octogenarian.

"Everybody knows you."

Blackwood's expression intimated that he didn't care for Novak's tone. The feeling was mutual and growing by leaps and bounds. Novak decided to come out swinging. He'd never been the timid type, especially with obnoxious egotists.

"Want to hear a funny story, Senator? An incident that I'm fairly certain the big newspapers in D.C. might love to print and distribute. Your little girl over there? She pointed her finger at me when I was eating my steak and minding my own business. I don't know her from a hole in the ground. I don't know why she chose me to involve in your family drama, but I do know I was drugged and dragged here to your den by the thugs that work for you. I don't want to be here, Senator Blackwood, and now you need to tell me why I was singled out and brought here against my will or I'm going to walk out that door and lodge a complaint with the local cops."

Blackwood was not impressed. He merely gazed at him, the picture of calm aristocratic dominance. Then he smiled. "So you're denying Irina's charges?"

That one caught Novak by surprise. "What charges?"

Blackwood studied him for a long moment. Irina stared into the burning logs, trembling all over, and three seconds from losing all grip on reality. The old man concentrated on relighting the meerschaum until the surrounding silence grew too long and laborious. He puffed the tobacco into flame and blew out a smoke ring that smelled like an exclusive London tobacconist shop. Afterward, he gave a put-upon sigh, nice and loud and long, and with a bare twinge of annoyance. "I've brought you here to do the right thing by my daughter. You're older than I expected, certainly not her usual type. I suppose I'm old-fashioned in my tastes, but so be it."

Novak glanced at Irina. She continued to shake and clasp her hands together as she rocked back and forth. He looked at her aged father. "What the hell are you talking about? I've never seen your daughter before tonight."

"Don't pretend innocence. It doesn't suit a man like you. You don't look like the type to deny your part in this disgusting mess, but I guess you are."

Novak was tired of the egomaniac pushing him around. He'd been curious at first, but now he was just tired of it. "Look, Blackwood, I don't know your daughter. I'm going to press charges on you and your men for taking me at gunpoint."

Blackwood frowned and made a show of placing his pipe in a cut-glass ashtray. "So you are categorically denying that you're the father of Irina's baby?"

Stunned by the ludicrous charge, Novak could only stare at him. At first he was speechless, and then he gave a contemptuous laugh. "That's ridiculous. She's just a kid, a strung-out junkie, if you haven't noticed. What is she, anyway? A high schooler? You got the wrong guy, Blackwood. If she's pregnant, check out the local football team, because I've never seen her before."

"Maybe you will admit the truth once my men have a go at you. Irina identified you as the father of her baby. You think I would not believe my own daughter?"

Irina jumped up and gave a laugh that sounded slightly insane. Everybody looked at her. "Well, shit, Daddy, get real, would you?" She was quivering now, and so was her voice, but she was glaring death and hatred at the old man. She looked so out of it now that Novak grew worried. Her lips were pressed tight, and she held her stomach, lashing out at him through gritted teeth. "Okay, you win! I lied about the big guy over there. He's not the father. I chose him because I knew you'd kill my boyfriend when you found out who he is. I wanted him out of town before your creeps beat him up. So just let this guy go. He didn't do anything to me. I don't know him, either. He just looked big and strong and able to take care of himself, so I chose him." Her face changed along with her voice. "Please, Daddy, I need my shot. Please, I can't stand it. I'm hurting bad."

Novak set his jaw and looked at Blackwood. He was supplying his own kid with drugs.

"What boyfriend are you talking about?" Blackwood demanded. "You're not allowed to have boyfriends, Irina. Tell me his name." Blackwood was angry, but calmer than his daughter, though that didn't take much. "You disobeyed me about going out with boys."

"Oh, yeah, Daddy, that's exactly what I did. I'm not allowed to get knocked up, either, am I? But I did, so ha ha. Now maybe I won't be so attractive to you, huh? Yeah, I'm gonna have a baby and the high and mighty Charles Blackwood can't do a damn thing about it."

After that outburst, Irina looked proud for maybe two seconds before she slid down on her knees and put her forehead on the floor. Novak watched Blackwood. His face had gone the color of tomato ketchup, and he was gnashing his teeth. "Who is the boy? Give me his name. Now, Irina!"

"No, no, no! I'll never, ever, tell you his name. Not in a million years. You can beat me all night long and not give me my heroin, but you'll never know who he is. I love him, and I hate you. Everything about you disgusts me. You're old and you're wrinkled and you're gross."

As disgusting as this whole thing was, Novak rather enjoyed the way Charles Blackwood's tanned face turned as white and hard as bleached concrete. Somehow the old man contained his rage, but it was simmering all right, just beneath the surface.

"Shut your mouth, young lady."

Blackwood glanced away from her, but didn't look at Novak or the guards. He was humiliated. Everybody sat still and said nothing. Irina started crying. The senator inhaled a deep, bracing breath, managing to contain the rage. Slowly, he stood up and walked over to where his daughter was sitting on her heels. He pulled her up. She stood there and glared unflinchingly up at his flushed face, hands on her hips. Without warning, he slapped her so hard across the face that it knocked the unstable girl off her feet. She fell sideways to the floor, stunned, then rolled over onto her stomach like a toddler, crying and mumbling curses at her father. A moment later she scrambled back to her feet and faced him again. She could barely stand, and her lower lip was cut wide open, bleeding profusely. She wiped at the blood running down her chin with the back of her hand, her eyes burning into Blackwood with unabashed hatred. "I hate you! You're not my real father! You're a monster!"

Blackwood hit her again, this time a punch to the face that sent her reeling backward onto a couch. This time she didn't get up. That's when Novak decided he'd had enough. He stood up, and when Blackwood turned on him, his face still twisted dark with rage, Novak punched him in the nose with a blow so quick and brutal that the Senator was flung hard against his chair, overturning a side table before he slid down to the floor, blood soaking the front of his velvet robe. The two guards had been too shocked to move at first, but then grabbed Novak. He shook them off and decked one with as much force as he'd used to hit Blackwood. Blackwood pushed himself up to sitting, slightly disoriented, as more guards rushed into the room and grabbed Novak's arms. Novak stopped resisting. He'd made his point.

The girl was on the couch, unresponsive, but Blackwood was up on his feet now and leaning against the back of his chair for support. His nose was bleeding and already starting to swell. He held a big white handkerchief to it. He was going to have two black eyes and a headache in the morning, and that was a good thing. Then the Senator looked at him, a man so famous for his bombastic oratory in the Senate chamber, but his voice came out low and trembling, much as his daughter's had.

"I want him behind bars. You hear me, Petrov! I want him in jail now! Tonight! And get that little bitch out of my sight. Lock her in her bedroom!"

When he said Petrov, Novak stiffened at the Russian's name. Somehow it rang a bell, but he couldn't remember why. Turning, he looked at the man who'd run into the room with the others. He was tall and lanky, maybe around six feet, with long arms and legs and a wiry build. He looked to be around fifty, maybe less. He had a shaven head, but Novak could tell by the barely visible hairline that he was not naturally bald. He had pale blue eyes that looked almost white in the firelight. He looked calm as an iced-over arctic lake, ready to do whatever was necessary. Novak felt he was a man to be feared.

Petrov frowned when he met Novak's stare. He looked as if he was trying to place him, too. Novak broke eye contact and returned his regard to Blackwood, who was coughing and spitting out blood. The girl lay unconscious on the couch. Nobody paid any attention to her, as if that attack was routine, something that happened every day. Petrov was in charge, probably head of Blackwood's security, because he ordered the men to seize Novak. Novak didn't fight them. He went along willingly, because he'd have a better chance of justice if he was arrested. In fact, he was surprised they didn't take the law into their own hands; they seemed the types. He could prove who he was and when he'd arrived at that marina. That would clear him of the girl's claim. Her face in the morning would verify that her father had hit her.

They marched Novak outside, slapping him in a pair of handcuffs that Blackwood seemed to keep handy. That was a bit concerning. Novak wondered if they were not taking him to jail, but out on some backroad where they'd beat him to death. As it turned out, he was wrong about their intentions. They drove him back into the strange Christmas town and ushered him into a sheriff's office that had flower boxes full of bronze-colored mums attached to the front windows. There, custody was handed over to a spiffy little shined-up deputy who didn't even inquire as to his name or the charges lodged against him. Apparently, in Hallmarkville, Blackwood's word was law, no superfluous questions asked. That couldn't be good news for Novak's immediate prospects. The deputy marched him back into the bowels of the jail and locked him behind bars in a cold cell. On his way out, he finally told Novak the charges: breaking and entering and physical assault and battery on the Honorable Charles Blackwood's craggy old face. Then Novak was left there alone. A moment later, the lights were turned off.

Novak shed his jacket and used it as a pillow. The bunk was hard and too short for his legs. It wasn't a bad cell considering some jails he'd been in—Cambodia and Brazil, for instance. He had spent many a night cooling his heels in various lockups around Southeast Asia and Africa and South America, so he took the false charges in stride. He could talk his way out of it, maybe, once any legit law enforcement officer showed up or Novak got a lawyer. He hadn't received his phone call, so that could mean a kangaroo court was not too far on the horizon, probably as soon as the sun came up, along with a judge's hasty decision to send him to prison. Nobody would be the wiser because nobody even knew Novak was there, so it could be just a good old-fashioned lynching.

The old man would not want bad publicity, especially when it concerned his young, strung-out, recently abused daughter whom Blackwood had violently assaulted right in front of Novak. Of course, the former politician could just have him taken out to the back forty and buried where his prized stallions grazed. On the other hand, Blackwood knew that Novak could have kith or kin who'd come looking for him, maybe important and bold enough to make waves. Worse for them, Lori Garner could show up and really raise some serious shit. Novak was counting on that.

Still, his acceptance did not mean he wasn't royally pissed off. He was eaten up with it, and it only grew stronger as he lay there in the cold darkness. He finally slept fitfully and awoke at dawn. Then he paced and listened for voices, but heard nothing and nobody. He lay back down and stared up at the ceiling, alternately cursing and worrying about Irina Blackwood's health after taking such a brutal blow. Finally, a police officer he'd never seen before made a big deal of presenting him with a mighty awful death glare as he unlocked his cell door. This guy was dressed in all black, a uniform that looked like a close derivative of German Gestapo garb. Novak sat up and looked at him. This was the sheriff himself, a short guy, maybe five-five or five-six, if that, but stocky and perfectly groomed, from his slicked-back black hair to his shiny black jackboots. The man stood there silently, probably trying to intimidate him, before he said in a loud voice, "You happen to know a woman by the name of Lori Garner?"

It's about time, Novak thought, but he was more than pleased to stand up and get the hell out of that place. "She here?"

"She's bailing you out and making a bunch of threats about some general she knows up in D.C. Come with me, you're being released."

Novak grabbed his jacket and followed him, glad she'd found him so fast. How she'd done it was a good question—likely the GPS. On the other hand, Lori was as smart as they came, and she did have her methods. She had been a woman chock full of surprises since the night they'd met on Bourbon Street in the French Quarter. She'd been injured and in trouble and gotten him embroiled in a big dangerous case. Looked like he was about to return that favor.

Chapter 3

When Novak was herded upstairs for release, he found Lori Garner standing at the front desk giving hell to the deputy on duty. She was not a tall woman, five feet five inches, but people tended not to notice that because of her erect posture and innate self-confidence. He thought she was beautiful with all that thick wheat-colored hair and her strong, athletic body. Her hair was brushed up in a neat bun today, and she looked sharp in her Army dress uniform. She wore a menacing scowl, not hiding her anger and impatience, but he could clearly see her relief when she caught sight of him. She had probably feared him dead and floating face down in some drainage ditch. He was lucky that hadn't happened. Despite the early hour and the fact she must have searched for him all night, she looked good. Her entire manner put across that she was not someone to be trifled with.

When the pint-sized sheriff showed up and unlocked his handcuffs, Novak moved over and stood beside Lori. She didn't say anything to him, just looked at him and shook her head. She was not pleased. He felt sheepish under her tacit reproach. Truthfully, he was simply grateful she had shown up so early. Their long-coveted reunion was not going to be the wine-and-roses romantic evening he'd anticipated when he'd stepped off his boat at National Harbor.

The duty clerk was dressed in a Gestapo outfit, too. He handed Novak his backpack and a large tan mailing envelope that was taped closed at the flap. The contents of the backpack were pretty much in order, but he tore open the envelope because his gun and cellphone were supposed to be inside, and he didn't trust anybody in a fifty-mile radius, especially not a bunch of crooked cops dressed up like Heinrich Himmler.

"Where's my weapon and cellphone?" he asked the clerk, sorting through the contents. "I want them back."

"That's everything we found. No gun, no cellphone."

"Yes, there was. You need to go find them and give them to me."

The guy shrugged his silver shoulder epaulettes, his smile remaining in place, pleasant and reasonable. "Please move along, sir, before you give us another reason to lock you up. You are lucky that we're overlooking your charges and releasing you into the custody of this officer."

"Where is my gun? It's a Kimber 1911, legal and registered, with a concealed carry permit. They took if off me at the restaurant."

The guy just stared at him, his courteous smile plastered in place.

Novak was agitated, and getting more so. He felt Lori's fingernails dig into his forearm in a way that he could not ignore. It was her attempt at painful encouragement to let it go for now. She turned around and headed for the front entrance. Novak followed, but he was not happy. There was information on his phone that nobody had a right to see, especially the guy named Petrov and Charles Blackwood. The phone was locked and he'd taken precautions for privacy, but he definitely didn't want it in the hands of criminals. He had to get it back. First, he was going to spend some time thanking Lori and placating her annoyance, and then he would take a hot shower, don clean clothes, and have breakfast. *Then* he would find a way to get it back. He was hungry and still miffed at having to leave half that steak on his plate.

Outside on the front sidewalk, Novak raised his face to the sky and inhaled deeply in the crisp autumn air. The temperature had dropped, and the early morning was cold. Lori turned to him with some hellfire accusations. "What in the hell are you doing here, Novak? There is such a thing as standing me up, and then there is what you pulled last night."

"Yeah, tell me about it. Look, none of this was my fault. I was sitting at my table, waiting for you and minding my own business. Then in walks this teenage girl who points me out to the guys with her and accuses me of being the father of her baby. Her friends were armed and ushered me out of the restaurant, drugged me, and I ended up in jail here, wherever the hell this town is."

Lori stared up at him. "That is just so ridiculous, Novak. Do you hear yourself? But it's not atypical since we're talking about you. I could make up a better story right off the top of my head in under a minute. You've had all night to come up with better excuses. Try again, and this time, tell me the truth."

"It's a long story. I just gave you the short version."

"Yeah, I'll bet you did. Okay, we've got a long drive back to D.C., and I do love your stories of woe. Don't you ever get tired of landing yourself in trouble?"

"This wasn't on me. Let's just get out of here. How'd you even find me in this place? Where are we, anyway?"

"It's called Blackwood, and I've never heard of it before. It's about three blocks long. As you might guess, there's more to the story. You see, I got a call from that filched cellphone you were so pissed off about inside the station. A woman's voice, real sweet, real deep southern, and oh, she's so worried about you and what they might do to you. Want to enlighten me a little bit about this unknown woman? Is she the mother of that baby you mentioned?"

"Irina called you on *my* phone? What else did she say?"

Lori gave him a look. "Well, *Irina* told me to come bail you out of this particular jail before they found you hanging by the neck, dead, inside your cell."

"We've got us a situation here. Like I said, I got sucked into this thing before I knew what was happening, and ended up arrested on trumped-up charges."

"Don't tell me, I already know. This sounds like one of your 'Damsel in Distress' predicaments. That it, Novak? This time it's poor little Irina needing your help, so you got yourself thrown into jail. Remind me never to be late on another date with you. Or *go* on any date with you."

"It's not that simple, but you're getting warm."

"Okay, give me the sordid details. Who is this Irina and when did you meet her? Is she an old flame?"

"Hardly. I never saw her before last night. She's just a kid, not even out of high school yet."

"Let's get in the car and you can tell me everything from the beginning." She looked behind them. "I don't trust these people. This looks like some kind of Disney production."

Novak agreed. Lori led him to an olive-green, hardtop Army Jeep. Novak opened the passenger door and got in. Lori rounded the hood, climbed in, and started the engine. She flipped on the heater. Novak started relating the details of the night before but kept it to the bare bones.

"Okay, that sounds halfway credible, I suppose. But surprise, surprise, I've got more news you aren't going to like one bit, besides you owing me two hundred dollars for bail."

Novak turned and looked at her. He was not in the mood for news he wouldn't like. He was not in the mood for any news.

"Your new friend, little Miss Trouble? She told me to come here, bail you out, and then for us to meet her at a Drury Inn just down the road from here. She says it's urgent that we show up and hear her side of the story. The way I heard it, it goes something like this: come, because it's a matter of life and death, somebody is surely going to die if we don't get there soon. That ring a bell, Novak?"

"Believe her. Last night, I watched her father hit her so hard in the face that she ended up on the ground."

Lori did not care for that. Her frown deepened, and her eyes latched on to his face. "I take it that's when you stepped in, took a swing at him, and ended up in jail on assault charges. That about the size of it?"

"He deserved worse than that. He's a rich, pompous SOB."

"So what do you want to do? Do we nix the hotel invitation and head back to the Beltway, or do we meet up with her and get ourselves embroiled in some illegal shit with people we hardly know? You choose."

"We're already involved, wouldn't you say? This is serious. I don't know exactly what's going on around here, but it's nothing good, believe me."

Lori pulled up at the curb and waited for a big mail truck to rumble by. Novak glanced back at the jail. The cocky little sheriff was standing outside the front door watching them pull away. As Lori made the turn onto the street, the little Nazi pointed at Novak, his thumb and forefinger formed like a gun.

"Maybe we should hear the kid out," he said slowly, trying to contain his anger. "There's more to this than meets the eye. I think these people are about as dirty as they can get."

"I agree. What you just described is child abuse and a probable felony. The father should not get away with it."

Novak looked at her. "If it's not, addicting her to drugs is."

"He's feeding her drugs? How do you know?"

"Because she said so right before he hit her."

"Well, that changes things up a bit. He can't get by with that, not in my book."

Novak relaxed some. Lori was a sensible woman. She would have done the same thing he had. "Thanks for coming and getting me out, Lori. I mean it. I'll pay you back."

Lori glanced over at him. "Forget it. You'd do it for me. In fact, since you saved my life once upon a time down in New Orleans...well actually, maybe it was twice, I'll spring for the bail this time. I'm making the big bucks now, you know, so no sweat." She slowed for a stop sign. "Tell me this. How long after you disembarked did you land yourself in trouble? Did you even make it out of the marina?"

Novak had to grin. He hadn't made it much farther than that. "Well, the ride to the steakhouse was uneventful."

"And after that?"

"After that, these people approached me while I was still eating, and the kid pointed me out. Like I said before, I was enjoying my T-bone and looking forward to a lovely night spent in bed with you."

"Yeah, that makes two of us. Good thing I asked for two weeks off. It looks like we're going to need it." She blew out a lungful of air, frustrated. "I do rather like the sound of falling in bed with you and getting some sleep right now, I have to admit that, and the sooner, the better. We're going to a hotel. Maybe we can kill two birds with one stone."

"Nothing I'd like better. Let's hear Irina out first and make sure she's okay. Then, the next two weeks are all yours."

"Okay, but maybe not at that hotel. I want to get you out of northern Virginia ASAP. You know, before you get arrested again."

"I've got questions that need to be answered. I feel sorry for that girl. She's a little bitty thing, and she took a hard hit last night. He hit her with his fist, too quick for anybody to react, and right in front of me. That makes me worry about what he might do to her behind closed doors."

"Well, that's an awful thought. Maybe she wants to apologize to you in person. They put you through a lot last night. She needs to press charges against her father, if he's abusing her. Maybe we can convince her to do it."

"I haven't told you the juiciest part yet."

"Yeah? That figures. Well, go ahead. Hit me with it."

"Her father? He's Charles Blackwood."

Lori jerked her face toward him. "Former Senator Charles Blackwood? The longtime Chairman of the Senate Committee on Armed Services? That guy? No way, Novak, please, say you're kidding me."

"I'm not kidding. Are you really surprised? Rumors of his corruption have been whispered around for decades. From what I witnessed last night, I don't put anything past him."

"Wow, that does change things a bit. Do you realize how powerful he still is? Anything else you need to share? Do it now so I can turn this car around and go home."

"Afraid so."

"Crap, go ahead."

"There's this guy working for Blackwood. I saw him last night. I think he's Blackwood's head of security, and my gut tells me he's dangerous. His name is Petrov. I don't know the first name. We need to find out everything we can about him. The name sounds familiar. I think he's a Russian, and there aren't all that many Russians in rural Virginia."

"Probably not. You want to get the goods on him right now?"

"Wouldn't hurt. I'd like to know who I'm dealing with, because I don't think we're done with these guys."

Lori had pulled over to the curb and already had her Dell laptop booted up. She punched in a few keys and worked her magic. "I've got one Petrov in our criminal databases. Vasily Petrov. Is that the guy?"

"I didn't get his first name."

"Is this him?"

She swiveled the tablet and showed him a photograph. It was old and not good quality. He looked younger in the picture and had long blond hair that hung to his shoulders. But he had the same eyes, cold and pale and intimidating. "That's him, but it's an old picture. He shaves his head now."

"It says here he's a former Russian operative. Looks like he got into hot water with the Kremlin a couple years ago. Went renegade for hire and has been linked to Syria, ISIS, and the Iranians since then. He was trained by the FSB and is known for killing with a steel icepick through the eye socket or up through the base of the skull to the brain. Holy crap, Novak. You sure this is the same guy?"

"It's him. His pale eyes give him away. Does our government want him?"

"What do you think? Shall I call him in?"

"Let's wait until I find out what's going on. I think he's up to no good out here in the Virginia woods so close to Washington, and I want to find out what he's doing with Blackwood. He's more than his head of security, I can tell you that." Novak paused and said, "Maybe he and Blackwood are dealing drugs or running guns. That girl was so strung out last night it was scary. She's still in high school, for God's sake."

"You didn't recognize this Petrov guy?"

"Never seen him before, but I've got an instinct for men like him. I knew he was bad the minute I saw him. I think he's the kind of guy who kills anybody who gets in his way. Right now, that would be us."

"Well, that's a good reason to drive right on past that hotel and keep going. How about we just tip off the Feds right now and be done with it? C'mon, Novak, you do see the wisdom in that course of action, right? Please say you do."

"Yeah, of course. I still want to hear what the girl's got to say before we take off or turn him in. The way her father hit her just got me. He could've killed her with that one blow, it was that brutal. She's so young and small and fragile, in a way."

"Is she really his daughter?"

"She got mad and started telling him off. That's when she said Blackwood wasn't her real father, so apparently, she's adopted. You should have seen the rage on his face right before he hit her. If he doesn't end up killing her one day, I'll be mighty surprised. Where exactly are we supposed to meet her?"

"It's a Drury Inn, somewhere around the turn off of 605. I don't know the roads around here, so I can't tell you how far anything is. She says it's not a town but a small tourist stop with a McDonald's and a Shell gas station. We can get a look at it on Google Earth, if you want."

"That sounds okay. We need to get there in a hurry, see what she wants, and then end this thing as quick as we can. You need to report Blackwood and Petrov to your general."

"That would be sticky, considering the power the Senator still wields at the Pentagon. But I'll find a way, I guess. Know what, Novak? I missed you. You're excitement, 24/7."

"Let's go check the girl out and see what she knows about this Vasily Petrov guy. He's the one I'm worried about. He doesn't fit in with the rest of Blackwood's men. They're mostly young guys from around here. A few looked more competent, and I suspect they came with this Petrov guy."

"What the hell, why not get involved? It's just more life-and-death stuff, the usual with you."

They arrived at the designated Drury Inn fifteen minutes later. The hotel looked deserted so early in the morning. Two cars were parked out front. A few more were next door at the McDonald's. Not a single person was in sight. Novak began to feel a wariness slowly crawling over him, like a thirsty man trying to make it to a watering hole. "This looks all wrong."

"Tell me about it. Where is everybody? A nearly empty McDonald's? That's a new one."

Lori turned into the parking lot, stopped, and looked around. "There's got to be somebody somewhere around here. Know what my gut's telling me? To clear out of here right now and never look back."

"Mine, too. But I do want to hear that kid out. She was so out of it last night that little she said made much sense. She said her father was sexually abusing her and withholding her drugs. Petrov is probably securing them for him, if I had to guess. I think that's how they control her."

"It doesn't sound like they're doing much controlling, not if she's hiding out in this hotel asking us for help."

Lori pulled around to the rear of the building. There was one car there, a white Mustang convertible with the top up. Lori backed the Jeep into a space, ready to take off in a hurry, if need be. He liked that about her, her foresight and preparation, but then again he liked everything about her. She would be ready when things got hairy. Still, there were no human beings anywhere to be seen. No tourists were carrying bags out of the hotel. Nobody was gassing up across the street. No cars were passing on the highway. The only movement was one stray dog eating something out of a discarded McDonald's sandwich box.

Irina Blackwood had big problems, but she also had close ties to dangerous men. She needed their help, all right, Novak already knew that all too well. He and Lori should have cut bait and gotten the hell out of town. Every bone in his body was telling him to go now, but his loathing for men like Blackwood and Petrov burned hot inside of him. And he thought Irina Blackwood just might be able to give him the ammunition he needed to bring them down.

Lori turned off the ignition and turned in the seat. "So, now what?"

"What room is she in?"

"She didn't say. She told me to ask the desk clerk for a key card that she was leaving with him."

"Under what name?"

"She said she gave him your name."

"Oh, that's just great."

Lori looked around. "What can happen to us in a hotel lobby?"

"You have to ask that? Really? You?"

Lori laughed. "Not really, no."

They got out of the car. The only sound was the American flag flapping on a pole in the brisk breeze. The chain was jingling music; everything else was quiet. They chose to enter from an unlocked side door that led them to the lobby. The décor was modern, done in dark blues and whites with shiny white marble tiles on the floor. Soft instrumental elevator music played in the background, selections that nobody could possibly want to hear. There was nothing unusual anywhere, and no sign of anything threatening, such as multiple men crashing through the front door with AK-47s. Novak waited by the elevator and watched Lori stroll over to the reception desk. She dinged the little bell on the counter.

Novak waited where he was, feeling naked without his Kimber. He didn't expect to get it back now, not if the police had confiscated it. Lori happened to be carrying legally at the moment, which made him feel better. The fact that she was the best shot he'd ever seen with a sniper rifle or any other gun helped his nerves. After a few minutes, a young man walked out behind the counter. He looked even younger than Irina. He still had on braces and a blue coat with the hotel's name emblazoned on the pocket. They spoke for a moment. Then he reached under the counter and brought out a small envelope. Lori took it. A moment later, she was back beside Novak.

"This place has a penthouse, believe it or not, and here's the card key. So la-di-dah, little Miss Irina has expensive tastes and money to spend."

"Well, Blackwood's loaded. She probably put it on his credit card or he owns this place, which wouldn't be good for our health, either."

"Let's go on up. We need to get this over with and get on with our romantic tryst that isn't happening the way it should be."

"You won't get an argument out of me. But not here. I am not shutting my eyes until we get a hundred miles from this place."

The elevator was as deserted as everything else in the hotel. Something about this tourist stop seemed to scare off tourists, as well as locals. Novak was getting that vibe loud and clear. The penthouse encompassed the entire sixth floor. What a waste of available rooms. He wondered if anybody ever stayed there, or if it was just a money-laundering establishment, or even Blackwood's private love nest. Their card worked for the penthouse floor, and the elevator doors slid open and revealed a large beige foyer totally devoid of furniture. A giant chandelier in the shape of Saturn hung in the center, replete with shining rings casting shadows on the walls.

A graceful archway led into a vast living area. Everything they could see inside was the same color: the dull tan of Egyptian sand dunes. The walls blended into the ceiling and tiled floor. They walked across the foyer and found Irina waiting for them inside the long living room. She was standing in front of a window with beige draperies that overlooked a panoramic view of the colorful autumn woods stretching as far as the eye could see.

"Thank you so much for coming, Mr. Novak," she lisped out through a fat, bulbous lip, awfully polite all of a sudden. Her voice was low, her manner quiet, and she looked directly into Novak's eyes. Her eyes were no longer wild and weeping. She had gotten her pills or injection recently, it appeared. Her calm manner told him that she was probably high but inwardly calm. It also told him that her father had used her for a punching bag after they'd dragged Novak off to jail. Both her eyes were bruised and turning black. The left eye was swollen shut. An ugly cut in the shape of her father's big gold Senate ring marred her cheekbone, the bruise dark purple against her pale white skin. She looked awful, and there were probably lots of other marks hidden beneath her clothes.

"I'm so sorry for what I did to you, Mr. Novak. I promise I am. I was just so scared and desperate and needed a fix. I'd gone way too long. I shouldn't have told them you got me pregnant."

"You need to see a doctor, Irina. He beat the hell out of you after I left, didn't he? It might have harmed your baby."

Novak glanced around the room, hoping Petrov wasn't lurking behind a corner with his icepick. That's when he caught sight of the young man lying on a red sectional across the room. He looked like a teenager, too, one that had been trampled by a herd of wildebeests. Somebody, probably Petrov, had worked him over and for a good long time. His beating made Irina's look like a playground scuffle. Under all those cuts and bruises and swelling, he looked slender and slight of build, certainly no athlete or tough guy. He looked like some nervous kid with a summer desk job as a gofer at an accounting firm, or a boy who had survived a car crash with a runaway semi. He didn't move or look at them, but kept his eyes closed tight. He came off as terrified.

Irina walked over to him and placed her hand gently on his fair hair. He still didn't open his eyes. "This is my boyfriend, Justin Dalton. He's hurting real bad right now. They caught up to him last night. They did this to him after Daddy beat his name out of me." She burst into tears at her own betrayal and went down on her knees beside the couch. She put her head on the kid's stomach and sobbed. Justin flinched at the pressure, so she sat back on her heels and wept harder.

Novak and Lori looked at each other. Irina had put up a pretty good tough-girl act the night before, but her protective walls were crumbling to dust. She was done holding her fears and bottled-up grief inside. For the first time, she looked and acted her age. In that moment, and against all reason and better judgement, Novak knew he was going to help her.

Chapter 4

"This boy is likely to have internal injuries, Irina. You need to get him to a hospital right now. It looks to me like you need to see a doctor, too." Lori knelt down beside Irina and put her arm around her, her tender heart getting the better of her.

Irina raised her swollen eyes, shining with tears that overflowed from her lashes and tracked down her bruised cheeks. At that moment, she looked about thirteen. "You just don't understand. I can't risk taking him anywhere that Daddy can find him. If he does, they'll kill him this time. That's what Daddy wants. Last night he told me I'd never see Justin again. So I snuck out of the house and drove around until I found him. You know what they did? They just left him in an alley to die, so I got him in the Mustang and brought him out here." She was crying again. "Daddy's beaten me up enough for me to know how to take care of him. I ought to be good at it by now."

Yeah, I bet you do know how to survive beatings, Novak thought, considering what he'd seen last night and the damage to her face that he saw now.

"Please sit down, please, just for a few minutes." Irina was still on her knees, begging now. "Let me tell you everything. Then I know you'll help us."

Novak wanted to hear what she had to say. Lori nodded, and they sat down together on a couch opposite the injured boy. They waited while Irina tried to compose herself enough to speak.

Novak didn't have much time to waste. "Okay, we're here and listening."

"You're still mad at me, aren't you? I can tell."

Irina's naiveté was back. "Hell, yes, I'm ticked off big time about what you did last night."

"I chose you because you looked so big and strong. I was in bad shape then. I didn't think they could hurt you the way they hurt me and Justin." Irina looked suitably contrite, Novak would give her that. He waited another moment, and when she just sat there and sniffled and wept, he became impatient, not sure what she was working up to.

"We're here, like you asked. You need to tell us what we need to know or we're leaving. Okay?"

She pulled up the tail of her red sweatshirt and wiped away tears. The front had a picture that he assumed was her school mascot. It looked like a black panther. "Daddy researched you after you left. I heard him say that you're a private investigator, and then he got all upset and worried about what you'd do. Is that true?"

Novak knew where this was going and didn't want to hear it. He'd heard similar halting, vulnerable requests for help. "That's right, I am, but I want nothing to do with your father."

"He thinks you're on to him. He thinks you're dangerous."

Novak scoffed. "Hell, Irina, everybody who reads the newspapers is on to him. He's a damn criminal and has been for years. He's just too connected to bring down. Everyone knows he's dirty."

"I know. But don't you see? I can hurt him. Me and Justin both can. We know things that other people don't know."

Novak glanced at the kid lying on the couch. He didn't look like he could do anything to anybody. He was lying there, unmoving, not saying anything. He didn't look at them or try to speak, or maybe he was in too much pain. Maybe Lori was right: the boy was broken up inside, his lungs punctured or multiple ribs broken, or both. His raspy breathing sounded like it could be a collapsed lung, but he wasn't coughing up blood just yet. Blackwood's men had pummeled him to a bloody pulp, all right. People had died from beatings this severe, and Lori was right about internal injuries. They needed to get him to an ER and fast. More than that, he needed some morphine for the pain. "Justin's not going to be able to do anything, not for a long time. So it would just be you against your father, Irina. You, all alone, up against him and all his men."

"I know, but not if you protected us." Irina stood up. They watched her battered face as she worked to check her ragged emotions. It took some effort, but then she took a deep, cleansing breath, and set her bruised jaw. "Daddy's not going to get away with this. He ordered his men to pick up Justin and hurt him bad. Just because I like him. They nearly killed him, you see that. They probably left him there to die. They'll come back if they find out he's still alive."

Lori's voice was gentle. "If you don't get him to a hospital, he's going to die, anyway. I've seen enough injuries like this to know that."

"But I can't!" she cried. "Everybody around here is scared of Daddy. The doctors and nurses, too. The minute somebody reports that Justin was admitted, they'll call Daddy and they'll come get him again."

Novak resigned himself. He had to help this girl. He could not sit around and let the boy die on that couch. "So you want to hire me to get him to the hospital and protect him while he's there. Is that what you want?"

"Yes, please, please, Mr. Novak. I can't go there or Daddy will beat me again and lock me up in my room. If you don't take him somewhere safe, he'll die. There's nobody I can turn to but you. I can't trust anybody around here. If Daddy wants Justin dead, they'll come back for him, they will. I know how he works. I've got to go home, too, or he'll get suspicious."

"No, no, Irina." Those were the first words Justin had uttered, proving he was conscious and listening. That was a good sign. When he spoke, his words came out slow and halting. "Uh uh, no way, Irina. You need to go with us."

"Daddy won't kill me. He loves me too much."

Novak glanced at Lori. She looked incensed, and spoke up. "Irina, take a good hard look in that mirror over there. Then tell us that animal loves you."

Novak didn't think Blackwood was above killing anybody, even his daughter, if she made him angry enough. "Looks to me like you both need somebody to run interference with these guys." He hesitated, not wanting to stick around, but he knew he had to. "Okay, I'll help you, but only until we can get both of you to a safe place where he can't find you."

Lori didn't hold back. "Novak's right. You both need to get the hell out of this town where that terrible man can find you. These guys mean to kill you, probably both of you. Why haven't you left before now, Irina? Or reported that monster to the police?"

"I wanted to, but he got me taking all these drugs, and I have to have it now. He won't give it to me when I don't do what he says." She looked ashamed. "That's how he controls me, with the pills and heroin."

Novak was disgusted but not surprised. He'd already guessed that's what was going on. "You need to go into rehab. That's your only choice now. What about the boy downstairs at the desk? Do you trust him, or has he already given you up to your father?"

"He would never. Mark and me are best friends, ever since grade school. He's scared, too, but he'd never tell on me."

"Does he know Justin's up here?"

"Yes, he helped me get him up here on the luggage cart. He's real scared of Daddy, but he wants to help us. Mark cried when he saw what he did to my face. I told him I wouldn't ever let Daddy know that he helped us."

"He hasn't come up here or checked on how Justin is?"

"No, and he won't. I know he won't unless they beat him up real bad and make him tell them."

"What was going to happen if we refused and walked out that door?"

"I don't know. They'd come here eventually, I guess. I know they're looking for me right now, probably. Please don't leave us here all alone. They'll kill him, and maybe me, too, or take me to one of our beach houses and lock me up there. That's why you gotta get Justin away from here. Daddy's crazy jealous of Justin. He can't stand it if I like anybody but him. We gotta go do it now. We've been here all night, and they'll find us soon. I know they will."

"They didn't kill him this time. Maybe they'll leave him alone now, as long as you stay away from him."

"Daddy's still mad about you, and now he knows I snuck out last night. He'll never let me be with Justin, or anybody else."

Novak didn't like anything about this, but the boy lying on that couch was seriously hurt. "Has Blackwood done this before? Ordered your friends beaten up?"

Irina nodded. "Once, he did, but I didn't get to ever have any boyfriends. I didn't dare disobey Daddy, not until I met Justin. We were keeping it secret and stuff, but Daddy found out somehow."

"How far are you along with the baby?" Lori asked.

"Three months, but it doesn't show yet. At first, I thought he might let us get married since I got pregnant, but then he got so angry, I couldn't tell him about Justin. So I rode around with them to see if we could find his car, and when they started getting impatient and pushing me around, we were close to that steakhouse so I just said my boyfriend told me to meet him there. I just made it all up, and I was going to say he wasn't there, either, once we got inside. Then I saw you, and you were looking at me, like, you know, like you knew I was in trouble and stuff, so I just pointed at you. You looked big and stronger than them, and I thought they wouldn't be able to hurt you. I'm sorry. I really am sorry, Mr. Novak."

Sorry didn't mean squat to Novak, not right now. "Okay, maybe we can take him to a hospital in the next town over, somewhere like that. What about you? Will you be safe here? Will they come here looking for you?"

"All Daddy wants is for me to stay away from Justin. If he has to kill him to do that, he will. If I go back home and say I'm sorry and beg him to forgive me, he probably won't send those guys out looking for Justin again. So you'll have time to get him to the doctor."

"Don't you have anybody you could go to or stay with?" asked Lori. "Surely you have an aunt or uncle or grandparents somewhere?"

"No, there's no one but Daddy. He got me over in Russia, he said, but I don't know if that's true. He didn't tell me anything about my real family except they didn't want me." Her voice hardened. "God, I hate Daddy. I hate him so much. I'd rather kill myself than stay in that house with him." She looked down and wouldn't meet their eyes. "He comes to my bedroom at night and does things. Bad things, but I can't stop him."

Novak's stomach rolled. He felt sick to even think about it. She had just given them another connection to Russia. Petrov had probably been involved in her adoption, if there really was one.

Lori did not mince her words. "You're saying that he sexually molests you?"

Irina's features dissolved into a grimace, and she still wouldn't look at them. "Don't you see? I've got to go back today, I've got to. It's like he owns me. I can probably sneak away again later this week if he doesn't force me to go down to Fripp Island with him. I think that's where he's going next. He's always traveling somewhere with that Petrov guy."

"What's Petrov's first name, Irina?" Novak asked her.

"Vasily. He's a horrible man. I'm scared of him."

"How long has he worked for your father?"

"He came around five years ago, I guess. I hate him, too. Daddy thinks he hung the moon, but his eyes just pin me to the wall sometimes. Anyway, once they take off, I can drive over and meet you, and then Justin and me can run away as soon as he gets to feeling better. I've saved up lots of money, and I stole some of Daddy's credit cards that he doesn't know about. We can make it to Mexico, if you'll just protect us for a little while, just until we get away. We've got passports. Our plan is to get married and sail down to Australia on a big cruise ship. He'll never find us there."

"He's forcing her...drugs," Justin muttered, shifting his body and groaning with the effort. "She's trying to clean up. He won't...take her to rehab."

Irina couldn't look at them. "Last night? After they took you away? They held me down and shot me up. Daddy says he owns me and that I'm his, and I'll always be his. He does own me. Don't you see?"

"He can't own you," Lori said. "Nobody can own anybody in this country."

"He bought her...when she was six." Justin wheezed and groaned, but that was all he got out.

Lori didn't buy it. "No way. That can't be true."

"It's true! He told me!" Irina pushed herself up and started pacing back and forth. She was wringing her hands. "He told me I came from a family in Moscow, and I sort of remember my mother's face and that she worked in this big house, I think. My real father was a soldier or something, but he wasn't around so I don't remember him. It's all real fuzzy. Daddy says he was there on a diplomatic trip, and my mother was a beggar out on the street. He said she offered to sell me to him, that she didn't want me anymore, and that she had too many mouths to feed, but I don't remember any of that so he's lying." Her face crumpled, and more tears came. "He said he'd always wanted a little girl like me to take care of. Yeah, he takes care of me, all right."

"That story sounds fabricated in order to keep you indebted to him," Lori told her. "Your own memories are the truth."

"Taking an adopted child out of a country requires a lot of red tape and is against the law, here and in Russia, I suspect. He'd also need a legit passport to get you out. The whole story sounds like his attempt to make you grateful. Did he mention how he managed to smuggle you through Russian customs and into the United States?"

"It could've happened, Lori," Novak told her. "Maybe not now, but back then. He was already a Senator by then. He could have pulled strings or paid off immigration officials to get her out. Maybe this Petrov guy helped him. Maybe they've known each other for a long time."

"Is he really molesting you?" Lori asked bluntly.

Irina's face flushed as she raised her chin. "Ever since he got me. He did things. The worst started happening when I was almost thirteen. Usually now it's when I'm so high that I can't fight him off."

"He's a bastard," Justin muttered, licking swollen lips.

Irina sat down on the floor and took Justin's hand. "I thought I could get away this time, but he found out. He always finds out. When he threatened to kill Justin, I couldn't bring myself to leave. Then I found out I was pregnant, so we had to get married, but Daddy went crazy. I didn't think he would. I thought he'd want me to get married to Justin to keep people from talking about me. But he just wanted to kill whoever had done it, and made me point him out. I'm sorry, Mr. Novak, that I chose you. I got you into trouble, but I didn't mean to."

Lori was angry. "They could have shot Novak outside that steakhouse, Irina, and asked questions later. What in God's name were you thinking?"

"How long have you been addicted to heroin? It is heroin, right?" Novak asked Irina.

"Since he started making me sleep in his bed. Pills, too, but I need the heroin more."

"Do you take anything else? What kind of pills?"

She looked away. "You know—opioids, hydrocodone, oxy, weed, too, sometimes. When I'm really strung out and need something, I let him give me whatever he wants to."

Novak had heard enough. "Don't ever go back to that farm, or you're going to end up dead. You need to get as far away from him as you can. Let's get you into a rehab center in another state."

"He'll never let me go. Not as long as I'm in this country. He's got ways to find me. People who work for him, Mr. Novak, real horrible people."

"Does he deal drugs? Run them, maybe? How's it work?"

"I'm sure he doesn't do it himself. He hires people for everything. Especially Vasily. He's the creepiest man I know."

"Why?"

"Because he's always trying to scare me to death. He's got these special gloves he likes to put on when he beats people up. He told me that's what they were for. He said it protects his hands. He told me he's got a special icepick, and he was going to find Justin and gouge out his eye with it. Then he'd beat him to death, and it would be my fault for messing around and being a slut. I'm not a slut. I *love* Justin."

Novak was ready to get them out of that hotel room. He tried one more time to make the girl listen to reason. "Irina, you need to get as far away from here as you can. You and Justin both. Petrov is going to kill you before this is over. Go with Lori and Justin. I'll stay here and stir up trouble for them to deal with."

Lori was quick to nix that idea. "Whoa, Novak. I'm not leaving you here."

"I told you, Mr. Novak. I've got to go back to the farm today. If I don't, they'll find us and kill Justin, and you, too, probably. They really will. They'll find us here eventually."

Novak believed her, all right. "Okay, we'll get him out of here. Can you get away later? You're sure?"

"Take Justin somewhere far away. Maybe down to Richmond. I can sneak out later. I do it all the time."

"What if you can't?"

Irina smiled, but it wasn't anywhere close to happy. "I've survived in that house ever since I was six. He loves me in his own nasty, perverted way, I guess." She looked away from their concerned faces. "I just need to steal a big stash before I go so I can ease off the stuff gradually. I can do it myself. Justin says he'll help me clean up."

"Justin's not going to be able to do anything for a very long time."

"I'll meet up with you wherever you take him. Find a hospital somewhere not too far from here, but not too close, either. Please go now, I know how Daddy works. I can get away again, I've done it lots of times, but if I don't go home right now, he'll go into a rage, and things'll go bad for me."

"How long did you say Petrov worked with your father?"

"For years. Five, maybe. He's his personal bodyguard...or that's what he says. How do you know him?"

"That doesn't matter."

"He's like a devil, isn't he?"

"Pretty much."

Novak thought it was interesting that Petrov felt secure enough working with Blackwood to use his own name. He was wanted here in the U.S. He seemed pretty comfortable hooking up with a former Senator.

"I don't like leaving you here," Novak said to Irina.

"I sneak out all the time. He'll think I'm so scared now after the beating he gave me last night. He usually doesn't knock me around this bad, just locks me in my room and lets me get strung out. He's mad because I brought you into this. He thinks you'll cause trouble, I heard him saying that to Vasily. I heard them say they need to get rid of you, so you need to find a safe place, too, Mr. Novak."

"We need to get out of here now," Lori said, walking to the window and looking down at the parking lot.

"I've played Daddy like this for years, Mr. Novak. If it weren't for the drugs, I'd have escaped a long time ago. That's why Justin was helping me. I can't do it by myself. I can't do anything without the drugs."

"How old are you, Irina?"

"I'll be seventeen in three months."

"That's still underage. I assume he legally adopted you at some point."

"He says it's legal. He says he's in love with me and that it's okay, you know, what we do, because I'm adopted and not a blood relative."

"Oh, God, this just keeps getting worse." Lori's face reflected her disgust.

"Okay, we need to go right now. We'll take Justin somewhere safe and let you know where later. Can you give us a number that Blackwood doesn't know about?"

"I use burners all the time. Oh, and I've got some of your things. I figured you'd want them back. I got them before I went out to look for Justin."

She walked across the floor and opened a desk drawer. She pulled out his cellphone and his Kimber. He was glad to see that gun, especially now that he knew Vasily Petrov might be coming after him. "Lori, go down and bring the car around the back entrance. I'll bring Justin out that way."

Lori didn't hesitate as she headed for the elevator. Novak turned back to Irina one last time. She was punching a number into his cellphone. "Don't ever call me. Leave a text, and I'll call you back."

"You sure you'll be all right?"

"Yes. He always catches me and punishes me, but then he relents. He will this time, too. Trust me. I know him better than anybody."

"Okay, but I don't like it."

"Wait, Daddy gave me some morphine last night because he felt bad after he beat me up. I need to give Justin some more before you move him."

Novak stood and watched her inject her boyfriend with an expertise that showed lots of practice. Justin tried to sit up, groaned, and lay back down. His pain had to be excruciating. The worst foreboding Novak had felt in a long time gripped him as he watched Irina lean down and kiss the boy gently on his battered cheek. Novak would help them, but he feared they were both going to end up dead, and sooner rather than later.

Chapter 5

Justin Dalton was only sixteen years old and looked like a brainy computer nerd. He was neither big nor tall, and had picked the wrong girl to love. After the morphine injection, the boy put on a brave front, assuring Irina he would be okay as he placed a pair of wire-rimmed glasses atop his broken nose. One of his arms was also broken, cradled in a makeshift sling made out of a pink scarf. With his naked eye Novak could see the break where it was pushing against the skin of his forearm. He rewrapped the scarf to bind that arm tightly to Justin's chest. Any movement of that limb would be excruciating. Justin knew that, too, because he clamped his teeth together and nodded that he was ready.

Novak knew it was impossible not to hurt this kid when he moved him. He'd had too many injuries and broken bones himself. He lifted the boy off the couch as gently as he could, but it didn't matter. Justin screamed with pain, and came close to passing out. The morphine had not taken full effect, and he never stopped groaning. Novak suspected he had multiple cracked ribs, and that intensified Novak's concerns about internal bleeding. Moving him without a backboard was dangerous, as evidenced by the blood at the corner of his mouth. If the boy lived through a beating this severe, Novak would be shocked. Petrov and his men had basically taken their time and beaten him to near death. Fortunately, the kid blacked out before Novak got him to the elevator.

"Don't take him anywhere around here, please. Daddy's got people everywhere. You need to take him down as far as Richmond, at least. It's less than an hour if you take I-95 South. He should be safe there, don't you think? Go to the VCU Medical Center on East Marshall. It's easy to find, okay? That's where I found out I was having my baby. Please, just be careful, okay?"

Irina was crying the whole time she told him all that. She followed them to the door, waving goodbye, sobbing as the elevator doors slid together and blocked her from Novak's view.

Lori was already out at the curb with the Jeep. She jumped out of the driver's seat when she saw Novak, and hurried around to open the back door. Novak settled the boy on his back as best he could. He hoped Justin remained unconscious for the duration of the trip. He shut the door and glanced around looking for Petrov, but didn't see him or anyone else. Again, the whole area seemed deserted, but that was good. He climbed into the passenger seat, and Lori took off.

"He's really bad off. I hope we get him to the hospital in time."

Lori nodded and turned on the blinker. "Did she say where to take him?"

"Yeah. VCU in Richmond. An hour or so away."

"God, I hope he makes it. She should have called an ambulance the minute she found him like this and had him medivacked somewhere else."

"She knew better. Those thugs would have shown back up before the ambulance did, bloody baseball bats in hand. Nobody would've lifted a finger to save him, not in any hospital with ties to the Senator. Looks to me like Blackwood owns everybody and everything in this part of Virginia, especially in that little make-believe town called Blackwood."

It didn't take them long to reach the Interstate, and Novak breathed easier once they were headed south at a high speed, with no tails behind that he could see. There wasn't much traffic this early, which was good. They had been lucky thus far, considering everything, and he hoped that held out. Novak had no doubt that Petrov had been the one who'd pummeled Justin and left him to die. Novak had seen Lori's intelligence on some of the Russian operatives. Their reputation of brutal cruelty to prisoners in the Middle East was well known. They had beatings and torture down to an art.

Obviously, Blackwood had no qualms about allowing Petrov do whatever he pleased, as long as his victim ended up in the ground. Anybody who dared cross the Senator was given over to his deadly henchman for a swift penalty, and Novak had to find a way to prove what they'd been doing. He settled back into the seat and tried to figure the best way to bring them down. Now that he'd learned more about Blackwood, he wanted to take him out. They needed to pay for what they done to those two kids. God only knew what else they'd done.

Novak pulled out his cellphone and found a map of northern Virginia. They were moving farther away from his boat at the marina. That might complicate things, but he might have to leave it there for a while. Once Justin was safely under a doctor's care in Richmond, maybe he and Lori could get a flight back to Washington. But no, that would leave the Jeep at the hospital, and he wasn't about to leave Lori anywhere alone. He'd have to worry about logistics later. Right now, Justin was in a life or death situation and had to remain their primary concern. They were on their way, and if they continued to make good time, maybe the boy would make it, after all. Even a Senator couldn't bribe everybody in a huge metropolitan hospital. That last shot of morphine was holding up so far. The boy hadn't moved. Novak needed to come up with a story that would satisfy the ER personnel. He couldn't tell them the truth.

Behind him, Justin strangled and stirred, groaning, then settled back, his breath rasping. Novak spoke the exact coordinates for the hospital into the GPS system, and then turned around and watched the road behind them. Nobody was following them, not yet, but they would as soon as they found Irina and got the boy's whereabouts out of her. She would tell them, but at awful expense to her body. They'd beat her even worse this time. She should never have returned to that farm. He should never have let her. After that, they'd come for them. Blackwood wanted this kid dead, and Petrov wouldn't stop until he was. Novak had to think up a reason to have them put Justin in a protected room.

In contrast to their dark task and the horribly beaten boy in the back seat, the autumn day was glorious, the sun high in the sky, bright and shining, the air outside windy and cool. Both sides of the divided Interstate were beautiful with the fall colors, and even more vivid in the sunshine. Novak couldn't dredge up much enthusiasm about scenery, or spending a romantic holiday alone with Lori, not anymore. He wanted this poor kid to survive and for Irina to get out of that hell house before she ended up dead, too. She was in a lot more danger than she knew. Willingly placing herself back under Blackwood's control had been a stupid move. If she pushed him too far, Blackwood would get tired of it as well as her. That's when he'd give the kill order and find another plaything to corrupt.

Novak had seen plenty of young people destroy themselves on opioids, both while in the military and in civilian life. It was a scourge that needed to be eradicated. The last he'd heard, several hundred Americans died of heroin or opioid addiction each week. Even worse was the fentanyl, the synthetic poison being smuggled into the country and sometimes mixed into the heroin, causing overdoses. He'd watched helplessly while a young girl had died of an overdose on a New Orleans street only a few months ago. He had since started carrying the antidote, naloxone, in his backpack.

He never wanted to see a young person perish in front of his eyes again. Irina just might be the one who needed it before her nightmare was over. Since Petrov was in the mix and Irina had been addicted, Novak believed the two men were into drugs somehow. He meant to find out.

Apparently, Lori had been thinking along the same lines. "Irina is young and naïve; she's underestimating what's going on here. She may have gotten away with bad behavior when she was younger, but loving another man and getting pregnant by him could be the bitter end for her. It would be the worst possible offense to a man as possessive and egotistical as Blackwood."

"Charles Blackwood's known for his pride and vanity. He sent men to murder Justin for loving her, and he almost got away with it. Her bringing me in was just a fluke that probably saved his life."

"She's next, Novak. Then Blackwood will find himself a new little girl in some other foreign country, and she'll end up just like Irina. We've got to stop this."

"We will. He's going down."

Lori glanced at him, then returned her attention to the road. "Well, I'm getting a little nervous. They don't seem to leave loose ends, and that's what we are."

"I've been watching. Nobody's following us."

"So far. Everything about this mess stinks to high heaven. Here we've got a revered former Senator involved in felony child abuse and sexual exploitation of his own underage, adopted daughter. God only knows what else he's doing. Now we've got an assault and battery with intent to kill, an attempted murder with the victim still alive to identify who did it. Irina's going to end up dead if she goes back there. We should call in law enforcement before they kill her."

"We should but we can't. We don't have any proof that they've done anything. They've got a record of me being inside their make-believe jail after assaulting the Senator. They'll put me up as the perpetrator. They'll make sure I take the fall. After we get Justin to the hospital, we can go back and find a way to get Irina out of that house. Don't ask me how, because I don't know. She feels safe, but they'll end up killing her, even though she won't believe it's possible."

Lori sighed and shook her head. "And to think I expected us to have a nice quiet getaway at that Victorian bed and breakfast. Damn it, you're a trouble magnet." She looked down at the instrument panel and groaned. "Oh, God, we're almost out of gas. I should've filled up yesterday. We've got to stop at the next station."

"We don't need to take the time."

"No, we don't, but it's better than to get stranded on the side of the road with an empty tank. I'll make it fast."

Ten minutes later, Lori turned up the next ramp, where there was a tourist stop with a big BP gas station and a Subway restaurant next door. Both looked busy, sitting off to the left side of the outer blacktopped road. A farm implement company sat just across from the filling station, but that was it as far as business concerns. The rest of the area looked like privately owned property, mostly covered in thick woods. Lori swung into the big graveled parking lot and pulled up at an open pump. Novak climbed out and searched the road for black Volkswagen SUVs or white BMWs. He saw nothing suspicious. His head told him it was unlikely Blackwood's men could find them this fast, but he was nervous because Irina had gone back there. If they made her talk and thought Justin could identify them, they would come after Lori and him, and it wouldn't take them long to catch up. He told Lori he would pump the gas while she went in and paid for it. Since the station was busy like most pit stops along the major Interstates, they didn't stand out.

Novak scanned the other people who were pumping gas. He saw nobody he recognized, nor anyone who seemed to be watching him. He pulled out the nozzle and gassed up, while Lori hurried across the busy lot and disappeared inside. Justin was not moving, but at least his chest was still rising and falling. The morphine was doing the trick now, but the difficult breathing was getting worse. Novak propped the nozzle to continue gassing the Jeep, and then opened the back door and gently moved Justin farther onto his side, so that he faced the front seat with his broken arm on top. He took off his windbreaker and draped it over the boy. The kid was alive right now, and that was about the only good news Novak had to hold on to.

After the tank was full, Novak got back into the Jeep and watched for bad guys. He knew they were coming. He just couldn't shake the idea that something terrible was going to happen before they could get the kid to Richmond. Lori was back within minutes with some bottles of water and a dozen glazed donuts. She started up the engine, and Novak grabbed a water bottle and drank down most of it. It had been a long, cold night lying on that jailhouse bunk, and his day was only getting worse. The station was crowded now, all the pumps engaged. The person waiting in the car behind them beeped his horn, so Lori pulled out in a hurry and headed for the exit lane.

The nice day had started going to hell, along with everything else they faced. Clouds the color of gunmetal hunched together like a massive frown on an angry sky. The portended storm had arrived and dulled the fall scenery, like a pall of depression settling over a deathbed. The temperature seemed to plummet all at once, with a hard wind blowing up out of nowhere and sending rain in windswept sheets against the Jeep's windows. People standing at the pumps zipped up their jackets and turned their backs to the blowing rain sweeping in under the canopy. Then a deluge hit all at once, as if released from a giant open spigot. A hard downpour pummeled the windshield in blurry sheets, sliding down the glass and running off the hood. Thunder cracked somewhere in the distance. Novak cursed—a storm was all they needed to slow them down. Recapping the bottle, he could not get his mind off Irina Blackwood and what was likely happening to her at that moment.

Lori noticed his agitation. He could tell she knew what he was thinking, which was not unusual. They'd spent several months sailing the Caribbean, just the two of them on the boat. They'd gotten to know each other's moods well. "You're worried about the girl. Go ahead, try to text her. You'll feel better if you know she's okay."

"I've just got this bad feeling, I can't help it. I trust my instincts. I think they're going to kill her."

"Text her, right now. Rest your mind. I can't see him just up and murdering his own daughter. She's been with him since she was six years old, or so he says. Maybe he went after Justin because he didn't want to have to hurt her."

Novak didn't believe any of that to be true.

"Do you really think they're going to murder her?"

"She's nothing but trouble for them now. She knows a lot about their business. She can name names and places. I know Petrov won't want to keep her breathing. He's hiding from the law, as it is."

"I still think Blackwood loves Irina too much to kill her. I guess that's what you call what he feels for her."

"That's not what you call it. Not even close."

"I know."

With the rain creating havoc on the metal roof, Novak got out the phone Irina had given him and punched in *u ok?*. He sat back and waited for a reply. "She's not answering. She's dead. I know it."

"No, you don't know it. Maybe Blackwood took the phone away from her. That's typical punishment for teens nowadays, I hear. Or she's hidden the phone and will check her messages later."

"Yeah, maybe. Or maybe he beat her to death with it."

"C'mon, Novak, quit thinking the worst, will you? He's obsessed with her in his own perverted way. He'll beat her, but killing her would create more questions that he wants to answer. You know, she has to know people in the area, like her high school teachers, friends, maybe social media connections. She should have come with us. I agree with you there."

Lori braked at the highway and looked through the beating windshield wipers for oncoming traffic. Cars were approaching slowly from both directions, so they waited for a gray Dodge truck to pass them. The rain began to let up a little, and the wipers were working better. Novak hoped the rain would stop completely. He could not get Irina off his mind. Lori had a point, though. Irina had been with Blackwood for years, had most likely disobeyed and angered him a million times, and she was still alive and breathing. After raising her for a decade, he had to care about her. Although that sounded reasonable, Novak didn't buy it. He tried texting again. There was still no answer. There was nothing else he could do about Irina, not until they got Justin checked into the medical center. They were about halfway there now. Novak turned to look at the traffic coming at them from Lori's side. That's when he saw a big white cab of a semi-truck, roaring straight at Lori's driver's seat.

Lori saw it, too, and tried to stamp down on the accelerator to get out of the way, but it was too late. The giant cab rammed the side of the Jeep so hard that they went sliding and scraping sideways across the gravel, pushed like snow in front of a plow. Novak's head whiplashed from the initial impact, and his airbag exploded against his face and chest, a devastating punch to the heart. Stunned at first, all he could hear was the shrill grinding of rending metal and smashing glass and flying shards. He heard Lori scream as the Jeep went over, tottering there a moment before crashing down on Novak's side. The passenger window shattered under him, and the windblown rain drenched Novak where he was strapped to the seat.

The truck's cab did not stop there, but kept gunning its motor, pushing the Jeep harder and harder until it began to overturn. The resistance finally gave way, and the Jeep landed upside down on its roof. The metal shrieked under the weight of the Jeep and then crumpled, crushing down to within inches of Novak's head. Novak's mind went reeling around like cartwheels, desperately trying to latch on to consciousness, but he couldn't seem to grab it. He hung upside down, held in place by the seatbelt harness.

Jagged streaks of light flashed in a strobe effect inside his skull, and he blinked as blood from a laceration on his head burned his eyes and blinded him. He wiped it away, his mind still reeling with shock. Then he remembered Lori. He found her in the driver's seat, also suspended upside down from the roof. Her nose and ears were flooding out scarlet streams of blood. She was hurt bad. Her eyes were closed, but he thought she was still breathing. Then he remembered Justin. The kid had not been strapped in. Justin was lying on the smashed-in roof of the car behind Novak. He was covered in blood, and definitely not moving.

Trying to shake off his confusion, Novak became aware of the big semi cab. It was still there. It had backed up and was sitting a few yards away. The driver kept revving the motor in a continuous threat, as if preparing for a second run at them. Novak couldn't think quite straight enough to know what to do, so he just hung there, his head bleeding onto the roof, his ears ringing over the roar of the truck's motor. After a few seconds, he got his bearings and tried to spot the attackers. The cab was still sitting there, looming over them like a vulture over a trapped rabbit. He tried to wipe away the blood blinding him, and saw a man's legs step down out of the cab.

It was Vasily Petrov. The Russian started walking through the rain toward the wreck. He had a silenced Ruger in his hand. The fear that brought up cleared Novak's head, and he scratched at his belt holster for his own weapon. Twisting desperately, he couldn't reach it because of the shoulder harness. Petrov had stopped on the other side of the crushed Jeep. He squatted down and peered inside the broken back seat window. When he saw Justin, he raised his weapon and pumped a double tap into the boy's head, and two more into his back. Novak clawed desperately for his weapon. Then Petrov turned his gun on Lori where she was suspended limp and unconscious on her harness. He lifted his weapon and pointed it at the back of her head. Novak touched the cold metal, pulled the .45 out, and held down the trigger. His slugs shattered what was left of the window glass, filling the Jeep with caustic smoke and the smell of gunpowder, the loud explosions of the guns nearly deafening him.

Petrov had ducked down. Novak saw the Russian scrambling back toward the truck. Novak started firing again, emptying his magazine, but he knew he'd hit Petrov because the man fell, got up, and limped heavily as he pulled himself up into the truck cab. The last thing Novak heard before daylight dissolved behind a black velvet curtain was the immense roar of the killer diesel truck fading away down the highway, and the last thing he saw was the concerned faces of people outside the windows. They were yelling and trying to pry open the door beside him. Then it got dark and quiet as all light and sound faded away to nothing.

Chapter 6

When Novak regained consciousness, he hurt all over and couldn't remember where he was. He tried to lift his head, but a debilitating onslaught of nausea hit the pit of his stomach. He gagged and lay still with his eyes squeezed shut. He sucked in deep breaths until the sickness subsided. After a couple of minutes, he opened his eyes and stared up at a white ceiling. Everything around him was white, like a snowscape. It wasn't the first time he'd awoken with no memory of what was going on, but this time his temples pounded whenever he tried to move his head. It felt like burning ropes pressed into his waist and across his chest.

He finally realized his bed was surrounded by white curtains. It looked like an Emergency Room cubicle. Someone outside the drapes was saying something he couldn't quite discern, and then there was a loud crack of thunder that rattled the curtain rods. Once that happened, Novak's recollections kicked in. The scenarios clicked through his mind in rapid succession like flipping pages of a book: the crash, the overturned Jeep, then the rest of the accident, rushing through his mind like storm waters sweeping down a steep rock canyon. Lori was hurt bad, he thought, alarmed. She had been hanging upside down and bleeding heavily. That memory scared him. His thoughts scraped like broken shards of thin glass as he tried to piece it all together. Then he relived Vasily Petrov striding toward the Jeep, peering inside at him and raising his gun. Oh, God, he'd shot Justin Dalton, but Novak couldn't remember about Lori. Had Petrov shot her, too?

Novak's confusion sent him into panic mode. He shot to an upright sitting position, and paid the price as his brain seemed to explode inside his skull. A hammer-hard pulse attacked his temples, and his stomach rolled.

Groaning and holding his head in his hands, he saw the young red-haired nurse in green scrubs standing at the foot of his bed. A man was standing beside her. She walked around the bed and stood on his right. She placed a hand on his heaving chest and pushed him back down.

"Everything's okay, Mr. Novak, please, you must remain lying down. You're all right. You're being taken care of in a hospital. This is the Emergency Room at VCU. You've been in a terrible car accident, but you're going to be fine. You've had a shock to your brain and cuts and abrasions from the flying glass. Your car overturned, and the exploding airbag hit you very hard in the chest and head. Please, calm down and try to lie still. Do you remember anything about the accident?"

Novak frowned, trying to remember as he massaged his aching temples.

"Please stay calm. You need to take things nice and slow for a while. The doctor has ordered a mild sedative in case you became agitated. I'm going to get it for you. Don't worry about being confused or frightened. Victims of head traumas often awake feeling like that. You're safe here. We're treating you for your injuries." She glanced at the man at the foot of the bed. "This is a police detective. He'd like to ask you a few questions about the accident if you feel up to it. Is that all right?"

It was not all right. He didn't know this guy or who he really was. Then he remembered Charles Blackwood's face and his Gestapo jailhouse. He was the one who'd sent Petrov after them. He wasn't going to tell this guy anything. The nurse leaned closer and examined the bandage wrapped around his forehead. Novak saw two of her, and knew then that he was still in bad shape. He wasn't fine yet, no way. Closing his eyes, he found that helped with his dizziness. His ears were ringing and his heartbeat was racing. He heard a slow, discordant clanging inside his ears, like the tolling of a cracked cathedral bell. Lori's bloody face came to mind and piled on more anxiety. The bell inside his head was killing him.

"What about Lori?" he asked the nurse. "She was in the car with me. Is she okay?"

The nurse continued to hold him down. "You've got to calm down, Mr. Novak. Yes, your friend survived the accident. She's not awake yet, but the doctors think it won't be much longer. The EMTs said she got the worst of the impact on the driver's side. You both have suffered concussions. You've got a deep cut on your forehead and another one on your chin. We've cleaned and stitched them, and they should heal up just fine. The doctor ordered X-rays and MRI just to be safe. The airbag hit you with such velocity that there could be internal damage, but we don't believe there is. But you will be sore for quite some time. Please try not to worry.

Ms. Garner is upstairs in the CCU. She's doing well and breathing on her own. She should wake up at any time now."

"What about the boy in the back seat?"

Even as Novak voiced the question, he knew Justin was dead. Novak and Lori were lucky they weren't lying in the morgue with him. They were targets. Petrov now knew that Novak had watched him murder Justin. They would come for him soon. Details were coming back into focus now. He and Lori had survived the crash. They were alive. How long they would remain so was the question. Petrov could be inside the hospital right now. He could be standing outside in the corridor, waiting to get Novak alone. Novak had to get out of there. He and Lori both had to get out.

The nurse was talking about Justin. Her voice had gentled and gone quiet. "The young man that was found in the back seat of your car didn't make it, I'm afraid. He was pronounced dead at the scene. I am so sorry to have to tell you that. Was he your son?"

Novak's stomach kept pitching and dipping and rolling. He shut his eyes and fought down the queasiness. He kept seeing Petrov shoot that poor kid in the head, watching it happen over and over, stuck like a faulty video. He opened his eyes when the officer spoke for the first time. He was standing beside Novak's head now, but on the opposite side of the bed. He was leaning close. He smelled like cigarettes. "I'm Detective Phil Harmon with the Richmond Police Department. We need to get a full statement from you, just as soon as you feel up to it, Mr. Novak. Do you think we could possibly do it now?"

Novak wasn't going to tell him anything, not until he figured out what to do. Justin had died from gunshots to the head. They could, and probably would, blame it on him. He had to be extremely careful with what he said. "I can't tell you. I don't remember much. Did a truck hit us? Tell me what happened."

Harmon didn't fill him in. "Do you remember anything after the truck rammed your military Jeep?"

"It rammed us? Why? I can't seem to think straight."

"There were multiple witnesses at the BP station who told us a white cab off a sixteen-wheeler drove right into you. Its trailer wasn't attached, according to those who saw it hit you. Your Jeep overturned and ended up lying on its roof. Do you remember any of that?"

"No, wait...maybe. I'm really confused. Why?"

"The witnesses also swore in written statements that a man got out of that cab, approached the Jeep, and fired a gun multiple times into the back seat. You don't remember that, either? Can you identify the gunman?"

"I'm not sure I saw that happen."

"You didn't see the shooter approach the car?"

Novak studied the detective's craggy face, not sure how far Blackwood's tentacles reached. "Where are we again?"

"You're at the Virginia Commonwealth University Medical Center in Richmond."

Novak wondered how influential Blackwood was with the Richmond Police Department. As a former Senator from Virginia, he would definitely know and hobnob with the current Governor and other politicos in the Capital. He had been a Senator from this state forever. Novak couldn't trust anybody. Not a single person would believe him over the Honorable Charles Blackwood. If he wasn't careful, Novak would end up in jail and charged with Justin's murder. Maybe that was Petrov's plan. He needed help, all right, but he sure as hell wasn't going to trust this detective.

"Can you describe the vehicle that hit you?" the cop asked.

"Um, I think you're right about it being a semi, but just the cab, yeah, like you said. No trailer. It was big and coming at us hard. I seem to remember that. It all happened so fast. I wasn't conscious for long, I don't think."

"Did you see who was driving the truck?"

"No, I don't think so." That was true. "It was over quick. I was knocked out at first, maybe."

"So you wouldn't be able to identify the truck if you saw it again? Or tell me why they would want to target you?"

Novak shook his head. That rapid movement sent barbed darts of pain through his temples and down the base of his skull. No, he was not okay, not by a long shot.

"Okay, just tell me what you do remember."

Swiping his tongue over dry lips, Novak felt the stiff suture threads on the gash at the corner of his mouth. He touched them lightly with his fingertips, and found they ran all the way down under his chin. His mouth felt stuffed with dusty cotton balls, and he was extremely thirsty but didn't think his stomach could handle water or anything else. He just wanted this cop to go away. "It came out of the blue. On purpose, though, I think they hit us on purpose."

It hurt Novak to take a deep breath, he found that out quickly, especially where the airbag had slammed him. He remembered his healing gunshot wound and felt his side. The recent scar had not reopened.

The detective was not finished. "Okay, Mr. Novak, like I said before, we got statements backing up your account. According to them, you were sitting at the exit waiting to pull back on the road when they rammed you.

Every single witness told us the exact same thing. We think we've already found the truck, by the way, abandoned in the woods about fifteen miles west of that gas station. No license plates, no registration, no fingerprints, so we figure it's gonna turn up as stolen. Lucky for you, there were lots of witnesses that put you in the clear on all counts. It just seems peculiar to me that they picked such a busy gas station to ram you and commit a murder, to boot. They had to know people would see it all go down." He stopped and watched Novak's face. "Would you happen to know why anyone would want to attack you like that? Were they targeting the young man in the back seat, you think?"

Novak was done with this guy. "Please, nurse, can't we finish this later? I'm feeling really sick to my stomach and just so dizzy."

The nurse stopped adjusting his IV line and sent a severe look at the detective. Her voice was firm. "Okay, that's enough, Detective. This man has a concussion and does not need to be agitated. Come back tomorrow. If he feels up to it then, you can question him further."

Unfortunately, the cop didn't listen. Novak was still piecing his thoughts together. He kept reliving the crash, the smashing, shattering, terrifying, thunderous impact that had sent the Jeep over on its top. He recalled hanging upside down, and how the blood had flowed down on the roof. The worst part had been seeing Lori suspended in her seat, bloody and unconscious. Petrov had been walking over to the Jeep. He'd fired into the back seat, and somehow Novak had fired back. After that, everything got muddied up and confusing. He'd gotten off some shots. Had he wounded Petrov? He thought he had, but he couldn't remember for sure.

The nurse was speaking to him in her soft patient-only voice. "There is one thing, Mr. Novak, that we truly need to know. It's important that we contact the deceased's next of kin, but no identification was found inside the car. Can you tell us his name? Please try to remember. It's important that we notify the family as soon as possible."

Novak didn't know what to do. The last thing he wanted to think about was that boy lying in a morgue on a metal slab. But giving Justin's name would lead to more questions. He could let them know later, after he got Lori safely out of the hospital. Petrov would come back for them, Novak was positive of that, and he would show up soon.

"That young man had nothing on him," Harmon added, ignoring the nurse's order to leave. "We need his name. Why was he traveling with you?" Harmon was getting impatient. "He died from gunshot wounds, Mr. Novak. Two slugs to his head and two more to the back. Witnesses heard the shots. They said there was return fire from inside the car and that the assailant was possibly wounded. Did you fire back, Mr. Novak? Do you know why he wanted to kill the man in your back seat?"

There was something off about this officer. Maybe he was there at Blackwood's discretion. Novak couldn't trust anybody. If he was Blackwood's man and took Novak in for questioning, Novak would end up in that noose planned for him in the little Hallmark town. One thing he did know: Petrov had been ordered to kill them, and he would have, if Novak hadn't opened up in time. Novak and Lori could not hang around long enough for Petrov to get a second chance. He was a pro, and not a man who ever gave quarter to anybody. If he wanted you dead, you'd end up dead. He'd be back, and they were sitting ducks inside their hospital beds. "I believe some guy did get out of that truck. I think I remember that."

The cop perked up. "What's his name? Did you recognize him?"

"I might have, but I can't recall it right now. You know, the dizziness." Novak wasn't dizzy now, but he was thinking fast. He looked at the police officer and considered spilling out the whole truth, simply identifying Petrov and Blackwood as the bad guys. Still, his gut told him not to do that. The Senator would deny everything, and Novak couldn't prove anything, not with Justin dead and Irina still under her father's thumb. Nope, right now, Novak couldn't and wouldn't trust anybody. "You know what, Officer? I think maybe we might've been taking that boy to the hospital. Yeah, I think that's it. Somebody had beaten him up, yes, he was terribly hurt when we found him—yes, I think that's right. We found him unconscious on the side of the road. We pulled over, and I'm pretty sure we were probably trying to get him to a doctor when it happened."

"I need to know who pulled that trigger, Mr. Novak." The cop didn't sound like he was buying into Novak's story. "Do you remember where you found the deceased on the side of the road?"

Novak wanted to get rid of this guy, find Lori, and get the hell out of that hospital and back to his boat before Petrov showed up. He kept feigning memory loss, but that wouldn't hold up forever. He had returned fire on Petrov, and that had left shell casings that matched his weapon inside the wrecked Jeep. They'd also find the Kimber 1911, if they hadn't already, and it would be taken into evidence, so he wouldn't get it back. That left him unarmed.

"I feel sick. My head is killing me. Nurse, please give me something for this pain," he said to the nurse, and that was all definitely true. He had to do something. He was unarmed and in a hospital gown. Canadian geese sitting on a frozen pond in front of a hunter's blind had better chances of survival than he did. "I'm seeing double now. Please, nurse, I can't do this anymore. I need you to give me something, please."

The nurse jumped the cop for hanging around. Her voice had a harder edge this time. "I am sorry, officer, but you're going to have to finish this interview tomorrow. My patient is not up to intensive questioning. I think you should let him have today to recover and come back in the morning. He should feel much better by then."

The cop looked disgruntled. "All right, I'll come back." Then he turned to Novak one last time. "We will need a full statement from you before you're released. You sure you don't know who the deceased man is? He's young and seems to have taken a violent beating before he was shot to death."

Novak picked up on the implication and didn't answer. He kept his eyes closed. The cop thought he'd beat up Justin. He was in for an assault and battery charge at the very least. He opened his eyes. "He was unconscious when we found him; yeah, he was beaten up, that's what scared us. He had a gun, too. It was stuck in his waistband. That's right, I do remember that. I didn't want to leave it at the side of the road, so I picked it up and stowed it under the front passenger seat."

"What kind of gun?"

"A .45 caliber, I think."

"What else did you find on him?"

"I didn't look for anything else. We were in hurry to get him help. I do recall that gun, though. The lady with me was armed, too. She works at the Pentagon. They need to be notified about the accident. It was one of their Jeeps."

"Seems your memory is coming back now, Mr. Novak."

"Yeah, a little bit at a time, but I'm so tired."

"That's enough." The nurse was adamant this time. "You're going to have to leave right now."

"Okay, just one more question. You say the victim was in terrible shape when you found him, but he was armed and unconscious. Why didn't you call the police, right then and there? And why would you stop at the BP station and pick up donuts, if you were in such a hurry to get him to a doctor?"

This guy was asking all the right questions, which was not good news for Novak. "I don't know why. Wait, we were out of gas. We were rushing him to the hospital, and when Lori went inside to pay, she grabbed some food and water, I guess, I don't know exactly. Nurse, can you give me something for this headache? Please, it's terrible."

The young nurse grew fierce. "Okay, enough is enough. This man has just woken from a traumatic accident in which he suffered a serious head injury. He needs time to recover without your badgering him. Leave right now. You can come back tomorrow. Do I have to call security?"

The detective appeared unconcerned with all that. He knew—and so did Novak—that hospital security couldn't make him do anything. The doctor could, though. He stared at Novak. "Don't leave town until we have a chance to talk," he said. "I hope you feel better soon, Mr. Novak."

"I don't think I'll be able to get out of this bed any time soon," Novak lied. He was getting out of that hospital bed the minute he could walk on his own.

The nurse had a sedative already prepared, and was injecting it into his IV line. "There now, Mr. Novak, this will relieve your pain and help you get some sleep."

Whatever she gave him worked fast. The tension in his body drained away, his limbs relaxed, and his headache subsided. He closed his eyes, hoping Petrov didn't show up and kill him before he woke up.

Chapter 7

The next time Novak opened his eyes, he had been moved into a private room. It was dark outside his windows. His headache had faded, and his thoughts were clear. There was no double vision, and he could sit up without groaning and clutching his head. Even better, there was no sign of Petrov. Unfortunately, a man that Novak had never seen before sat in a wheelchair that he had rolled up close beside the bed. He had on blue hospital scrubs and white tennis shoes, and was watching a New York Rangers hockey game on the television affixed high on the opposite wall. The sound was muted. Novak did not want to talk to this guy. He felt okay, but nowhere near a hundred percent. It was quiet outside in the corridor, so it must have been late. Who was this guy? A nurse, an orderly? He was mildly surprised the hall nurse had allowed some stranger to come in and watch his television. Maybe he was waiting for somebody. Novak shut his eyes again.

"You feel better now, do you not?"

Novak considered feigning sleep but wanted to know who this guy was and what he wanted. He turned his face toward the guy without lifting his head. "Who are you?"

The man remained seated. He didn't look as big as Novak, maybe five feet eight or nine, or even smaller. He was stocky, with the kind of big rough hands and bulky arms of a dirt farmer who fought hard scrabble earth for years. He looked fit, though, and totally relaxed with his legs stretched out and crossed at the ankles. His thick fingers were intertwined and resting atop his stomach. He was smiling. Problem was, there wasn't anything to smile about. Novak sure as hell wasn't smiling. The man had the bare hint of a foreign accent, one that Novak had a sneaking suspicion was Russian.

There seemed to be lots of Muscovites running around in northern Virginia all of a sudden. He did not like the feeling that he was unable to defend himself if this guy meant him harm. Tensing up, he waited for those big rough-hewn hands to clench around his throat. Novak needed to get out of bed and find some kind of weapon, because he was still drugged up, and if this guy wasn't one of Blackwood's henchmen, the next guy would be. The effects of the sedative were slowly wearing off, but he was still at a definite disadvantage. If this man had come there intending to fight him or inject him with something lethal, Novak was in trouble. He could have done that while Novak was asleep. So why hadn't he?

"Hey, Will, please—I know you're trying to figure all this out. Please do not fear me. I mean you no harm. You will have to defend yourself, however, when Vasily Petrov shows up here with his steel icepick. I'm surprised he hasn't come for you yet. He's had the time to kill you, so why hasn't he? I suppose they think you and your pretty lady friend upstairs are too busted up to go anywhere, so they're taking their time."

Novak tried to digest all that. He asked again, "Who are you?"

"That doesn't matter."

"It matters to me."

On edge, Novak glanced around the room. Everything seemed all right. He didn't sense imminent danger. The guy had his hands in plain sight, so he wasn't reaching for a knife or pistol. Novak searched for a call button, but found that it had been moved from the bed to the side table, well out of his reach. "Look, I don't know what you're talking about. How about handing me that call button? I need a nurse."

"Sorry. I can't do that."

Novak examined the guy's face. He stared back. His eyes were big, black and luminous enough to reflect the television screen. He looked fairly young—thirties, maybe older. White-blond hair that looked bleached because of his dark brows, close-to-the-skull buzz cut, and a dark blond scruff along his jawline. His voice was the rumbling kind of deep bass, but he had the calm and quiet demeanor of a scholar. Novak was in no shape to take on him, or anyone else for that matter. He would probably have to, sooner or later. He flexed his arms and figured he could put down the guy if he got in the first blow. He played stupid. "Who's Petrov? What do you mean?"

"Come now, my friend. Don't play silly games. Better to not take me for a fool or incompetent. I know what you and the woman have been doing. I know who the deceased kid inside your car is, and I know why he was almost beaten to death."

He knew a lot, all right—too much, in fact. His English was good, but his accent was definitely Russian, barely discernible but probably originating from the north—somewhere around St. Petersburg would be Novak's guess. He had lived and worked in Russia for almost a year. They had been protecting a diplomatic mission with the cooperation of the Kremlin. His guess was that this man was a member of the GRU, Russia's military intelligence service. They were all taught English as part of their job. He looked and acted the part. He doubted the guy would admit it. "Who are you? Why are you here?"

"Do not be alarmed. I am here to help you, my friend. You need to believe that and trust me. So listen well, Mr. Novak. You need to get out of that bed right now so the two of us can go upstairs and get your girlfriend and take her out of here. We cannot leave her behind, or she'll end up with a bullet in her head like Justin Dalton, or poison in her IV."

Novak felt alarmed, if that's what the man was going for. "Is she okay? Did she wake up?"

"Yes, about an hour ago, I guess. The way I saw it, she felt pretty much the same way you did when that detective was questioning you down in the ER."

"How do you know so much about me?"

"I've been following you, ever since Blackwood's men grabbed you at that steakhouse."

Novak didn't like that. "Why? I don't know you. I've never seen you before."

"I'll tell you that and everything else you wish to know, but only after I get you and the woman to a safe house."

"And if we don't trust you and don't want to go along?"

The man stared at him for a long moment, then hitched a small shrug. "Then you will both end up dead. Tonight, most likely. This place has very weak security. Almost non-existent. I was able to move about freely once I put on these clothes and stole an ID card. Nobody even questions my presence. Even I was surprised at how easy it is to infiltrate your American medical centers."

Nothing about any of that sounded good. "You're going to have to tell me more than this before I step a foot outside this room."

"Just know that I am a friend to you. I also want to bring down the Senator and his criminal organization, for my own reasons. I think you can help me do that. Therefore, you are valuable to me. I don't want you dead this early in the game."

What the hell? Novak couldn't decide whether or not to believe him. He couldn't trust him; that was a given. He also knew Petrov would soon show up and put a bullet in him. He was the only witness to the cold-blooded execution of Justin Dalton, and could identify Vasily Petrov as the killer. Petrov would kill Lori next, a loose end that needed to be eliminated. She knew who was involved, and that was her death warrant, plain and simple.

"You're thinking he'll come with a silenced handgun and shoot you both in your beds. Right? But you're wrong. That's too risky for a man as careful as Vasily. They'll make some kind of diversion, and while the nurses are busy, they'll inject you with a special drug that kills in seconds, without leaving a trace at autopsy. They deal these kinds of drugs, so they're handily available to him."

"You're Russian. Petrov is a Russian. How do I know you're not working with him?"

"You don't, of course. But ask yourself this, Novak: why would I sit here and wait for you to wake up? Why wouldn't I have already injected you and your girlfriend? I've had plenty of time and the means to do it, with no one the wiser. If I wanted you dead, you'd have been dead the minute they put you inside this room."

The guy was right. "Where do you want to take us? What safe house?"

The Russian did not hesitate. "No need to know the particulars. I have a secure place. It lies to the east of Blackwood's horse pastures. It's perfectly safe there. He and Petrov do not know of it."

"I don't think I want to be that close to those guys. You know, since they're gunning for me."

The Russian stared at him. Novak watched his face for signs of subterfuge. He didn't see anything but a bland, serene expression. This guy looked and acted like a trained operative. He spoke like one, and had the cool confidence of a man who could take care of himself. Novak felt certain that's exactly what he was. But the man was right. Novak needed to get Lori out of that hospital bed and somewhere safe. Her Jeep was totaled, and the Pentagon would send soldiers down to get it. All their possessions were now in the hands of the police. Once they were safely away from the hospital, Novak had easy access to money and plenty of it, in his offshore bank accounts. This man was telling the truth about one thing. He could have killed Novak while he was unconscious. Novak didn't trust him, not one bit. He didn't particularly want to go anywhere with him, but he wanted to get Lori out of the hospital before it was too late.

"Who are you? Why do you want to help us?"

"I suppose it does not matter if you know my name. I am Stepan Sokolov. I came here to help you, you can believe that. Maybe this will make you believe me."

Novak watched him pull out a Ruger similar to the one that Petrov had used to shoot Justin in the head. He placed it on the blanket beside Novak's hand. "Now you're armed. If I make a move against you or the woman, you can shoot me. But I won't harm you. I need your help more than you need mine, or I'd never take this big of a risk in coming here to rescue you."

Novak was partly reassured. He'd wanted a weapon, and now he had one. He picked up the handgun, checked the magazine, and racked a shell into the chamber. Sokolov didn't seem to mind.

"As I said, Novak, time is of the essence. We're wasting it with all this idle chit-chat."

That was true. "Okay, but don't think for a second that I trust you."

Sokolov actually laughed. "You think I trust you? I do not."

Novak threw back the covers and swung his legs over the side of the bed. A barrage of pain hit him. He winced, stood up, and staggered a little.

"I have medications on hand that will help your headaches. You both are going to have plenty of them, trust me, but your concussions are deemed moderate. I'll take you up to the woman's room in this wheelchair. That would be the best option."

"I can walk." Novak hoped that was true.

"The wheelchair would look more legitimate if a nurse such as myself is pushing a patient upstairs to visit his friend."

"All right. Where are my clothes?"

"They probably cut them off you when you reached the ER. I stole some scrubs for you and the woman."

Sokolov reached into a plastic bag and pulled out a green V-necked shirt and drawstring pants. "These will be too small for a man your size, but it's the largest I could find. We can put a blanket over your legs."

Ten minutes later, Sokolov was pushing him down the outside corridor. As they passed the nurse's station, Sokolov smiled at the two nurses sitting behind the desk. They smiled back. "I'm taking Mr. Novak upstairs to see his friend. He wishes to make sure she's okay. We won't bother the lady, I promise. He only wishes to check on her."

"Do you need help?"

"No, I can manage. Thank you very much. That is kind of you."

The man had effortlessly changed his accent. Now he spoke in a deep Texas twang and sounded like an Amarillo cowpoke. Impressive. Novak kept the Ruger hidden under the blanket over his knees, but he had his finger on the trigger. His head was killing him again, pounding like a kettle drum. The painkiller was wearing off. He felt uncomfortably weak and more than a little disoriented, but tried to shake it off. He didn't think this guy was there to kill them, but he could have been. Novak had to be ready if he tried something. It was after visiting hours, so the rooms they passed were dark, the corridors quiet.

Lori had been given a room a few doors from the elevator. When Sokolov rolled him inside, Novak stood up and braced a hand on the wall, trying to right his spinning equilibrium. He'd had worse concussions before, so he knew what it felt like. He'd live, especially given time to rest. He was more worried about Lori's condition. She was in the bed, either asleep or unconscious. She was lying on her back. Her left arm was strapped tight against her chest with a dark blue sling. "I thought you said she had come to."

"She did."

"Is her arm broken?"

"No, it's a dislocated shoulder that will heal. They put it back in place. Go over and wake her up. I'll watch at the door. When they come for you, they'll come at night, probably just before dawn. They'll step inside this room, inject her with poison, and be gone in less than a minute."

"You sound like you've done it before."

Sokolov just shrugged.

Novak made his way to the bed. He leaned down close to Lori. Her face was as white as a summer clover and covered with small stitched-up cuts and dark bruises. She looked awful. "Lori," he whispered. "C'mon, wake up."

Lori opened her eyes. It took her a moment to focus on him. "Will? Thank God. We've got to get out of here. They'll come for us. Are you okay?"

"Yeah, I'm all right, just beat up a little, like you. How bad do you hurt?"

"I felt pretty rough at first, but they gave me painkillers to help my headaches. That air bag hit me like a concrete barrier."

"You think you can walk?"

"I don't know. I feel lightheaded when I move my head too fast. Who's the guy by the door? He came in here earlier but left real quick when I tried to sit up."

"I don't know for sure yet, but he's offered to help get us out of here. He told me Blackwood's goons are going to show up any time, and he seems to know a lot about them."

"Who is he?" she asked again. Her words slurred.

"Says his name is Stepan Sokolov."

"Sounds Russian."

"He says he is. I think he's telling the truth. Probably GRU."

"I don't like this. I don't like him. I don't trust him."

"Me neither, but he knows a lot about Blackwood, and he says he's on our side. He says he wants to bring the Senator down. We need to get out of here, in any case."

"I'm not going to trust any Russians."

"Let me help you get up. We've got scrubs for you to put on, but you better keep on that gown. It's getting late. We need to go."

"The nurse said cops were here earlier, waiting to question me."

"Yeah, me, too. Another reason to get out now. Sokolov gave me a weapon, if that makes you feel better."

"I'm too dizzy to think about it."

"C'mon, let's get you in the wheelchair."

Lori's body was sore, and she moaned every time she moved her dislocated shoulder, but Novak got her off the bed and helped her sit down in the wheelchair. Sneaking her past the nurses would be the problem. He didn't even have time to get her out the door before a fire alarm blared on. The shrill siren wreaked havoc in his head. Lori groaned and held both hands over her ears.

"Sorry," Sokolov told them, entering from the corridor. "We needed a distraction to get out of here unseen. Nobody will think a thing about us pushing her out in a wheelchair if there's a fire alarm. Let's go."

Within minutes, people were emerging from their rooms, looking frightened. People were shouting and pandemonium was brewing. "There's a fire in the kitchen, and the smoke is toxic," Sokolov cried out to the nurses as he pushed Lori past them. "Get the patients downstairs to the parking lot, stat."

That sent the nurses running. The three of them fit right in with the burgeoning frenzy. Nobody stopped them as a full evacuation went into effect. They got to the elevator first and rode it down to the lobby. Within minutes, they were outside in the parking lot while first-floor patients were wheeled out at every exit. Nobody noticed them or tried to stop them.

Sokolov led them to a white Range Rover that he unlocked with a key fob. Novak pushed Lori's wheelchair with one hand, and steadied the gun in his other, ready to fire. He searched the cars around them and didn't see anybody suspicious. Behind them, the hospital staff rushed about, and police sirens screamed somewhere off in the distance.

"We'll ride in the back seat, and I'll have this gun pointed at the back of your head the whole time," Novak told Sokolov.

"You're welcome," the Russian said sarcastically. Then he laughed as he got in the driver's seat. So he was a fun guy.

Novak glanced around as he helped Lori settle into the back. He hadn't been kidding the Russian. He was armed now, and he would use the gun if this guy turned out to be one of Blackwood's trigger men. So far, so good, though. Sokolov had gotten them out of that building with no questions asked. If Blackwood had ordered a hit inside their hospital rooms, they would be hard pressed to find them, unless the Russian was driving them straight to Petrov's custody. He sat with his arm around Lori, the other clutching the Ruger. Lori was holding her head. If the guy turned out to be legit, he'd have to fill in the missing puzzle pieces, because Novak was too tired to figure out Sokolov's angle.

Chapter 8

Stepan Sokolov kept up the friendly chatter, pretending they were long lost college buddies. Lori never said a word, just huddled under a blanket, her eyes closed, her head resting on Novak's chest. She didn't buy what the Russian was selling, not for a single second. Novak knew that without being told. He didn't feel many friendly vibes, either. Instead, he kept himself alert, scanning the street behind them, all the while expecting a double-cross. Still, he did have a loaded weapon. He'd checked again. What Novak wanted was answers. Three blocks away from the hospital, he said, "Okay, Sokolov, we're out now. Let's hear the rest of your story."

"Please call me Stepan."

Novak wasn't going to call him that. They weren't friends and probably would never be. Novak turned again, looking for a carload of armed thugs. Sokolov remained on back streets that were dark and untraveled with everybody asleep. They drove north on I-95, retracing Novak's route from the previous day. He tensed up considerably when they got on the road that took them back to Blackwood's horse farm. But the Russian continued right past its entrance, drove about two miles farther along, and then turned onto a dirt road to their left. The acres around his safe house looked to be heavily wooded with bushes and overhanging branches scraping the sides and roof of the Range Rover. Minutes later they ended up at a rundown old farmhouse that seemed to be set down out in the middle of nowhere. Sokolov pulled up to the front steps, stopped the car, and identified the place as his little cottage in the forest. It was too dark to tell much about the house except it looked old, circa 1930s or 1940s, maybe. Like something out of *The Grapes of Wrath*. Novak didn't care much about how it looked; he was more concerned with its proximity to Blackwood's estate and all the armed men milling around there. Novak gripped the Ruger tighter, tensed up and on edge, fearing he'd made a serious mistake in judgment. Still, instinct told him Sokolov could be trusted, at least for the moment. Novak opened the back door and helped Lori out. She was weak and wobbly on her feet, and shivering all over. He wrapped the thermal blanket around her shoulders, but she refused to be carried. She still complained of an awful headache. Then she told him she was fine, but she wasn't okay, not even close. Keeping a cautious eye on Sokolov, Novak led her up the three steps onto the tiny front porch. The Russian had gone ahead. They waited while he unlocked and pushed the door open. Stepping back, he gestured for them to precede him.

"Don't think so. You go first."

"You will soon realize that I am no enemy to you. You need an ally right now, and I am the only one you can trust."

"I'll wait for you to prove that."

"You are wise to be cautious, but you're a bit overly so."

Novak didn't respond. Sokolov walked inside and flipped on a ceiling light. The attached five-bladed fan began to rotate slowly before gaining momentum. Novak stood in the threshold and examined the room, found it non-threatening, then led Lori to an easy chair near the front door. It was not exactly warm inside the house, but it felt better than the cold night wind channeling through the treetops. The interior looked shabby. The walls appeared to have been painted and repainted, papered and repapered, over and over, for decades. Some owners had done better jobs than others, considering the multitude of paint stains on the old hardwood floor. The boards squeaked with every footfall, but that usually came in handy when being stalked by killers. Novak's body ached in every single muscle. It was screaming to lie down and rest. So was his head. Lori kept shivering, and looked a sickly shade of white. He hoped to God he hadn't made a mistake by taking her out of that hospital too soon.

"We've got to get her to bed and let her rest," he said.

"Yes, that is true. She does not look so good, does she, my friend? But she will feel better in the morning." Sokolov hovered close to them like a nervous landlord. He looked concerned, but that could be easily faked. "You'll both feel better tomorrow. There is a guest bedroom just over there. The bed is comfortable, and the linens are fresh."

"You sayin' you have guests out here?"

"At times I have friends who come visit."

"What friends?"

"You wouldn't know them."

"Yeah, I'll bet I wouldn't. Is anybody supposed to turn up tonight or any time soon?"

"No, rest assured, you are perfectly safe here. Please, go now, let your woman rest. My room is upstairs." He flung his arm out in a vague gesture at the enclosed stair to his left. The door that led to it was standing open. "The lock on your bedroom door works," he continued. "I will give the woman a weapon, as well, if she feels insecure while here. They won't find us, though, I swear that to you. I've been using this house for months. No one from the farm has questioned my presence here. I will put my hand on my Bible and swear it to you."

"Funny, I wouldn't peg you as a religious man."

"I am a Russian Orthodox Christian. I attended church regularly as a boy. My mother was a godly woman. Then I was in espionage for so long that I lost faith in all things for a time."

Novak considered lying down with Lori and getting some rest. Any car approaching could be heard out here in the quiet woodland. Stealthy men approaching through heavy woods on foot would be a much different story. No way would he get much sleep tonight.

"Please, the woman is shaky. Take her in there and let her lie down. Her color does not look so healthy."

Novak decided Lori would be safe enough behind a locked bedroom door with him armed and sitting beside her. While Sokolov got busy arranging kindling for a fire in the old red brick fireplace, Novak opened the door to the small bedroom and checked it out for surprises. The walls were covered with old-fashioned wallpaper: a pattern of red roses and violets intertwined with white lace ribbons. It reminded Novak of a room inside the mansion he'd inherited on Bourbon Street in the French Quarter. In this room, the paper was peeling off in places, but everything looked clean, including the white sheets and down comforter. There was a side table beside the bed and a blond dresser with a round mirror spotted and darkened by age.

Lori sagged on her feet, pretty much at the end of her rope. Novak picked her up and carried her to the bed. He threw back the covers and placed her down gently. He covered her up, and she rolled onto her good side and closed her eyes. He took a minute to check out the closet, then peered out both locked windows, taking a last look at her before he rejoined Sokolov. The Russian had finished building the fire, and the logs were burning hot. Novak moved closer and warmed his back to the flames, keeping a close eye on the Russian.

"She just needs sleep, my friend," he told Novak. "I give you my word this place is a safe haven for her."

He kept giving his word about everything, which meant zero to Novak. Time would tell if he kept it. "I am not your friend. You need to understand that. I don't trust you or your word or anything else about you. I needed help getting Lori out of that hospital or I wouldn't be within ten miles of this place."

"You think I do not know these things. I find that the intelligent thing to do. You do understand that sedatives are still in her system. That is making her appear weaker and woozier than she really is. When she awakes in the morning, she'll feel much better, and you will see that she will be fine. I have worked at hospitals. I read her chart while she was unconscious. Her concussion is moderate but her bruising is severe because of the seatbelt restraint, similar to your own injuries. She will be all right, given time. The same can be said for you. You were very lucky to survive a crash like that."

Novak frowned. This guy was coming off as weird. What was with all the concern for two veritable strangers? That was a danger signal that Novak couldn't ignore. Sokolov stood up and walked into the adjoining kitchen. Novak kept waiting for something bad to happen. He sat down and kept the Ruger in his lap. He could see Lori in the bed through the half-open bedroom door. A few minutes later, Sokolov was back, holding a cold bottle of Mamont Vodka and two short glasses. He sank down in an overstuffed chair across from Novak. "You need a drink, Novak. You deserve one."

Novak watched the Russian pour the liquor. He handed the first glass to Novak. Then he slouched back on the couch, propped his foot on his opposite knee, and tossed down his drink in one deep draught. He sat back up and refilled his glass. Novak didn't touch his. He was not going to impair his reflexes and mix alcohol with the remnants of the sedatives he'd been given. He needed to be alert and wary of this guy. He felt fairly clearheaded at the moment, but occasionally a fog steamed up his mind and obscured his clarity. He needed sleep. He did not need vodka. They sat there together for a while, neither saying anything. The only sound was the popping and crackling of burning wood. The heat felt good.

"I watched that semi cab ram your Jeep," Sokolov told him at length. "I thought all of you would be killed. Especially after I saw Petrov get out of that car with his gun."

"How do you know him? Was he a colleague in your spy games?"

"We both served our country, yes. We belonged to a special paramilitary unit for a time. We performed difficult and highly classified missions. Black Ops, I believe is what you call them here. Vasily was the most infamous man in our ranks, known for his utter ruthlessness. We did not know each other well, not back then. He was already an officer, and I was a new enlistee. He was trained by members of the old KGB. He is dangerous when crossed. Actually, he is dangerous at all times." Novak wasn't going to share military secrets with this guy. "Yeah, I figured that out. So let's get down to what's what. Who are you? Why are you here? Why are you going to so much trouble to help me?"

"One thing's for certain, I am not your enemy. To the contrary, I am the farthest thing from that. I'm on your side. You have no need to worry about my betraying you." His eyes held Novak's, their black depths reflecting firelight like two glowing white stars. He looked and sounded sincere. "I am also the only one who is not out gunning for you and your woman right now."

"Yeah, we'll see about that."

"When you aligned yourself with Irina, you became a target. Just like poor young Justin."

Novak waited for Sokolov to tell him something he didn't know. "What will it take to make you believe me?"

"The whole truth might do the trick. Look, I don't know you from Adam, never have laid eyes on you before tonight. I don't know if you're legit, or if you're playing me for a fool. I do know we've made some enemies around here. Feel free to fill me in on the particulars of that, since the guy gunning for us is your old army buddy." He stopped and waited for answers. Sokolov only stared back at him. "So what's your angle in all this, Sokolov? Better yet, why are you so reluctant to answer my questions?"

"I need your help more than you need mine. You're no use to me if you are dead. Neither is the woman in the bedroom. I know she works at the Pentagon for an important General, which could be helpful to me down the road." He trickled another portion of vodka into his glass. "I took you out of that hospital because I knew Petrov would return to finish the job he started at that petrol station. He always takes care of loose ends, and that's what you and the woman are right now."

Novak was tired of talking. His head was absolutely killing him, thudding jarringly like a broken fan, and he was worried about Lori. "I'm only going to ask you this one more time. Who are you? Why did you involve yourself with us? Why are we here? What do you want?"

Sokolov laughed. "And here I thought you'd be thanking me for saving your skin."

"I'll save the gratitude until I know who the hell you are and why you're doing this."

"Fair enough, I suppose. I would do the same."

They moved into another unblinking staring contest that lasted a full minute before the Russian stood up and threw a log on the fire. He poked and stabbed at the grate until the flames shot up. Novak got up and moved to the front window, and looked out at the road. Once the fire was roaring and throwing out heat, Sokolov turned and faced Novak. "Okay, I'll tell you everything. Once you hear me out, you can leave this house, or stay and help me save Irina's life, whichever you choose."

Novak waited. He needed some sleep, and they were wasting time.

"I bear you no ill will, if that's what you're worried about."

"You keep saying that. I don't believe you, and it seems you're avoiding telling me the truth. Why is that?"

"I need your help. I am alone in this. My movements inside your country have limitations, while yours do not."

"Okay. And?"

"All of this is about Irina. You see, they'll kill her eventually, now that she's old enough to cause them trouble. It's already started now with that boy, Justin. She's been pliable enough until now. Unfortunately, she is an impetuous child. The Senator is growing concerned that if she throws one of her tantrums, she'll do it in public, or go to the cops, or maybe even contact the press. I want to get her out of there before she gets hurt or worse—Petrov kills her."

Now Novak was interested. "What's it to you?"

Petrov looked down at his glass. He raised his somber eyes to Novak's face. "She's my daughter. I've been searching for her for years. I finally found her earlier this year."

"Irina Blackwood is your...*daughter?*"

"I can't say one-hundred percent that she is, not without a paternity test, but I know it in my heart."

He was actually serious when he said that. "You do realize how that sounds, right? Enlighten me. How could you not know?"

"Because I wasn't home when he took her. Now that I've watched her and followed them, I know she's being abused by that monster. Even if she isn't my child, I want to get her out of there. She's an innocent they've corrupted since early childhood, and he's victimizing her in every possible way."

Novak knew what that meant. He also knew it was true. Irina had told Novak herself. "So I'm just supposed to believe all this and get involved with a gang of Russian murderers? That's why I'm here?"

"It's the truth. Irina doesn't know who I am, of course. I doubt if she even remembers me. I was gone most of the time after she was born, and it was a long time ago. Blackwood kept her first name but I doubt he's told her what her last name was or anything else about me and her mother."

"She knows she's adopted. She told us Blackwood bought her for a few rubles off a Moscow street. She said her mother sold her."

"Lies! My wife would never do that."

"So what *is* the truth, Sokolov?"

"The truth is, Blackwood saw her, wanted her, and stole her away from us. I was not in Moscow at that time, but deployed to Somalia. My wife was a maid inside his house when he stayed there on a Senate diplomatic mission. He took Irina out of the country."

Novak was having trouble with his story. "That doesn't sound credible, to say the least. He was a U.S. Senator, in Russia on official business, but there are limits to diplomatic privilege. Kidnapping children is one of them."

"Not if you're dirty and doing criminal favors for a foreign government."

"You can prove that?"

"Of course not. I may never be able to prove any of it, and it doesn't matter anymore. I just want to get my daughter back before Blackwood tires of her and she ends up dead."

"How old was she?"

"Almost six. It was ten years ago."

"So all this time passed before you show up here looking for her?"

"I was still with the military at first and unable to get back home. I wasn't sure who took her, and when I started asking questions about Blackwood, his friends in my government didn't like it. They trumped up terrorist charges and threw me in prison. I got out two years ago. After that, they put a watch on me. It was almost impossible for me to get out of Russia."

"How did you get here?"

"I have ways.

Great, Novak thought. *This guy is probably a suspected terrorist.* "Yet here you are plotting a kidnapping of a senator's daughter and asking me to help you. No dice. I want nothing to do with this, or you."

"I infiltrated your country via the Canadian border. I came across on foot."

"I want nothing to do with you, Sokolov."

"I'm not a danger to anyone except Blackwood. I don't plan to stay here any longer than necessary. My wife wasn't sure it was Blackwood who had taken our child. Irina just disappeared one day. My wife knew that he had become overly fond of Irina and liked to hold her on his lap and feed her sweets. There was little she could do after our child disappeared. But it happened the same day Blackwood returned to America. I knew in my heart that he'd taken her. When I got out of prison, I started researching Blackwood's past. I've been gathering proof here, in this house, for several months. Now that she's grown up, Irina closely resembles my wife at that age. I know she is our daughter, and she is in danger. Blackwood will get tired of her, and he'll eventually end her life."

Novak wanted to see Sokolov's reaction, so he told him the truth. "Irina told me herself that Charles Blackwood has been molesting her."

The muscles in Sokolov's face contracted and went hard as he set his teeth. The pain in his big dark eyes was easy to read. He watched the Russian struggle with his emotions. His face reddened with contained rage. "I know what he is doing to her. It's hard for me to wait even a day to get her away from him, but I have to. And after I do, I'm going to kill him for what he's done. I swear to God, I am. I promised my wife that I'd find her, and now I have. My hope is that she'll remember me or something about her early years with us, but I can't count on that. She was so young, and I was always deployed. A DNA test would prove it, if she'd agree to cooperate. But I fear she won't. Blackwood abducted her, and I'd like to bring him down and Petrov along with him, but I think he's too powerful here in his home country for that to happen. Just so long as I get Irina away from him, that's got to be enough for me."

"You've got bigger problems than that. Blackwood's got her addicted to heroin, and God only knows what else, so she's totally dependent on him. She thinks he loves her, but when she finds out he had her boyfriend murdered, she'll leave him. That's when he'll have her killed, and he'll kill us if we try to help her."

"All that is true, I know that it is. I need you to help me. She needs you to help me. I don't know you or why she turned to you, but she must trust you. If I am with you, she will trust me. She will believe me. What is your interest in her?"

"I have no interest in her. She identified me as the father of her baby so Justin wouldn't get killed. It was a random thing. Lucky me."

"She's with child?"

"Yes, and that's what got Justin murdered. I got caught up in this mess through no fault of my own. I've seen nothing but grief ever since."

Novak rose to his feet. "Okay, I've heard enough. We're getting out of here. Good luck with the kid, Sokolov."

"Wait—I am only here for my daughter. Nothing else matters. I worked in espionage while in service to my country for years before I went to prison. I admit that. I am not ashamed of it. It was honorable. But your CIA knows about my work here and will pick me up if my presence becomes known. I am no longer interested in espionage. I'm only here for my daughter."

Novak shook his head. "You're saying that you're a known Russian agent here in the United States illegally? That's what you're telling me."

"That's right. I worked here for a time, and yes, I spied on your government, but that is long past. They never could prove anything, but they just kicked me out of the country on the suspicion that I associated with Russian agents. This was all long before Irina was taken."

"What was your mission here?"

He hesitated. "I was tasked with setting up sleeper cell units back then, but I never did gather any kind of intel myself. They were contacted through other channels."

"I want nothing to do with you. I'm getting Lori, and we're getting the hell out of here."

"Wait. There's something else you must know."

Novak didn't want to hear anything else. This thing had become more complicated than he'd expected, and he had expected the worst.

"I can make a deal with you."

"I don't make deals with people like you."

"You might this time."

Novak sat down, reluctantly willing to listen to Sokolov's deal. On the other hand, he was leaving this house before dawn, no matter how the Russian played his hand.

Chapter 9

Sokolov sat down directly across from Novak. He made a show of leaning in closer in order to show how earnest he was. "Let me tell you what I did while I was in your country."

"I've heard enough already to know I could never trust you, not in a million years. You'll be lucky if I don't call ICE and the CIA as soon as I get out of here."

The Russian ignored that. "Years ago I was assigned to help Vasily Petrov place Russian sleeper cells on the East Coast. Most were family units trained to speak American English and schooled in your culture. We completed our mission successfully. After I was expelled from America, I moved on and served in Somalia and Syria." He stopped. "Those sleepers? I think some of them might still be in place, or Vasily has formed new ones for his own purposes."

"I'm going to turn you in, Sokolov. You should never have approached me and told me all this."

"No, you won't do that. Because I need your help bringing him down. Most of the families I helped put in place here returned to Russia long ago. Some defected and disappeared into the heartland of America, and we don't know where they are. You need to help me locate the ones still operating. Do you want to know why?"

"I can guess."

"Because Petrov is doing all this unsanctioned by my government. The Kremlin has ordered them found and taken down."

"So you're still working for the Russian government? They sent you here to get him?"

"Not exactly, I went to a trusted friend at the Kremlin who works in foreign intelligence and asked her to help me locate my child. She told me that Irina was here, and that Petrov was working for the man who took her, a powerful American politician. I agreed to let her know if Blackwood is still using the sleeper cells for his own benefit so Moscow can shut them down. Her superiors will look kindly on her if she can bring Petrov in. The last thing they want is for Petrov's drug smuggling to become a diplomatic problem for them. I believe now from my surveillance that he has possibly turned some of his cells into a drug pipeline. I need your help to destroy it. First, however, I'll help you track these people and give you information that will help you find them. They are bringing drugs into your country, I am sure of it. Tons of them: cocaine, heroin, meth, opioids, even fentanyl. I think they're into human trafficking as well. I only want my daughter. That's all I'm here for. Petrov has committed treasonous acts in the past against the United States and Russia. I don't care what happens to him."

"What kind of treasonous acts?"

"He's ordered or committed atrocities everywhere he's been. I saw him kill a whole village in Somalia. He just mowed them down: men, women, and children. I tried to stop him but couldn't. The Kremlin wants him dead, and they don't care how it's done. So do I, but he's not my priority. My daughter is and always will be my primary concern."

Novak studied him. Sokolov was not lying now. Novak believed him, but wasn't sure why. He knew he shouldn't. He had just admitted to being a former Russian espionage agent and even worse, Petrov's colleague. His grudge was personal.

"Say I do help you take Petrov down. How can you get Irina out? She's back in Blackwood's house of her own free will, because, trust me, I tried to talk her out of going there. I think she still loves Blackwood. Probably another reason is that he gives her all the drugs she wants. That's going to change, once we tell her that her father had Justin murdered. I saw it happen, and I think she'll believe me. That might just make her cut ties and believe you."

"Yes, that's what I hope. She would never trust me. But she turned to you for help, did she not? So I think she'll believe you if you approach her. Once she's out of their control, I'll help you locate the family cells he's got running the drugs. I'm pretty sure he'll have set it up the same way we did the original sleeper cells."

"Working with you will be treason. No way will Lori be a party to this."

"She doesn't have to be. She's still injured. You can take her somewhere safe and come back here. We'll take them down together and turn them all over to your CIA." Sokolov's face was serious. "As I said, I believe that stopping the flood of opioids coming up the coast would be reason enough for you to help me."

Novak wavered because that was true. The opioid epidemic was a terrible thing. He found himself wanting to take Petrov down and stop the drug trade. It was tempting.

"This will have to be just you and me, and your law enforcement can wrap it up later. Russian intelligence thinks they're moving the shipments straight up the Atlantic seaboard, probably from Florida. They say they like to target schoolyards. Since Petrov's involved, I concluded they're new cells being used as drug mules. Family units would be good cover. I don't know how they're doing it yet, but I'm working on it." He leaned back and took a deep breath, probably sensing Novak's interest. "You and I have common goals. I want Irina out of their control before we destroy the pipeline. You want the drug pipeline destroyed. We can make both things happen if we work together."

Novak stared into Sokolov's eyes. He believed him. Novak already knew the opioid devastation was destroying American communities. It was a scourge and a tragedy. A woman in Lori's office had lost her teenage son to a drug overdose only a month ago. Lori would probably help them take down these criminals. She would definitely want Irina away from that pedophile father. Still, he planned to keep her out of it, if he could.

"Okay, say I help you do all this. How about we just contact the DEA and give them everything you know? They need to be involved from the get-go. You can tell them your story. I'll back you up once you show me enough proof."

Sokolov laughed. He looked amused. "I am an enemy of your country. Years ago, I helped Petrov set up agents here, but they've been inactive for a long time. This time Petrov's started it up again for his own benefit. If you report this to drug enforcement, I will spend the rest of my life in your prison system. I've had enough prison. I'll never go back."

"Maybe that's where you belong."

"Maybe I should get a chance to help destroy a network that was never intended to transport drugs. It was just to watch, infiltrate, and relay information. These guys target children. I think some of them are used in worse ways."

"How many families do you think are involved?"

"Back then, we set up ten in each loop. Mainly around Washington, Baltimore, and New York. Petrov might do it the same way. I don't know yet how he's operating, but I think he is."

"And the cells you set up are no longer functioning."

"No, they are long gone. My friend told me that before I came here. This is suspected to be Petrov and Blackwood's drug network using his contacts. You know I am putting my life in danger by telling you these things."

"Do you have proof Blackwood is abusing Irina? I saw him hit her, but that's probably not enough to bring down a man like him."

Sokolov frowned. "Yes, I have been watching. I think he will certainly kill her, if she threatens to expose him. I know that the senator has taken other kids out of my country and other countries as well, on the pretext of giving orphans good homes. It was part of his payoff for collaborating with them. Some of these kids eventually turned up dead or dropped out of sight. One little girl drowned while at the beach. Irina has apparently lasted longer than the others, but she will end up dead, too, Mr. Novak. Charles Blackwood is a practicing pedophile. She's intrigued him, but now she's causing trouble and has the means to expose him for what he is. That would destroy him, so he'll have to get rid of her. Then he'll find another innocent child to corrupt. She has gotten too old for his prurient tastes."

Blackwood made Novak sick to his stomach. He didn't want to believe he was capable of such depravity, but he did. "Tell me more about yourself and what you've done."

"I told you about setting up the sleepers here. After that, I was recruited into the special unit in Somalia and put in intelligence. That's where I was when he took Irina. When I got home and could do something about it, I went to my superiors and convinced them Blackwood had our daughter. They wouldn't do anything because of his powerful position in your government, and warned me not to pursue it or my wife and I would be jailed. That's what happened. My wife died while I was behind bars. So Irina's all I have left."

"You're in a hell of a lot of trouble, Sokolov. Does Blackwood know who you are and that you're out here so close to him?"

"I'm better at my job than that."

"First good news I've heard since you started talking." He downed the vodka and let Sokolov refill it. It was calming his ragged nerves now that the sedative was out of his system. "So you were active in Russian intelligence and an enemy of the U.S."

"I was. I was doing what I thought was right at that time. I am not so sure now. I wish to atone for some of the things I did while in the army. All I want is my daughter back."

"Where will you take her?"

"Somewhere no one will ever find us."

Novak made his decision. He didn't want to work with Sokolov, but if he knew how to bring down a major opioid pipeline operated by pedophiles, he would. "Okay, if I decide to buy into this, what happens next?"

"As I said. We will find a way to get Irina safely away from them, and then we bring down Petrov and Blackwood and everybody working for them."

Novak scoffed. "And you think that's going to be easy?"

They gauged each other a moment. Sokolov looked more relaxed now. "Novak, you showed up at Blackwood's out of the blue and caused a big stink. What's your connection to him? Whatever it was, he now wants you dead. That puts you firmly on my side. What did you do to him?"

"Nothing. He's upset because Irina told him she was pregnant and accused me of being the father. That's why Justin is dead right now. She told him I was the father in order to protect her boyfriend. I never saw any of them before that night at the restaurant. When I saw Blackwood hit her, I slugged him and knocked him down."

"Yes, I know."

"How?"

"I'll show you presently. That's why she thought she could trust you. Am I right about that?"

"She was terrified they'd kill Justin, and tried to get us to get him out of town. Turns out she was right. He's dead with a bullet in his head. Lori and I both know who did it and why, so now they're gunning for us. You, too, if they find out you pulled us out of that hospital."

"We must destroy them together. I have information you'll need to put them behind bars. My background makes it impossible for me to give it to your authorities, but you can. Fate brought us together on the side of what is right and good."

"I don't believe in fate. Blackwood's untouchable except for Irina's testimony. Even then, his political connections and media friends might get him by. You'll never pin anything on him that sticks. But you're right. I do think he'll kill her. If not now, then eventually."

"I'm going to destroy him and Petrov and their drug network. I need you to help me, but if you don't, I go it alone."

"How do you know about the drugs? You sure that's what's going on?"

"I've watched Petrov make a few drops. Mostly around this area and in D.C. His men were selling pills laced with fentanyl to kids at a middle school in Fredericksburg. I saw that myself. You're trained to take care of yourself, as am I. I think you want to get Irina out, or you wouldn't have listened to me or come with me tonight."

"All I know about Irina is that she got me mixed up in her drama and cost me and my friend concussions, and now we're on the suspect list for killing her boyfriend."

"Enough reasons to take Blackwood down. He's the one who signed that kid's death warrant. He gives Petrov his orders. He'll come after you and your woman again, and this time he'll get you, and he'll get away with it. We have to get him first."

Unfortunately, Novak knew all that was true. He was angry he'd been sucked into this guy's problems, but he did want Blackwood and his henchman as bad as Sokolov did. He just wasn't sure hooking up with a former Russian agent was the best way to do it. Probably not good at all, truth be told. He would have to trust Sokolov and his whole outlandish story, and some of it seemed a bit iffy. "Maybe I'll help you, Sokolov. I'll think about it. I want Irina out of there, too. We're not going to break any laws to do it. If you pull a double-cross on me, I'll hunt you down."

"And I will do the same with you. That is granted. We don't have to break American laws to do this. We can turn over evidence to whichever agency you wish. But Blackwood and his people will die."

"Just murder everybody and be done with it, huh? That your take on all this?"

"Precisely. They are the worst of men. They corrupt everything they touch. Especially little children."

Novak couldn't argue with that. They were worse than Sokolov, but this guy was no angel, either. Neither was Novak.

"I'm not promising you anything. I want to hear more and see more, and look over whatever proof you have. I don't want Lori involved. I'm going to take her somewhere safe before we do anything."

Sokolov nodded. "That is a wise decision."

"No kidding. Just for the record, I still don't trust you."

"You will learn to. Just do not think to betray me."

They were off to a great partnership, Novak thought, wishing he'd never stepped foot off his boat a few days ago. So be it. Blackwood and Vasily Petrov were both monsters. They were going to end them and everything they stood for.

Chapter 10

Novak pulled a chair up close to Lori's bed and thought about what he should do. She was resting peacefully, still sleeping off the painkillers. He was contemplating a dangerous course of action, and had halfway decided to join forces with Stepan Sokolov. If even one-tenth of what Sokolov had said was true, somebody needed to get involved, but it wasn't going to be Lori Garner. She had been invaluable to him many times since they'd met, but it wasn't in the cards this time. Petrov was not your run-of-the-mill criminal. He was fully capable of committing murder without hesitation. Lori was never going to meet up with him, not if Novak could help it.

Besides, she had gotten the brunt of the injuries in that wrecked car. Convincing her to sit this thing out and let him go it alone would be the problem. She wouldn't like that, and probably wouldn't listen to reason. He looked up when she shifted slightly and moaned as a result. Her eyes flew wide, and she looked around wildly, scared. Novak rose before sitting down on the edge of the bed. She calmed at once when she saw him.

"Everything's okay. How do you feel?" he asked softly.

"Not so good."

"Headaches?"

"My shoulder hurts worse, but my head's pounding as if it were trapped in a drum."

"You need another painkiller. I have some in my backpack."

"You know what, Novak? This thing sucks to high heaven. We've got to quit ending up like this." She squeezed her eyes shut.

"Yeah, I know. It's getting old, all right."

"Are you hurting?"

"Not like you are. That truck rammed the driver's seat. Your side got the worst impact. Do you remember much about it?"

She kept her eyes shut. "Not so much after I came back out of the gas station. Maybe that's a good thing. Maybe I don't want to remember it."

"I hope you don't."

"One of us always ends up in the hospital," she murmured, so low he could barely hear her. "This time it's me. Last time it was you. Time before that it was me. We're taking turns, Novak. Being polite." She attempted to laugh things off, but it didn't come out that way. Her face was still that frightening waxy white color, and she did not feel well. For the first time, Novak had a bad feeling about her injury. She was tough as they come, but this time she'd hit her head a little too hard. Concussions could be dangerous, and he'd been forced to take her out of that hospital too soon. His determination to sideline her doubled. He needed her in a safe place, out of harm's way for the duration of this case. "Wish it had been just me this time."

"Me too." Another feeble joke that wasn't funny, but he smiled. Lori turned her head and gazed at him. "What in the world have we gotten ourselves into this time? Do I even want to know?"

"Well, nothing about it is good. That's for damn sure. You don't need to be involved, not until you get better."

"I hate like the devil to admit this, but I don't think I'll be much help to you, not for a few days, anyway. Not until this headache lets up. I can't think straight or lift my head without getting sick to my stomach. Every muscle and joint in my body hurts. Did I break something in my shoulder? I'm having trouble remembering things."

"You dislocated it, but the doctor fixed it. It's going to be a problem for a little while. Keep the sling on, and it'll heal faster. Don't worry about anything until you get better. This thing has gotten ugly very fast." He squeezed her fingers. "Hey, I'm sorry I got you into this. I mean it, Lori. This is my fault. All of it."

"You got suckered in. Not your fault."

"Do you think you can get out of here tomorrow?"

"If you help me."

"I'm going to take you somewhere safe." He stopped, debating how much to tell her. She didn't need to lie around worrying, but she had to know some of it. "Sokolov thinks they're going to kill Irina soon. I think he's right. She's causing them trouble and involving outsiders in their private business."

"What's that Russian's stake in this? I don't understand who he is or why we're with him."

"He told me Irina is his daughter. I'm not sure I believe him, but the rest of his story halfway makes sense. I think he's bad news, but not as bad as the Petrov guy. He's the one I want to bring down. *He's* the one who shot Justin to death."

"Not the news I wanted to hear. So what happens next? What are you going to do?"

"Right now, we both need to rest and get some sleep. In the morning, I'm driving you back to my boat. After that, I'm checking you back into a hospital, somewhere far away from Blackwood's influence. I want you to be safe while I help Sokolov get Irina out of that house." Novak felt his suppressed rage welling up every time he pictured Petrov firing those bullets into that young kid's head. "I watched Vasily Petrov execute that poor boy in cold blood. He didn't hesitate one second. Then he turned his gun on you, and I opened fire. They're trying to kill all of us, and they're not going to stop until they do. Sokolov is giving me a chance to take them down first."

"How?"

"You don't need to worry about that. I won't do anything unless I believe it will work. And I'm not trusting that guy out there completely. I'll be watching him."

"I wish you wouldn't go after those people...but I know I can't talk you out of it. I'm okay lying low for a day or two, or I have to be, I guess, but only till I get my legs back under me. I can still shoot, even with my shoulder strapped into a sling. But I have to be able to focus my eyes on the target, and I can't even focus on your face right now."

"You don't have to. I'm getting you to a safe place."

"I can make do without the hospital stay if you keep me supplied with those painkillers. I'd rather stay on the *Sweet Sarah*. Nobody will look for me there. I'll be armed, anyway. Just drop anchor somewhere. I'll be fine."

"I'd rather take you back to your apartment in D.C. Let the army take care of you."

She shut her eyes again. "Let's just figure this all out in the morning. I'm too wiped to talk anymore."

"Go to sleep. I'll be right here."

"Well, don't leave me alone with that Russian creep. I think he's weird."

"I'm not going anywhere."

She didn't answer him. Her eyes remained closed.

"You sure you're okay, Lori? What did the doctor tell you?"

"He said to take it easy and rest the shoulder, and that it would take some time to heal. Quit worrying about me. You need sleep, too." After that, she lay still, and the room went quiet. Novak stretched out on the bed beside her, on top of the comforter, fully clothed. He kept the Ruger loosely in his hand. He'd locked the bedroom door and closed the curtains, but he still felt uneasy. Sokolov had not proven himself yet.

Lori started awake from her doze and moved closer to him. "What about the cops?"

"They've already questioned me. I've got a feeling they'll be out looking for us first thing tomorrow morning."

Lori didn't say more. Novak shut his eyes. This thing was not going to end well. All he had wanted was a good steak, damn it. He hadn't even gotten to finish eating that T-bone before all hell had broken loose.

* * * *

Well before dawn the next morning, Sokolov tapped softly on their bedroom door. Novak grabbed his weapon and jumped up. When he opened the door a bare crack, the Russian held up a big brown bottle of pills. "Hydrocodone. I thought your lady might need some for the road."

Novak looked at him suspiciously, unwilling to take them. He didn't know what was inside that bottle.

Sokolov smiled. "I have no reason to want to hurt the pretty lady. These are what I said they were, only painkillers. The bottle is still sealed." He held it up. Novak still hesitated. "Okay, look, I will take one myself, if it makes you feel better."

Novak watched him break the seal and swallow a pill without water. Then he took a second one. After that, he took the bottle. "I hope you don't run into trouble because you're going to be as looped as Lori now."

"I have a high tolerance."

Trustworthy or not, Sokolov was right: Lori was going to need relief on the ride back to the marina.

"Where are you taking her?"

"Somewhere they'll never find her. I'm staying with her until she's settled in and I feel good about her security. After that, I'll come back here, and we'll go get these guys."

"Yes, you do that. Keep your woman far away until we get this done. I'll stay here and continue surveillance until you return. But if I see Irina, I'm going in to get her before they hurt her again."

"Don't be stupid, Sokolov. You can't do it alone. That would be suicide. Wait until I get back. I won't be gone longer than a day or so, maybe. Blackwood's got a dozen men surrounding him. Don't get reckless, or Irina surely will end up dead."

"Maybe you sell my training a trifle short, my friend."

Novak didn't have a clue about his training, but Sokolov had gotten them both out of that hospital safely enough. His skills weren't shabby, not by a long shot. Novak's primary concern was getting Lori out of harm's way as rapidly as possible. Within the hour, Lori was fully awake and felt well enough to make it to the car. She had to lean heavily on him, but she made it all the same. They were going to use another car that Sokolov had hidden in an overhang shed out back. It turned out to be an unremarkable four-door white Ford Fusion with current Pennsylvania license plates. Novak didn't ask Sokolov how he'd managed that. More spy skills, no doubt.

The morning was so damp and foggy that Novak could barely make out Sokolov where he stood on the porch, watching Novak help Lori lie down on the back seat. It wasn't long enough for her to stretch out, but she got comfortable on her good side with her knees bent. She would have a halfway comfortable ride, if and when she downed enough drugs. She took the pills Novak gave her with a bottle of water without urging, but until they took effect, Lori was in the mood to talk. Now that her mental acuity was on the mend, she had more questions than Novak wanted to answer. He filled her in on a portion of what Sokolov had revealed to him. She kept her voice low, but watched the Russian through the front windshield.

"I don't trust him. I think he's lying about everything. He's a former Russian operative, for God's sake. My guess is that he's still one and playing us for fools."

"I'm not convinced, either, but I'll give him a chance to prove it. He says he loathes Petrov and intends to bring him down by any means necessary. That's what I want. He says Blackwood's fronting a big drug-running operation that includes selling fentanyl-laced opioids to kids. If that's true, I want to smash it up and put away everybody inside it. If Blackwood's fed up with Irina, Sokolov says he'll put a gun to her head without missing a beat. I don't want him to kill that young girl. I'm not going to let that happen."

"I don't like any of this. Oh, God...Go after them on your own, Novak. Don't trust this guy. You don't know anything about him."

"I'm getting you out of here, so you don't have to worry about him. I'll find out soon enough if Sokolov's telling me the truth. You just take care of yourself and feel better. I'm going to watch my back. You don't have to."

"I'm going to worry myself about your back all the way to my grave."
Novak got in the driver's seat. Sokolov smiled and waved goodbye as
if they were taking off on a holiday full of fun and laughter. Novak was
distinctly glad to get away from him. Once they were driving down through
the speckled shadows cast by the trees with lots of leaves fluttering down on
their windshield, Lori became quiet. Novak didn't want to explain himself
further because he was going on blind trust this time. That would be hard
for her to understand. He rarely did that. In fact, he never did that. He
shouldn't have been doing it now, and he knew it. Lori was right in every
warning she'd given him. He drove fast, staying on the less-traveled state
roads and off the major highways and Interstates, which cost them some
time, but was ultimately a safer route.

The sun was up and the sky was sunny and clear, another gorgeous
autumn day by the time they reached National Harbor and parked the Fusion
in a space not far from the *Sweet Sarah*. Novak got out and checked out
the boat from stem to stern before he took Lori aboard. Nothing had been
disturbed that he could tell. The safety precautions he'd set for intruders had
not been triggered, so he felt comfortable that nobody had been snooping
around on deck. He unsnapped the hatch covers, got everything ready to
sail, and then walked back for Lori. She was awake now but still groggy,
so he picked her up and carried her aboard the boat and down below. He
would have preferred to leave her inside some private hospital with tons of
security guards. On the other hand, it was highly unlikely that Blackwood
and Petrov knew Novak owned a boat or where he had put in. They sure
as hell couldn't know where he intended to anchor next, because he hadn't
decided yet. If he was leaving Lori alone somewhere, it would be in a
private cove where nobody would ever think to look for her.

After sleeping the entire drive, Lori roused a bit, so Novak helped her
dress in a warm sweatshirt and sweatpants that she'd left aboard. He settled
her in the master cabin with a mug of chicken noodle soup, a cup of hot
tea, and Sokolov's bottle of wonder pills. After she went back to sleep,
he walked over to the marina's office, settled the bill, and then motored
his boat out into the Potomac River, heading south to the open ocean,
glad to bid the place goodbye. It took a long time to navigate the river,
but he finally made it out onto Chesapeake Bay. Several miles offshore,
he fixed the sails and headed off south along the coast, the sun hot on his
head. He had decided exactly where he would lay anchor. Novak had an
old detective buddy from the NYPD named Jeffrey Summers. He owned
a private marina on an inlet, not far from Virginia Beach. From there, it
wouldn't take Novak long to drive back to Sokolov's safe house. Lori could

recuperate safely under his friend's watch. Novak trusted him. He visited Summers and his wife every time he sailed up the East Coast. The cove wasn't exactly uninhabited, but it was well off the beaten path. Jeff would be there to take her to the hospital, if something unforeseen happened. It wasn't the perfect set-up, but he felt comfortable leaving Lori there. She wouldn't be alone, and she had a gun that she definitely knew how to use. She would not hesitate to protect herself, and he doubted that anyone could get the jump on her. Those were the positives. He tried not to think about the negatives.

Chapter 11

Jeff and his wife, Angie, were out on their private dock to meet them. Novak had phoned ahead, and Jeff had agreed without a moment's hesitation. Lori took to both her hosts right away, probably because they were also military veterans who'd served in Iraq and Afghanistan, and were proud of it. After that, Novak felt better leaving her in their care. He hung around for the lobster boil they'd already prepared and shared some of the story with Jeff, but not enough to make him a target. Afterward, he borrowed Jeff's second car, an old Nissan sedan, and headed back to Sokolov's safe house. The drive was going to take a couple of hours, but the solitary road trip gave him time to consider everything he knew so far. Most of the time, he mulled over various ways to rescue Irina from the devil who'd taken that poor kid and abused her since she was a little girl. That ate at Novak more than anything else.

Despite her head injury, it appeared Lori wasn't taking it all that easy. An hour into his drive back, she texted Novak with some background history on Blackwood's Senate career and business dealings. He pulled off at a big rest stop and skimmed through the information. Other than Blackwood's horse farm and his mansion in Georgetown, his major investments were in real estate holdings. She had included a long list of residential properties purchased for investment and beach rental opportunities. The sheer number of beach houses the Senator owned seemed ridiculous to Novak and immediately raised his suspicions. Most of them were located at well-known Atlantic Coast hotspots, including Myrtle Beach, Hilton Head, Fripp Island, and Amelia Island, to name just a few. That lined up with Sokolov's theory about drugs being passed along the coastline. Rental properties were not in themselves unusual, but this guy had way too many, which were way too close together. Novak was pretty sure these properties had a great deal to do with the opioid pipeline, if there really was one. Proving it was the problem, and that would take time and round-the-clock surveillance. First things first, they had to get Irina out from under Blackwood's power before it was too late. She was going to end up dead, sooner or later. Novak knew it in his gut—she didn't have a chance, just like her boyfriend hadn't. She was becoming Blackwood's pain in the ass instead of his sweet little underage plaything, and he didn't like it. Murder was his favorite method of disposing of unwanted problems, or so it was beginning to seem. She would be on the kill list soon, if she wasn't already.

Novak had no trouble finding Stepan Sokolov's woodsy little hidey hole again. It bordered Blackwood's horse pastures and private woods, just like he'd said. Sokolov had found a good place to stand watch, right on top of Blackwood's every move. The fact that he was a well-trained espionage operative was showing more and more all the time. He knew exactly what he was doing. Whether he could be trusted was another story completely. Time would tell. Novak turned off the blacktop road and drove back through all that swaying dappled sunlight streaming through all those beautiful autumn leaves, until he pulled up into the same scraggly front yard that he'd left on that foggy morning.

In the bright daylight, he realized the outside of the house was in worse shape than the interior. It was either unpainted or all the paint had peeled off. Some of the shutters were hanging askew, and many bannister slats on the porch were missing. It looked exactly like a place he might choose to burrow in and hide, if he were in another country illegally. Right now, the Russian did not look like the typical farmer where he sat on the front porch in an old rocking chair, dressed entirely in green camouflage, holding a high-powered rifle across his knees. A country bumpkin or stupid redneck Stepan Sokolov was not.

Novak stopped the car at the porch steps. He turned off the motor but kept his eyes riveted on the Russian. The rifle was attached with a giant, telescopic scope. No way could he let down his guard with this guy. Glancing around, he put his hand near his own weapon, searching the undergrowth around the clearing for Petrov's thugs. Sokolov had been a successful spy for decades; a double-cross was definitely possible. Still, if this guy could help Novak take down an opioid network that had killed even one American child, Novak would work alongside him.

Irina Blackwood wasn't Novak's highest priority, but she was for Sokolov—at least that's what he'd said. Novak had some doubts about all the sentimental father-daughter drivel he'd been fed so far. Whether the familial ties were true or not, that teenager did not deserve what life had given her. She was in big trouble. She thought she could handle Blackwood, and she probably had manipulated him easily enough when she was young. Now she was a thorn in his side.

"Welcome back, my friend," Sokolov greeted him, as Novak mounted the front steps.He stopped at the top and looked around.

"You're sure this place is safe?"

"Of course, one of our agents bought this property decades ago with KGB money. They've been watching Blackwood's farm for years. That's how Petrov got to know Blackwood was corrupt. He's been dirty since his broadcast days, and that only got worse after he was elected. Good news for us, though. I'm sure your people did the same thing in Russia."

They had, of course. They still did. Novak had lived for a time in a safe house on the outskirts of Moscow. But he wasn't going to trade spy stories with this guy. "Okay, I'm back. So what's your plan? How do we get Irina off that farm without getting her killed?"

"No clue. I was hoping you had some ideas."

"That's not what I wanted to hear, Sokolov."

"Please, call me Stepan. I will call you Will."

"I'm not calling you Stepan. We're not buddies. We're never going to be buddies. I'm working with you because you have information I need to bring down Petrov and the guys in that truck who tried to murder us. I'd rather bring in the Virginia State Police, to tell you the truth, but I can't, because Blackwood's got a long history in this state, which means they'll never believe me over him. We are not in a budding friendship, Sokolov. We're too experienced in this game to ever completely trust each other. After we destroy these guys, I don't care if I never see you again."

"You appear quite judgmental for a man who has committed many of the same crimes as me. But you can trust me. I served my country bravely, as you did yours. In time I lost the patriotism I once felt for the Motherland. She failed me. This will be a difficult and trying alliance, you and me. But we do need each other."

"Yeah, whatever. What are we going to do now?"

"I do have ideas; I only wished to hear yours first. A few I think are failsafe. An assault on the horse farm is not well-conceived. It's much too well protected. Infiltration at the perimeter will be difficult, and a frontal assault even less desirable. We cannot simply barge in there and grab my daughter. It would be wiser to wait until they travel to one of his beach properties. Fortunately, he often moves his retinue around, especially on weekends. They're headed south, and that's when and where we'll strike.

As you found out the hard way, Blackwood's men surround him night and day. They're his private army, and they do exactly what they're told, or Petrov executes them where they stand. That man is ruthless when it comes to discipline. Once they leave the farm, fewer people will be with them. Security becomes more lax, and that will be our best opportunity to strike."

"Are they on the farm now?"

"They left there this morning."

"Irina, too?"

"Yes."

"How do you know?"

"Would you like for me to show you?"

"That would just be peachy, Sokolov."

Sokolov smiled. "That is sarcasm. I have already set up round-the-clock surveillance in the attic, and positioned cameras in the woods behind this house. It was the first thing I did when I set up here. Come, I will show you."

The narrow steps leading to the attic were concealed behind an old door. The stairs were enclosed, and so narrow that Novak had to turn his shoulders sideways to get through. He felt claustrophobic, not to mention vulnerable to anyone coming up behind him. Sokolov preceded him, and was already at the top. Novak climbed the last few steps, not sure what he'd find. He had his gun ready. He holstered it when he stepped out into a big room that ran the length and breadth of the house. It had unfinished studded walls and open rafters. It smelled like new lumber and paint.

It also resembled a NASA control room for Apollo 13. Novak was surprised at the amount of electronic equipment. Old and new maps of the United States were tacked on bulletin boards nailed to the studs, and clipped newspaper articles were pinned to the walls. A row of brand-new Dell computers sat on a countertop across from one twin bed made up with a blue coverlet that looked hand-crocheted. This place had been here a long time and was a spymaster's dream. "How long has this room been in use, Sokolov?"

"I told you we've owned this property since the Cold War days. My new computers are locked up. I purchased the very best. They're over there, in that cabinet." He pointed to a tall built-in safe secured with a keypad lock.

"If this was KGB property, how come Petrov doesn't know about it?"

"He wasn't assigned to this area. He ran things up around New York mostly. I was assigned down here."

"How many other people know about this place?"

"A few people maybe, but they've moved on or been recalled home years ago. It has sat here empty until I came and tidied it up. Nobody will come out here."

"I hope you're right. They might take a bullet if they do." Novak watched the Russian, looking for signs of deception. But he probably wouldn't see any. Sokolov was no fool. Novak needed to remember that.

Sokolov punched in the code and pulled open the doors. Inside, there was an elaborate surveillance system similar to the ones seen in Five-Star hotels and restaurants. There were eight screens, all revealing various rooms inside a house. Novak leaned closer. "Is that the house at Blackwood's farm?"

The Russian nodded. "I managed to plant secret cameras in the major living areas of his house. This is the living room, and that one is the kitchen. I wired up both Irina's and Blackwood's bedrooms. There's also a surveillance camera in the stable and the bunkhouse beside it. That's where the guards sleep."

Novak stared at the small screens as Sokolov booted up a thirty-inch monitor in the middle. He could see men moving about inside the bunkhouse, some asleep on beds and others getting dressed. He could see a female cook dressed in white standing in the kitchen of the main house. Everything was being recorded. Impressed, Novak looked at Sokolov. "How in the hell did you get those cameras inside that house?"

"This was what I did during my stint in your country. I've bugged hundreds of houses through the years, sometimes with our targets watching me the entire time. For Blackwood's house, I used the excuse of a possible gas leak. They have gas fireplace logs in nearly every room."

"Nobody recognized you or suspected you? Petrov didn't recognize you?"

"I disguised myself, but the servants there are used to service people coming in and out. The Senator travels so often that they have the gas and water lines disconnected at times. I bugged their landlines as well, but they rarely use them. Blackwood never stays anywhere for long. He goes from one property to the next. They leave only a skeleton crew behind, usually one maid, the cook, and a guard or two. The horse trainers and stable boys never see the inside of the big house. They work hard all day and sleep in the bunkhouse with the guards. The last thing Blackwood expects is somebody infiltrating his home, especially out here in the Virginia woods. He thinks he's too powerful to be brought down. He is, I suspect, unless you know how to get incriminating tapes."

After that, Sokolov's expression sobered, and he looked away from Novak's regard. Novak assumed he meant proof of Irina's abuse. He felt his stomach react to the idea. If that's what was on the tapes, he didn't want to see them. He couldn't imagine what it would do to Sokolov, if he was in fact her real father. "What about Petrov? We bring him down first and Blackwood falls, too. Are you sure he didn't recognize you or remember something about this place?"

"We met many years ago. He helped to train me, but I was one of many recruits. I avoid the house if he is there, though I don't believe he'd recognize me now. I've changed—*he's* changed. He's always around Blackwood and Irina because his primary job is to protect them, making sure Irina stays in line. He is kind to her at times. I don't know if he still runs a network in New York, but he might, or it could be in Washington. That would be more likely. I think not, however, because he is no longer sanctioned by the Kremlin."

"But he's into smuggling drugs?"

He nodded. "It would be perfect, don't you see? If they're using all his beach properties to transport opioids, they can line the coast from north to south with safe houses in which to move the product. We engineered family units that fit in with their neighborhoods. Some may still be operating. I would suspect, though, that he's using new people. Petrov had many contacts here and in Canada."

"Using them as drug mules?"

"I'm sure they're moving the drugs. No telling what else they're smuggling. As you know, human trafficking is now a lucrative business."

"Let's just get Irina out first. She has free rein to do whatever she likes most of the time, or she used to. She kept Justin hidden from them in a hotel just down the road from here. She had to have freedom to do it."

"She sneaks out at night mostly, usually through the pasture behind the house. I've seen her do it. Justin used to pick her up out on their entry road. They watch her, but not close enough. If Blackwood catches her, she pays a dear price when she gets home."

Sokolov got angry thinking about it. Novak didn't ask what that bastard did to her because he didn't want to know. Sokolov told him anyway, his words ground out through clamped teeth.

"Blackwood is big on corporal punishment. He likes to put her over his knee." He stopped there. "He does this to my daughter that he stole from me, my only child, and there is nothing I can do about it as long as she continues to stay with him."

"He's a depraved bully. We'll get her out of there, and he'll pay for what he's done."

"Molesting her and beating her is how that son of a bitch gets his fun. He tells her he loves her the entire time he's beating her. That it's all for her own good. When he gets really angry he slaps her or punches her with a closed fist."

The visuals that cropped up in Novak's mind made his flesh crawl. He'd heard rumors that the senator was a sexual predator, but nobody had ever accused him publicly. He stared at the bedroom monitor. The hidden camera was focused on Irina's big white canopy bed. "How can you stand to watch that?"

"I can't. It's all taped, but if I ever sat down and watched him hurt her that way, I don't know what I'd do. So I record, but stopped watching it after the first few times. I have learned to be patient. I am setting things up now. I will kill him when the time is at hand. I hope that is soon."

"I won't stop you. We'll get him, and we'll get Petrov." Novak looked at Sokolov. The Russian evaded his eyes. Novak's distrust bloomed full-flower. "I find it less than believable that you can walk into that house and plant cameras all over the place without raising suspicion."

Sokolov lifted a shoulder in careless disregard. "It is not easy, but I can do it. That's on tape, too, if you want to watch me work. I trust you now. You could have turned me in yesterday while you were gone from here. You knew where I was, and you knew my background. You did not do it. That is because you want to help me."

Novak didn't answer. "How long were you a mole in this country?"

"For several years. I moved around a lot and set up sleeper cells with people the Kremlin trained. Nobody ever suspected me of anything. Petrov did the same. My loyalty to the Motherland ended when I found out my government allowed Blackwood to take Irina out of the country as a toy for his own sick perversions. I was the one they jailed."

"I can understand that."

"I doubt we can bring Blackwood down, not right now. The tapes I made are the only thing I believe can do that. I will try someday. We can destroy his drug business, though, and when we do that, Petrov will go down with him." He caught Novak's gaze. "But I want them both dead. I want to do it myself. Petrov also has a price on his head now. If we're lucky, Moscow will find him first. He is a traitor in every sense of the word. That's why he hides out here in the forests of Virginia under the protection of a powerful politician. They'll deal harshly with him when he's found. That's why we must get to Irina. Then I'll take her and disappear forever."

"I hope it's that easy."

"As long as I have these tapes, Blackwood will end up in prison. I made copies to send to media outlets in case of my death. I just need to get Irina first. You are my eyewitness to Petrov's murder of Justin Dalton."

"Where is Blackwood now?"

"They left the farm not too long after you did. Not to fear—I know where they're going, because I attached a GPS tracker on his car. It is a habit of mine."

Novak nodded. He often did the same, carrying multiple GPS trackers in his backpack. Knowing the exact locations of your targets all the time was the name of the game.

"Their first stop was at Nags Head in North Carolina," Sokolov continued. "Then they drove on to Myrtle Beach. They're still there, but they're going to Fripp Island next, because I heard the cook telling the guard about their plans. By the time we catch up to them, that's where they'll be."

"That's in South Carolina."

"You've been there?"

"I've been to the Marine base at Parris Island outside Beaufort. I know Fripp isn't too far from there. Do you have those places bugged as well?"

"Not yet, but they are easy to surveil, especially on Fripp. I have a beach house there that I bought many years ago. In the other places we can rent condos and watch their movements from there."

"So you just sat here and watched them take Irina away?"

"I'm not ready to rescue her yet. I need your help. Fripp Island is a wildlife refuge and residential island. His beach house sits right on the ocean among many others, including mine. In the past, Irina has had free rein while there, as long as she doesn't try to leave. They shot her up with heroin before they left, so she'll be out of commission for a time. We'll be down there and set up to get her by then."

"You aren't afraid he'll kill her before we get there?"

"He relented in his anger when she begged for forgiveness. If she thwarts him again or tries to find Justin, he'll turn her over to Petrov. I'm sure of it. She's never done anything like this before. He'll only give her one more chance. We can get her out before that happens."

Novak hoped he was right about that, or that kid was going to end up dead.

Chapter 12

The drive down to Fripp Island took most of the night. The fastest route was south on I-95. Sokolov took the wheel of his Range Rover. He was a careful driver, never exceeding the speed limit, maybe because he didn't have a U.S. driver's license and was in the country illegally. They didn't say much. Novak stared straight ahead, thinking about Lori Garner's state of health. He finally gave in and punched in her number, just to soothe his mind. She picked up on the first ring, told him she was feeling better, that her headache wasn't quite so awful now, and that she was enjoying getting to know the Summers, so he should stop freaking out and worrying about her. The last thing she said was to hurry up and expose Charles Blackwood for the disgusting bottom-dweller that he was, sooner rather than later. This conversation made her sound more like the amazing woman he knew so well. Afterward, he sat back and relaxed. That's when his mind moved on to what he might be facing in the days to come.

At the same time, he kept a cautious eye on the former Russian operative sitting next to him. He expected something bad to happen, something that Novak wasn't going to like. He wondered how much and what parts of Sokolov's story were true. Despite his serious misgivings about the man, he believed enough of his story to stay inside that SUV. When Lori texted him additional information on his new ally, most of it lined up with what Sokolov had already revealed to Novak. The guy had been wanted by the U.S. Government for espionage for over a decade. That news caused Novak to feel better, and worse.

Novak stayed alert. None of this quagmire had a damn thing to do with him, other than his desire to bring down Petrov. Irina Blackwood's lies had sucked Novak in nice and deep and brought him into a doubtful league with a Soviet spook. If he could help him put this whole operation down, he had to go along with it. He wanted to exact justice for Irina, too. Together, they had a good chance to accomplish that. That was the only good thing. Fripp Island turned out to be a six and a half square-mile barrier island in the low country of South Carolina. It had a population of less than a thousand people, but that number exploded as tourists swarmed in to enjoy its warm beaches. Located about twenty miles out of Beaufort, it was close to the Marine base on Parris Island where he'd spent time training. So he was familiar with the surrounding area and the climate, but knew very little about the nearby tourist hot spots.

Stepan Sokolov grew talkative about the time they hit Beaufort's city limits. He suddenly became a tour guide. He said that the island was not commercialized, but was fairly laid back and quiet. According to him, it was about a hundred miles south of Charleston and about half that distance north of Savannah. He told Novak how he'd used his beach house there as a holiday escape in the old days when he was undermining Americans. Novak wished he'd shut up. Everything he said galled Novak because he had chosen to work with a former enemy spy. It went against his grain and everything he believed in. On top of that, Novak was about to step foot inside a place that had probably once been a Russian safe house. For all he knew, Americans might have been held and questioned inside, or even killed for information. He felt himself stiffening up.

The first sight he got of the island showed a seascape with waterfowl flying over wild marshes. A long bridge took them over to the island proper. As they drove over the water, a Great Blue Heron flew parallel to their vehicle, its long wings flapping lazily before it veered off. A small guard house was situated at the island end of the bridge. A security man stood inside behind a sliding glass window. He wore a tan uniform with *Welcome to beautiful Fripp Island* embroidered in script on the pocket flap. A sign instructed them to stop at the booth, so Sokolov rolled to a standstill and slid down his window. The guard greeted them with a big friendly smile and asked where they were going in his pleasant South Carolina drawl. Sokolov gave him a street address on Tarpon Boulevard and glibly lied about his name. The guard checked a clipboard, was satisfied, and waved them on. He told them to enjoy their stay and not end up sunburned. Sokolov laughed and told him he'd brought lots of sunscreen. He was such a convincing liar that Novak's already wavering trust took a nosedive into a pool of suspicion.

As they drove along, Novak decided the island lived up to its reputation as the perfect vacation spot. It seemed to cater especially to families with kids. All the golf carts they passed were jam-packed with youngsters, and they passed a lot of them on the road. "What's with all these golf carts?" "Most of these rental houses provide them so tourists will be apt to park their cars and run around the streets in the carts. Thus no traffic to speak of, and the children love it."

This island would be a nice place to retire, Novak decided, or in Sokolov's case, to hide inside a foreign spy nest. The neighborhoods looked neat and orderly, every street lined with gray or yellow or white Charleston-esque houses built up off the ground in case of coastal flooding. They looked nice and welcoming, usually two or three stories high with well-kept emerald lawns, lots of saw palmetto palms and waterways intersecting the island with private boat docks behind some of the residences. Most had wide front verandas and multiple cars parked in the driveways with license plates from all of the country. Novak suspected there were lots of family reunions going on.

They came in on Tarpon Boulevard and stayed on it. Lots of people were out and about, biking or walking, most of them dressed in shorts and bathing suits. Since the island was also a wildlife preserve, tame deer loitered about everywhere, grazing in front yards, stopping traffic when they crossed the streets, and even meandering about on a golf course, where one errant ball could be a death knell. Ponds and waterways intersected the island all over the place, with warning signs indicating the deadly presence of alligators. He hoped all those moms and dads walking around kept a tight rein on their small children and pets. All in all, it looked like a pleasant little paradise surrounded by the sea, everything neat as a five-star hotel, with every indication of a safe and pleasant holiday destination. That is, except for the former Russian assassin and corrupt ex-senator running drugs in their Mister Rogers' Neighborhood.

Sokolov became chatty again. "There's a nice golf course here. Sixteen holes, and the greens are fabulous, that is, unless you encounter an alligator sunning on the fairway. I used to play. Nice place to live full-time."

"Are you trying to sell me a time-share at your house, Sokolov?" Novak was watching for the senator's car and memorizing the route to the beach house, just in case he had to get out in a hurry.

Sokolov chuckled. "No, I am not interested in selling. I like it here too much. It's a wildlife sanctuary, you know."

"Yeah, I noticed. How come you just happen to own a house close to Blackwood's? That seems pretty coincidental to me."

"Not so much. We bought my place years ago only because it was close to him, and he was our target at the time. He was still a broadcaster back then, but he was influential and eventually was brought around to join us. When he became Senator, his value to us increased exponentially."

"No kidding."

Sokolov smiled, as if reminiscing about the good old spying days. He was really beginning to get on Novak's nerves. He wondered if this guy had ever murdered an American citizen. He figured Petrov had done so, plenty of times. He had a feeling Sokolov might have also been designated a sanctioned killer at one time or another.

"Just trying to break the ice, Novak. Earn your trust a bit. We're stuck together for a time, whether you like it or not."

"I don't like it."

"That's mutual, of course. We'll never be friends. I do know you were a good soldier. Of course, you had to be if you were on a Navy SEAL team. Hating Blackwood and Petrov is all we have in common."

"Yeah, there is that fun fact."

Sokolov shut up for a few minutes. Then he said, "If he wants Irina dead, he'll probably do it while they're here on the island. We can't let that happen."

"Why here?"

"Because I've talked to people who have surveilled him in the past. That old man has brought other young girls out here with him, girls even younger than Irina. Sometimes they simply disappeared while here, never to be seen again. Nobody reported them missing; nobody seemed to know they'd ever been alive and well. They would be observed in his car on arrival, but then vanish overnight. Our people searched for their bodies, believe me. They believed he dumped the bodies out in the ocean, but they could never prove anything, one way or the other."

Novak could believe that. He was ready to believe anything. "We're going to get Irina out." He glanced at Sokolov. "Seems a bad place to commit a murder. Why here? Way too many tourists running around everywhere."

"He managed it somehow. Both our houses are down at the end of the island, where it's far less commercialized. No restaurants or businesses down there. Look around, Novak. See how happy and carefree everybody is. No one would suspect the Russians have landed." He grinned, then sobered at the hard look Novak gave him.

"Is this where you stay when you sneak into my country to kill people?"

"I don't make a habit of killing people, no more than you do. From time to time, I came here. I liked it, so I bought this house when we shut down most of the sleeper cells."

"You think they use this as a primary depot for passing the drugs?"

"Probably, but it certainly won't be the only one. He owns beach houses from New England to the Florida Keys. It's odd for him to own so many in similar places while rarely renting any of them. That raised our suspicions, of course. He's using them for something other than weekend trips, and I say they're all part of a drug pipeline. We have to identify each and every one and shut them all down. It won't be easy, as far apart as they are. That's probably why they're doing it this way."

"Have you personally witnessed him passing drugs, here or at the farm, or anywhere at any time?"

"No, why would I? See that family walking over there on the side of the road? The ones eating the ice cream cones? For all we know, they could be his mules. There could be drugs in their backpacks. Nobody checks people's bags around here. Nobody checks anything. Then there's that great big ocean right over there. Who would be expecting a drug runner to pass product in this vacation paradise?"

"So you're saying he's moving drugs from one beach house to the next?"

"Exactly. All at busy, popular beach resorts. I don't know if I'm right or if I can prove it. They're good, and they're careful. I think they'll be using family units like the one we just passed."

"Still seems a dangerous way to operate. You really think they're involving children in these families?"

Sokolov nodded. He slowed down when a baby deer ran across the street after its mother. "Petrov liked to use families—the children make good cover. Normal American families, just out for fun in the sun. Looks innocent, don't you think?"

"Did you use children in your operations?"

"No, but he always did. Those old networks are gone, but if he did start up a new one, there would be kids involved. I hope they're not trafficking those children, but I wouldn't doubt it, not when it's Vasily Petrov and Blackwood, with his vile perversions."

"How close is your house to his?"

"Four houses north, right on the beach. Oceanfront properties on Tarpon are built close together. I had a widow's watch built atop the roof for easier surveillance."

"I ought to just shoot you right now."

"Yes, of course. But my espionage occurred a long time ago when I was young. I could shoot you for the same thing, could I not?"

Novak said nothing.

"You must know the statistics, do you not, Novak? Heroin overdoses kill hundreds of Americans every week, maybe more by now. Most of those drugs come through at your southern border, so that leaves this route less scrutinized, except by the patrols of the Coast Guard cutters. Petrov will have found a way for his couriers to look perfectly innocent to them and all other law enforcement officers."

Novak knew those statistics and that opioid use was now in epidemic proportions. It was a terrible problem that needed to be solved, especially if these criminals were targeting kids.

"Up top on the roof, we can see straight over into Blackwood's place. He's got big side windows on the second level deck that we can see through, and the decks are open, so we can watch whoever comes out, as well as anyone on their stretch of beachfront. Having a telescope in the widow's walk raises no suspicions. Lots of houses have them to watch the tankers and ships out on the horizons. I'm hoping we can video a drug drop."

"That's gonna take round the clock surveillance."

"Yes, of course, it will. We can take turns sleeping. He won't stay here very long, although he seems to like this place better than the others. It may be as long as a week, maybe longer. I can't figure that. I hope we can spot a courier and follow them to the drop."

"How long is the beach?"

"Three miles, I guess, something like that. We'll need to conceal our identities with ball caps and sunglasses. They could possibly recognize us. They've seen you close up and personal. Petrov knows you on sight now, knows you're a threat. Your size and height alone will give you away. I've learned how to melt into the woodwork, so I doubt they'll know I'm anywhere around."

"You can't be sure Petrov doesn't remember you. You were on the same team."

"Years ago we were, but we only met briefly a time or two. I was a new trainee among many others. He was an important figure in Moscow back then. I was a cog in his big wheel. I was still patriotic at that time, and ready to give my life for Mother Russia. There's no way he'll remember me."

"You better hope he doesn't."

"They took my daughter, just stole her away in the dead of night. They didn't know Irina was my daughter. Blackwood saw my beautiful baby girl, wanted her, and took her. Petrov made sure my wife stopped complaining. He beat her so terribly that she never regained hearing in her right ear. Until she died, she lived in terror that he'd come back and kill her."

"Nobody in your government made any effort to stop them from taking Irina out of Russia?"

"No. It was easy for them. My wife was never the same after that day. Even after I returned from deployment and started searching for Irina. She died while I was in prison. Years passed before I found out the truth about who took our daughter."

"I take it you've got a plan worked out now."

"I'm working on one."

"Work faster. We can't hang around here long and not be made."

"Like I said, our surveillance is twofold. If this is a depot for opioid trade, we need to document that and incriminate everyone involved."

Novak looked around the idyllic setting. He agreed with Sokolov. This place was perfect, as any popular island resort would be. Choosing a place like this, with this kind of small town ambience and a long beach providing access to open seas was a smart move. Add to that the boats darting around everywhere offshore, and any craft coming north from the next tourist spot would never be noticed. Nobody in their right mind would suspect a long-time famous former senator would be running a drug operation out of his vacation homes, even with constant whispers of his corruption. "They transfer from resort to resort, right? It's coming into the country from the sea."

"That's my guess. My focus has always been on Irina. Bringing down the drugs is yours."

"How often does Blackwood come down here?"

"Every month or so, he visits them all, starting at Nag's Head and traveling south from there. Sometimes he goes north instead, with stops at Atlantic City and Newport. He visits these places too often for it to be a normal thing. That's what makes me suspicious. The good thing about it is that Irina is often alone out here. His men hang around, but don't dog her footsteps like they do in Virginia. We can probably approach her without being seen. I don't think she knows yet that Justin's dead, so she's probably waiting for a chance to sneak away and go back home. Other than by boat, there's only one way off the island, so she's stuck here for the time being."

"I'm betting she knows plenty about how they're passing drugs."

"She has to. But she's addicted and is afraid to turn them in."

"You think that's why he addicted her?"

Sokolov nodded. "He did it strictly for control. She's headstrong. I think he forcibly injects her when she tries to wean herself off the heroin. I've seen him hold her down and do it on my surveillance tapes. He's plain evil."

Blackwood was going down hard. Novak was sure of that much. He didn't like the idea of sitting around on a beach and hoping to get a glimpse of some drug deal. "We need to force action here. Take her out of his control, get her somewhere safe, and then come back for Petrov."

"You need to be more patient. I'm surprised you're not. I didn't peg you as impetuous."

"I'm not patient, no, but I'm not stupid, either. I'll act as soon as I see a good opening."

"You cannot put my daughter in danger."

"I don't intend to."

"We need video evidence showing the dealers pushing the drugs."

"That takes too much time."

"Time we've got. I know how Petrov does things. He's slow and methodical. That's the way he'll set this thing up. He never hurries anything. That's why he doesn't get caught."

Sokolov crossed an intersection at Bonito Drive. They had been passing plenty of big and fancy beach houses with glorious views of the Atlantic Ocean. It had to be expensive to live out there.

"This is home." Sokolov turned into the driveway of a large, two-storied gray clapboard-sided house. It was long and narrow with tiny side yards, but had lots of tropical foliage and palmettos hugging the half-moon driveway. Novak could see the widow's walk high above the roof. It was enclosed with white bannisters, and would be the perfect place to set up a surveillance post. Sokolov knew what he was doing, all right.

Inside, the beach house was hot as hell, but beautiful all the same. Expecting it to be unused and closed up with Cold War-era furnishings, he was surprised by the large airy white rooms and windowed walls, all closed to the sun, making it dim inside. It must have cost Sokolov a small fortune, even years ago. Sokolov moved around, turning on the air conditioner, pulling sheets off the furniture, yanking open the wood blinds and shutters. The windows were tinted glass, which prevented glare and provided privacy. Though the view was magnificent, the house had few furnishings. The living room had one long couch and two recliners, and the kitchen had a granite island. Both bedrooms on the main floor looked comfortable, with king-size beds and mirrored dressers.

The second floor had four bedrooms with nothing inside. An enclosed stair at the end of the hall led up to the open-air widow's walk. They climbed the steps and came out into the hot sunlight and brisk ocean breezes. The smell of the sea filled Novak's senses. He wished he was out there on his boat surveilling the island, instead of here. The roof was about even with some of the tallest palm trees. They could sit up there and observe anything that moved down on the sand for the entire length of the beach.

It was midday, and he could see at least a hundred people at the other end of the beach where there was a cluster of tall condominiums. Everyone was sunning and swimming in the surf or playing beach volleyball. Lots of tide pools glistened and reflected the sun like silver mirrors. Some mothers were sitting in them with their babies, while the infants splashed in seawater warmed by the sun. A long line of ten brown pelicans flew by at eye level. Sokolov had been right. This end of the beach was relatively deserted.

Sokolov went back downstairs, returning a few minutes later with a honey of a high-powered telescope. He quickly set it up on a tripod and pointed it out to sea. "That's Blackwood's place down there. See the beige stucco house with two decks and the brown roof?"

Novak could see it well. It looked nice enough, though smaller than Sokolov's house. Both the Senator's decks were high off the ground and extended a ways over the sand. Both decks were deserted. One guy was fishing in the surf two doors down, and one couple was sitting on a blanket not far from him. Nobody moved in or around Blackwood's house. It looked closed up and empty. "You sure they came here? Looks like nobody's home."

"They're here, all right. My tracker puts their car inside that very garage. I think they're here to get Irina back under control. Their garage faces Tarpon, but they usually leave some of their cars parked outside on the driveway. They'll show up out on the beach eventually. Especially Irina, unless he's got her locked in her room. He does that when she's being difficult."

"How long have you been watching them?"

"Several months."

Novak pulled up a folding beach chair and focused the telescope out at sea, then slowly moved it back toward Blackwood's house. Up close, he could see through the windows. Nothing moved inside. The place looked unoccupied. The glass windows facing the water, which he couldn't see well, would be a treasure trove after dark when the interior lights came on. He would be able to watch what they did from the beach if the tide didn't come in too high. He felt his muscles start to relax.

Sokolov could be right with his theory. This could be a prime location to move those drugs. With new tourists coming in and out on a daily basis and condo rentals changing hands every week, nobody would be around long enough to notice irregular contacts made from a house at the quiet end of the beach. Nobody would think twice about strangers showing up. He sat up and set his gaze out on the deep blue waters of the Atlantic, where whitecaps flashed like white diamonds. If he had to set up a drug operation from here, that's where they'd pass the drugs to the next runner, right out there, far past the breakers, boat-to-boat. The beach house was just a depot, all right. They set up binocular cameras on the widow's walk and inside a second-floor bedroom window. The house was huge and could sleep at least twelve, but that was good. Novak could have his own floor without listening to the constant chit-chat of the Russian. He would sleep gun in hand for the foreseeable future. It didn't take long to set the place up to spy on their prey. The widow's walk was by far the best spot.

Novak gave Sokolov credit for the excellence of his set-up, but he still found it a mighty big coincidence that Sokolov happened to have a beach house located only yards from Blackwood's place. His story made sense, but Novak still wondered. He was unsure about a lot of things that his new Russian cohort had told him. Mainly, Sokolov was acting awfully chipper for a father whose daughter was in so much trouble and had been so for a decade. He seemed fine with taking things slow and easy while his child was being molested by a perverted old man. He said he'd been unable to watch Blackwood and Irina on his tapes, but had he? He seemed a little too calm and collected, even for a jaded ex-spy. None of those questions sat well in Novak's mind.

Sokolov could and should have moved a long time ago to get his kid out of that hellhole. Novak would have. Irina liked to drive around in her convertible, didn't she? Why not approach her back then at the horse farm before Justin ended up in the morgue? Why hadn't Sokolov done it? That was a good question that he needed to answer. Novak's trust in the man disintegrated more with every passing hour.

Chapter 13

Throughout the first day they watched Blackwood's beach house around the clock. All remained quiet, inside and out, most drapes drawn, and nobody to be seen. Novak and Sokolov each took turns at the roof, while the other caught some sleep. The beige stucco house appeared like all the others lined up to face the sea, except that no one came outside to wade in the surf or laze around on the beach. There was no sign of Irina, Blackwood, or Petrov. Novak got worried, thinking that Sokolov was dead wrong about the Fripp Island property.

But on day two, there was a big change. Early in the morning, Novak spotted Irina when she walked out onto the upper deck. She was wearing a tiny red bikini, and carried a water bottle and a paperback book. She looked impossibly skinny, almost anorexic, and yet she was with child. He watched her lie down on a chaise longue and appear to fall asleep. She looked no worse for wear after returning to her father's house, not from what Novak could tell. That was a definite relief until Blackwood showed up and joined her on the deck. He wore a terrycloth robe over a bathing suit and came out of the same room that she had. Sitting down on a deck chair, he leaned close to her, apparently having a lot to say. His face looked serious, and more angry by the minute. Irina kept her eyes closed, looking sullen and defiant, unresponsive to whatever he was telling her. They were definitely still at odds, all right, but it wasn't coming to blows. Not yet, anyhow.

After a time of fruitless barking at her, Blackwood stood up, palms planted on his hips. He looked old and bitter and frustrated as he stalked back into the house. Irina showed no reaction to his departure. At that point, Novak hoped that Irina remained alive long enough to get her away from him. She didn't appear to have been beaten up again, though, or she was simply high out of her head. So they were keeping her supplied with heroin. If she continued her willful obstinacy to whatever Blackwood was steamed about, they'd probably eventually withhold the drugs until she decided to cooperate. Novak had a sinking feeling that inside that house, Blackwood didn't mind acting on his true interest with that poor teenage girl. Although Sokolov didn't express those sentiments aloud, his beet-red expression told Novak that he believed sexual abuse was still going on. That was probably why Irina was given her brief bits of freedom. She had been forced to accept her fate a long time ago, and was resigned to do what he wanted.

Novak kept watching. He felt as if something awful was about to happen. Later that morning, he perked up when a carload of visitors showed up in a dark blue Camry. It was a family unit—father, mother, and two children. Both looked between five and ten years old. The parents were dark-haired, while both kids were towheaded. All had deep tans and were dressed like everybody else out on that beach. They all climbed out of their car and went inside Blackwood's house, as if they were simply paying a call to friends who lived on the beach. More likely, they were drug mules paying a supply call on a gang of armed thugs. It was looking more and more as if Sokolov's theory of family drug runners was right on target.

Several days passed with the same family arriving at Blackwood's house around the same time, late morning into the noon hour, always all four of them. They would always enter through the front door in broad daylight. The parents carried totes or backpacks with beach towels draped over their arms, as if they were headed out to the sand. After their arrival, Novak never saw either parent out on the porches or on the sand, but the two children usually appeared on the lower deck before running down to play on the beach. Irina sometimes came out with them. Novak had a feeling she was the designated babysitter while the parents filled beach bags with illegal pills and heroin. Each visit lasted several hours, and then they would trail back to the car and drive away. Today, they were still closeted inside. Novak looked around the street for unusual activity. The houses across Tarpon Boulevard were quiet, nobody outside, and the beachfront had three groups of people, with none anywhere close to Blackwood's place.

"You see, I was right," Sokolov said to Novak as he climbed the last few steps to the widow's walk. He had a pair of high-powered binoculars on a cord around his neck. He handed Novak a cold Bud Light, then sat down and fixed the field glasses on Blackwood's house. "They've got heroin inside that house, and God only knows what else. I think we've identified our first family of mules moving his drug shipments."

"Well, they sure as hell aren't typical tourists. Do you think those kids are really theirs?"

"Maybe. Or maybe they're just human cargo. As I told you before, child trafficking is big business and the most terrible crime of all. If this pipeline is as far-reaching as I suspect, they can be transporting all sorts of things up here from Central and South America. Mexico, without a doubt. Nobody would dream they're drug mules. Nobody would think to search the car of a well-known senator. It's a good set-up, I'll give them that. These people probably have to pick up enough product for all the dealers around Fripp and maybe even in Beaufort, but I think most of it is going farther north with other mules."

"We need to follow that blue Camry back home, so we'll know where to call in a raid when we're ready to act."

"Yes, I agree. They may live here or in a nearby town, or they could be renting a condo this week."

"I'd say they have a permanent place, but not out here on the island."

"They're not hiding their visits to Blackwood. They come in the light of day when anybody can spot them. We're just the only ones who've followed Blackwood and kept track of who shows up to see him. They're moving a shipment soon. I can feel it."

"Yeah, it's a good cover." Novak took a drink of beer and set it aside. "We need proof that it's a drug operation. Irina is in that house. She's our best witness. She knows everything that happens inside. She has to. We definitely need to get her out of there and to a safe house before we bust them."

"I've already got photographic evidence. I got close-ups of this same family last time I followed Blackwood down here. I'm not sure the kids are the same. I seem to remember an older boy that time, a teenager, I believe. We need to get the entire operation nailed down, and then you can present it to your DEA, or FBI, if you want."

"You make that sound easy, and it won't be," Novak said. "You think Blackwood hasn't incorporated safeguards. He's corrupt, as bad as they come, but he's not stupid. Think about how long this has been operating without anybody being the wiser. Think about it, Sokolov—we need to get Irina out or she'll be charged, too, after we bring it all down."

Sokolov became testy. Novak watched his face with interest; the Russian had kept his feelings flat and hidden most of the time.

"I know all that perfectly well. Of course, she's got to come out first. I've said that all along. Then I'm going to take her so far away from here that they'll never find her, much less accuse her of anything. Even if they do arrest her, she's an addict and minor, coerced to do whatever he said. I want him behind bars or dead."

Novak leaned back in his chair. "You're thinking best case scenarios. This could all go to hell in a million different ways. But you're right. We need to get her out and to a safe place before we go in. And we need to see how the drugs move on and off this island. Where do these people go? How do they pass it? My bet is out there off the coast. We need to take our time. Maybe I ought to pay them a visit tonight and see what I can find out."

Sokolov was against the idea. He shook his head. "Too risky. If they see you, they'll shoot you down and dump your body. Nobody will be able to prove anything. That's the way they do it, believe me. Their guards will see you."

"They won't see me. I'm better than that. I want to know exactly what they're dealing and how their couriers pass the dope. Maybe that family is getting instructions on when and where to meet the next courier. If they're staying here on the island, they're not going far. That means they're passing it on from right here at Fripp. If they live on the mainland, I want to put a GPS tracker on their car, as well as any other car that comes into that driveway. They're bound to be couriers. If we're serious about bringing this thing down, I want every single person working for him busted."

"You've got GPS trackers with you?"

"In my backpack. I need them in my line of work."

"I keep some on hand, too. The minute we take Blackwood down, he'll give up the rest. He won't go down alone. He's a coward who bullies women and little girls."

"We're going to need proof on every single courier for this to stand up in court. If we can find out all the transfer stops along this pipeline and where the drugs initiate, we can present an open-and-shut case. That's what I want. These kinds of people have skated far too often in the past because they hire slick lawyers. You can bet Blackwood has the best attorney firm in D.C. on his payroll, and it will be as corrupt as he is. If we get Irina out and keep her clean, her testimony will be devastating for all of them. Hopefully, she can identify by name and location all the drug runners he deals with."

"Okay, we'll follow them. I just want her away from him. I think she's going to run soon—she'll be worried about Justin, and doesn't have any way to find out where he is or if he's okay. I don't want Blackwood to kill her before we can take her out, and he will if he catches her trying to sneak off. He's losing patience with her. You can see that as well as I can."

"You got a plan worked out for getting her out of here, Sokolov? If you do, I want to hear it."

"It's not complicated. We contact Irina on the beach somehow and tell her what's going on. She doesn't know me, so she won't trust me, but she *will* trust you. You've got to make the first contact."

"Yeah, that sounds great, except I'll never find her alone. Everybody inside that house has seen me that night when they took me to the horse farm. When she's out there with the kids, guards will be watching her. After what she pulled with Justin, Blackwood will never let her out of his sight again. Or worse, he'll grow tired of her and get rid of her. So we've got to do something before that happens."

Novak's phone vibrated in his pocket. He pulled it out. The screen showed his picture of Lori. Good. He wanted to see how she was doing. "I need to take this downstairs. I'll be back in a few minutes."

Novak punched in her call as he descended the steps, then moved out into the living room near the big windows. "Hey babe, I've been thinking about you. How do you feel?"

"Wonderful. Headache's all gone. Shoulder still aches, but not so bad. I've taken off the sling. Bedrest and TLC and hydrocodone is not overrated, let me tell you."

"Good. Better take it easy for another week or so, though."

"What about you? You got Blackwood in handcuffs yet?"

"No, but we're getting close to proving he's up to his neck in drug running. I think we'll have enough soon to burn his network to the ground, if we take time to connect all the dots."

"That sounds good. Where are you?"

"Still with Sokolov, out on Fripp Island."

"That's a nice place. I was there once a long time ago with my family. How about me coming down there and helping you screw things up for him?"

Novak wanted to say yes in the worst way, but he didn't. "Better heal a bit more first. We're watching Blackwood's beach digs, and trying to get a feel for how and when he's running his pipeline. We think he takes them up the East Coast by boat, one step at a time."

"What about Irina? She okay?"

"She's here, but they watch her constantly. We're trying to figure how we can get her out alive. We may need your help when we're ready to move."

"How do you plan to do it?"

"Not sure yet. Hoping to get her alone at some point."

There was a moment of silence. "Well, actually, I've had a good idea. It occurred to me last night after I went to bed. I'm extremely tired of hanging around here, although Jeff and Angie have been wonderful, feeding me home-cooked meals you'd die for. So, how about I haul anchor and bring the *Sweet Sarah* down there? You can find a way to get the girl on board, and I'll whisk her out to sea before they have time to blink."

Novak considered it. To be honest, it sounded like a plan that could work. Blackwood would not be expecting that, and Lori could handle his boat almost as well as he could. He had taught her the basics of navigation when they'd spent a couple of months island hopping in the Caribbean. Lori was a more than capable sailor to make a short voyage parallel to the coast, even if she was handling the boat by herself. Still, she was not at a hundred percent yet, regardless of what she said. "You'd have to sail her down here by yourself. You think you're really up for that?"

"You know good and well that I can do it, bum shoulder and all. I did it all the time down in the islands. It's a short sail anyway, easy as pie. The coast always in sight."

"Yes, but I was with you down there."

"I told you. The painkillers keep me comfortable enough. Jeff can help me get underway, and I know I can manage this easy of a trip. Irina will be safe out on the water after you take her—why would they suspect her to be on a boat? You can continue surveillance on the house from wherever you are. Blackwood doesn't even know you have a boat, right? Irina probably doesn't, either, so they won't think to look for her out on the water."

"Yeah, that makes sense. We don't know yet exactly when we're going to try to contact her."

"Why not now? What's stopping you?"

"Because she stays inside the house most of the time, and a guard's near her when she's out on the beach. I might have to go inside and take her out."

"You've done that kind of stuff before with no problems. I've seen you. I believe in you, Novak."

"Bet you say that to all the guys."

"Let me come down there and save the day, Novak. You must miss me terribly by now. Besides, you owe me a big juicy steak."

"I owe myself a steak. I don't think I can ever stomach one again, though. It's too dangerous."

Lori laughed, but she was right. Sokolov got on his nerves big time, and he still wasn't sure he could completely rely on him. He'd rather Irina be out on his boat with Lori. He decided to let her do it. "Okay, you know where Fripp Island is?"

"Of course. I've already put the coordinates into your GPS system and found the best refueling stops if I need them. You taught me to think of everything, you know. Please, let's go back to St. Barths as soon as we slap Blackwood in prison. I don't think they have two-ton semi cabs there."

"You got yourself a deal. How soon can you set sail?"

"I'll cast off as soon as we hang up. Quit worrying, I know this tub's your baby. I won't sink her or run her ashore, I swear."

Novak smiled, realizing he was all in for her joining them now that she felt better. "If you run into trouble, any kind at all, promise me you'll just tie the boat up somewhere and call me. I'll come get you."

"Okay, but that's not gonna happen. No way."

Novak punched off, but misgivings hit him almost at once. If Lori came to Fripp Island, he was putting her right back in the line of fire. He shouldn't do that. He should've told her to stay put where she'd be safe. Still, her arguments all made perfect sense, and she was not coming ashore anyway, so maybe it would work. Now it was time to move.

As soon as the sun went down in a fiery panorama of golden streaks and gloriously backlit clouds of pink and purple, darkness fell slowly over the island until night lay around them, black and still as death. Novak bided his time until people had been off the beach a while. Even better, the courier family was still there, their Camry parked out on the driveway. It would be a perfect opportunity to put a tracker on their vehicle. He donned black clothing and gear and left Sokolov atop the roof watching the house. He went out the front door and kept to the shadows. It was dark enough to conceal himself all along the street. Most people were congregated inside, or watching the starry night skies on the oceanfront. It was quiet, no cars moving along the street, no pedestrians out walking. Somewhere in the distance, he heard a child laugh, probably in the house two doors down, where a huge family reunion had been going on ever since he'd arrived. Those people were having a great time. They were a happy bunch celebrating being together, unlike the sick family inhabiting the beige stucco house.

The beachfront homes were built close together. There were some windows and porches on the front of the beach houses, but he never saw anybody hanging out on the street side. He crept past the house next door. It was a rental, occupied by two families who were probably sharing expenses. The kids were toddlers, usually playing in the sand close to the adults. Tonight their place was dark and silent because they'd driven off somewhere earlier that day.

The front side of Blackwood's place was also deserted. Two cars sat in the driveway: the blue Camry and a white Ford Explorer. The garage door was open, which surprised Novak. It usually wasn't. It also made him wary. The porch light was off. Maybe they considered themselves safe on this private island and expected no trouble. That would be good news for Novak, but not something he could count on. He hunkered down in the shadows at the side of the house and listened. Nothing, no voices, no other sounds coming from inside. He got down on his hands and knees and then duck-walked around the back of the Camry. He pressed the GPS tracker up inside the back wheel well. Once he was sure it was good to go, he moved to the Explorer and did the same.

Hunkering down, he still heard nothing from inside. He moved along the side of the parked cars and eased into the double garage. The light was off, and Blackwood's big black Lincoln was sitting there all by itself. He quietly tried the doors. It was unlocked, so he did a quick search of the car and found nothing. He returned to the shadows outside and stopped for a moment, thinking maybe it had come off a bit too easy. It occurred to him that they might even be able to bug this house. Sokolov had seemed good enough at that at the horse farm. That could give them all the evidence they needed to incriminate the senator and maybe even give them video evidence of the courier transfers.

Feeling more confident, he moved down alongside the beige stucco wall toward the beach, staying beneath the big windows, even though the drapes had been pulled closed. At the back corner, he darted a quick peek at the deck standing about ten feet off the ground. Nobody was on either porch, but the drapes were open. Big squares of yellow light fell over the deck furniture, but there were still plenty of shadows in which to hide. He bent his knees, then jumped up and grabbed the wood railing on the bottom deck. He quickly pulled himself up and over, landing lightly on his feet in the shadows below one side of the windows. He hunkered down and waited for an alarm. Nothing happened. There were no security cameras, so he moved to the dark outer edges of the deck. The tide was coming in high on the sand, the breaking waves drowning out any sounds he made.

Crouching behind a lounge chair, he could see inside the main living area of the first floor. He was astonished that nobody was standing watch out back. Guards were usually patrolling everywhere around the senator. Inside the house, four men and the courier couple were sitting around the dining room table playing cards. They were talking and laughing and drinking beer. The two children were watching cartoons on a big-screen television at the other end of the room. Nobody was looking out on the deck. He tensed when he saw Petrov descend some stairs and sit down on a tall barstool. The Russian set his beer on the counter and pulled out his cellphone, staring down at the screen. There was no sign of Blackwood or Irina.

Easing back the way he had come, Novak jumped up and grabbed the upstairs balcony rail and pulled himself up far enough to climb onto the deck. Glancing back at Sokolov's place on the widow's walk, he couldn't see him, but he knew the man was watching with a night-vision rifle scope. The upstairs deck ran the length of the back of the house. He knelt in the dark for a moment. Four sliding glass doors stood in a row down the deck. He assumed all led to bedrooms, but the rooms were all dark. He moved down to the end, where a thin slice of light fell across the deck through drapes that had been left open a couple of inches.

He could see Irina inside, lying on a bed. She was covered partially by a sheet and looked stoned out of her mind. Blackwood sat in a chair beside the bed, wearing the same white terrycloth bathrobe and smoking a cigar. Novak could smell the cloying, sweet odor of his tobacco. The monster was just sitting there staring at her. When she moved slightly, trying to lift her head as if coming out of her stupor, he picked up a syringe and injected her with more drugs. After that, she didn't move at all. She probably wouldn't be able to for a long time. But she was still breathing; Novak could see her chest rising and falling.

Novak wanted to kill Blackwood. Every fiber in his body longed to end the perversion this man perpetrated on innocents. He squeezed his eyes shut and tamped down his burgeoning rage, wishing he had never looked into that bedroom. Still, it was better he saw them together rather than Sokolov. He didn't want to see what happened next. He wanted to burst in there, put Blackwood down for good, and get that kid out of that house forever. But he couldn't, not now. She would be dead weight, hard to get off the deck without alerting the guards. Novak could handle Blackwood easy enough, because he was a weak, overweight, and evil old man.

Still, he couldn't risk it now, not if they wanted to identify and destroy his operation. It was sick and depraved, what that man had been doing to that young girl. Putting Blackwood in the hospital would be gratifying, especially while Petrov and all his guards played cards downstairs. But Sokolov wasn't ready, and Lori wasn't anywhere close to the island with the boat, and wouldn't be for a while.

Novak set his teeth and backed away. It would be better to get her when she was alone and conscious and able to walk without him having to carry her. He swung a leg over the rail, determined to get her out as soon as Lori showed up. He wasn't willing to wait longer than that, and he wasn't going to tell Sokolov what he'd seen. Irina's real father was better off not knowing what was going on inside that bedroom.

Chapter 14

Novak's next glimpse of Irina came the following late afternoon. For the first time since they'd been on the island, the teenager descended the deck steps alone and walked down the beach toward Sokolov's house. This time, she wore a one-piece black bathing suit and was barefoot, carrying a beach towel in one hand. She was listening to music through ear buds attached to her phone. She spread out her towel directly in front of the house next to Sokolov's.

Her face was sunburned, her eyes sunken, and she looked so listless that Novak was alarmed. She appeared exhausted and ill, but definitely not as spaced out as she had been the night before. She was still coming down off heroin, she had to be. This was their chance, maybe the only one they'd get. Her freedom on the beach was probably the result of Blackwood and Petrov having left the beach house earlier that afternoon. Novak had watched them drive off together in the Lincoln almost two hours ago. According to Sokolov's vehicle tracker, they were playing golf on the other side of the island.

"Oh, my God, Novak, look at her. She looks sick. Look how thin she is. He's killing her with drugs."

Novak looked at her sunken belly—he had a feeling she was sick because she was no longer pregnant. He didn't know when or where or how Blackwood had managed it, but he'd ended her pregnancy. He didn't comment or conjecture to her father. "She's an addict, and has been for years. She's going to look worse than that if she doesn't get clean. Forget how she looks, it's time for us to move. Take a fishing rod down to the beach and wade out, maybe fifteen yards from her. Do you think she'll recognize you?"

"I doubt it. I was out of the country most of the time when she was little."

"Then I'll make contact. The guards are watching her, trust me. Why they let her come out there all alone bothers me."

Novak gave the Russian time to grab a rod and walk down to the water. He watched him enter the shallows barefoot and throw out his line. Novak waited a few more minutes before following him with a beach umbrella and towel. He had pulled on a New Orleans Saints ball cap, and thrown on a windbreaker and shorts. He didn't glance at Irina where she sat, about ten or twelve yards away and slightly in front of him. He shoved the umbrella into the sand. She never even glanced at him or anything else. She seemed in a complete daze, unable to notice anything, focusing only on the cresting waves. She looked dejected and depressed. Novak hoped she wasn't sitting there contemplating suicide. That's what it looked like.

There were two men out on Blackwood's lower deck. Keeping one eye on them, Novak angled the umbrella to shield him from their sight. Irina had removed her ear buds as she sat in the sun, as stiff and still as a slab of stone. The tide had receded to daytime levels, but the surf was loud enough to drown out his voice from the guards. He lay back on his elbows, weapon at the ready in case the worst happened. Few other people were at this end of the beach, so it was probably his only chance to contact her. After a couple of minutes, he called her name without looking in her direction. When he did glance at her, Irina had not moved or looked at him. He called to her again, a little louder, and this time she roused from her stupor and looked at him.

"Act like you don't see me," he called out. Blackwood's men were talking and drinking beer but still keeping an eye on her.

She stared dully at him.

"It's me, Novak."

That got through to her. She perked up, frightened, jerking her head around to glance at the guards. She didn't give him away, just placed her head on her bent knees and smiled. It looked pitiful and strained. The drugs were going to kill her if she didn't get help soon.

"Don't look at me. Look out at the water."

Novak glanced again at the men. One had his face tilted up to the sun. The other was watching Irina, but didn't seem to be aware of Novak.

"Listen to me, Irina. We're here to get you out of that house. You understand me? Nod if you do."

She nodded.

Novak said, "Are you okay? Did they hurt you?"

"I'm sick. Daddy gave me too much last night. How did you find me? Can you get me out of here, really? Daddy's gone but he's coming back soon. How's Justin? He's okay, isn't he? Is he here, too?" Novak didn't want to answer her rapid-fire questions. He glanced at Sokolov. The Russian was staring at his daughter, but he was also aware of the guards. "Can you get out of the house and meet me here around midnight?"

"I don't know. Daddy hangs around me at night." A dark flush rose to color her pale cheeks. Novak knew what that meant. Her words flooded out after that. "Daddy and Vasily are gone somewhere. I don't know when they'll be back. Please, can't we just do it now? Is Justin okay? Is he here?" Novak looked out to sea. "We can't do it now. A boat's coming, probably tonight. If we get you aboard, you'll be safe. Tell me where's he getting the drugs he gives you. Is he picking them up here?"

The question scared her. Her face was easy to read. "People come see us, you know, families. They talk to Daddy, then they go away. I think they bring stuff in. I hear him telling them when to go out for the drop. I don't know where or anything. He keeps me locked upstairs in my room, but sometimes I get to go outside and watch the little kids."

"Do they move the drugs on boats?"

Irina sat up straight, agitated. "I don't know. I don't know anything else. I guess it's in boats."

"Turn away from me or they'll get suspicious."

She obeyed.

"At what other beaches do you meet up with these families?" Novak asked.

"You know, all the popular ones like Hilton Head and Amelia Island and Jacksonville."

"Can you get out tonight without being seen?"

This time her answer was slow in coming. Her face revealed nerves and uncertainty. She started sobbing. Novak's muscles tensed. "Lie down, Irina. Turn over on your stomach so they can't see you're upset. They'll get worried if you cry."

"No, they won't. I cry all the time. They're used to it."

She flipped over, shoulders shaking with emotion. She hid her face atop her folded arms. Novak watched the men. They were clueless, guzzling beer and laughing.

"Please do it now. Daddy's angry all the time, and he made me go to this doctor—" she began, stopping mid-sentence to weep harder. She didn't have to say anything else. Novak knew exactly what her father had forced her to do. She got control back a moment later. "He says he'll kill me if I ever look at another man. He says he's tired of me, and all I do is cause him grief. He said I'm old and ugly now, and nothing but a junkie." Blackwood was beyond despicable. If Lori didn't show up soon, he'd take that kid out by car. "We'll get you out tonight if you can get down here without being seen. Can you do that?"

She nodded. "Justin's going to be so sad about the baby. We wanted it so bad. We were going to name her Britney, if it was a girl." More tears flowed. She put her cheek on the towel and wept again.

Novak felt for her, but she was going to alert the guards if she didn't cut it out. "Calm down, Irina. We're here to help you, but you're going to give us away."

"Is Justin with you? Is he all right? Why won't you tell me? Please tell me!"

Novak couldn't bring himself to do it. She was already distraught, and the news that he was dead would send her over the brink. "No, he's not here. Look over there. See the guy fishing? He's going to help us. You can trust him."

"Did you get Justin to the hospital? Did they fix him up all better?"

"The guards are looking. I gotta go. Remember, tonight at midnight, out here on the beach, right here. We'll be watching for you. Listen, Irina, if you don't see a sailboat anchored offshore, don't come down. It will be lighted up where you can see it. If it's not out there, don't come down to the beach. We'll try to get you out tomorrow night."

"What if Daddy finds out?"

"Just be careful. Go out your bedroom door and climb down on the far side of the deck. Have you snuck out before?"

She nodded.

"Then you know what to do."

She shut her eyes and asked no more questions.

Novak waited a little while longer, then stood up and brushed the sand off his shorts. He took down his umbrella and strolled slowly down toward Sokolov's house. As he climbed the steps to the low deck, he glanced back. Irina was still on her stomach, watching him. He hoped to God she didn't tell Blackwood they were on the island. If she got strung out enough, that could happen. Otherwise, the die was cast. Lori would be there soon. When she showed up, they could move.

Around dusk, when the daylight was nearly extinguished as the sun dipped into the sea beyond the horizon, the *Sweet Sarah* loomed up as a dark smudge against the darkening sky. Novak sat high in the widow's walk and watched her approach. Lori sailed the boat like an expert, dropping anchor about two hundred yards off the beach. When she called him, she reported that all had gone well, and that she was ready whenever he gave the signal.

Novak waited until it was dark and quiet all along the beach, then walked to where the incoming tide was creeping up high on the sand. He waded out to chest level and swam out to the sailboat. Lights shone from every window in Blackwood's house. Sokolov was watching for trouble from the roof. Novak settled into a slow and steady crawl stroke. When he got close, he could see Lori sitting cross-legged on the swimming platform. Once he pulled himself up, she hugged him tight and laughed. "Well, now, you are a sight for sore eyes," she said.

"You look a lot better than you did the last time I saw you. You feel okay? You sure? Have any trouble getting here?"

"Piece of cake. I feel better now that you're here. What about you? You sounded worried on the phone."

"I get nervous when we're depending on Irina to hold up her end of things. She's so shaky that she might screw up. We really need to get her out of here tonight. You game to take her out on open water?"

"Of course. That poor kid has suffered enough, especially since she's pregnant."

Novak shook his head. In the dim glow of the running lights, he could see by her expression that Lori understood. "Oh, no, she lost the baby?"

"I think Blackwood lost it for her. She said he took her to a doctor."

"My God...that man is the devil incarnate."

"He keeps her high most of the time. She's in bad shape, so we need to take her now before he loses his patience and hands her over to Petrov. According to her, he's tired of her."

Lori was concerned. "Okay, how do we get her out here?"

He went through the plan briefly. "I told her around midnight, but it all depends if she shows up. If he injects her, she won't be able to think straight. This end of the island's dark that late. The tide comes in high, but we can still get her out here."

"Does she know about Justin?"

"I couldn't bring myself to tell her. She's already close to losing it."

"No, don't tell her until we get her out of there .I don't think she could take it, either."

"I'm taking the Zodiac back in to the beach. We'll bring the girl out here in it and Sokolov will probably insist on going with you. She's too weak to make the swim. He probably can't, either."

They talked a while, during which Novak made sure everything was ready. Then he took the rubber boat back to shore, and Lori went below to prepare a cabin for Irina. Novak wanted to get her to a rehab as soon as he could and let a doctor bring her down. She was not well physically, emotionally, or any other way. If they could get her off the drugs for good, maybe she'd have a chance, but only if they could get her as far away from Blackwood as she could get. In her present condition, the hell of withdrawal was going to be difficult. He hoped she could get through it. Sokolov wanted to get her out of the country ASAP, and that was probably the safest bet.

As the hours dragged by, their nerves were as tense as tight wire. Close to midnight, Sokolov turned off all the lights and locked up the beach house. They'd already stowed their gear in the boat Novak had dragged up to the back deck. Once everything was in place, both of them sat down near the boat and waited. Out on the ocean, *Sweet Sarah* was lit up like the most popular playhouse on Broadway. Irina could not help but see it. Maybe that would give her the courage she needed. Lori was prepared to set sail the moment they got the girl on board. All they had to do was get Irina out there, and she'd be gone without a trace. Blackwood would never find her.

Midnight came and went with no sight of the girl. Novak's stress level was maxing out. He watched the house with a night scope, finally catching a glimpse of her running down the sand toward them. Novak jumped up, ready to drag the Zodiac into the water, but then he saw the man coming after her. It looked like Vasily Petrov.

Sokolov saw him, too. "Damn it, Petrov's going to stop her."

They hunkered down in the dark and watched. Novak was ready to intervene. Irina had seen Petrov, having stopped and turned to meet him. They talked together for a minute. It didn't look like he was going to hurt her or drag her back to the house. Petrov just walked along with her at the water's edge. When they were about thirty yards from Novak, they sat down together on the sand. The tide was rushing in high, almost to their feet. They sat there a moment, and then Irina lay back on the sand. Petrov leaned over her.

"Oh, God, he's shooting her up." Sokolov jumped up, ready to run to her aid, but Novak stopped him. "Wait—maybe she gets an injection every night. She's not fighting him, maybe she's playing along. If he leaves her there, we can still make it out to the boat."

Worried now, too, Novak crouched down in the shadows, ready to move if he felt she was in danger. Sokolov was shaking with fury, and could barely restrain himself. After a while, Petrov stood up and walked swiftly back to their place, leaving Irina sitting alone at the edge of the water. Not long after that, Novak saw the Lincoln's headlights flash across the beach as it backed out the driveway and drove away. The other two vehicles followed it. That meant the guards were leaving. Novak was surprised they'd left her on the beach alone. He looked back at the girl. She was not moving, the incoming rivulets lapping over her feet. At that moment, he realized what they'd done.

"We've got to move now, Novak. They're gone."

"He just overdosed her, damn it! They've left her to die out there."

"Oh, God," Sokolov cried, already running down to her.

Novak followed in a panic. If they didn't get to her fast, she was going to die—if she wasn't already dead. He grabbed his backpack out of the boat and jerked out the Naloxone, ripping it out of the package as he ran down the sand. He fell to his knees beside her. He could barely see her face in the light of a distant dusk-to-dawn light a few doors down. Her eyes were shut, and he didn't know if she was still breathing. Sokolov was trying to rouse her, but couldn't get a response. He put his fingers on the pulse at the side of her throat. He could barely feel it, but it was there.

Novak quickly injected the antidote into her other arm. The drug would block the opioid receptors in her brain quickly and bring her out of it. He'd seen it used on other overdose victims. She should have revived immediately, but she didn't. She lay unmoving. Novak started slapping her cheeks and yelling in her face. When she finally twitched her eyelashes, Novak pulled her up to a sitting position. Her eyes opened, vacant and nonresponsive at first, but then they fluttered and she gagged. She was alive and awake, albeit incoherent and confused. She threw up on the sand, and Novak washed her face off with the salt water pooling around them.

"Go get the boat! Quick!"

"You sure she's okay?"

"Yeah, she's back. Hurry, Sokolov! We've got to get her to an ER fast. This was supposed to look like she overdosed herself. He left the damn needle in her arm."

Novak scooped the girl up and in seconds, Sokolov was back and pushing the boat into the surf. He held it steady while Novak lifted her over the side. Then Sokolov scrambled in and held Irina's head on his lap, probably the first time he'd touched her in years. Novak pushed the Zodiac out deeper and pulled himself inside. He fired the motor and headed out to *Sweet Sarah*. When he glanced behind him, the houses on the beach lay still and dark, all the tired tourists sleeping peacefully in their beds, unaware that the monsters among them had driven away.

Chapter 15

While Novak raised anchor and prepared to sail, Lori got on the satellite phone and found that the nearest hospital was on Parris Island. She got through to the Brigadier General at the Marine Corps Recruit Depot there, got him out of bed, and tossed around her Pentagon credentials again in a nice, respectful way. As extra incentive, she threw in Novak's exemplary Navy SEAL service record. The Commander was impressed enough to order a base ambulance to be waiting for them at the closest possible dock, ready to rush Irina to the nearby Naval Hospital Beaufort. Novak made good speed, sliding past Pritchards Island and around the tip of St. Helena Island into Port Royal Sound, where the Navy corpsmen would be waiting with the ambulance. Sokolov rode with her while Novak and Lori finished docking the boat.

By the time they reached the hospital, the Naloxone they'd administered had done its job. Irina was resting well and breathing normally. The doctor told them if they had gotten to her half an hour later, she might have ended up dead.

She was in a private room. Stepan Sokolov was sitting close to the bed, holding his daughter's hand. Novak stood back, watching them, pretty sure that the kid would survive, and maybe even end up living a decent life. After a moment, he walked out into the corridor where Lori was sitting, her Dell laptop open on her lap.

"Thanks for arranging this, Lori. I don't think I'd have that much clout."

"My new job does have some pretty cool perks. My one star is popular with his colleagues, which is most handy, I have to agree."

"You able to pick up Blackwood's GPS signal?"

"Yep, they're right across from here at Hilton Head. I've found a house on that beach with a deed under Charles Blackwood's name. Looks to me like they're staying put there, at least for the time being. Probably meeting with couriers like they did on Fripp. Maybe they're over there waiting for the news to break about someone finding poor Irina overdosed on the beach."

"How far is that from here?"

"Not far, if we go by boat. Driving will take a little longer."

"Okay, let's go. Sokolov says he's staying with Irina until she's out of the woods."

Lori looked around, and lowered her voice. "You think he can keep his mouth shut about his less than American past profession?"

"He's got more sense than that. Nobody here is going to question him, not with a one star General backing his right to be here. Do you think Petrov will come finish the job?"

"No, they probably think she's dead. They were thinking her body would wash out to sea. If they figure out she's alive, then they'll come looking for her. She should be out of here by then."

"Good thing Sokolov knows how Petrov operates. He'll be on alert. He said he's going to find a safe place for her as soon as she's released, which will be soon."

"Let's go. I want to take these guys down."

"It's not going to be quick or easy."

"Is anything we do ever quick and easy?"

"Nope."

It took some time to get back to *Sweet Sarah* and head for Hilton Head Island. Daylight had dawned by the time they arrived off the beach, so they anchored a good distance off Blackwood's beach house, but close enough to watch his movements. This place was bigger and fancier than the one on Fripp Island. It was built with multiple levels, about as elaborate as any designer could make it. It had a big rectangular pool and a boardwalk that led out to a beautiful white sand-beach called Coligny. The place had two wings that probably housed bedrooms. In Blackwood's case, those guests would all be his henchmen.

Lucky for Novak, there were only a few palm trees blocking his view. The major difference that Novak could see was that more guards seemed to be patrolling, though they were all dressed in tropical garb, their cool linen shirts hanging open to hide their weapons. That told Novak this could very well be a major hub in his operation. Nothing much happened at the house until early afternoon. That's when the visiting family appeared, all with dark skin and hair. Maybe they lived on the island or somewhere nearby.

"He's upped his manpower in there considerably. It'll be difficult to get close to him here. More traffic, more tourists, more hotels."

"Yeah, I know," Lori answered. "There's one hotel close by that would give us a good vantage point. Let's grab a room that overlooks his place so we can video their movements. That will give us irrefutable evidence. We've got to get that at every stop along the pipeline, as well as some clear photos of the couriers. If we can do that, I can start digging up everything online about the players."

"It looks like the set-up is pretty much the same everywhere they go. Blackwood owns the property. The couriers show up and get their marching orders. Sokolov thinks Petrov's recruited people like they used to do for Russian sleeper cells. He also thinks these kids might be a part of a human trafficking ring working in concordance with the drug smuggling. I hope he's wrong, but it does make sense. Who would know? Maybe that's how Blackwood gets his new playthings."

"Oh God, I can't even bear to think about him with Irina or any other child." Lori's face reflected utter abhorrence.

"I don't want to dock the *Sweet Sarah* at a public marina. They're sheltered, but would be hard to get out of in a hurry. Once they find out Irina's alive, they'll be looking for whoever got her to safety. We'll be safer anchored out here offshore."

"They could notice us out here, too. They might already suspect it's us. They would've investigated you by now. Don't you think?"

"Yeah. They know I'm an investigator, so they'll look for me under every rock. They could find out about this boat. Just get pictures of the family that's inside right now. We need to follow the couriers to wherever they go next. If we can nail down their home addresses, it'll be easier to round them up. Won't be that easy, though. I'm still hoping that Irina can tell us more once she feels better, but that's not going to be any time soon. I'm going on the assumption that they transfer the drugs out here on the water. Otherwise, why use all these beach properties? It would be safer for them to meet in some nondescript house in a quiet neighborhood."

"They must have access to a boat, but this house doesn't have a dock. I say they launch somewhere else nearby or rent a different one every time at some public marina. We need to get on shore to that hotel and follow the family. You said they came to Blackwood's house several days on Fripp Island, right? They'll be the ones who lead us to the actual drop site."

"Pack a bag and we'll lie low for a while and see what happens around that house. It's still early. We'll anchor the boat off the hotel shore and take the Zodiac in. We can grab a room and watch from there until we figure out who's doing what. I'll take watch so you can get some rest."

Lori refused to sleep until they got to the hotel. They called for a reservation in a giant Westin that was busy and swarming with happy tourists. Families and couples milled around everywhere, especially at the pool and on the beach. There were blue cabanas set up within yards of Blackwood's house, which they could use without being noticed. He made sure the room Lori booked had a corner balcony with an ocean view and a good vantage point over Blackwood's driveway. He wanted to see when the couriers arrived each day and get pictures of their vehicles. He'd have to get closer to photograph the license plates and place the GPS trackers.

They took the Zodiac to shore around noon and pulled the rubber boat up under the shady cluster of giant palm trees on the hotel's property. After that, they checked in, posing as a married couple under the false name of Gloria and Henry Milton, and paid the doorman to keep an eye on the Zodiac. They paid cash for the luxury corner suite on the top floor facing Blackwood's house. Once inside, Lori wasted no time collapsing on the silky sheets of the king-size bed. She was asleep in minutes, and didn't move for three hours. No doubt the painkillers she'd swallowed right before she disembarked from *Sweet Sarah* had something to do with that. Novak ordered up sandwiches, a fruit platter, and a large pot of coffee. He drank most of it during his first hour on watch. He'd have to hit the rack soon, too. He could make it fine on a couple of hours' sleep, a knack he'd been forced to cultivate in the military, but this time he hadn't slept at all for going on eighteen hours. He had to crash soon.

Nothing of interest was going on at the beach house. Blackwood's men were congregated around the pool, behaving like college frat boys on Spring Break. All of them had on swim trunks and sunshades. Some of them sat around on the multilevel decks. They were the ones on duty. Some were out front on the sand or wading in the surf. Their carefree behavior probably meant Petrov and Blackwood were gone somewhere or they wouldn't be goofing off that openly. That theory disintegrated when his two main targets strolled out onto the upper deck of the wing nearest the hotel. Blackwood held a martini glass. Petrov was drinking from a beer can. Novak focused his binoculars on their faces, and tried to read their lips. Sometimes he could do that fairly well if he was close enough, or at least get a feel for the conversation. Not this time. One thing was for certain—they didn't look like two men mourning the overdose death of Blackwood's adopted child.

He continued to watch for the rest of the day. Lori woke up, stumbled in to see what was going on, and went back to bed. Although she denied it, she was not fully recuperated; handling the boat alone had been harder on her than she wanted to admit. She finally woke up around dusk, showered, and ordered dinner from room service. They sat down and ate together on the balcony, then Lori took over watch while Novak hit the bedroom. He slept four good hours before he woke, and that was enough.

The next day the same courier family showed up. They drove into Blackwood's driveway in a fire-engine-red Volvo. They were not afraid of being seen. Novak watched them get out of the car. The same four people got out. The man and woman, and two children, the boy looking about eighteen, the girl about six or seven. Once they disappeared into the back of the house, Novak and Lori headed downstairs and called for a rental to be brought to the front entrance. It took fifteen minutes for an employee to show up driving a white Corolla. They drove it out to a parking lot at the back of the hotel, in a spot that lined up with Blackwood's driveway, from where they could see a good distance down the beach road.

It took almost an hour before the family emerged and backed the Volvo up, turned around, and headed down the road toward them. Novak and Lori slid low in their seats as the family drove past their position. Novak started the car, expecting them to head inland away from the ocean. That didn't happen. Instead, the driver stayed on the beach road. They followed them a mile past the beach houses and hotels until they reached a big marina.

"Bingo," Novak said. "They're renting a boat. Get ready. They're going to make a drop."

"They're taking their kids along. These people are awful excuses for human beings."

"The children have to be there to alleviate suspicion. Let's see where they take the boat. We'll have to rent one, too. They're inside the office now. Call in and have a boat waiting for us, or we'll lose them. Tell them we want a fast one."

The Volvo was parked in a spot a few yards down from the front office. The entire family got out and headed inside. Novak eased his car into a space next to the Volvo. He got a tracker out of his backpack and got out of the car. A moment later he was back with the GPS tracker secure in the Volvo's wheel well. Then they waited. Ten minutes later, the family came back outside and trailed a uniformed employee down the length of the first floating dock. At the last slip, they stood and chatted a moment before the man stepped down into a sleek red-and-white motorboat. Mom and the kids followed him and started strapping on life preservers. The man had evidently boated before, seeing how he expertly backed the boat out of the slip and headed slowly toward the channel that led out to open ocean. "They do make the drops at sea. You were right," Lori said. "We've got to hurry or we'll lose them. Boats are zipping around everywhere out there."

A quarter of an hour later, they were aboard their own speedboat, one with a bigger motor and more horsepower. They also rented a bunch of fishing gear as cover, just like the couriers had. It took them a while to locate their prey with binoculars, but Lori picked them out where they were floating about a mile offshore. Other boats were using the area for swimming, and some were fishing. Novak kept going right past them, while Lori kept her binoculars trained on the father of the group.

"Both kids are in the water now. So is the woman. The man's scanning the horizon with binoculars, but he's not looking at us. He's watching the south horizon for somebody, mark my words. We're going to see the meet."

A hundred yards past the red-and-white boat, Novak steered the prow seaward in a wide arc and pushed down the throttle. The boat jumped, then flew toward the horizon. Once they were far enough out to waylay suspicion, he turned off the motor, and the craft settled gently back to bobbing on gentle waves. "You see anybody yet?"

"They're putting out lunch. A couple of big buckets of KFC. More than they can eat."

"Keep watching. They didn't come this far out here for nothing. Somebody is going to show up."

"You can count on it."

It took over an hour of watching and waiting before a big white cabin cruiser showed up just south of them. It was traveling in their direction at a moderate speed. There was nothing out of the ordinary at all, but Novak's gut told him that boat would soon make contact with the family. He focused on the man at the helm. He was big with a dark tan, and looked perfectly normal for a man out boating. He had on black swim trunks, a New York Yankees cap, and mirrored sunglasses hanging around his neck on a white cord. A woman and two children were sitting in the stern, their dark hair blowing wildly in the wind. For all intents and purposes, they were just a normal American family out on the water, enjoying the salt air on a sunny afternoon. It was good cover, he would give them that.

Novak examined the big cabin cruiser for its name. He found it lettered on the stern in big black letters: *Family Time, Savannah, Georgia*. Nothing appeared suspicious about her. A few other craft were anchored farther in toward the beach, and a few more sped about here and there. On *Family Time*'s stern, an American flag flapped in the wind, but Novak focused his glasses on the small pennant fluttering beneath it. It was triangular and black with a white trident, just like the one under the flag on the red-and-white boat. It wasn't a nautical flag, because Novak knew them. It was a signal. If those two boats hooked up, Novak was certain that was how they recognized each other.

"Lori, look at that pennant the cabin cruiser's flying. Have you seen it before?"

"Not that I can remember."

"Take a look at the pennant the couriers put up. It's one and the same."

Lori trained her glasses on the small boat. She smiled. "Yeah, I see that. It tells them who to meet. I bet they never know who is coming or which boat. So they can't identify the other couriers if they get caught. But it sure as hell will give us a way to nail them to the wall."

"The Coast Guard cutters can pick them out anywhere once they know their signal flags."

"Exactly. They'll hook up any minute now. Mark my words."

Novak moved over to the stern bench where Lori was on her knees, her binoculars resting on the back of the seat. He got down beside her. The cabin cruiser was slowing now. Moments later, the man at the helm steered the boat into a nice tight turn that put them up close against the smaller one. While the two men lashed the boats together, everybody else waved, laughing and calling out, as if they were two families who were meeting for a picnic at sea.

"Well, it's clever, that's for sure," Lori murmured softly. "Two big, happy, drug-dealing families having a finger-licking good time. Who would think they've got illegal drugs aboard? Nobody would ever guess."

"Problem is, we've got to prove it. They're probably celebrating the money they're getting paid for this drop. And it's plenty, let me tell you."

Lori sat back on her heels. "Do you think those little kids belong to those parents? I can't imagine real parents subjecting their own children to this kind of danger."

"If they're based on those old sleeper cells, and Sokolov thinks they are, then most likely they are theirs. If they're not, the worst case scenario is those kids are for sale, too. Petrov and Blackwood are the kind of men who'd traffic them."

"I hope you're wrong. But if you aren't, I hope they all get the death penalty."

"I think it goes deeper than that. Blackwood has a personal interest in child trafficking, and we'll be able to prove it before this is over. I won't stop until I get him on that charge. He's also the safety net if anybody else gets caught. He wields a lot of power and can pull strings to get them out on reduced charges, at the very least. Most of these couriers are probably addicts. We've got to get an idea on how deep this thing goes and where they get their product. Are you getting close-ups of these guys?"

"Yeah, and videos. We might be able to put names with faces using our facial recognition software at the Pentagon. I think we should contact the DEA right now, Novak, before this goes any further. Give them everything we suspect and let them take the reins. I have contacts in Washington that I trust implicitly with this kind of information. My general would help me line things out."

Novak shook his head. "Not yet. Eventually, maybe. We don't have enough proof. I want to get every stopping place, every contact, north to south, east to west. We'll keep following them until we can nail down points of connection and the names of the boats. I'm guessing they use assumed names when they do it. That's smart, too, but most marinas will have names and dates and hopefully security cameras that can ID them."

"So what do we do now?"

"Keep documenting everything they do. If we get authorities involved right now, things could go bad fast. Law enforcement would have trouble coordinating and staying out of sight. Besides, Blackwood had the whole sheriff's office in his pocket up in that town in Virginia. Stands to reason, they've bought off dirty police and judges."

"I still think we should hand it over. We're not equipped to pull off this big of an operation."

Novak kept his eyes on the two boats. He was not going to convince her, so he wasn't going to try. "I want Petrov myself. He overdosed that kid and left her to die out on that cold beach by herself. He murdered Justin and would've killed both of us inside that Jeep if I hadn't been armed. I want to take him out myself."

"Does that mean you want to kill him yourself? Look, Novak, I'm not into vigilante justice. Just so you know that from the get-go. I'm not going to stand by and let you gun him down in cold blood. Not when we can legally put him away forever."

"I didn't say I was going to gun him down."

"No, but that's what you meant."

Lori knew him all too well. He would like to be the one who put a bullet in that devil's head, but he wouldn't unless he had to. Novak could never convince Lori of that, so he changed the subject. "How often do you think they make these connections out on the water?"

"It'll take a lot of surveillance to get any idea of the length and breadth of this thing. My guess? I'd say their network stretches all the way from Florida to Maine, maybe even into Canada. If I'm right, these transfers at sea have to go on every few days. Probably at different times and places with different couriers showing up. It's a pipeline, so it's got to have some kind of schedule and somebody pulling the strings to make it work."

"I don't think the GPS coordinates are driving the meetings out here. It's the trident flag they hoist. I say we follow the guys in the cabin cruiser and see where they go. The ones coming up from the south are most likely passing the drugs—most of the heroin and opioids are coming out of Mexico and Central America. They'll be moving it along as fast as they can, tag-teaming their way up the coastline and transferring product at the busiest tourist spots where they'll look like vacationers. We need to follow them all the way down to Florida."

"Where's the next transfer? You have any idea, Novak?"

"I'd say somewhere in north Florida. A busy place. Jacksonville Beach, maybe. Or it could be Fort Lauderdale. Or Amelia Island. Any popular beach community will have marinas with boats they can rent for the day. We've got to tail them. That's the only way, since everything changes for every drop."

"That's going to take time. I have to be back at work at the end of next week."

"It's going to get dangerous the deeper we delve. If you're safe in Washington, I'm all for it."

"I don't want to leave you alone with this, but I don't want to lose this job, either. I really like what I'm doing."

"You won't lose it. In fact, if we pull this bust off, you just might get a promotion and a medal."

"I'll take both, plus a raise. Just don't start killing people if I'm not here to stop you."

"I don't go around killing people. You know that."

"I just want you free as a bird and out of prison so we can go sailing again."

Novak smiled. She was beginning to love the sea as much as he did. He liked that about her.

The people aboard the two boats appeared to be having a great time. They seemed to know and like each other, which indicated maybe they had met before. Most of them were swimming off the stern of the cabin cruiser, laughing and splashing like old friends or extended family. At one point, Novak and Lori got into the water to keep their cover intact, but they had a video camera fixed on their targets the whole time, recording the date and time.

Novak was soon back aboard, watching with binoculars when the two men disappeared below decks on the cabin cruiser. When they came back topside, both were carrying large red Igloo ice chests. They loaded them on the smaller boat, where the two women poured in bags of ice, then stowed food on top.

"Okay, they just made the transfer," Novak told Lori.

"Yeah, and we got it on film."

"Now they'll wait a bit and take off back the way they came."

That's exactly what happened, but it was closer to an hour later. The boats had lowered the black pennants now. The small boat remained at anchor, the family waving goodbye to their drug-smuggling buddies. Novak waited until the cabin cruiser was a mere dot on the horizon due south of them, then weighed anchor and set sail. The Hilton Head couriers were back in the water, splashing and playing, and didn't seem to notice Novak's departure. He was relieved to see that they had the same two children with them, so at least those kids were not human cargo. It seemed to him that these drug mules were acting a bit overconfident, or were new at smuggling—or maybe they had just been lucky and never gotten interdicted by a Coast Guard cutter. Their apparent nonchalance would someday turn out to be a mistake.

Novak hugged the coast far enough out to avoid most boat traffic for the rest of the day. The big cabin cruiser eventually came into sight through Lori's field glasses. By their direction, it appeared they were also keeping parallel to the coast, while bypassing Georgia completely. They were heading into Florida waters, just as he had predicted.

Hours later, when he caught up to them, they were stopped off Jacksonville Beach. The sand was teeming with sun worshippers, and the cabin cruiser cut its engines and moved down a canal that led inland, probably heading back to a marina. They could own the boat, but that would be risky. This pipeline was too well thought-out to allow that kind of mistake.

"Okay, this is their next base, at least for this trip. I think they're using the same towns, but most likely different marinas. This family will probably wait a few days until they receive drugs coming up north. That's going to give us time to get back to Hilton Head, check this boat in, and bring *Sweet Sarah* down here. We can sail down overnight and watch from out here on the water."

"Are you planning to follow them all the way to their source? That's where we will contact the authorities. Right, Novak? I do not want you to go at this alone. It's too big. These guys are organized. We're going to end up dead if we take them on without law enforcement having our backs."

"I'm not going to take them on alone. We're just gathering information right now. The FBI and DEA will need more than we've got to coordinate and raid the homes of these couriers. I think their starting point may be somewhere in the Florida Keys. That's where they'll bring in the drugs first. It only makes sense."

"From Mexico?"

"Probably, we'll soon find out."

"That could take time."

"I've got the time. You need to go back to work and let me keep you posted."

"Well, I must say, I didn't expect to spend my vacation out here chasing drug dealers. Strike that—knowing you, I should've known something like this would happen."

Novak nodded. "I'm going to make up lost time with you, once I've got these guys rotting behind bars."

"You bet you are, unless, of course, we're both dead by then."

"There's always that."

Chapter 16

Novak called the marina and told them he was leaving their rented speedboat at the Westin, and authorized the charge for not returning the boat to the marina. They got into the Zodiac and took it back to the *Sweet Sarah*, pulled anchor in a hurry, and sailed south again, keeping one eye on the GPS signal attached to Blackwood's wheel well. The Senator and his gang of goons were already on the move, driving south on I-95, probably on their way to Jacksonville or the next stop after that. The dark-haired family was still at Blackwood's beach house on Hilton Head, no doubt waiting for their next arrival of poison, death, and destruction.

Novak felt a white-hot knot of suppressed rage growing down deep inside his chest, scalding his emotions as he realized the enormity of destruction perpetrated by Blackwood's drug empire. His only relief was his determination to bring it crumbling down atop the old man's head.

The GPS trackers were proving to be golden. They knew where Blackwood was all the time, providing he didn't get out of the car somewhere, which Novak was pretty sure he wouldn't. Novak was certain they were headed to the next drop. It did surprise him that Blackwood took this much direct involvement, instead of kicking back and riding his thoroughbred horses, reaping all the benefits while others took the risks. He felt Blackwood was either keeping a close eye on his people, which meant he didn't trust them—another good thing—or he was instrumental in some way to the day-to-day operations. Novak didn't think it was the latter, but couldn't be sure yet. He still believed their ultimate destination was Miami or Key West or somewhere in that vicinity, but he didn't know how many more stops they would make along the way.

The fine weather held, with bright and clear blue skies, brisk southerly winds ballooning his sails, and warmer temperatures the farther south they sailed. White cottonball clouds scudded ahead of them, pushed around like sky-strewn tumbleweeds. The hot sun felt good on his bare skin. He'd never liked cold weather. He almost wished he and Lori were simply out on a cruise, with no cares or worries, just having fun and making love. Too bad that wasn't the case. They were no longer happy-go-lucky. They both were dead serious, all business, thinking only of the endgame. They wanted to destroy Senator Blackwood and everybody around him. It would take some time, but once they'd gathered enough evidence to turn over to the Feds, they could bring down every point of transfer, every courier family, and every single facet of it. Novak wanted to be able to hand over Blackwood's entire syndicate, wrapped up in a big red bow.

As it turned out, the black Lincoln bypassed the city of Jacksonville and stopped just down the coast at Daytona Beach. Again Novak anchored the sailboat offshore, but close enough to surveil the beach. They were able to pinpoint the exact address according to the GPS signal and set up surveillance. This time they didn't catch the actual transfer, but they got good photo evidence of the family of four who visited him at the beach house. Novak had no doubt they'd be out on the ocean, flying that significant black trident pennant high in the wind. They tagged the make and year of the courier's car so they could trace it to an address later. The extended days Blackwood and his entourage spent there gave them time to remain right on his heels and document every move. They knew now for a fact that drugs were moving up the coast, boat-by-boat, resort-to-resort, but Novak wanted to nail down the initial source before he returned north. He wanted the exact point of distribution and where it was coming from.

The winds continued to hold when they went on the move again. He hugged the shoreline, not wanting to drift out into the Gulf Stream, which flowed close to this part of Florida. They seemed to fly over the waves, making excellent time. When Blackwood reached Miami, he surprised Novak by not stopping there, but heading down Highway 1 to the Keys. They just might be able to beat the Lincoln to Key West. Feeling a bit more in control of the situation, Novak asked Lori to phone Sokolov and get an update on Irina's condition. She should have been out of the hospital and in rehab by now, hopefully making good progress. She made the call on his sat phone, and by the look on her face when she hung up, he knew something had gone wrong.

"What happened? She's still okay, isn't she?"

"Irina's gone missing. Somebody must have gotten to her."

Novak could only stare at her in disbelief. "How? Where the hell was Sokolov? He was there to protect her."

"Nobody knows where he is, either. He's gone missing, too. The hospital suspected foul play and called the cops. There's a BOLO out on them."

"Either they took off together, or they're both dead. That's the way Petrov would play it. If at first you don't succeed, kill everybody in and around your target."

Lori kept shaking her head. It made her ponytail swirl around. "I don't think they're dead. Maybe Petrov found them and sent men out to kill them, and they botched the hit somehow. That would force Sokolov to take her and go on the run. Those thugs aren't exactly military material. They could very well have flubbed it. What it probably means is that they know she's alive, that she survived the overdose."

"I can't believe they could've found her that fast. They were both in that car headed south."

"Maybe they had somebody watching us, or somehow got a tracker on this boat."

"I'm almost positive they didn't know I even had a boat, much less followed me without out one of us knowing. Doesn't seem likely, or they would have tried to put us down the first time we got near their couriers."

"The nurse I talked to said Sokolov was in Irina's room the night before last. She said he'd been staying overnight since she'd gotten there. Two hours later, she said they were gone without a trace. Nobody saw them leave. Nobody saw anything. No sign of them on the hospital security cameras, either."

"That doesn't make any sense. Was Irina okay when she disappeared?"

"The nurse said she was better but not out of the woods. She's a long-term addict, Novak; she'll never be free of it, not without a lengthy stay in a good rehab center. Maybe not even then."

"Blackwood's guys could be holding her. If they are, Sokolov is already dead. He would die to protect her. We haven't spotted Petrov for a while. He could've gotten a flight back up there to do the job himself. He's good at assassinations. The question is, how did he find them so fast?"

"Somebody had to have tipped Petrov off. Guess who that sounds like to me? Your so-called friend, Sokolov. I never trusted that guy, not for a single second. He's way too slick. I told you that. You didn't listen. So what do we do now?"

"We don't know for sure Sokolov had anything to do with it. It's more likely that he's dead."

"True, but he was the last person seen with her inside that hospital room." Lori sighed. She leaned back in the seat and stared out at the distant horizon. "The nurse also told me that Sokolov rarely left her bedside. Apparently, he was the picture of fatherly concern. You're right to say that doesn't sound like a man planning to turn her over to a bunch of brutal killers."

"No, so maybe it's simpler than we're thinking. Maybe they got nervous and went underground once she was well enough. Maybe Sokolov sensed the bad guys were coming back for them. Maybe he found out somehow before they could get her."

Lori didn't buy it. "Thing is, if he got her out, why not call us and let us know? Why isn't he picking up that phone you gave him? More likely, he's playing both ends against the middle. Worst case scenario? He's just a damn liar that we never should have trusted in the first place. How well do you really know him anyway, Novak? You sure he's not working for them? You check him out?"

"I checked him out first thing and found nothing, one way or another, other than his background in espionage. It doesn't make sense for him to be working for them. Why would he help us get the girl away from Blackwood? He went to a lot of trouble to do that, including leading us to where they were."

"And how did he know that? He was a Russian operative, right? Setting up cells in the United States? He's just as much an enemy to us as Petrov. They both were trained by the GRU, right?"

Novak knew that Lori's dislike of Sokolov was visceral, and had been all along. She was smart to be suspicious. "You could be right. I don't get why he'd go to so much trouble convincing me that Irina's his daughter if he's working for them. He helped us get her to the hospital. That doesn't make sense, either, if he wants her dead."

"He's given you no concrete proof to back up any of his story, has he?"

Novak frowned, not wanting to believe he could be so wrong. "Nothing black and white, but he told me where to find them and what was going on with the drugs. Why would he carry it that far?"

"Hell if I know. I do know they're both gone now under mysterious circumstances. Either he's got her somewhere or he delivered her into their hands. Maybe he gave her up to save his own neck. If that's true, that poor kid is definitely dead now."

Novak considered everything she'd said. He had always considered himself a good judge of character. Sokolov had come across as fairly legit. "No proof, one way or the other. Again, why would he show me where she was, only to give her back to them?"

"Maybe it's something else, a whole different track. What if she's a Russian national, a criminal over there, or some dissident on the run whom their government wants dead or in jail? Maybe they want to use her to blackmail Blackwood. He was privy to international secrets; maybe he still is. Maybe she's an agent herself, groomed from birth. Sokolov and Petrov were spies, for God's sake. Blackwood knows lots of state secrets, believe me, and they could be using her to coerce his cooperation. We need to turn this thing over to the CIA, right now. It's too big for us."

"Espionage plays a part in this, I agree with that. I'm just having trouble figuring out the who and why of everything." Novak concentrated on steering the boat, but his thoughts riveted on their problem, because he knew Lori could be right. It could all be connected to espionage, with people manipulating him the whole time. Sokolov could have duped Novak with the abuse story so he'd help get her out, but Novak had seen the senator hit her with his fist. "It's possible they are using me, but there would be better ways. I was a totally random player until Irina pointed me out inside that steakhouse."

Lori mulled it over in her mind. "Well, maybe you weren't a random player. Maybe they knew all about you, your history with the SEALs, your military record, your abilities, everything. Maybe you were their target all along."

The possibility of being played for a fool made Novak sick to his stomach. He considered her theory. "No way. They couldn't have done that. I spent the last four months recuperating at Lake of the Ozarks, out in the woods of rural Missouri. Few people even know where Lake of the Ozarks is, much less that I was there. You saw how remote the place is. The Russian government wouldn't give a damn about me anymore. I've been out of the game way too long."

"What about Petrov? He was at the other end of what you did on your SEAL team. He could want you dead for that alone."

Lori had always been good at poking holes in theories and clearing away the fog. She was making him look at this whole thing in a new light. She could very well be right. Still, to go to this kind of extreme to trick Novak into some elaborate plot just seemed ridiculous to him, unless their plan was for Novak to end up dead. If he was working in league with the Kremlin, Petrov would have had the means to find Novak, even in the wilds of Missouri. Or the Syrians, or the Iranians—all those countries had done business with him. Following Novak's boat without him knowing would not be difficult, either, not with Russian satellites in the sky.

Still, Novak had no reason to think anybody was after him. He was always wary of being followed, and he hadn't seen anything out of the ordinary, not even on his voyage from New Orleans to D.C. On the other hand, a GPS tracker attached to the hull of his boat would not be something he'd easily spot when he had no reason to suspect trouble. If they were being tracked, they still were, this very moment. Lori's theory was beginning to sound feasible.

Lori took the sat phone back down to the main cabin, leaving him alone to think things through. Novak fixed his gaze on the vast blue water stretching out in front of him. Far away at starboard, long tan beaches stretched out along the coast as far as his eye could see. He got a mental picture of Irina the last time he'd seen her, lying white and bruised and unresponsive in that hospital bed. She was already jaded and used and weary from a childhood spent in hell. Her lot in life had been worse than imaginable, and he feared it might already be over at the tender age of sixteen.

Novak wavered back and forth, not sure what to believe. It was an unusual feeling for him, to feel out of touch, to fear he'd been so easily manipulated. Lori's take on everything made sense, but there were still things that made him doubtful. He felt there was more to this than met the eye, but which way did it go? He hoped she was wrong about Sokolov. He had believed him, had felt the man's desire to free his daughter had been sincere. He hoped Sokolov had simply moved Irina somewhere safe, that she was still alive and getting better. His gut kept telling him they could both be dead. If Blackwood and Petrov had gotten them, there was no question they were, probably left to rot in the backwoods of South Carolina or weighted down at the bottom of the Atlantic.

When Lori came back topside, Novak said, "You may be right. Can you use your contacts at the Pentagon to see if you can find out if Sokolov's still connected in Moscow?"

"I can try. My security clearance certainly won't warrant that level of intelligence, but I have some friends in high places. Lucky for you."

"I do, too, but they might not be as eager to help me as yours. Last time they got involved, it didn't turn out so well for them."

"Why am I not surprised?"

Novak grinned, but it took serious effort. If she was right, and the Russian government was sanctioning this entire pipeline, things were going to get sticky. Criminals running illegal drugs up the East Coast was one thing. If the Russian secret service was behind it, it turned into a whole different ballgame. How the hell had he ended up smack-dab in the middle of a Russian conspiracy theory? What if everybody involved were spies, including Irina? Had she enticed him to help her for ulterior motives? What if she hadn't been stolen as a child? The adoption story had come from her and Sokolov. He had no verification if any of it was true. Again, the one pertinent but elusive question plagued his mind: why him? Even if Petrov wanted him dead for some unknown reason, he could have done it without all these complicated machinations. There had to be answers, and Novak had to find them before everything came crashing down on his head.

Chapter 17

They tracked Blackwood's car all the way down to the Florida Keys, ending up at the Oceans Edge Resort Hotel & Marina in Key West. The Lincoln was now sitting in a reserved parking space in front of a huge white yacht. Novak found a place offshore, out of the cruise lanes, but close enough to observe what was going on at that hotel dock. He used his binoculars to get a close-up look at the boat. It was a beautiful ocean-going yacht, black and white, sleek and fast, with smoked windows, and maybe sixty or seventy feet long. That boat must have cost Blackwood some big bucks. Novak's guess was that it was purchased straight out of some offshore bank account where Blackwood kept his misbegotten drug profits.

"You think Blackwood can afford that monster boat?" Lori asked him, taking a sip of her iced tea.

"Not on a retired senator's cash flow. But he could if he's dealing drugs or providing a shill cover for a Kremlin game. More likely, it belongs to whoever he's getting his product from. If that's the case, we're probably not the only ones surveilling him right now. You can bet the DEA is somewhere around here, hiding and watching everybody who goes up and down that fancy railed gangplank."

"Yeah, not to mention the FBI. Maybe they're on the job now, so we can go home. Think about it, Novak. Like I said before, this is getting too complicated for the two of us. I hope we don't get caught up in their dragnet when they lower the boom."

"If the Feds are out here watching, it'll complicate things, all right."

Novak didn't want to become entangled with law enforcement red tape, but he also didn't want to lose an opportunity to find out the source and name of Blackwood's opioid suppliers.

It was almost three o'clock in the afternoon, very hot out on the water despite the ocean winds. Novak felt his bare skin burning, but it felt good after the autumn chill of New England. They were near a group of sailboats about the same size and weight as *Sweet Sarah*, anchored in a protected spot, and that gave them good cover. They were both lying on their bellies atop the main cabin now, each watching the yacht with high-powered binoculars. The name was right there for all to see, in big reflective gold letters that pretty much nailed down its place in Blackwood's empire: *Trident Point*. It was listed out of Key West, Florida. The pier the hotel used was not a private dockage but open to the public. There with other boats of similar size, it would be less noticeable. He examined the nearby boats, but he was pretty certain that the Lincoln was parked in front of the black-and-white yacht.

Lots of people were moving around aboard that yacht, a real hive of activity—guards, most likely, each dressed in spotless white nautical uniforms, replete with fancy gold-braided epaulettes on their shoulders. All were armed, too, not concealed or hidden, their pistols secured in belt holsters. Somebody aboard that yacht was important. Novak believed that to be Charles Blackwood, or better yet, his contact from Mexico who arranged their shipments.

"You think he's got Sokolov and Irina tied up on that thing, below decks somewhere, maybe?" Lori asked, sitting up and wiping sweat off her brow. She was whispering to him, spooked by her own envisioned scenario. Her face was starting to sunburn after weeks spent working inside.

"Maybe they're all aboard. Maybe they're all co-conspirators. I think the people on the yacht have been waiting down here for Blackwood to arrive. Not sure why they'd choose a dockage as public as this one. Blackwood may not be the owner, but I think he is. To answer your question, I think it's unlikely Sokolov and the girl are aboard. I think they're dead, and it's back to business as usual."

"Somebody stayed behind to get them? That's what you're thinking?"

"Yeah. I'm beginning to feel like they've already gotten rid of them. We'll never find their bodies, not if Petrov was in charge."

"I just cannot see Blackwood murdering his own daughter."

"Maybe he didn't order the hit. Maybe Petrov got fed up with her and fixed it to look like she overdosed herself. He's not above doing that."

"Oh God, I just want this to end. I especially want Petrov. I'm so ready to take them down. I'm going to see if I can find out if the DEA's infiltrated Blackwood's organization. There might be an undercover agent onboard that yacht. It could even be Sokolov."

"Don't think so."

Novak watched her get up and disappear below decks. She was dead on. He wished he'd never craved that steak. He might never eat another one without a gun gripped in his hand. Whether they had targeted him specifically that night or he'd been a random victim like Irina had sworn he was, Novak was in too deep to get out now. This was too important, and too many people were dying from the drugs they smuggled. As Lori reappeared holding her laptop and sat down under the awning, he refocused his glasses on the yacht.

"There's a lot of movement on the stern deck now," he told her. "Looks like the stewards are getting it ready for afternoon cocktails, and if we get really lucky, they'll have a big powwow with all the players around that dinner table. Now that would be a nice photograph to show the Feds."

Novak kept watching. A group of men were milling around at the stern seating area, about ten of them. Most of them looked like guards or crew members, judging by their pristine white uniforms. The other guys had come out of the main salon wearing dress slacks and linen tropical shirts patterned with palm trees, leaping dolphins, and beach umbrellas. Three of them sat down around a glass-topped table. A steward scurried over and filled stemmed goblets from a magnum of champagne cooling in a silver bucket. The armed guards stood around the railings at a distance from the table, facing out, as if the meeting were private. Other men aboard in various areas were dressed in white T-shirts and white jeans. All of them carried guns.

If FBI agents were watching this meet, they were getting their money's worth. Novak snapped a bunch of pictures, zooming in on each man's face. The wind was blowing inland, ruffling the hair away from their faces, giving him good, clean shots. Then he moved back to the men at the meet. He recognized Blackwood, with Petrov sitting on his right. There were two others now whom Novak had never seen before.

Lori climbed back to the roof and lay down on her stomach close beside him. Novak said, "Snap some pictures of the guy in the pale blue shirt. And the one in the black T-shirt with the dolphins. We need their identities. They're dirty, in this thing up to their necks, believe me."

"Oh, I believe you. I already got them from the stern. Want me to go down and run them now?"

"Yeah, I want their names and countries of origin. I hope they don't pull anchor and sail tonight, but they might. If they do, they're meeting someone out at sea."

As evening approached and the sun dipped low with one of its famous fiery red-and-gold Key West sunsets, sending swathes of water-colors out over the fading blue sky, everything on shore was bathed in pastel shades of pinks and lavenders and golds. Lights began to come on around the harbor and the big hotel they watched. The four guys still sat hunched around the table; after having dinner and several breaks, they were back, deep in serious conversation. Novak wanted to hear what they were saying in the worst way. Whatever their subject, it was damn important to each of them. It didn't appear they were in agreement, nor that they were particularly happy with each other. The new guys both looked Hispanic, maybe of Cuban heritage, judging by the cigars smoking between their fingers. That guess was a stab in the dark—they could have been anybody from anywhere. On the other hand, Key West was ninety miles north of Havana, so Novak was betting on Cuba being the final leg of the pipeline.

When he caught movement on the gangplank, he refocused his glasses on the man descending to the long dock. At first Novak didn't recognize him, but when his target passed beneath a dusk-to-dawn lamppost positioned at the bottom, Novak could see him as clear as a spotlighted deer. Stepan Sokolov was coming blithely off that yacht for anybody to see. Novak was stunned to see him there. He watched the Russian chat with the armed guard standing duty. They conversed a while before Sokolov strode on down the pier toward the big parking lot behind the marina slips. Novak never took his eyes off him. When Sokolov reached a late-model, dark green Ferrari, he opened the trunk, rummaged around inside, and pulled out a knapsack. Then he headed back to the boat. As he walked up the gangplank, Novak lowered his field glasses and glanced at Lori, where she was bent over her laptop right below him, hard at work searching for answers in the Pentagon's facial recognition database.

"I just saw Sokolov. He's alive, right over there, cozying up with Blackwood and Petrov."

She raised her eyes to his face. She looked as shocked as he felt. "What? He's down here? Is Irina onboard, too? Did you see her?"

"No. She's either locked up below deck, or a part of this whole thing. Or she's dead, weighted down with concrete blocks on the ocean floor, compliments of our friend Sokolov."

"Oh, my God. Has Sokolov been playing us this whole time?"

"I'm beginning to believe you were right, Lori. I don't know why he approached us, but he's been lying from day one. He wanted our help getting Irina back, so he gave us that sob story about her being his daughter so we'd help him. Like an idiot, I handed her over on a silver platter. I'm

pretty damn certain she's dead. I have no idea who he really is or why
he got us out of that hospital. None of this makes any sense whatsoever."
    "She can't be his daughter. If she were, he could never deliver her back
into the hands of the devil who's been abusing her. That has to be a lie.
He's got to be just another one of Blackwood's flunkies."
    "He told me he had video proof of Blackwood molesting her, but I didn't
want to watch it. I did see them in a bedroom together on Fripp Island, and
you can bet that's what was about to go on. Maybe she's not anybody's
daughter. Maybe she's Blackwood's lover and has been all along. This
whole thing could've been some kind of trap for us. Why they'd go to this
kind of trouble, I cannot imagine."
    "A more important question to me is, why us?" She glanced around at the
other sailboats anchored around them, suddenly paranoid about their safety.
    Novak followed suit. Most of the boats were still battened down and
completely dark, the owners probably staying in the hotel or sightseeing
in town.
    Lori looked worried. "You think they know we're out here, and have
been watching us watch them?"
    "I don't know, but I'm gonna find out."
    "How?" Now Lori's voice was wary. She was spooked, all right.
    "I'm taking the Zodiac into the hotel, and then I'm going to get Sokolov
alone and have a little heart-to-heart with him. He's going to tell me
everything I want to know tonight, trust me on that."
    "I'm coming, too. You'll need backup with that many guys."
    "Not if I get him off by himself. I need you to stay out here. Watch my
back, but keep your rifle beaded on him. That's the best way you can help
me. By the way, don't hesitate to pull the trigger if he gives you cause."
    "You're too angry to go after him now. Wait until you cool off a little bit."
    Novak said nothing. He wasn't waiting. His anger lit his resolve.
    "How do you intend to get him off by himself? Are you thinking of
infiltrating that yacht? Might I remind you of the number of armed men
aboard that thing?"
    "Not unless I have to. It'll be easier if I wait for him to come ashore
again. I can take him in the parking lot. It's nearly always deserted." He
put down the binoculars and shook his head, so furious at possibly being
duped so thoroughly that he wanted to kill somebody. Sokolov would be
his first choice. "He retrieved a bag from that car, which probably means
he didn't sail here on the yacht. We know he wasn't in the Lincoln with
the others, not unless they picked him up somewhere along the way. That
could be the case. I've got a feeling he took a flight down here and met

them when they docked. That means once he got Irina out of that hospital, he got rid of her. I'm going to make him tell me where she is and what he did to her."

"You're upset that you trusted him. I understand that. But you need to stop and think this through, Novak. She could be alive, right over there onboard that yacht, or he could've put her into safekeeping before he came down here. We just don't know. That boat looks impenetrable. You've got to take time and plan out how you can get him when he gets off. One more thing, Novak: I'm going with you. Don't even try to argue."

"No, you're staying here. You need to keep trying to identify the men Blackwood's meeting with. Now I feel we've got to turn all this over to the DEA. I think those men at that table are the sellers who provide the product for his pipeline. They're negotiating terms for the next shipment right now, out in the open for anyone to see. Who would expect that to happen outside a busy hotel? Who would have cause to storm that boat and arrest them for drug trafficking? We need their names because they're the important players. I want to know where they're going next. I can handle Sokolov, so quit worrying about it. I'll stake out the lot and place a GPS tracker on his vehicle. If he took Irina and told her he was her father only to gain her trust and murder her, I want him worse than I want Petrov."

"You're not planning to kill him tonight, I assume?"

"Of course not. I don't kill anybody unless they're trying to kill me. Or you. Which Petrov has already done once. But tonight, Sokolov's going to tell me the truth."

"Well, talk to him and then turn him in. This whole thing is blowing up soon. The Feds could be watching him right now, and they don't need to see you do something they have to charge you with. They'll call you a co-conspirator. You'll never see the light of day again."

Lori was right, of course. He knew that. He wouldn't kill the man, but he could grab him and force him to tell him what he wanted to know. Novak was pretty sure that Sokolov had taken a teenage girl out of the hospital and murdered her, most likely on Petrov's orders. The two men were Russians, both formerly in espionage, and they had worked together. They were probably still working together; Novak had been naïve to think otherwise. Rage kept boiling and brewing inside him. He had to calm down and regain control. He didn't usually let emotion get the better of him. This time he felt extremely foolish, so he was having a hard time beating down his humiliation. He was their fall guy, all right, and had been all along. He would be the one who got the blame for everything, including the girl's murder. Lori would, too, since she'd used her credentials to get Irina help at Parris Island.

"Just stay out here, Lori. Keep your rifle ready and watch me like a stalker. You don't need to be seen anywhere on shore, and especially not anywhere on that dock. Text me if you see anything coming at me. If it looks like I'm in trouble and about to go down, call 911 and make up a story where I'm the good guy. Then call the Key West police and ask for Detective John Ebertson. He's a friend."

"Let's call him right now. I don't like this. You're putting yourself up against their whole team."

"Just stay here and keep watch." He softened his voice. "Please, Lori, do what I want this time. I'll be all right. I know what I'm doing."

Lori was not a woman who gave up. "You're too angry. Don't deny it, either. Get your temper under control. I'm speaking to you as a soldier now, Novak. You go in all hot like this, you'll make mistakes. You cannot be rash right now."

He knew that, of course. "I'm rarely rash, Lori. My anger's there, but it's under control."

"Novak, you are *not* in control."

Novak grimaced, tired of her arguments.

Lori took a deep breath. "I'm just worried about you. The fact is that you're usually calm, utterly ice-cold when you go after somebody, and that's why you always come out ahead. Right now, you're nowhere close to that, which puts you at risk."

"I know what I'm doing. Stay out here. Keep out of sight with the lights off. Keep your eyes open and watch me all the time with the scope. If they know you're out here, they'll send a kill crew. We're dealing with the big guys now. They won't hesitate to protect their livelihood."

"I know that."

"Good. I need you to watch my back. I'm going to rent a car first, so I'll be ready to follow him if he takes off. He might've stashed the girl down here somewhere, who knows? She could still be alive, but I can't count on it. If he's here with Blackwood, I think she's long dead, probably by Sokolov's hand."

"Just be careful. Please."

Novak left her there. Both of them had calmed down. They were ready. He did need her to keep watch from out on the water. Besides, Lori Garner had been hurt too many times since she'd hooked up with him. She'd been hurt this time, too, but that was the last time he was going to let that happen.

Within the hour, Novak sat inside a 2019 Honda Civic, black and chrome with concealing dark-tinted windows. He had it delivered to the street parallel to the water, then parked it at the back of the hotel's marina. He chose a shadowy space near the rear entrance, where he could just barely make out the running lights of *Sweet Sarah* with his binoculars, and also get a good picture of *Trident Point's* stern deck. Everything else around the dock was dark except for the portholes of docked boats.

The same four men were sitting at the table, smoking cigars, probably half-drunk by now. They took periodic breaks where they all disappeared below. The guards remained on duty at the railings. As time passed, it appeared the four players had come to mutual agreement, seeing how their conversation now appeared friendly, convivial. They laughed together as they drank their way through a lavish dinner. He did not see Irina Blackwood or any other woman anywhere aboard. This was strictly a private business meeting only for the main players.

Perhaps an hour passed before he caught sight of Sokolov. He picked him up where he sat on a cushioned bench under a canopy. His back was turned to Novak, so he hadn't noticed his presence until he stood up and moved to the dining table. He bent down and whispered something into Petrov's ear. Petrov nodded, after which Sokolov walked away quickly and headed down the gangplank. This was the moment Novak had been waiting for. He slumped down behind the steering wheel as the Russian spoke to the guard without lingering this time. He took off with long strides toward the Ferrari, unlocked the door, and climbed inside. A moment later, his headlights flashed on, and he backed out of the spot, heading for the front exit.

Novak waited until Sokolov pulled out onto Peninsular Avenue. Novak started the Civic and headed for the same exit. Minutes later he was behind Sokolov, but lagging three cars back. When Sokolov stopped at a traffic light, Novak tried to get his bearings. They were still on the same street heading inland. They started moving again, passing a mobile home court and a busy McDonald's. Sokolov was driving under the speed limit, clearly in no hurry. He didn't appear to notice Novak or try to lose him, so Novak figured he wasn't aware he was being followed. That was good. Two blocks down, he pulled up to a Burger King drive-through window and ordered food. Maybe he wanted a snack before he killed Irina. He'd rot in an American jail forever if he murdered that teenager. No way would Novak let him get away with that.

They continued driving on a circuitous route, passing trailer homes, luxurious golf courses, and a community college, until Sokolov finally turned into a dark middle-class neighborhood. Sokolov made his way through the streets to Azalea Drive, ending up at a modest brown house surrounded by clustered palms. There was a wood fence out front with brick pillars. The Russian turned into a bricked driveway, stopping in front of the entrance. Novak drove past, fervently praying that Irina was inside that house. He still held out hope that she was alive.

Novak made a quick circle of the block and drove past the house again. The lights inside were on now. The house looked made for infiltration. The fence and thick tropical foliage and palms were perfect cover. There was a light shining to the right of the front door, behind a big plate-glass window covered with draperies. Novak drove around the block once more, trying to see into the backyard. He kept killing time, afraid the Russian would take off again for the yacht. Thirty minutes passed, and he stayed put.

Novak parked the Civic down the street after his next pass, choosing a house on the opposite side. A 'For Sale' sign was planted in the yard. The property appeared vacant with dark, undraped windows. No cars were in the driveway or carport. He pulled out his weapon, checked it out, and racked a round into the chamber. Then he got out, holding his gun close beside his leg, finger along the trigger, hoping Sokolov didn't have nosy neighbors. He breathed in humid, muggy, hot air, the temperature cloying even so late at night. Huge gray moths flitted and buzzed, murdering themselves on street lights crowned with mist. They were set a good distance apart, filling the street with lots of shadows. Sweat dripped down his neck, running down his back under his T-shirt. There was no breeze, only the chirping cacophony of a million insects and tree frogs. He moved along cautiously, avoiding the circles of light illuminating the sidewalks.

Once he was directly across from Sokolov's house, he stood hidden in the shadows under a trio of palmetto trees and watched the windows. Nothing moved in or around the house. No other lights came on or went off. Finally he crossed the street, searched the eaves for security cameras, saw none, then crept up through the foliage at one side. The neighboring houses were hidden behind the fence. No way could they spot him easing through the dark, let alone observe anything else going on in that yard. Sokolov's house was small, only one story with a crawl space. The backyard was tiny, the grass dying, choked out by weeds. It didn't appear that Sokolov stayed there often. It had to be an old safe house, or maybe it was a storage facility for the opioid shipments. Maybe it was a prison, a death row for Blackwood's captured enemies.

The back door was locked tight. No light shone from what must have been the kitchen. He moved closer, his back to the wall. Then he froze as a hushed voice came out of the darkness, right behind him. "Don't move. I got you dead to rights." It was Sokolov's voice. He was close, maybe a foot off to Novak's right.

Novak didn't wait. He ducked down, spun around, and lunged. He got the smaller man around the waist and took him down, forcing his weapon up at the same time. It went off through a silencer, tearing off palm leaves above them. They went down hard, tangled together, Novak on top. Within seconds, Novak had the advantage due to his superior size and strength. The Russian had been caught by surprise. He fought hard to shove Novak off, but he was too big. Novak chopped his wrist and the gun fell free. He forced his forearm hard against Sokolov's Adam's apple until the man started choking for air and quit fighting. Novak hit him hard in the temple, then gave a quick jab to the nose. He heard it crunch under his knuckles.

As the blood sprayed, Sokolov groaned and choked but didn't try to fight. When he got his breath back, he spit out blood and struggled. Novak clubbed him in the forehead with his gun butt, and that was the end of the fight. Sokolov sagged, only half-conscious. Novak grabbed a fistful of Sokolov's shirt and dragged him bodily to the back door. It was locked, so he put one shoulder against it and gave it a hard shove. When it banged open, he pulled the smaller man into the kitchen, shut the door, and looked around. A night light burned on the stove, but everything else lay in darkness. Sokolov started coming back around, but his struggles were weak. He was gasping for breath through his injured nose. Novak jerked him up in front of him and flexed his forearm tight around the man's neck.

"Stop fighting, or I'll finish you right now."

The Russian must have believed him, because he sagged limply. Novak thrust him down in a kitchen chair. He pulled out the roll of duct tape he'd brought, secured his arms and legs, and slapped another strip over Sokolov's mouth. Then he quickly switched on the overhead light and searched the house, checking for prisoners. He found nothing and nobody, just a lot of empty rooms. Irina was not there.

When he got back to the kitchen, he stood over the woozy Russian, ripped the tape off his mouth, and stared down at his bleeding face. "I actually thought you'd put up a better fight, you being a trained Russian operative and all that. Pretty weak show of skills, Sokolov. I had you pegged as a better fighter."

Sokolov gagged on blood when he tried to talk. He swallowed it down. "Not that kind of operative."

"Really? What kind then? The kind that murders abused little teenage girls? After we left, you took Irina out of that hospital and murdered her, didn't you?"

Sokolov started shaking his head. "I didn't. I'd never kill her. I have killed only a few people in my life."

"Irina didn't deserve what you and Blackwood did to her. She was an innocent child when you snatched her and corrupted her in the worst ways possible."

"No, no, you got it wrong."

"I don't think so."

"Irina is not dead. For God's sake, listen to me, man. I couldn't kill my own daughter. How could you even think I could do something like that?"

"You had me at first, but I don't think she is your daughter, not anymore. I think you work for Blackwood, and have all along. You played me for a fool, using those two teenagers to pull me in."

Sokolov leaned his head back, trying to stop the bleeding. He coughed and spit out more blood. Novak was not affected.

"Where is she? Where'd you bury her body?"

"I swear to God. I never hurt her. I just needed information. That's why I took her out of the hospital. I knew she wouldn't tell me anything until she got desperate for the heroin. I knew you wouldn't let me force her to talk that way."

"Damn right, I wouldn't. Who the hell are you? What do you do for Blackwood?"

"I don't work for Blackwood." He paused a second, as if trying to think straight, or maybe just to figure out his next lie. "Petrov's an old friend of mine, that's true, I admit it—or he used to be one back in the old days." He took a deep breath, his eyes closed.

"Where?"

"Syria. He was, I guess you'd call it, a mentor."

"You were whispering to him on the *Trident Point,* looked pretty buddy-buddy to me. What did you tell him? Why did you come out here tonight?"

"I'm playing him, not you. I swear it on the Holy Virgin."

Novak laughed, but his amusement died quickly. "You expect me to believe that? Where is Irina now? Is she dead?"

"She's alive, I swear to God. She's safe. I left her in a place where they're taking good care of her."

"Where?"

The Russian clammed up. Now the blood from his nose was just a trickle. "If I tell you now, you'll kill me, or leave me out here to die."

"Maybe I will. Maybe I won't. I will for sure if you don't tell me what I want to know."

"Let me explain. Please. Just listen to me."

Novak pulled out a kitchen chair and sat down where he could see the back door and the archway into the living room. He kept his firearm pointed at Sokolov's heart. "Make it short. I'm not hanging around for your buddies to show up."

"I'm on your side. I've been with you from the beginning."

Novak shook his head. "Yeah, I can see that. You and Petrov both are my best buddies."

"Not him. He's the villain in all of this, not me. Please, you've got to believe me."

"Where is Irina?"

"Okay, okay. I'll tell you. She's being cared for. She's in sort of a rehab center, but…not exactly. Listen, you can call her, if you want. I've got her number. She'll tell you herself that she's fine, that I didn't lay a hand on her."

That surprised Novak. He wasn't sure he believed him, of course. It sounded like a trick. "That sounds great. What's the number?"

"First, just let me tell you some stuff. Let me explain what's going on and why I kept you in the dark. I couldn't tell you everything."

Novak studied the man's injured face. It was already bruising and starting to swell. The look in his eyes seemed legit, desperate, but that was because he thought Novak might shoot him. He ought to be afraid. Novak was more interested in answers, and he wanted the truth for a change. He was tired of flying blind in this thing. He didn't work that way. He wanted to know what he was caught up in. "I'm listening, Sokolov. Don't feed me lies. I've heard enough."

"I'm telling the Gospel truth now. I swear it on all the holy angels."

"You sure got religion fast. Go ahead, tell me everything."

Sokolov looked relieved. He started talking. Whether any of it was true, Novak had no way of knowing, but he would listen to his story. It had better be worth his time.

Chapter 18

Sokolov stared down at the floor. He was feeling the cut on his mouth with the tip of his tongue. The bleeding had stopped, but the man's shirt was wet and shiny red. "Okay, okay. This is the truth. I'm done playing games. I am playing Petrov. I have no interest in hurting you and your girl."

"That didn't tell me a thing."

"You don't know Petrov like I do. You don't know what he's capable of. I won't be a part of it, anymore. I want to bring him down, probably more than you do."

"Is Irina your daughter or not?"

"Okay, you're right. She's not my kid. Blackwood just snatched Irina off a Moscow street when she was little, just like she said. She wasn't the first he picked up for his perversion, and she won't be the last unless we stop him. She's special to him, though, because he adopted her and kept her around all these years. He gets the kids overseas. Sometimes he pays off their parents. If they don't want to let him have the child, Petrov beats them up until they agree. Just like they did to Justin. They're poor and can't do anything about it. He's always had diplomatic immunity that smooths his way to take the children out of the country, while greasing palms at government levels."

"Why did you lie? Why not tell us the truth from the beginning?"

"Because I needed to get information out of Irina. She's not my daughter, no, but she's the one who took my baby girl."

Novak watched his eyes. They were bloodshot and swelling, but they looked calm now. He searched his face and body for signs of deceit, but he couldn't find any yet. Maybe that was because Sokolov was good at it. The man before him no longer appeared frantic. He gazed straight back at him, ready to cooperate. "Irina took your real daughter? That's your new story? Why would she do that?"

"I don't know why. I guess because Blackwood told her to. That's what I want to know. I want to know where my baby is. I want to know if she's dead or alive. I found out they took her through an old army buddy who's at the Kremlin now."

"I'm asking you again. Why does Irina want your daughter?"

"She didn't. From what I could figure, her father told her to get Katerina over to the car. She says she did it because she was strung out and he was withholding the heroin as punishment. I got that much out of her after you left the hospital."

Novak felt his anger flaring up again. He waited a moment to get it under control. "What else did she say?"

"She said Blackwood took Katerina to the farm until he got tired of her. He was trying to groom her like all pedophiles do. She was afraid of him, homesick, and she cried and screamed if he tried to touch her. He didn't like her after that, thank God." His voice actually broke this time.

Novak said nothing. It took some time for Sokolov to regain his composure. He started talking again. "Irina told me that my daughter's with one of the couriers. She says they take kids out for the drops and use some kind of black pennant or something to recognize their contact. Apparently, they meet up with different people each time. The drugs are transferred boat-to-boat, all the way up the coast. I guess you've already figured that out, right? They take little kids so they'll look like families and allay suspicion. My daughter's being held by one of those drug dealers, Novak. Probably living with a bunch of addicts. I've got to find her and get her out, and then I'm taking her as far away from here as I can get."

"Which family is she with?"

"I don't know. That's what I'm trying to find out."

"So you're saying Blackwood abducted your girl the same way he took Irina years ago?"

Sokolov nodded. Tears were welling up now, rolling down his cheeks. His grief looked legit. He found himself wanting to believe Sokolov's new story, although he knew he probably shouldn't, not with Sokolov's track record. "My baby girl was in the wrong place at the wrong time. It's that simple. They had opportunity, and they grabbed her. They had no idea she was mine. It wouldn't have mattered if they had. Katerina was out on a walk with my wife. They were sitting on a park bench. Blackwood saw her and thought she was a beautiful child. He wanted her, so he took her. That's what Irina said happened. Nobody was there to stop them. My wife didn't know who they were." He looked down. "Irina cried when she told me. She said they pulled up, and Blackwood told her to get out and bring Katerina back to the car. He gave her candy to give to her. My wife refused and started to walk away, but Irina dragged my girl back to the limo. When my wife tried to stop them, Petrov hit her so hard that he put her in a coma. It took months for her to come out of it, and then she couldn't remember much for a long time. When she finally told me that the limo had diplomatic flags on the front, I found out Senator Blackwood had been in Moscow and had flown home the same day my daughter was taken. I learned through my friend that Petrov was working with him, and there was a witness to the abduction. She lived in a house across the street and identified Blackwood. She told me about Irina, too, but I had no idea who she was until I started watching the farm."

"So how do I fit in?"

"I didn't see you until I followed Irina and her bodyguards to that steakhouse. I had no idea who you were or why they took you. I thought they might lead me to Katerina that night, but they picked up you instead."

"How did you know Petrov?"

"We worked together in Syria, like I said. He was a coordinator with the Assad regime. I wasn't there long and didn't really work with him. I was sent to gather intelligence. I found out later that he started working for Blackwood. I came here, reminded him of our past association, and asked for a job. I thought that would help me locate my daughter. I didn't know anything about their drug smuggling at that point. I had no idea he had developed a pipeline using families. Petrov based it on our old sleeper cells."

Despite his misgivings, Novak believed him. "These people who go out on the boats, they're the actual drug mules, is that it? They move the product to the next rung on the ladder. Do you know their names or where they're based?"

"Some of them, I do, but only the few that I've met with personally. Most of them are addicts. The children are used for cover. I think some of them are trafficked in from South America. God, it all makes me sick. As far as I can tell, none of them are actual families. The kids are their captives. They're victims, too, all of them."

"How did Petrov hook up with Blackwood?"

"I suspect Petrov approached him, hoping to survive the trouble he's in at home. He murdered a few too many people down in Syria. Some of them were his own Russian operatives, and he covered it up. When they found out, he fled for his life. Russia's got a price on his head. That's why he's hiding here and using Blackwood as insurance. He trusts me and thinks we're still friends like in the old days, but I want him brought down. When my government finds him, they'll kill him."

"He doesn't know Katerina is your daughter?"

"We worked together before I even got married. He doesn't know about her, and I don't want him to. He was the one who hurt my wife. I want him dead, but I have to find Katerina first. I think they'll kill her if they find out she's mine. They'll kill me for sure if they find out I'm working against them. She might already be dead. That's my biggest fear. They murder those who cause them trouble or don't cooperate."

Seeing him shake in frustration, Novak believed his story. Nobody could fake the pain flickering on Sokolov's face. "What exactly do you do for Petrov?"

"Whatever he tells me to. He's been worried about you from the beginning. He thinks you've got connections that can bring him down. You weren't supposed to come out of this alive, and neither was your girlfriend. I guess you know that."

"Yeah, I noticed. So my involvement was random? That's what you're telling me?"

"Yes, Irina chose you to take the heat off Justin. She told me that you were big and looked tough, and she thought you could hold your own with those guys. She was thinking of herself and her boyfriend, and that's all. She didn't know you, and she didn't care what happened to you until she saw you slug her Daddy after he hit her. That's when she decided you could help her escape that house."

"Yet they had me at the horse farm and didn't kill me."

"Petrov wanted to, right then and there. Blackwood wouldn't let him. They wanted you dead because you'd seen and heard too much. They planned to hang you in the jail and call it suicide. The Senator said it would be easier to explain away. That was going to happen until Lori showed up so quick, waving around Pentagon credentials and threatening a federal investigation. Blackwood couldn't risk that, so they had to let you go. You were supposed to die in that car crash along with the boy. You and Lori both. That was the cleanup."

"Did Petrov order you to befriend us when we were taken to the hospital after the wreck?"

"No, that's when I decided to intervene and help you. They seemed almost afraid of you, which is not customary in a man like Petrov. Your woman presented a threat that they could not allow to happen. All these things were to my advantage if I joined up with you against them. They would have killed me eventually, anyway, once they realized I knew they had taken my daughter."

"That's why you got us out of the hospital that night?"

"Everything I told you that night was the truth. They were coming there to kill you before dawn. You'd both be dead now if not for me." Novak kept watching those big expressive black eyes. They remained steady on his face, without a hint of deceit.

Sokolov was not finished. "You both would've suffered heart failures during the night. They have drugs to inject into IV feeds. These people are good at what they do, and they would have pulled it off. Petrov and Blackwood both wanted you dead by then. You were trouble they didn't need. They couldn't let you go. You knew too much."

"Give me Irina's number. I want to talk to her."

Sokolov recited it from memory, and Novak punched in the numbers. A woman answered. She sounded like Irina. "Stepan? When are you coming back for me? I hate it here. I'm scared Daddy's going to find me."

"Sokolov's not coming back for you, Irina," Novak told her.

There was momentary silence on the other end. Then her voice came back, one that revealed the girl's nerves were shot. "Mr. Novak. It's you, isn't it? Did you kill Stepan? Oh, no, you shouldn't have killed him! He's helping me get away from Daddy. He's the one who helped you, too, back at that hospital."

"I didn't kill anybody. Not yet, anyway. He's sitting right here in front of me. I bloodied him up some and got the answers I wanted. Tell me exactly what happened after we left you at the hospital."

In essence, she reiterated the same story that Sokolov had told him, but in different words. He didn't think they'd rehearsed the story. Her telling was interrupted several times by her usual sobbing theatrics, and none of them touched Novak's emotions this time. The girl had a lot to answer for.

"Where are you?" Novak asked bluntly, cutting off her phony weeping. It didn't take her long to calm down enough to talk, seeing how it had all been a show. He decided she should be an actress, if she managed to stay alive that long.

"I'm in a convent. Way up here in Quebec City. They can't get to me here. The priest said so. Daddy can't get to me here, can he, Mr. Novak? Stepan said he couldn't."

Novak was pretty sure Blackwood and Petrov could get to anybody, anywhere. Irina being in Canada wouldn't deter them. "If Sokolov told them you were dead, they'll stop looking." He looked at Sokolov to verify that conjecture. The Russian nodded. After hearing his story, Novak had figured out that much. "Yeah, he told them you were dead. You should be safe enough up there."

"Please don't hurt him. He's just trying to find his daughter. I helped Daddy get her, but I don't remember much about it. I was so screwed up when it happened, I swear to God I was. I do bad things when I need a fix, really bad things that I don't even know I'm doing. I do anything Daddy wants when I'm strung out."

Novak's stomach turned. The whole thing was sickening. The girl had lived in a hell she hadn't asked for and didn't deserve. She might be a little jerk at times, but she had been horribly used and abused for most of her life.

"I don't trust Sokolov, but I'm not going to hurt him unless he tries something stupid. I need him at the moment."

Sokolov appeared more than relieved to hear it. He shut his eyes and sagged back against the chair.

"Ask him when he's coming back to get me. These people are real nice and stuff, and they got a doctor here who comes and tries to help me clean up, but it's so cold up here and there's nothing to do. No TV, no Netflix, no nothing. Just books."

"Stay there and don't talk to anybody about anything. You understand me, Irina? Don't talk to your daddy on the phone, or Petrov, if they come to get you. Don't call them for drugs, you understand me? You do that, and you'll end up dead."

"Yes, sir, I won't, I promise. Stepan told me that, too. I'll stay here and try to get better. I won't talk to them, no matter how bad I'm messed up. But I hate it here, there's nothing to do. It's so boring."

"Just do what you're told. If they find you, they'll kill you."

"Okay, okay, I will. And Mr. Novak…I want you to know I really am sorry I picked you out for those guys at the restaurant. I shouldn't have done it. But I'm so scared of Mr. Petrov. I knew better, but I needed to shoot up so bad that night. I was so sick."

"Yeah, I'm sorry you did, too."

Novak hung up. He wasn't sure he believed her. She'd have said anything if it got her what she wanted. She'd already proved it. Junkies never told the truth, anyway. "Okay, Sokolov, I believe some of your story, though I probably shouldn't. I'm taking you with me. We're going to walk out of this house and down the street to my car. Don't try anything or I'll shoot you. Believe it."

Now Sokolov was eager to please. "I do believe you. I won't, I swear to God, I won't. I want to go with you. Petrov's going to find out who I am, sooner or later. I'm already a dead man if they find out I'm double-crossing them."

"Just do what I say and keep your mouth shut."

Novak took his time taping Sokolov's hands behind him and slapping duct tape over his mouth. It looked like he could breathe through his nose well enough now. It was all a safety precaution. He walked him out the back door, down the sheltered side of the house and across the street, then down the sidewalk to the Civic. Nobody appeared to notice. Everybody was inside, probably watching late-night television or sound asleep. Novak saw no one peeking out their windows, no one calling the cops with their cellphones. He opened the trunk.

Sokolov started protesting under the tape, but Novak wasn't going to risk him yelling or trying to escape. He pushed him in the back, and Sokolov fell in forward, writhing around. Novak tossed his legs inside and slammed the trunk shut.

"I told you I didn't trust you," he muttered.

Looking around, he saw no signs of alarm. He got into the driver's seat, started the engine, and headed to the deserted beach where he'd left the Zodiac pulled up high on the sand.

Chapter 19

"So now we're *kidnapping* this guy?"

Lori's voice was so incredulous that Novak felt like laughing, but couldn't quite dredge it up. She stood at the stern rail and stared down at the Russian, where he was bound in the bottom of the rubber boat.

"Relax, Lori. We're just going to get some answers out of him. That's all."

Novak secured the Zodiac at the stern, grabbed the Russian by the back of his shirt, and hauled him up on deck. Dragging him below, he dropped him without much ceremony on the floor in the main salon. Novak did not believe everything this guy told him, but his story about his real daughter rang true. There were lots more questions that he needed to ask.

Lori followed him down the steps. "You're going to cost me my cushy new job at the Pentagon," she accused him. "I didn't sign up for illegal abductions."

Novak turned to her. "This guy is a former Russian espionage agent who is currently inside the country illegally while working with drug smugglers. The Pentagon will probably give you a commendation for turning him in."

"Sorry, but I'm unlikely to believe anything he says."

Novak shrugged and pushed Sokolov down on the couch. He ripped the tape off Sokolov's mouth. The man groaned with pain.

"I'm telling you the truth, I swear to God." His lips looked inflamed. He kept licking his sore mouth. "I'm on your side now. I've been so every step of the way. You've got to believe me."

"No, I don't." Lori sat down on the couch across from him, arms crossed over her chest. She didn't look eager to hear his tale. "I trusted you less than Novak did from the moment I saw you. I was right then, and I'm right now. You're a traitorous dirtbag."

Sokolov stared silently at her, then looked up at Novak. Under the circumstances, he appeared in control. His voice sounded normal, and his eyes were holding steady. "I saved both your lives at that hospital. You'd both be dead now, if not for me. I hope you'll remember that."

"Keep telling yourself that." Lori turned to Novak. "You shouldn't have brought him aboard. He's working with them, and they'll come looking for him here. What are we going to do now? Turn him in to the authorities?"

Novak pulled up a chair facing his prisoner. "I'm going to find out everything he knows and see if we can believe any of it. Depending on what he coughs up, I'll decide whether or not to let him go or turn him over to Homeland Security. As I said, he's here illegally. That's a serious crime, and they'll want to know what he's been up to while here. If we turn him in, that will put you in the clear with your general."

Sokolov didn't like any of that. "You can't do that to me, Novak. Please, just listen and believe me. I can help you put Petrov away for good. I can tell you things that will help you bring him down—dates, places, people he works with. You can take it all to the Feds. Put him away forever. I hope you do. The world will be a better place when he's locked up."

Novak looked at Lori. "Anything going on aboard *Trident Point*?"

She shook her head. "They're all in bed by now, I guess. It's been dark and quiet since around midnight. Guards are still patrolling the decks and surrounding docks. They don't seem to miss our friend here. Maybe he wasn't supposed to come back tonight."

"Will they come after you?" Novak asked Sokolov. "Are you supposed to report back tonight?"

"No, I'm supposed to take a flight out of here tonight."

"Where to?"

"Nantucket Island."

Novak frowned. He hadn't been expecting that. He'd been expecting him to say he was headed back to Virginia. "Why Nantucket?"

"If I tell you everything I know, will you let me go find my little girl before they kill her?"

"Maybe. Maybe not. If you don't, I'm turning you in. Then you'll spend the rest of your life behind bars and never find her."

"You've got to believe me. She's in terrible danger. All I want to do is find her and get her out of here."

Lori scoffed. "Looks to me like you've been playing both ends against the middle. Just like all spies do."

"I have at times, I admit that. I came here to find Katerina, and that's the only way I could do it. I don't care what happens to Petrov and Blackwood. Are you kidding? I hope they both land in prison or end up dead."

"What's going on up at Nantucket? Who were you going to meet there?"

Sokolov stared at Novak, then glanced around the cabin. That's the moment he decided to lie. Novak could read it on his face. "If you lie to me now, Sokolov, I swear I'll turn you over to the CIA tonight. That's a promise."

Sokolov hesitated. Novak could also ascertain the moment he made the decision to cooperate. This guy was too damn readable to be a good agent. Maybe he got that way when he was bloodied up and bound. Novak began to wonder if Sokolov had manufactured his espionage background.

"Okay, here's the truth: Nantucket is the major distribution point for drugs flooding into New England. It's where Petrov deposits the product and gets it ready to ship to the mainland. Nantucket's a touristy place like those beaches are, but nice and quiet and quaint, off the beaten track. Nobody would ever suspect an illegal drug operation out there. Blackwood's had his estate there since before he was a network anchor. It's been a family place for a century, passed down from father to son. He's the model citizen on that island, influential and respected, and he's got a warehouse on his grounds, or somewhere out there. Who would suspect he's using it as a depot for opioids? He's been doing it for years now."

"What about *Trident Point*? Who owns it?"

"Who do you think? The Senator, of course. He'll stay down here a while in the Keys on that yacht. He likes the weather here."

"They think you killed Irina, right? Is that what got you back in their good graces?"

"I was never out of favor. They trust me and have no reason not to. I told them I was going to befriend you. They wanted me to. They wanted to find out what you knew. Especially Petrov. He seemed to remember you somehow, but couldn't remember where."

Lori looked angry. "That's right, we saw you whispering in his ear this afternoon, all cozy-like. You're working with him, and you've been two-timing us all along."

"I was playing everybody. I'm a trained spy. That's what I do. Think about this. It's to my advantage to land on your side. They took my child. I'm only here in the States to find her. I had no choice but to play along with them or I'd never find her."

Novak kept trying to gauge how much of this story he was willing to believe. Lots of lies had come out of the Russian's mouth since he had entered the picture. No way could Novak believe everything he said. That would be stupid. "Tell us more about Petrov's pipeline. Are the drug shipments coming up from Mexico?"

Sokolov was not holding back anymore. He was spilling out everything with no reserve. "Yes, and from Guatemala and Nicaragua, as well. All of it passes through Cuba. The fentanyl is manufactured in China. That's where it comes from. There's a little seaport down the coast from Havana. That's where they transfer the drugs to a fishing boat, which then takes it out to sea. All of it goes up the coast to Nantucket Island off Cape Cod."

"It's passed from boat to boat, right?"

"The *Trident Point* meets that Cuban vessel somewhere out in the Florida Straits. It's always a different area, and always in international waters. It's been going on for years now."

"Causing the deaths of thousands of Americans, mostly kids in high school or college. You proud of that, Sokolov? You proud of all the families you've destroyed?"

"I haven't been involved in it long enough to be responsible. I only want my daughter back. She's my only child, and she's headed for a life of hell, just like Irina's. If they know she's mine, they'll know why I'm here, and we'll both end up dead. That's why I had to take my time, earn their trust, and do it this way. I had to look like I was one of them."

"How many drugs are we talking about?"

"More than you could ever imagine. The boats at those resorts? They make transfers every other day, all of them. Mainly it's opioids, especially heroin. Some is cut with other stuff, too, even fentanyl. I know they're also dealing oxycodone, crystal meth, and marijuana."

"You know for a fact that the fentanyl comes out of China? You can prove that?" Novak asked.

"Yes, it's a particular synthetic they make, twice as powerful and twice as deadly. I don't know how they get it into Cuba, but it comes up here by the crate."

Now Lori was interested. "So they pass these drugs onto Blackwood's yacht and take it back to Key West? Is that what you're telling us?"

"Yeah, Blackwood's a famous senator. The Coast Guard's not going to board his boat without absolute proof. Why would they even suspect him? Blackwood moves it out fast because he doesn't want to endanger himself. Except for the Nantucket compound, he keeps his hands pretty clean."

"How long has this been going on?" Novak asked.

"Years, I guess. At least a decade, but that's just a guess. I don't really know. Law enforcement hasn't been suspicious, or they would've busted them by now. Petrov set up the system himself. He personally recruited all the mules. All of them also have legitimate jobs during the week."

"Tell us exactly how they do it?"

"I think you've already guessed. Those families pretend to be vacationing, but they use different popular beaches where they won't be noticed. They move around so nobody gets suspicious."

"We saw a drop, but I want to know more information about those couriers."

"It runs like clockwork. I've been up and down the coast with Petrov enough times to know where most of the couriers show up. You can follow them home and bust them there. There might be some couriers that I don't know about. It's a big operation. Petrov keeps things under wraps so he can stay in charge. Blackwood doesn't talk about it at all. He knows it's going on and pockets billions, but he's going for deniability if things fall apart."

"Are they looking for us now? Do they know we're here, or that we're on to them?"

"No. Petrov got shook up for a while because he flubbed the Jeep accident and was seen shooting Justin. It shocked him when you opened fire, because he told his men to take your gun at the jail. You got him in the leg, but it was just a flesh wound. He says he'll find you someday and make sure you pay for that scar. They don't know where you are, or they would have sent somebody out here by now."

"Well, I hope you're right." Lori rose and looked out the porthole at the yacht. "It's still quiet at the dock."

"Don't get too relaxed. They're looking for you. That's what I'm supposed to be doing."

"How soon will they know you didn't arrive in Nantucket?"

"I report in every night. So we have until tomorrow night. Or I could just lie, but I would probably be found out if they called the guys on the island. If they catch me lying, they'll suspect you're involved. Petrov feels threatened by you."

"Tell me about every drug transfer that you've seen personally—time, place, routine, the whole works."

"I'd be naming nearly every beach resort on the Atlantic. It's big, I tell you. I have no idea how many mules are operating at any given time."

"Be specific. Going north from here in Key West."

"It would be easier to identify the families they're using. Couriers know little about their counterparts and just meet up with them because they're flying a certain kind of flag. Always different people but the same procedure. Petrov keeps everybody in the dark. You know, they only know their part of the equation."

"What kind of flags?"

"White trident on black flags. Actually, the ones I've seen are pennants."

Novak knew that was true. The rest of the story he wasn't so sure about. A lot of it corresponded with what they'd already found out, so it was beginning to look legitimate.

"And you think one of these mules has your daughter as part of his fake family?"

Sokolov nodded. "I have her last school picture in my wallet. Look at it. I'm telling you the truth."

"How old is she?"

"Eight."

"So you would recognize her if you saw her?"

Sokolov looked indignant. "Of course, I'd recognize her. Why wouldn't I?"

"Because we've snapped pictures of some of these people, and she might be one of them."

That got Sokolov excited. "Really? Let me look at them! Please, Novak. You've been following the pipeline? How did you know to do that?"

"They've become overconfident, and we've been careful. We changed boats right along with them, keeping our distance. It's a well-considered operation. That doesn't mean we can't bring it down."

"I don't think you can."

"Why?"

"There are too many pieces to the big puzzle. None of them knows everybody else, probably not even their real names. How can you prove anything?"

"I don't have to prove it. I just have to find enough evidence to give the Feds about the times and locations and method of transport, and let them do the rest of the work. They'll salivate at the idea of catching these people, especially when they hear they can get Blackwood. They've conjectured the Senator was dirty for years but never could prove it."

"It's going to be hard to catch all of them."

"That's where you come in, Sokolov. You're going to tell us names, dates, places, everything you know."

Sokolov's eyes narrowed. "And what happens to me if I do that?"

"You give us what we need? Show us where to go? We'll find your kid and get you both safe passage out of the country. Anywhere you want to go, name your destination."

Lori took umbrage. "Wait just a minute, Novak. That's a little much for me to swallow."

"I'm willing to agree to that," Sokolov said quickly. "I know a lot I can give you, but not everything you want."

"You help us bring these guys down? You've got a new life with your kid."

"That's worth everything to me. Petrov will be difficult to corner. He moves around a lot. He just watches, keeping his fingerprints off the actual drops, just like Blackwood. Make no mistake, he is calling all the shots, but it's unlikely you can tie him to anything."

"We've got photographic evidence that he runs with Blackwood and visits all his beach houses. If you think the Senator won't turn evidence on him when he gets caught, you're mistaken. He'll save his own neck, trust me. They'll all make deals."

"He's his personal bodyguard and lieutenant. That's his cover and safeguard. He'll say that's why he's with him. He's made sure he'll come out clean if the pipeline goes down."

"Yeah, that might work, until the Feds find out who he really is and what he's done in the past, that his own people in Russia want him dead. Do you still have the tapes of them inside his mansion at the horse farm?"

"Yes, but I can't give them to you without incriminating myself."

"We'll find a way."

Lori said, "Does he have any kind of routine? Petrov, I mean?"

"He moves around. He'll take a flight out soon, probably up to Nantucket, maybe a couple of stops first in Boston or New York. He's got safe houses all over the place, just like I do. He's learned to be careful. That's why he's still walking around with nobody the wiser."

"You said the Kremlin is after him. You sure about that?"

Sokolov nodded.

"Maybe we'll help them find him."

"We better do it soon. He's a formidable enemy, Novak."

"Tell me all the stops you know about. Lori, get everything he says on record. I want your voice on tape, Sokolov, as an insurance policy, since you're known for double-crossing people."

She got out her phone and set it to record. Novak did the same with his cell, not taking any chances. Sokolov started talking. "Key West first, and then it goes north up the coast, step by step. The route changes every time. I've seen transfers done both at Daytona Beach and Jacksonville, but they usually skip Miami. Too much heat and drug interdiction going on there. Amelia Island, sometimes. Fripp Island, Hilton Head, Nags Head, Atlantic City. I'm telling you, they have no constant routine for their drops. Different families travel to different places and rent boats. It's been working for years without a hitch. If anything, it works better now."

"That's all the places you've seen yourself?"

"No, I heard Newport mentioned a couple of times."

"Anywhere in Virginia?"

"Virginia Beach. They alternate marinas where they rent boats and always use false names. No family goes back to the same place twice in a row. It'll take a hell of a lot of surveillance and following these people around to nail down everybody. That, or just catch Petrov and force it all out of him. It's his baby. He makes it tick."

"That would be my preference."

"I'll help you do that," Lori said.

"Me, too," said Sokolov.

"You do know that we can't—and don't—believe everything you say. Why would we?"

Sokolov studied them. "I can prove what I say is true."

"Be my guest."

"I've got a tracker hidden on *Trident Point.*"

"Okay, now I'm interested."

"I put one inside Petrov's backpack, too, sewn into the lining. He's smart, but he'll never think anybody can get that close to him. He carries that bag everywhere."

"Where do you come up with all these trackers?"

"Where do you come up with yours?"

Novak looked at Lori. She appeared encouraged, eager to get a final takedown in the works.

"Look, Novak, both of you—listen to me. I used to be a spook for two decades. I keep what I need close at hand. Don't you?"

Of course Novak did. He hadn't been a spy, but he kept an emergency backpack with him most of the time, just like Petrov did. One full of anything he might need on the run. "Prove it. Show us the GPS positions."

"Give me my phone, and I will. No problem."

Novak knew that finding Sokolov's daughter was the key to his cooperation. He believed that was Sokolov's only reason for taking a chance by sneaking into the United States. That had to be the major priority for him. And now they had the means to find out. If Sokolov's picture matched one that Lori had snapped on their surveillance runs, it would be proof he was telling the truth. If they got her location, they could get her back for him. But the fact that Novak now had the means to track Petrov's every movement was too good to be true. He wanted that guy, and now he could find him in whatever filthy hole he crawled down.

Chapter 20

"Okay, Sokolov, what's your phone's password?"

"Let me loose, and I'll show you what I've got. I'm on your side now. What's it going to take to make you believe me?"

"Nothing's going to make me believe everything you say."

Novak took a moment to consider. He glanced over at Lori to get her take. She nodded okay. "All right, I'm going to cut you free, but I'm going to keep a gun to your head, so don't try to give us up to them. You understand?"

"Oh, yeah, don't worry."

Novak pulled his weapon and kept it pointed at the Russian. Lori grabbed a steak knife from the galley and cut through the tape bindings. Once he was free, Sokolov stood up, stretched, rubbed his wrists, bent down and back up, trying to get his blood circulating again. "My hands are numb, man. Why'd you make it so tight? I can barely feel them."

Lori did not commiserate. "Well, boo hoo, Sokolov."

Sokolov sighed. "I hope I can soon convince the two of you of my good intentions. I've never had complete loyalty to Petrov, and especially not to Blackwood. I just want my daughter back, that's the only reason I came here. I had no other choice but to work for them until I found out what they did with her. After she's safe, I'll be happy to put a bullet in both their heads and never think twice about it."

"You would probably do the same thing to us," Novak said. "You have no idea where Katerina is now?"

"Of course not. If I did, I'd have her with me and be long gone by now. I couldn't question them about her, you know that. I had to wait and see if I could find out where she was on my own. I now think she's with one of the courier families. That's all I have to go on. She's not on the yacht, because I searched it when I set up the GPS on Petrov and the boat. If he finds them and thinks it's my doing, he'll come for me."

"Okay, let's get this over with." Novak handed Sokolov the phone he'd taken off him earlier. When Sokolov pulled up a screen, Novak pressed his gun against his temple. "Don't even think about alerting them to us. You won't live for another second if you do."

"Stop with the constant threats, already. I get it," Sokolov grumbled as he poked in commands.

Novak watched the screen carefully. Within seconds, two dots popped up, blinking with steady signals. They were nearly on top of each other.

"That's the yacht with the backpack on board. It'll stay this way until Petrov disembarks for his flight north."

"You're positive?"

"Absolutely. They're going out soon to meet the *Jose Blanco*. That's the name of the Cuban vessel that brings out the drugs from that port near Havana. I think it's called Matanzas, or something like that. Check it out if you've got a way to do it. They make these transfers regularly, but out in open water."

"Let me see that," Lori said. Novak handed the phone to her. She was the resident computer guru, so Novak let her do her thing. She examined the screen, punched in commands, then nodded. "He's got that ship bugged all right. Ditto for Petrov—or his luggage, I should say. High-quality GPS signal, too. Right now, anyway. Better than yours are."

Sokolov smiled. "I'll give you my dealer's name in Portugal, if you like. We'll know exactly where they are until the batteries run out, and that won't be for a couple of weeks, so we don't need to waste time." Sokolov appeared pleased with himself. "Now are you satisfied, Novak?"

"Looks legit, but don't think it makes us buddies."

"Oh, I would not think so. Do you trust anybody, my friend?"

"Not you." Trustworthy friends had been few and far between in Novak's life. Lori, Claire Morgan and Nicholas Black, his SEAL buddies, and a few from the NYPD, but that was about it.

"Have you ever been on the yacht during a Cuban transfer?"

"Yes, one time. Before you suggest it, don't follow them out there. If you do, they'll spot you. They're heavily armed in case they're stopped, and that's when they're the most careful. But it's the same boat every time, and now you've got its name. Petrov trusts no one. The next time *Trident Point* ventures offshore, all you have to do is call the U. S. Coast Guard and their jig is up, as you Americans like to say."

"You believing any of this?" Novak asked Lori.

"I'm beginning to. I can't believe I do, though. Not with this two-timing little weasel."

Sokolov feigned hurt. "I thought we were friends after I got you out of that hospital."

"Quit assuming things like that."

Sokolov looked back at Novak. "Your woman is a smartass."

Novak ignored that. "So now we can sit right here, watch the transfer via these trackers, and know when they'll start transporting it up the Atlantic Coast."

"Exactly. And you're welcome."

Novak liked that idea, because it meant they could watch for the first transfer to a smaller boat right here in Key West, and follow it to its next drop. That's how they could get photographic evidence. They needed to find a way to follow the courier families back to their safe houses. If they could get that information to law enforcement, a full-fledged takedown would be easy to coordinate.

"So what information do you have on my daughter? I told you everything I know. Please tell me you know where she is."

"I don't know where she is, not yet."

"Then I'm done cooperating."

"I've got pictures of the families at the drops we've witnessed. All you have to do is point her out. Then we go get her."

"Let me see. I want her out of there. I want her out of this country."

Novak hoped he found the girl's picture so they could get her out before they brought the pipeline down. The three of them sat down at the dining table, and Lori opened her laptop and pulled up the photos she'd taken of the families.

"I didn't get shots of every single courier. There could be more families that we didn't see, or there could be other kids that they leave at home. They might not want your daughter out in the public eye if she's a kidnap victim. These are only the people we saw at the beach, or ones we were following when they raised that trident pennant. The photos aren't the best quality, but you should be able to tell if any of them are her. That is, if anything you've told us is true."

"I'm telling the truth. If she's one of them, you can match her to her school picture. I have it in my wallet."

Lori swiveled her laptop around so that she could scroll through the first pictures in front of them. Sokolov watched the screen, and Novak watched Sokolov. The Russian was leaning in eagerly. His face revealed disappointment. "No, neither of them is Katerina."

"The second family was photographed on Fripp Island. They came with two young girls, so maybe she's with them."

A moment later, Sokolov shook his head. "No."

He went through two more sets without luck.

"These are from Hilton Head Island. They brought an older boy and a girl."

Sokolov looked at each picture carefully, and then he froze. His face twisted with emotion, and he shocked them both by bursting into tears. "That's her. Oh my God, she's grown so much. But it's her, she's so beautiful." He kept wiping away tears with his fingers. His outpour was raw and hard to watch, but revealed a lot to Novak. "I cannot believe I found her. We've got to get her out of there. Now, before they move her somewhere else."

Or worse, Novak thought. "They won't move her without cause. Petrov knows nothing about you working with us now, or that she's your daughter. Are you sure he doesn't suspect you?"

"He's trusts me, I think. It's hard to tell with him. He's guarded." He kept his eyes on his daughter's picture. "She looks okay. Just so very thin. My God, I'm so relieved she's alive and well. You've got to help me get her away from them, Novak."

No way was Sokolov's relief at finding his daughter faked. "We will. Soon. But not until we get photographic evidence of the yacht meeting up with the Cubans. How close can we get to them without being seen?"

"That's not a good idea. I told you already. They are the most careful at that point. They'll meet in open water where it's unlikely to be observed. Coast Guard cutters and drones patrol the coastal waters. They avoid them and get closer to Cuban waters. I think the Cuban government might be getting a kickback."

"Even so, it's surprising they haven't been searched," Lori said. "One call to my general and we could intercept them in the process of loading the drugs on the yacht."

"Getting Petrov and Blackwood and their entire crew in one fell swoop would simplify things considerably," Novak said.

"No, no, listen to me. We can't do that. Petrov will get a call out in time, and the entire pipeline will fade into the woodwork. He'll know I tipped off the authorities. We have to wait until next time, after I get my daughter out of the country. They meet up once a week or so. It won't hurt to wait that long."

"I think it's risky to wait, but it will give us time to get back to Hilton Head and get your daughter out before we bring the whole thing down."

"Is the GPS tracker still on the courier's car?" Sokolov asked him.
"Yes, we're tracking several of them in different states. We couldn't get them all, but that one's for sure. They went to an address inside Beaufort and have stayed there most of the time; I've been checking. If they're still there, we've got them. After that, I want to go after Petrov and Blackwood. I can't get them down here, not on that fortified yacht, no way. So where do you suggest we try to take them, Sokolov?"

He shrugged. "I don't think you can get to Blackwood. You'll have to let them get him during the law enforcement bust. Petrov's careful, I warn you, but he can be surprised if you do things the right way. I do know his plan is to head up to Nantucket as soon they return to Key West on the yacht. That's probably your best chance to find him alone. He likes it up there, likes to go out to eat at some of the restaurants on the island, things like that. Nobody would expect any kind of attack on Blackwood's compound out there. It's Blackwood's summer home, nice and quiet, and it's been in the family forever. No one would ever suspect he's moving drugs out of that house. It will not be as heavily guarded as most. Not out in the open, anyway. Too many guards do nothing but raise suspicion in a small, insulated place like Nantucket."

"We need to bring my general in on this," Lori told them. "Tell him everything and get a coordinated effort together to hit all these safe houses and the yacht at the same time. It has to come down all at once, or most of them will be forewarned and get away scot free."

Novak didn't want to do that. He didn't like bringing in so many agencies at once, especially where the Feds were involved. They had a tendency to leak information, and that could ruin the whole takedown. Sokolov felt the same way.

"I don't trust the CIA to keep it quiet."
"Of course, you don't," snapped Lori. "You're a damned Russian spy."
"That doesn't make me a bad guy. Just a loyal patriot to the Motherland."
"Like hell it doesn't."

Novak listened as they bickered back and forth. They were never going to like each other. Lori was right about this, though. This was a big bust, and it had to be well-coordinated because there were so many people involved. Petrov would have a failsafe warning system locked into place. This was too big for the three of them to coordinate, but not so much for the power of the Pentagon. "Lori's right, Sokolov. Washington will have to call the shots on this thing. Lori, I want you to fly up to D.C. and present all the evidence we've gathered so far. Give it to your boss, confidentially, in person. He already trusts you enough to bring you aboard in his new position. Leave my name out of it—it won't do you any good in some corridors up there. They'll arrest Sokolov the minute you mention him, so keep him out of the conversation."

"I've got to give them exemplary proof if I expect them to act. What are you going to do?"

"First off, I'm gonna get Sokolov's daughter back. Once she's in a safe place, I'm going after Petrov. I should be able to get to him before you guys can put together a coordinated operation to bring them down. How long do you think that will take?"

"Using government hierarchy? Are you kidding? Forever, or even longer. Still, I've got all the evidence they'll need to legally proceed right here in my laptop. That'll speed things up. How much time do you need to take care of business?"

"Less than a week if we get lucky, two at the most, if she's still in the Beaufort house. Maybe longer. It depends."

"That's doable, I think. I'll need to fly up to D.C. tonight."

Once tentative plans were drawn up, Novak began to feel better. Lori would be home and out of danger, which was good. He could keep an eye on Sokolov himself, which he would do with diligence. Within the hour, Lori was packed and had driven his Civic rental out to the airport. She would fly out an hour after she got there. Sokolov and Novak kept watch on the *Trident Point*'s movements. At five o'clock that morning, the crewmen cast off the moorings, and the yacht moved slowly out of berth, headed for Cuban waters. Novak pulled anchor and headed up the coast toward Hilton Head Island. It had begun.

Chapter 21

Novak watched Sokolov for signs of nerves. The courier family lived in a house on Calhoun Street in Blufton, near Hilton Head. They had found it easily enough. The blue Camry with the GPS signal was sitting in the driveway. At the moment, he and Sokolov were crouched down behind a thick bed of azaleas growing at one side of the house. It was approaching eleven o'clock at night. Most of the houses were already dark, their vehicles parked out front or tucked into garages. Nobody stirred on the sidewalks or anywhere else. There were streetlights to avoid, but plenty of shadows they could use for cover.

"Ready to roll, Sokolov?"

"I just don't want Katerina to get hurt."

"I can't guarantee that. You sure she'll remember you?"

"I'm her father."

"One who was deployed most of her life. She hasn't seen you in a while."

"She'll remember me. We were close when I got to be with her."

"Do you have a plan in case she doesn't?"

"I've got a picture of her with her mama and me."

"Keep it handy. We can't take a screaming kid out of that house in a neighborhood as quiet as this one. Okay, let's do this."

Novak crept closer to the house with Sokolov right behind him. Sokolov had handled himself well thus far, and that was what Novak had expected since the man had worked as an agent. But that was a long time ago, and this guy was anxious and afraid for his child. A married couple had Katerina. At least, Novak assumed they were married, but they could be just two criminals working together. If Petrov had put Sokolov's daughter with them after Blackwood had cast her aside, they would not be model citizens, but probably armed and dangerous. The teenager that he'd had last seen out on the ocean with them at their last drop was not inside the house. Nearly an hour ago, he had driven off in a convertible with a couple of other boys. "Okay, you know the plan. I'll distract the mom and dad at the front door while you go in and get your daughter out as fast as you can make it happen. Head back to the car with her as soon as you can."

Sokolov had been uncharacteristically quiet since they'd arrived. Novak took a deep breath and hoped for the best. He had a bad feeling that something might go wrong. They could not risk incarceration by the local cops at this point, not on a charge of child abduction, which is what it would look like if they were apprehended. Right now, Lori was busy setting things in motion to bring Blackwood's drug empire down around his ears. They needed to get the girl out, nice and quick with no trouble, then get the hell out of town. Problem with that was Sokolov. He didn't appear up to anything at the moment. In fact, he was as nervous as a cat set loose in a dog pound.

Novak stopped and placed his hand on the other man's shoulder, hoping to calm him down. He could see the way Sokolov's chest rose and fell, heard his raspy breathing. Once, Novak had had a sweet little daughter he'd loved as much as Sokolov loved Katerina, but she had died along with his wife and son when the Twin Towers had crashed to the ground on 9/11. Even now, years past that awful day, he felt the horror rising up inside him. Neither of his children got to grow up. They hadn't even reached school age, but he knew that if either of them were held hostage in a house with criminals, he would feel the same trepidation that the Russian was now showing.

"I've got to ask you, Sokolov. Can you do this or not? If you can't, I need to know now. I can go in there alone and get your kid. Say the word and I will."

"No, she wouldn't know you. She'd be scared. I can do this. I'm just a little nervous, is all. I don't know what they might have told her about me and her mom. What if they told her I just gave her to them? Or that I didn't want her? What if she hates me and won't come with me?"

"That's up to you. I wouldn't leave my child in that house with those people, not in a million years."

"I know. Of course, I know that. Okay, okay, I'll go in the back door, just the way we planned it."

"Just make it quiet and find her fast. She's probably already upstairs in bed. I'll distract the two adults at the front door. Everything will go easier if you can get away without them knowing we took her."

"I know, I know, but you've got to keep them busy. It might take some time to convince her."

"You better convince her quick. C'mon, let's get this over with before the older kid and his friends come back. That would just mean more people we have to deal with."

Novak pushed his gun into his belt holster at the small of his back, dropped his shirttail over it, and then stood up and walked to the sidewalk until he stood in front of the house. He looked around, found nothing going on, then walked down the sidewalk and climbed the steps to the covered front porch. He could see the couple inside as clear as day. The picture window was large, the drapes partially open. They sat together in the living room. It looked like they were watching television. He remembered the lady. They were definitely in the right place.

Tonight she had on black sweats and was barefoot. She was sprawled on a couch the color of a ripe eggplant. The man was kicked back in a blue-and-red plaid recliner, and both were smoking pot. Several glass bongs, hypodermic needles, and other drug paraphernalia were scattered around on the coffee table in front of them. They were just a couple of typical drug-dealing dirtbags, smoking their product while waiting for their next drug drop. It was a sickening sight, especially with a small child somewhere in that house. Now he knew where they lived. The Feds would bring them down soon, right along with all their drug-dealing friends.

Novak tapped a knuckle lightly on the front door and waited. He hoped Sokolov was already inside and had made it upstairs to the girl's bedroom. He'd had plenty of time. A moment later the door opened, and the strong, pungent smell of marijuana rolled out in a wave. The woman was smaller than she had looked on surveillance. She had to tilt her head back to look up at him, standing not much taller than five feet. Her eyes were dark, and her pupils were dilated. She looked scared when she saw him. She took a step back and stopped there, her hand still on the doorknob. Novak didn't move. She was spooked.

"Keith," she called out. "Some big guy's out here."

Keith showed up three seconds later. He pushed the woman behind him as if he thought Novak was going for her throat. She hovered there, watching and wary, but not afraid to hang around and see what happened. Novak adopted a pleasant expression. He was pretty sure this guy was armed. "I'm sorry to bother you folks, but I was looking for Apple Street. I've gotten all turned around somehow and can't find my way back downtown to my hotel. I saw your light was on, so I figured someone was still up. I know it's late, but my phone's dead, so I'm kinda desperate."

Keith relaxed visibly. He looked stoned out of his mind, but halfway
functional. Most of his drug-robbing enemies invaded homes in packs
with weapons drawn, no doubt. That was what he was used to. He had
pulled on a windbreaker since springing out of that recliner, so Novak
assumed he was hiding a gun. Novak turned slightly so he could reach his
own weapon if something went wrong. Keith was still sizing him up, but
was no longer tense. "You've come too far this way. Turn around and go
back to Boundary and take a left. That should take you back downtown."

"Okay, let me just get those directions set in my mind."

The man looked past him at the street. "Where's your car?"

"I parked it just up the street there. I was going to ask at another house
but their lights went off about the time I got out. So I saw yours were still
on and walked down this way. Again, I'm really sorry to disturb you."

Novak was about to ask him to repeat the directions, stalling for time,
but he failed to get the words out. A child screamed, and the horrible shriek
reverberated down a staircase that Novak could see from his spot at the
front door. Katerina had not recognized her father. For an instant, all three
of them froze in place. Then Novak moved first. He drove his fist hard
into the man's solar plexus, and then as he bent over, gasping for breath,
Novak brought up his knee and got him in the face. Keith collapsed hard,
facedown and lay still. The woman took off down the hall, screaming as
if the hounds of hell were after her.

Novak shut the door and chased her, but she grabbed something off a
table in the living room and whirled on him. The silenced Luger went off,
and Novak threw himself down just in time. The bullet missed his head by
a fraction. He charged at her and tackled her bodily to the ground. They
landed near the coffee table, knocking off the bongs, which shattered
on the hardwood floor. She fought him as if he were a demon, and she
knew what she was doing. If she hadn't been stoned out of her mind, she
might've gotten away.

Even so, she landed a hard undercut to his chin that sent his mind
bouncing around inside his head, but he managed to get a grip on the gun.
It went off again, the bullet hitting the ceiling and raining plaster down on
them. He wrested the gun out of her hand, but not before she kicked him
hard, aiming for the groin. He evaded that maneuver and flipped her over
on her stomach, getting an arm around her throat. He squeezed off her air
until she stopped fighting, maintaining the pressure a few more seconds
until she went limp. When he was sure she was done, he stretched her out
on her back, checked out the front window, and found nothing moving on
the quiet street. He bounded upstairs at a run.

The house was silent now, but he still led with his weapon. He started checking out the bedrooms, finding the little girl's at the end of the hall. Sokolov was inside, sitting on the bed with the girl on his lap. She had both arms around his neck, as if she'd never let him go. He was rocking her back and forth. They were both crying, but Novak was more interested in who else might be inside that house. "Get her packed up and let's get the hell out of here. We're wasting too much time. I'm going to clear the bedrooms."

Novak moved down to the next room. It obviously belonged to the teenage boy. The walls were covered with posters of superheroes and sexy starlets posing in tiny bikinis. Of more interest to him was the glass bong in plain view on the bedside table. There was also evidence that the kid had been shooting up heroin. Remnants of weed and cocaine rested in bowls strewn around like candy dishes. Maybe he wasn't a high schooler, after all. Maybe he was a dealer just like the other two were. Maybe he was Katerina's guard. He searched the room and found more paraphernalia, along with supplies of weed, pills, every drug imaginable, a good portion already in small plastic bags and ready to sell. Maybe that's how Petrov paid his couriers: free drugs they could deal to kids in the suburbs. More drugs were sitting out in the open inside the master bedroom. This was a pathetic family of criminals. He hoped the little girl had not suffered living there.

"We're ready now," Sokolov said from out in the hallway.

"Take her out to the car and be ready to go. I'm going to clean up a few things here first." They fled down the steps and out the back door while Novak scooped up the glass bong and several bags of pills and headed downstairs. The man and woman had not moved. He placed more drugs and paraphernalia on the coffee table, then dropped some pills and weed on the carpet. Then he went to the hall, picked up Keith, and dragged him back. He dropped him face-first on the floor in front of the couch. The woman was small to have fought so hard. He picked her up and eased her down on the couch. He put the bong on her stomach. Neither of them appeared to be seriously injured—at least they were still breathing. They would have big problems when they woke up, especially when the cops that he was about to call showed up. He rubbed drug residue on their hands, and then wiped his fingerprints off everything he'd touched. Once he was satisfied, he washed his hands in the kitchen sink and left the front door slightly ajar before exiting out the back.

As soon as Novak reached the car, he told Sokolov to get in the back seat with the kid. He took his place in the driver's seat, started the motor, and pulled away from the curb. He didn't gun it, didn't speed away, but drove slowly and carefully. When he got about three blocks from the house, he pulled out the burner phone in his pocket. He dialed 911, tried to disguise his voice when he reported a violent home invasion at a known drug house. He gave them Keith's address, telling them to hurry. Then he hung up, disabled the phone, and tossed it into bushes at the side of the road. After that, he drove away, keeping one eye on the rearview mirror. He didn't breathe easy until he was back at the harbor where he'd left *Sweet Sarah*. So far, so good.

Novak let Sokolov and the girl off on the beachfront, then parked the rental at the end of the lot. They took the Zodiac back out to the sailboat, and Novak felt a hell of a lot better when they were safely on board. Nobody was out on the beach. He heard no sirens, no cops pulling up behind him with flashing lights. They'd made it.

Sokolov led Katerina below, his arm draped around her shoulders, holding her close. Novak followed them. He grabbed some blankets out of a locker and handed them to Sokolov as he led his daughter to the couch. They sat down together. Novak backed away and put on a pot of coffee in the galley. He fixed the girl some cookies and hot cocoa as he listened to Sokolov speaking softly to her in their native Russian. He felt better about their chances of getting away unscathed, but he was cautious enough to keep an eye on the porthole so he could get ahead of incoming trouble. The ocean and beach looked dark and deserted. He hated to subject the kid to more emotional stress right now, but he needed answers, and she was the only one who could give them to him. He poured out two mugs of coffee, filling the third with the cocoa and popping a marshmallow on top. He took them over, and sat down across from the little girl.

Sokolov looked up at him. "I can never thank you enough, Novak. I can never repay you for helping me get Katerina out of there."

"I'm glad she's okay. You need to get her out of here and take her to that convent where Irina is. Keep them both safe there until I contact you again. I can handle the rest of this on my own."

"What more will you do?"

Novak watched the child. She wouldn't look up at him, but kept her eyes downcast. Her hair was long, waist-length, dark and curly, and hung in a veil over her face. Her hands were trembling until she cupped them around her mug. She was not in good shape emotionally, but looked okay physically. What child would be okay after what she'd been through?

"You know what I'm going to do," he answered Sokolov. "I want Petrov. He won't expect me anywhere near the compound in Nantucket. He'll think nobody knows about it."

"You need help to do that. Let me take Katerina up there and come back."

"No, no, Papa, please don't leave me." The child became distraught at once.

"Listen to your daughter. She's the one who needs you." Novak hesitated. The girl relaxed again, and Novak watched her take a delicate sip of the chocolate. She ended up with marshmallow on her nose. She wiped it off with her hand.

"I need to ask you some questions, Katerina. Will you talk to me for a minute?"

That caused her to tense up. She almost spilled the chocolate. She steadied it again and answered him, avoiding looking him in the eye. When she spoke, it was in heavily accented English. "What if they find me again? Bobby told me they'd kill me if I ever tried to get away. He said they'd kill my mama and papa and everybody else in my family."

Novak assumed Bobby was the teenager. "They won't find you. Your Papa is taking you far away before daylight. Just tell me a few things that I need to know and you can go with him right now. Please, I need your help to get these people who took you away from your family. I want them in prison, where they can never hurt you or any other little girl again."

She raised her lashes. They were long and black and revealed the most captivating blue eyes. She was a beautiful child. That's why Blackwood had targeted her on that Moscow street. Her gaze was troubled now, and her mouth quivered, but she nodded assent.

"Okay, we already know those people you lived with pick up drugs when you go out on the ocean in the boat. Are you aware of that?"

She shook her head. "We go to the ocean sometimes, but I thought it was just to swim and have a picnic." She looked down again. "But I do know about the drugs—Keith and Kate and Bobby smoke them all the time. They take lots of those pills. They make me stay in my room, but they never hurt me." She got quiet again. "Are they dead now?"

"No. They were trying to stop your father from taking you home, so I had to do something. They'll be all right when they wake up," he assured her.

"What about that old man who had me first? I won't have to go back there ever again, will I?"

"No, never. You'll never see him again."

Sokolov hugged his daughter closer. Novak waited, then gentled his voice. "You need to tell us everything you know about those people you lived with. And the people they were friends with. Did other families come to visit at your house?"

"Nobody ever came there. Except people who wanted to buy those pills and things. They came to the back door, and Bobby sold them what they wanted, I think. None of the people in the boats came to our house." She took another sip and nibbled on a vanilla wafer.

"Okay, did you hear any names when you were out there on the ocean? Did they call each other anything?"

She nodded. "Yes, sometimes we met a family named Monroe. They were nice. They laughed a lot." Her fearful gaze lifted and latched onto his face. "You won't hurt them, will you?"

Novak couldn't promise that. They weren't the major attraction as far as he was concerned, but they were still going to end up in jail. He didn't answer. "Do you know where they live?"

"We went to their house one time. It took a long time to go there."

"Where was it? Do you remember the address or the street, or what town it was?"

"It was in Savannah. The street's name was Brown Pelican Drive. I remember because I saw one of those birds sitting on the pier right before we left. They fly in a big long line right over the water sometimes."

"Do you remember anybody else?"

She considered the question thoughtfully. "I remember visiting the beach at this pretty house. I played in the pool with Bobby and Kate. She asked me to call her mommy, but I never did. She's not my mommy. She slapped me once for talking too loud when we were waiting for Keith to meet somebody out on the beach."

"Do you know who that was?"

"No. He made us stay inside the car and walked down the beach all alone in the dark. It was the same beach where we swam. I saw a boat out on the water, but I couldn't see Keith anymore. It was too dark."

"Okay, you're really helping us, sweetheart. What else do you remember about the people they met?"

For almost fifteen minutes, she told them stories of driving out to the beach at night, about taking motorboats out on the water where they swam and fished and had picnic lunches with other families. Petrov's system operated like clockwork, well-oiled and efficient. And Katerina had been with this family for over a year. They had moved lots of opioids and heroin in that time period. Novak jotted down names and incidents on a notepad. Katerina was going to be a prize witness when this thing went to court. He hoped she could hold up to testifying, but he wasn't sure she could.

He hoped Sokolov would allow her to stay in the country, but he wasn't counting on that, either. Her father was going to want to take her as far away as he could get her.

"You've been a big help, Katerina. Finish your cocoa and let me talk to your daddy a minute, okay?"

Once they stepped aside and huddled together in the galley, Novak lowered his voice. "You need to take her and get out of here tonight. Take the rental car and hide out with the two girls at that convent, or whatever it is. Make sure they both stay healthy. You got that?"

"Yes, but I warn you, my friend, don't try to take Petrov alone. Do not do that. Not without backup. He's a monster, a cold and deadly killer. He likes hurting people, and he's good at it. He uses an icepick in the eye or at the base of the skull. Just so it penetrates the brain."

"I know what he is."

Sokolov glanced at his daughter. His face softened. "She's going to be okay, I think. Thank God."

"Get her out of here before something goes wrong or somebody shows up and tries to stop you. I'm heading to Nantucket now."

"He'll be up there eventually. He likes it there. He might have his own place, but I'm not sure about that. He went off alone a lot when we were there last time. He's got another safe house in Quebec, in case he has to flee the country. He's got everything planned out for any eventuality. He's always been like that, a planner."

"Yeah, figures. But this time everything is coming down around his ears. Now get going before somebody shows up. I'll take you in on the Zodiac. Drive all night. This thing is far-reaching, and they'll bail out Keith and the woman as soon as they know they're in jail. Let's go."

Novak took them to shore and watched them drive off. When their taillights faded in the distance, he took the Zodiac back out to *Sweet Sarah*, pulled the rubber boat aboard and stowed it in place, then pulled anchor and set his course north to Nantucket Island.

Chapter 22

Novak grabbed up the sat phone on the first ring, eager to talk to Lori and make sure she was okay. He also wanted to know what she'd found out. "Lori, where in the hell have you been? I've been trying to call you."

At the other end of the line, he heard her amused laugh. "Wow, you really did miss me, huh?"

"You were supposed to call me when you got to Ronald Reagan Airport in D.C. It's been three days. I get nervous when I don't hear from you, especially when I know dangerous men are out there trying to kill you."

"Chill, baby. I'm fine. My boss listened to me, looked at the evidence we've gathered so far. He's completely on board with presenting it to his superiors and taking down this whole thing, lock, stock, and barrel. He's as excited as we are."

Novak felt his body relax. "Good, good news. What's next on your end?"

"He's got to get approval and signatures from just about everybody at the Pentagon and beyond. It's going to happen, though. Everybody up here has been screaming about the opioid epidemic. We'll end up heroes if this comes off well."

"Are you okay? Any more headaches?"

"You know I'm fine, but thanks for asking."

"Anybody try to give you trouble?"

"No, the flight up here was uneventful. A military jeep picked me up at the airport with an armed guard in the front seat. What about you? Are they coming after you?"

"Not yet, but it's going to happen eventually."

"Where are you now?"

"Sailing north to Nantucket as fast as the winds will carry me. Luckily, they're brisk and steady, and the weather's been fair so far."

"Will it hold up, though? It's storming like crazy outside my office window."

"So far. Blue skies dead ahead."

"You could dock somewhere and take a flight. Faster and easier, I'd say."

"They might be watching the airports. I can't take chances right now. I can control what happens while I'm on this boat. It's going to take days for you to put the bust together, right?"

"Yes. You should have time to get there if the weather holds. What about the Nantucket ferries from the mainland? Couldn't you go in that way if you flew out there?"

"They'd be stupid not to have somebody watching who lands out on Nantucket. I would be, if I were them. If that's their major point of distribution as Sokolov says, there are a lot of drugs storehoused somewhere on that island. He says they've got several buildings in Blackwood's compound. I'm going to find out what's inside them. Did you dig up those addresses and the other things I asked for?"

"Yes, believe it or not, his places are not cloaked in official secrecy. He must feel perfectly invincible. Who could blame him with his credentials? He's got houses all over the place, sticking to the story that he's a real estate investor. Who could say different? As far as Nantucket, he's got a big compound on the north shore. It's off by itself, and the images I've got show me it's up on a rise above the beach on Nantucket Sound. Not a cliff, really, but a grassy slope with shrubs and some trees that can give you cover if you have to go in that way. There's a cluster of houses just down the beach, sort of a little village almost. Blackwood's place has got a boardwalk along the top and steps down to the water. There's this dock sort of thing, too, but it's not very big. I can text you the GPS and some Google aerial shots of the layout, as well as some tourist photos I found."

"You're nothing but a genius, Lori."

"You need to remember that and praise me more often."

"I prefer to praise you in other ways."

"Me, too, now that you mention it. We just can't seem to get around to that, not when you go to steakhouses."

"We'll make up time. That's a promise." Novak meant it. He owed Lori a nice vacation, wherever she wanted to go. She was spending her time off gathering information for him instead of having the nice romantic getaway they'd planned.

"Yes, sir, you certainly will."

"It's a date. Okay, send me the pictures and maps. I've still got a long way to go. Will that mess up your end of things? Is the takedown going to be a simultaneous one?"

"Yeah, but you know how slowly the Pentagon works. We're going to have to cut through a hundred miles of red tape before we get the go-ahead. My boss is gung-ho and ready to move on this thing. In fact, you might be right about that promotion if things go according to plan. Still, he's got to get everything sanctioned and lined up to strike all at once. But he's good at those kinds of maneuvers. He wants to take everybody along the pipeline at the same time, or as close as we can. That means I'm lining up proper law enforcement agencies in every jurisdiction. It's not going to be easy, and I'll be surprised if something doesn't leak or go wrong. If it does and they burrow in their holes, we're done for."

"How long before they think they can put it together? I've got to have time to get there and evaluate their set up."

"You'll have it. I'm only halfway through figuring out who has jurisdiction at these places. We've got to get all the local law enforcement agencies on board, but they will be a source of leaks, too."

"Have you pinned down each stop?"

"I'm running all the names and photos we've got so far through all our criminal databases, but I think most of his people are working under aliases. They'd be stupid not to, and these guys aren't shortsighted for as long as this has been going on. We still might get some matches on facial recognition with former Russian operatives and see if any of them are still skulking around in the U.S."

"Petrov won't make dumb mistakes. He's careful."

"You got Sokolov's daughter out, I take it."

"Yes. He's on the way to the convent where he stashed Irina for safekeeping. I hope he follows through and makes it there. Never know what to expect with him."

"He's hasn't betrayed us yet. This thing is so damn far-reaching. If we pull this off, it'll be a miracle. You know what else, Novak? You better make it through this alive. I'm warning you. You could wait for reinforcements when you get up there. I can make that happen."

"No, I do this one alone." Novak knew she'd argue, so he said, "Are you really feeling okay?"

"I'm fine, please—let it rest. My state of health is A-OK. What about you?"

Novak still had some headaches, but he attributed that to stressing over bringing those guys down. She didn't need to know that. "I'm fine, too. We're both tough."

"How much time will you need to get there and map out the inside of that compound?"

"Another week, at least. Ten days tops, unless I hit a vanishing angle."

"A what?"

"It's a nautical term. That's when the wind tips a sailboat too close to the water to right itself and it capsizes. In other words, a freaking disaster."

"Did you just say *freaking?* My word, I am rubbing off on you. And I thought I knew all your nautical terms." She laughed a bit. "That sounds like what's been going on since you stepped foot on the dock in Maryland. Yes, sir, a vanishing angle is heading right for us. My Jeep certainly capsized. It's totaled, but luckily I'm not going to have to pay for it. Hope I can pull all this off on my end."

"You can. You always come through."

"All I want is a nice warm beach and a hotel with a king-size bed. And you."

"Sounds good. After I take down Petrov, that's what we'll do."

"He's only a part of the whole. This is bigger than him."

"Not to me, it isn't. He was going to kill you in that Jeep. He killed that boy without blinking an eye. He's got to pay for that."

"Wait, you're not saying you're going to murder him, right? I misunderstood that."

"I'm telling you that I'm going to stop him, no matter what it takes."

"Bring him in. He'll rot in a federal prison for the rest of his life if he doesn't get the death penalty. Better yet, let the Russians have him. They won't go easy, let me tell you."

Novak kept quiet. He'd have liked to see Petrov in the ground. He had wreaked havoc on more innocent people than they'd ever know, and for decades. He'd always escaped punishment. Not this time.

"You know, Novak, I hate the thought of visiting you in jail for the next thirty years. It would put a crimp in my love life."

Novak smiled. "I won't go to jail. I'll sail into the sunset before they catch me."

"I hope you get out of this thing in one piece. So what are your plans when you get to Nantucket?"

"I'm going to case out the island, find whatever warehouse Blackwood's using. I'd blow it to hell if it wasn't full of evidence. I'll leave capturing the good senator on his luxury yacht up to the Coast Guard."

"All that sounds so sweet to my ears. Just watch your back. Or let Sokolov help you."

"I told him to stay put and protect those girls. They're both eyewitnesses to Blackwood and Petrov's crimes. We need them safe and sound so they'll agree to testify. Sokolov wants payback for those guys, so he'll definitely keep them safe."

"Hang in. All we need are some high-ranking signatures and a good plan in place before we move."

"Just give me time to get up there. Stall your boss if you have to."

"That I know how to do. Be careful, Novak. I mean it. And keep me informed so I'll know you're still breathing."

"You got it. Ditto."

They hung up, and Novak felt much better. He turned his gaze to the north horizon. Even with refueling stops and managing to get some sleep, he just might make it up there in excellent time. Any change in the fair weather or a mechanical breakdown would be calamitous. Time would tell, but he was praying for clear skies and favorable winds.

Everything did go exceptionally well. Weather, boat, and wind held up for most of the next week, and the blue hump of Nantucket Island showed up on the horizon one week and seventeen hours later at midmorning. He had only been to the island one other time, and had stayed for only a day or two. He remembered the marina he'd used and how to get to it, but there were marinas everywhere, most of which had whole colonies of sailboats anchored in the deep water off their slips. He wanted to approach on the south shore and drop anchor at a marina across the island from Blackwood's place—just a bit of caution on his part—but he didn't like to take chances. He felt it unlikely that Blackwood's people could be watching every boat dock on the island. On the other hand, bad luck often happened of the blue.

Novak felt confident he could get there undetected and rent a car. The marina where he was heading used to have a few on hand for their customers. Things had gone well so far, but in Novak's world, this run of good luck would not last. Now everything depended on how careful Petrov was. From what Novak had seen, it seemed that Petrov put his personal security before everything else. He was the man running things on the island. So he would be out and about. Novak had to keep his head down and stay alert. Petrov was a formidable enemy, something that Novak had to remember.

When he got closer to the cove where he'd anchored before, he called the marina there, owned by a man named Hap Carlton. He was a friendly older fellow whom Novak remembered and liked well enough. He requested a spot out in the water among the other anchored sailboats. He arrived there without incident, dropped anchor, and took time to batten everything down. He set his usual booby trap alarms so he'd know if anyone had been aboard, steered the Zodiac into a slip near the office, and settled up his tab in advance. Hap Carlton was working the desk and was pleased to rent out an older model Oldsmobile that he'd bought years ago. So far, so good.

Nantucket Island lay about thirty miles off the southern coastline of Cape Cod, Massachusetts, an old whaling port that had been famous back in its day. The island was still as colorful and quaint as it probably had been in the past, but now it was trendy and hip with bookstores, restaurants, and cozy streets that took visitors back in time. It was a beautiful storybook setting, with its gray-and-white shingled houses built up on the hills over rugged white beaches strewn with seaweed, driftwood, and shells. The trees had turned, and the hills were vivid with fall colors and bright chrysanthemums in all the window boxes.

Nobody paid any attention to him as he got into the car and found his way to Polpis Road, which ran along the Nantucket Sound. It passed a lot of nice places edging the sea, and Novak had no trouble locating the heavily fortified gate that blocked off the entrance road to Blackwood's compound. He drove past it, pulling over a quarter of a mile or so farther along. He drove the car into a thicket of wind-stunted pine trees, grabbed the backpack holding his gear, and headed up an overgrown hiking trail that meandered its way over a gentle rise.

A few minutes later he came out on a spectacular view of Nantucket Sound. Below him, a deserted rock-strewn beach stretched out in both directions. The waves were coming in heavy, with whitecaps dotting the ocean all the way to the horizon. A storm was brewing out there, one he was glad the *Sweet Sarah* had missed. He hoped the worst of it skirted around the island. No one was on the beach or in the water, probably because the water was cold. He could see the neighbors' houses, all gray-and-white with window boxes, stacked like blocks up the hill. Blackwood's stood off by itself on a point that jutted out farther than the rest of the coastline.

The surf was coming in high and dangerous, not to mention thunderous, with rip tides he could see in the crashing waves. The surf bombarded the sand and encroached on the docks that lay at various spots along the beach. Far out on the horizon, he could see the storm was a bad one, with dark clouds gathering and spears of lightning forking down into the sea like crystal arrows. He was going to get wet before this day was done. There was a trail along the crest, but it was overgrown with weeds and straggling bushes. He noticed some wind-twisted trees dotting the slope down near the water that he could use for cover. With binoculars he could see Blackwood's house clearly. It was also gray-and-white, enclosed by a rock wall that had probably been stretching across that ridge for more than a century. Blackwood's compound had a larger dock than the other houses. He had a pretty good idea what that dock was used for. Novak found a spot behind some bushes and retrieved his field glasses from the backpack. He focused them on the house. He estimated it was maybe sixty yards away from his position. It was identical to most Nantucket homes, only bigger. It had several outbuildings inside that wall. Novak figured the place had once been a prosperous farm or some kind of lookout point. Now it appeared to be a nice warm little drug den befitting a dirty, corrupt former senator from Virginia. Little did Blackwood's neighbors know that the big gray house and matching garage probably held a multimillion dollar stash of opioids, heroin, cocaine, and deadly fentanyl. No telling how many teenagers on this island and in neighboring Massachusetts had died from what had once been stored inside that compound.

There were a few guards loitering about, but not as many as he had figured. They were dressed as day workers or handymen, but every single one was armed. Their weapons rested in leather holsters in open carry. They did not look like Secret Service agents, though. These were private bodyguards. They strolled around the property, sitting on the wall to smoke cigarettes or lounging on one of the three porches. They were not expecting trouble. Nobody walked the beach, which Novak found ridiculous. That's where he expected their shipments came in, most likely late at night, just like the rum smugglers had done it in the old days. No way could they risk bringing product in on ferries or at the airport. The drugs traveled north, boat-to-boat from Cuba, and this is where they ended up, right down there on that dock.

Novak made his way closer, keeping out of sight as best he could. The hill was grassy, the land uneven and rocky, and there weren't many trees that had stood up strong against the pounding sea winds. He wanted to get a bead on the far side of the house. When he couldn't get close enough without being spotted, he returned to the Olds and drove past the driveway in the opposite direction. He gained a similar viewpoint on the rise on the other side, and that's when he discovered the steps that led from that tiny beach below the compound up to the buildings above. They were steep and wound around a bit, and would not be difficult to ascend with bags of drugs unloaded at the beach, which he assumed was how they did it. He had a feeling Lori might be watching him right now on one of those big military satellites used at the Pentagon. If she was, they would also be able to watch the drug shipments coming in. He wanted to get closer, but would have to wait for nightfall.

He holed up in a little dip in the slope that hid him from the guards, but he stayed alert, hoping Petrov didn't have foot patrols walking the sand. While he waited, he went through various scenarios on how he could destroy the operation and get Petrov at the same time. He hadn't seen him yet, but it was only a matter of time. Sokolov said he was coming up there, and that he ran things inside that compound. Dark seemed to take forever to fall, but Novak stayed put, eyes peeled for any incoming boats, though he was pretty sure he wouldn't get that lucky. If they made transfers along the coast every other day, and he knew they did, it stood to reason that a shipment would arrive here just as often. He wanted to blow the entire place to hell, but he couldn't or he'd give the bigger bust away. He couldn't take down anybody until Lori's people pulled the trigger on the comprehensive takedown. He didn't like waiting for them to get their act together, as that meant more time for things to go wrong. He had enough C-4 with him to blow everything to smithereens inside that rock wall, and everything in him wanted to destroy every inch of the place, but he would wait for Lori's go-ahead.

That didn't mean he couldn't be impatient.

Chapter 23

Dusk crept across the water like an intruder in dark attire, and the day slowly went to black. Stars appeared, bright pinpoints in the heavens, white crystals scattered on beds of coal. The sea was magnificent, with a beauty that never failed to strike awe in Novak. Nantucket Island was a gorgeous place. Far out on the horizon, the electrical storm still marched toward him in its throes of atmospheric rage. Lightning bolts struck the sea, one after another, as if Zeus and Thor and Odin were all hurling their weapons at the earth. The dark sky lit up in quick three-second intervals, backlighting mounding clouds before the charged electricity danced its way across the horizon.

Novak was glad he could watch the approaching gale from where he sat, and not in his boat navigating through those turbulent, stormy waves. He heard thunder, low and rumbling, and hoped it came no closer. When it was dark enough to move around without detection, he stood, slipped on his backpack, and focused his night-vision glasses on the compound. It looked nice and quiet and deserted inside that low stone wall. He could not see the guards now. No one was down on the beach, due to the storm winds and heavy surf. High tide was coming in fast, and the strip of sand below Blackwood's property had disappeared under rising water. He couldn't scale the hill to the wall without detection, so he was going to try to make it to the steps. That meant entering the water and swimming around the craggy rock outcropping impeding his way. The boardwalk to the beach was not affected; it looked like the perfect place to tie up a boat and unload drugs. The moon was out but obscured by rain clouds, keeping things nice and dark. That was good. He descended the slope, keeping low, trying to get a better vantage point. He wanted to know if Petrov was inside. He had yet to see him.

Removing the gear he would need from the backpack, he secured all of it inside a waterproof bag and waded out into the shallows. The water was cold, a little wild, but it pushed him down where he wanted to go in a hurry. He swam up to the lower part where the boardwalk was already submerged, got atop it, and squatted there, watching for guards at the top of the stairs. Nobody was outside the wall in that area. The lack of security gave him concern. It didn't sound like Petrov to leave the place this vulnerable. From what Sokolov had told him, the man was never nonchalant about his personal security. He waited a few more minutes, watching and listening, then removed his gun, racked a round, and took his flashlight before quickly climbing to the top.

Once he was outside the wall and hunkered down, he found the gate in front of him had a lock. Novak had no trouble picking it. Afraid of hidden alarms, he felt around the edges of the gate for wires, finding none. The people inside had to feel less than secure with this kind of protection. He saw no security cameras either, only a few lampposts here and there.

Unlatching the gate, he ducked through quickly and got down inside the shadows against the wall. He waited for a hidden alarm to scream his presence. Nothing. All he could hear was the roar of the ocean below him, as well as the insane flapping of an American flag attacked by stormwinds. High tide was encroaching behind him, rising slowly on the steps. The storm was getting closer.

Still, there were no guards anywhere to be seen. He stayed where he was a few more minutes. Lori's satellite image of the compound had been clear about the arrangement of the structures inside the wall. There was the typical Nantucket house, big with two stories and lots of paned windows facing the sea. It stood dark and quiet, with no lights on inside. There was a big garage, some kind of storage shed adjacent to it, but he couldn't see anyone around anywhere. Where had the guards gone? Maybe he was wrong about this place. Maybe they stored the drugs somewhere else on the island. He kept his weapon up and ready. Three dusk-to-dawn lights threw off some pools of light, but it was easy to avoid. The wind was obstructing any noise he might be making. The yard had more sand than grass, but had been partially sodded in the backyard.

Novak crept down the wall until he got closer to the big house. The tarmac driveway came in at the front gate and curved up to the front of the house. He found the first guard standing in front of the barn, under a light over the door. He was young, early twenties, maybe even younger, just a kid. Novak pegged him for a boy who'd grown up on the island and was out there making pocket money. He did not look like a professional, not even close. When he walked toward the house, Novak realized he wore a red football-letter jacket with award patches sewn on the sleeve. He sat down on the front steps of the house and lit up a joint. Novak could smell the smoke from where he was hiding. If Petrov was hiring these kinds of guards, he was losing his edge. Maybe he was a night watchman, and Petrov brought along his own bodyguards. Still, it was strange, and made him second-guess whether the drugs were really stored there.

Making his way around the house, he was certain Petrov was not in residence yet. He should have been, according to Sokolov, which again put Sokolov's story in doubt. Out back, he found one light burning inside. It looked like it was over the kitchen sink. The place looked empty as far as Novak could tell, but the house was a big rambling place with lots of rooms. The second floor was all dark, but the place was big enough to house a lot of people. So where was Petrov? He had flown out of Key West more than a week ago. Lori had checked. He could have been staying somewhere else on the island. Maybe the compound wasn't the right place, after all. Sokolov could have been lying. Maybe they stored the product in a warehouse on one of the wharves. That seemed more dangerous than up here on their private property, unless the island's law enforcement had been paid off. Now that the DEA and Coast Guard were about to get involved at Lori's end, he wanted to take Petrov down before all hell broke loose up and down the coast.

It could be that Petrov had found out Sokolov was double-crossing him. Maybe he had somehow gotten the location of the two girls and was on his way to Quebec. That made sense to Novak. This pipeline had worked well for years, so they had to have a way of gathering intelligence. If they'd caught up to Sokolov, he was already dead, and the girls would be soon. Or Sokolov could have unwittingly led them straight to that convent. Novak didn't like to think that had happened, but something was wrong.

Lori was still tracking Petrov with the GPS device in his backpack. She had called Novak just the night before with news that Petrov had flown north, with several stops to meet with couriers along the way. They were getting addresses left and right from his visits, so those couriers would go down soon. Then he'd stopped in Atlantic City and Newport, Rhode Island. She was encouraged, thinking they had eyes on all the couriers now. Her last text that morning had placed Petrov landing at Logan Airport in Boston. Novak had felt certain the man had been heading to Nantucket. So where had he gone? The delay put a crimp in Novak's plans and Lori's, too, because she was waiting for him to get Petrov before she gave the all-clear for the comprehensive bust at all fronts.

Undecided on how to proceed, Novak decided he needed a peek inside the barn. If it was their drug warehouse, he wanted to know it. The Feds could get a warrant for the compound, but it would take time. It would be nice for them to know it was full to the eaves with illegal drugs. He looked out at the dark ocean, and could still see lightning forking down into the waves. The surf was roaring below him now, and he felt the first sprinkles of rain. If Petrov didn't show soon, Novak needed to go find him. It sounded like he was the only person still in the wind. Lori had located nearly everyone else involved in Petrov's drug operation.

The unexpected delay gave him time to check out the barn. When he found the doors unlocked, he knew it wouldn't be the main depot. He ducked inside and shined his flashlight around the interior. It looked as if they used it strictly for a garage for when the Senator was here with his entourage. It had a concrete floor, and the air inside smelled like motor oil. He saw no indication of drugs, but found a storeroom located at the back. Inside, the shelves were filled with canned goods and cases of bottled water, sodas, and beer. That didn't mean there wasn't a trapdoor somewhere inside the place, but he didn't have time to search for it—he heard vehicles approaching. He dropped down and froze. That was bound to be Petrov. He had to get out of that barn, and fast. He eased through the front door, where he saw the young guard now standing up and walking toward the locked driveway gate to the inner sanctum. Over the top of the wall, Novak could see headlights that were reflecting off the windows of the house. There were two cars, both coming fast.

Novak took cover behind some firewood stacked at one side of the house. He barely made it there before the gate opened and the cars rolled inside, stopping in front of the house. He kept his finger near the trigger, his nerves jumping. After that, everything happened so fast. The first vehicle was a black Ford SUV with Massachusetts license plates; the second was a Chevy Blazer, also with state plates. The cars looked shiny and brand-new, and Novak figured they were island rentals or maybe Blackwood's personal transportation, seeing how he was a permanent resident.

Novak peered through a space between the logs where he could see the front of the house. Two armed guards climbed out of the first vehicle. Petrov emerged from the back seat behind the driver's side. Novak stiffened when he saw the second man. Stepan Sokolov got out and waited for Petrov to come around the hood and join him. Novak could not believe it. He frowned. Had Sokolov duped Novak again? His jaw clamped tight, and he felt like a fool. He had never been an easy man to trick, but Sokolov had played him twice.

It took momentous effort not to lift his weapon and shoot them both where they stood. He heaved in a couple of bracing breaths and forced himself back under steely control. He kept his eyes glued on the second SUV, now fearing that Irina and Katerina would be dragged out and forced into the house. It didn't happen. Four more men got out of the Blazer and assumed positions around the house and barn. The two Russians walked down to the barn together, chatting as if close comrades, and disappeared inside the front door. Every nerve in Novak twitched to come out firing and put everybody down. He shook the urge away; he knew that would be suicide, that it would endanger the coming bust. He struggled to get his emotions in check. He had to be smarter than that. If he reacted angrily or rashly, he would probably die. So he stayed where he was and waited for his opportunity.

The compound had gotten busy. The pothead kid had disappeared. Novak wasn't worried about him. He watched Petrov's men open the trunk of the second car and unload several suitcases that Novak assumed to be crammed with pills and heroin. Maybe he had been wrong about the drugs coming in off the water. Maybe they brought them in by ferry, in plain view of all the other wealthy people who made their home in the gray-and-white, shingled and flower-bedecked cottages. Charles Blackwood was an exalted senator—who would suspect he had crawled out of hell? He was probably at the top of Nantucket's Who's Who list. Or maybe they transported it in both ways: courier boats in the dead of night and suitcases full on the ferry. He maneuvered himself to a better position and snapped photos. His two targets had come out of the barn now, standing in an elongated rectangle of white light flooding out the barn doors. They stood there a while chatting together, as the guards carried several suitcases into the barn. Another guy took two smaller bags into the house, one of which was Petrov's bugged backpack. Lights started coming on in the windows.

Outside, the activity waned as everybody headed into the house. One guard stayed behind at the barn, and another stood in front of the house. The cars remained parked in the driveway. The rain was still holding off, so Novak contemplated getting another look inside the barn. He wanted to know what was in the luggage taken inside. He couldn't risk it yet. Now his main desire was getting his hands around Sokolov's throat and choking answers out of him. The fact that the girls were no longer with him did not look particularly good for their health. They were both probably dead, either buried in shallow graves or wrapped in chains and dropped overboard. The visual got to Novak. He had made a terrible mistake in judgment that had cost those girls their lives. Hidden in deep shadow, he tried to decide on his best option. The coastal sting was coming, but not just yet. If Lori had a hand in coordinating the takedown, it would come off without a hitch. She was that good. His only worry was the number of federal agencies involved, and the possibility of a snitch getting word to Blackwood and Petrov. Right now, he wanted Sokolov so bad he could taste it. The man was good at lying, but why wouldn't he be? He had lasted as a spy for years before he'd given it up. This time he had either double-crossed Novak or Petrov, or played them both for fools. Sokolov was slick and dirty and would pay for his betrayal, hopefully tonight.

Novak shook his head, remembering how loving Sokolov had been with Katerina. He was her father. He had to be. They knew each other that night. He wanted to believe that she was safe somewhere, that Sokolov was playing Petrov, but it was getting hard to convince himself of it. He needed to question Sokolov before he put a bullet in his brain. He needed to get him out of that house alone. They had no idea Novak was on the property, not yet. Maybe he could get into the house, find the guy, and make him tell him where the girls were.

Watching the windows, he could see a man preparing food inside the kitchen. The other guards were sitting at a table in front of a long set of casement windows. Neither Petrov nor Sokolov were with them. After a while, the man standing at the barn was relieved, and the new guard said something to him in Russian. The other man laughed with him. Novak couldn't understand everything he'd said, but he knew they were talking about women. They chatted and smoked cigarettes, on all accounts seeming to feel safe and secure. *Good,* he thought, *let them get comfortable.*

After a while, the first man walked inside and sat down with the others. He could hear them laughing and talking. When they started eating, things got quiet until three other guys came outside and took up positions along the wall, two in front and one at the back gate. The one in back strolled along the wall's perimeter and watched the waves crashing below. The others kept their attention on the entrance road. Unfortunately for Petrov, nobody seemed to consider that an armed intruder might already be inside the walls.

Not long after, Novak moved to a position closer to the house. He found a concealed spot where he could watch the back door. Only one lamppost was out there and he could avoid it. Sokolov had a habit of smoking a special brand of Turkish cigarettes right before he went to bed. He had done it every night that he'd been with Novak. So maybe Novak would get lucky and the man would do it tonight. He settled down, well-hidden, listening to the rhythmic beat of the surf, and waiting for Sokolov to appear. He kept his gun ready; he knew he would come. He tried to remain loose and relaxed and ready to move, hoping the Russian would exit through the back door and walk down into the yard. That's what he usually did. Novak could take care of him there with nobody the wiser.

Almost an hour later, Novak got his wish. Sokolov exited the back door, crossed the open porch and descended to the yard. He stopped at the bottom of the steps and lit his cigarette. Novak could see his face clearly in the flare of his lighter. The familiar smell of that strong, potent tobacco wafted out to him. It was an unpleasant odor, and it clung to Sokolov's clothing all the time. Novak would have recognized it anywhere. After a moment, Sokolov strolled down a sandy path toward the seawall. Novak followed him. Once he was within a couple of yards, Sokolov sensed his presence. He swung around and came face to face with Novak. His gaze dropped to the gun Novak held pointed at his heart. He dropped his cigarette and lighter, holding up both palms in front of him, a defensive stance that would not stop Novak's bullet. The Russian's voice was a frightened whisper. "Wait, Novak, this isn't what you think."

"I think it is. Where are the girls? Did you kill them or did he?"

"They're safe, I swear to God, they are." He looked back at the house, keeping his voice low. "I'm not back with Petrov. For God's sake, Novak, you've got to listen. I didn't know where you were, but I figured you'd come out here alone. I knew you'd need my help. I've been trying to spot you since we got off the ferry. We've been down at their depot. I can give you the name of the street. I've got it all down in my phone. I swear to God that's the truth. Look, he's got too many guards out here for you to shoot me and get away alive. You need me. I'm on your side, I swear to God. You've got to believe me."

"You really think I'm that stupid? I know a double-cross when I see one."

"I double-crossed him, not you. They're on to you, man. Petrov put out a hit on you the minute I got you out of that hospital. I can't believe you came out here alone. That's crazy, man. You'll never get out of here alive."

"I got in. I can get out."

"The guys we brought in. They're trained mercs out of Moscow. Don't underestimate them."

"Where's Petrov?"

"Asleep, I guess. He was up all night down at the warehouse. Look, you've got to believe me. You need me to get this done. Did you get the names of all the couriers?"

Novak had never completely trusted this guy, but somehow he wanted to believe him again. What was the matter with him?

"You want Vasily? Is that it? I can deliver him to you. Just say the word."

"Who's down there?"

They both jerked around at the sound of the guard's voice. A man was heading down the path toward them. Novak ducked back behind a tree and got ready to put him down. Sokolov stood where he was and called out the man's name.

"It's me, Dmitri. Stepan Sokolov. I'm just having a smoke before I turn in."

"I thought I heard voices."

"No, I'm out here alone. Probably just the wind whistling. Sorry to alert you. I'm about ready to go back inside."

The guard looked around. He hesitated. "Okay, no problem."

The guard turned and walked back toward the barn. Novak waited where he was, but the guy didn't come back. No alarm was raised.

"Do you believe me now?" Sokolov whispered.

Novak stood up and faced the Russian, not sure what to believe.

"It would have been easy for me to point you out just now. Why wouldn't I if I wanted you dead? I'm still on your side. I always have been. How could you doubt me after what they did to my Katerina?"

Novak began to waver. It was not easy for him to believe the guy. He kept his voice low. "Why are you here with him? Where are the girls? You were supposed to take care of them."

"They're safe at the convent, just like I told you. Both of them are fine. I came down here to help you. I told you I wanted to when I left, because I knew you'd be in trouble if you came alone. Why else would I be here?"

"You tell me."

"Is the sting happening?"

Novak wasn't going to tell this man what was about to go down.

"Look, I've got a GPS tracker on Petrov's car now," Sokolov went on. "I'm traveling with him because I don't want him to get away. I know where he's headed from here. He's taking me with him, and you can follow us. He's got a cabin up in the Maine woods, somewhere close to the Canadian border. He always stops there and picks up his false ID, and then goes to a safehouse he's got in Quebec City. That's your best chance to get him when he's alone. He never takes anybody with him into Canada. That's an old KGB route across the border. I know exactly where it is, because I've used it."

"You really think I'm just going to forget all this and trust you, Sokolov?"

"Why didn't I just give you up a minute ago?"

"Probably because I would have shot you dead before they got me."

"Then don't follow us up there. Let me kill him myself once we get out in the woods alone. If I'm taken into custody here in the U.S, I'll never see Katerina again. She'll be stuck in that convent forever. I'm wanted by your government, as you well know, just like Petrov is." He glanced back at the house and reached into his pocket. Novak's finger moved to the trigger, but the Russian only withdrew a cellphone. "Here, take this. It's got his GPS trackers on it. It's a burner, but it'll lead you right to Petrov's backpack if you go after him. I've got the addresses of his safehouses listed on there, too. I took pictures of the dealers we met in New England the past few days, and everybody else I came across who were helping him. Here, take it. Send the data to your girlfriend. I've got to get back inside before Petrov comes looking for me. He's already suspicious."

Novak took the burner and watched Sokolov hurry back to the house. He waited to see if he gave the alarm. Nothing happened, so Novak watched the guard move out in the other direction. He ran for the wall, scaled it in a hurry, and got the hell out of that compound while he still could.

Chapter 24

Novak wasted no time getting back to *Sweet Sarah*. He pulled up Petrov's GPS signals and found them blinking, still at the compound. Taking Sokolov's burner phone, he went through the files and found it had everything the Russian had said would be there. It also had the address of the warehouse where the drugs were stored on Nantucket, and pictures of Petrov inside overseeing the shipments. Novak felt better now that he was in possession of the new information, but was still uneasy. Sokolov always had an answer for everything. This time Novak wanted to believe he now had important evidence that Lori could use, but only if it turned out to be true.

Novak had never been one to trust on blind faith, and only did so if he knew the person to be honest. He rarely relied on anybody, and certainly not on a short-term acquaintance. Despite all his misgivings, he found himself wanting to believe Sokolov yet again, when he probably should have never trusted him. He delved into the phone's information once more, realizing it held clear and incriminating photographic proof of drugs and money changing hands. That's when he texted all the addresses and pictures to Lori. It didn't take long for her to get back to him. Fifteen minutes later, his cellphone vibrated.

"Hey, you get those goodies I sent you?"

"You bet, I got them. Wow, Novak—why didn't you just send me this stuff in the first place? Would've saved me some serious time."

"I just got it from Sokolov. He showed up at the compound. I confronted him, thinking he had double-crossed us, but he says he's still playing Petrov."

A couple of beats passed before she spoke. "Well, is he playing him or not? He could be playing us. If that's the case, I can't rely on distributing this information to law enforcement."

"I'm not a hundred percent positive one way or the other. He's smart, crafty. He could be lying. But I feel like he's telling me the truth. Guess we'll figure that out once you verify what he gave us."

"I'll send it along to the appropriate people and tell them we think it's above board. That's all I'm willing to do. We're getting closer now to shutting this thing down for good. Some of the mules live in small communities inland from the coast. We've got to get local law officers lined up to raid them, take them in, and let some of our guys pick them up later. That will delay the takedown here."

"For how long?"

"A few days, probably not more than that."

"Good. They've got drugs up here, too, in that warehouse. I couldn't find any at the compound, but it's worth getting a search warrant for the house and barn."

"What did Sokolov say about Irina? Is she all right?"

"He swears she's safe at some convent, and so is Katerina. I think they're both in Canada, probably Quebec City. I'm following Petrov and Sokolov when they leave the island. He told me Petrov's got a cabin in Maine. He seems to think it's not a drug house, but a safe place for Petrov to hide out when he crosses the border or goes on the run."

"Where is it exactly? Want me to arrange backup for you out there?"

"Not sure yet. It's supposed to be a place the Russians have used for years, close to the Canadian border crossing. They used it to get in and out of the U.S. with false credentials. He gave me the means to follow them, so I'm going to. The cabin sounds like a good place for us to take Petrov down. He won't expect anybody to know where it is. Sokolov says Petrov never told anyone for fear of a CIA mole or a double-cross. He trusts Sokolov because of their past association."

"Okay. Good God, Novak, just be careful and don't get yourself killed. I'll let you know when we're ready to pull the trigger."

"Stay right where you are, Lori. These people are ruthless. Let other people do the dirty work this time. You stay safe and sound inside the Pentagon building and surround yourself with guards."

"I will, Novak, unlike you, always running toward danger." She laughed softly. "One thing for certain, nobody's going to get hold of me down here in the bowels of the Pentagon complex. I'm coordinating things, but my general is looking over my shoulder night and day. It's in his best interest that this thing doesn't go belly up."

"Stay there, please. I don't want to worry about you getting shot again."

"Hey, Novak." She lowered her voice. "I know I say it a thousand times, but don't get killed. I want to go back to St. Barths. We had a fine time there, remember that?"

"I remember. We'll do it again. Keep me posted, and watch your back."

Novak hung up. He stretched out on the stern bench with Sokolov's phone still open on Petrov's GPS signals. He fell asleep out in the cool night air, and didn't awake until cold raindrops spattered his face. He moved under the canopy as the downpour started in earnest, and rechecked the signals. There was no movement yet, and the marina around him lay dark and quiet.

He was up again just before daylight. The rain had let up, and the wind had died down during the early morning hours. The boat rocked gently on waves coming in from turbulence out on the open water, but the swath of thunder and lightning had veered out into the Atlantic away from Nantucket. The remnants of the storm were deluging the north part of the island. He brewed and drank a pot of coffee, then ate some toast. He was cleaning up when a text came in on Sokolov's burner phone. Sokolov warned him that he and Petrov were flying up to Portland, Maine that afternoon, where they would rent a car and drive north to Canada. He added in a second text that allowed Novak to follow their GPS signals, verifying their travel route.

That left Novak undecided about what to do. Almost everything Sokolov said or did from the beginning made Novak feel twitchy, but not enough to ignore their travel plans. He had to follow them, and he had to be careful.

After pulling down ocean charts and checking weather patterns and tides, he decided that sailing to Portland would be too time-consuming. The quickest voyage he drew up was nearly thirty-six hours on the water, so he decided to leave *Sweet Sarah* right there in Hap's marina and fly out. He wanted to arrive in Maine before the two Russians, so he took the first available ferry across to Cape Cod. He needed to beat them there, rent a car, and be ready to trail them up through Maine. If it turned out that Sokolov was lying, Novak had decided to take that risk.

Novak called Lori and asked her to arrange the flight out of Cape Cod to Portland, and check flight manifests for Graham Turner, which was Sokolov's American alias, something else he'd found in that burner phone. Not long after that, she called back with Novak's plane ticket and arrangements for a four-wheel drive truck to be waiting for him at the Portland airport. More important, she reported that two men, one under the name of Graham Turner, the other under Joseph Lorde, had seats together aboard a plane leaving three hours after Novak's flight took off. So Joseph Lorde was Petrov's cover identity. He could beat them up there with plenty of time to get ready before following them up to that cabin. He felt relieved, and was very grateful for Lori's help. She went on to say that her people were going to spring the bust in forty-eight hours, at 5:00 a.m., EST. He was pleased it was happening so fast, but it meant the capture of Petrov would be his solo responsibility. He relished the idea of bringing that killer in.

Four hours later, he sat in a Ram pickup truck at a Subway parking lot near the ramp that would take him onto Highway 201 and eventually up into Canada. He kept a close eye on their GPS signals. So far, they were doing exactly what Sokolov had said they would. When he saw they were on the 201, he waited about ten minutes before driving up the ramp and following them. Of course, he didn't know if it was them inside that car. It could have been somebody else carrying Petrov's backpack. He was going on nothing but trust now, something he knew he should never do with Stepan Sokolov. For all he knew, this car could have been a diversion and the two Russians could be long gone.

Novak kept following them. He would soon see if he was being played for a fool. The Atlantic storms had brought a cold front that swept into the whole of New England, so he had on a down jacket he'd purchased at the airport. He had also filled his backpack with everything he figured he'd need if he had to go it alone in Canada. He kept the GPS up and running, keeping a close eye on it. They were still traveling north, right at the speed limit, still ahead of him on Highway 201. They were within twenty miles of the border now.

After a while, he watched the GPS signal for a turn off the highway. It came not long after they hung a right on a rural state road. That's when Novak knew for sure they were heading for the cabin. They had a good reason for going there, or Petrov wouldn't have taken the time. Something had to be going on in the deep woods, and Novak didn't like to think what it might be. He hoped they hadn't stashed the two girls out there. The idea was alarming. He pressed down on the accelerator, but kept it just over the speed limit. He did not want to get pulled over and ticketed. That would waste time, and he could lose them.

Both sides of the highway were cloaked by seemingly impenetrable hardwood forests, the brilliant leaves dulled under cloudy skies and wet weather. The tops of the trees tossed violently under strong westerly winds. Leaves fluttered over the roadway and hit his windshield, and he had to avoid several broken limbs lying out in the highway. He passed a couple of pit stops with gas stations and fast food joints, and a few small towns that weren't much more than spots in the road.

Right after they'd driven through a fairly good-sized town, Petrov turned again and headed off on a road that was not named on the map. Novak knew it had to lead into the cabin. He reached that turnoff point about fifteen minutes after Petrov. There was an old rusted mailbox lying on the ground. It had been broken off halfway up the post, probably by kids driving along, knocking it down with a baseball bat. Most of the writing was scratched out, but he could still see the last name: Adams. Novak slowed down, turned, and stopped. He let his truck idle just off the highway. Their signal had stopped, and not too far into the treeline. Novak had to be cautious now— Petrov would be watching for tails, and could have set up booby traps or cameras. The man was paranoid, and that penchant had kept him walking free for decades. He would know how to protect himself.

Novak pulled back out and drove maybe half a mile before he found a similar logging road that headed back into the same tract of woods. It looked unpassable, clogged with overgrown bushes and brambles. He pulled in far enough to conceal the truck in a thicket of pine trees. Climbing out, he donned the backpack, and started through the woods on foot. He hadn't gone thirty yards before he heard the crack of a gunshot. He dropped down instinctively and drew his weapon. There was no second shot, but he could hear the sound of a car starting up. Within seconds, he saw a black Ford Explorer barreling into sight a good distance away, headed back to the highway. Novak stayed low until it roared out onto the main road in a squealing, skidding turn. Only the driver was inside, but he couldn't tell if it was Petrov or Sokolov.

If it was Petrov and he was alone, that meant Sokolov was stranded at the cabin, or they kept a spare vehicle out there. Novak's gut told him Sokolov was out there and in big trouble. He took off running through the tree trunks, angling in toward the parallel road, tripping on tangled vines and fighting sharp sticker bushes that tore at his clothes. When he gained the other road, he stopped and listened. Nothing moved—no birdsong, no traffic sounds filtering from the highway, nothing. He took off for the log cabin sitting alone in the distance. All he heard was the wind crackling through branches far above him and the crunch of rocks and dead leaves as he ran through them. The house was small and built of logs, sitting in a hardscrabble, rocky clearing. There were no paths, walks, or driveway, just that rocky road. There were no cars, either. The place looked deserted and closed up. He hunkered down again and watched, not sure who or what might be waiting inside. He wasn't optimistic that it would be anything good for his health.

The front door was standing open. He ducked down and ran up to the side of the front porch. No one appeared, so he inched up to the door and ventured a quick peek inside. He kept his weapon up, ready to return fire. Inside the one big room, Stepan Sokolov was lying on the floor, his sweatshirt soaked through with blood. He appeared to be trying to make it to the door, a gun clutched in his hand. He was conscious. He struggled to turn on his side, and pointed his weapon at Novak. Novak ducked down, but Sokolov didn't fire.

"Help me." His words caught in his throat, and he rolled back onto his stomach, groaning in agony.

Novak knelt down beside him and shrugged off his backpack. He could already see torn flesh, and the gaping exit wound on Sokolov's upper back. It hadn't hit the spine, or the man would be dead. Blood was pooling beneath him, but the bullet had missed his heart. Novak shifted him on his side and pulled up the sweatshirt. A pulsating crimson stream poured from the single bullet hole in his upper torso. He was bleeding out and fast. There was so much blood now that Novak feared he was already too late to save him. It depended on what internal organs had been hit.

Jerking gauze bandages out of his backpack, he tore off the wrappers and held a wad of them tightly against the wounds. Then he started wrapping long strips of gauze around Sokolov's chest, trying to slow the bleeding. Sokolov writhed with every touch, now only half-conscious. "I've got morphine, Sokolov. I'm going to give you a shot of it and get an ambulance out here."

"It's no use…too much blood…I'm dead…" He was weak, but he caught hold of Novak's sleeve. "Promise me…promise you'll get him, promise me…He's going after Katerina. Don't let him get her…"

"You're not gonna die. Just lie still." Novak finished taping the makeshift bandage in place, then dialed 911, telling them about the morphine and describing the old mailbox he'd seen out on the road as their turn-off point. The operator wanted him to stay on the line, but he hung up. "They'll be here in minutes, Sokolov. They'll get you to an ER and into surgery, and you'll be fine. We're not that far out of town. You'll going to make it. Lie still and try to calm down or you'll bleed out faster."

Sokolov wasn't calming down. He was working himself up into a panic. "He's going after Katerina…He knows where I took them. He's going to kill them."

"How does he know?"

"I don't know. They're at the convent…go quick…"

"Why'd he turn on you? Does he know you're working with me, that I'm following him?"

Sokolov shook his head. His eyelids were squeezed tight, his groans terrible now. "He made an excuse to stop here and then he just shot me… said I was a witness…Nobody would've ever found me." He stopped there, trying to breathe, then roused up again urgently. "I should've known he'd do this. He's tying up loose ends…thinks things are going to hell because you're after him. He's killing anybody who can identify him."

"Where's he headed after Canada?"

"Damascus."

"Where are the girls? You gotta tell me, Sokolov, or they'll end up dead. I've got to get to them first."

"Quebec City…the old convent…he's headed there, but I don't think he knows where they are…but he can find out. He's got friends…You've got to stop him."

"What contacts? Who?"

"Russians, still up there…He'll find her…they're with one of them." He stopped again, panting heavily now. "The border's not far…go now and you can get him before he crosses. You can't get through the border…with the gun…leave it. I got a safe house…near Old Town. Look in the burner for address…weapons there…codes for house…everything." He stopped, his breathing hitched on what Novak feared was his last breath, but then spoke again. "Go, go…"

"I'm not leaving you until the ambulance gets here."

"Kill him, Novak…promise me…save my kid."

"I'll get him."

That was it. Sokolov shut his eyes and lay still, but he still had a pulse. "Where are they? What convent?" Novak said down close to his ear. "You've got to tell me."

He mumbled, but Novak heard him. "In the old church…in phone… hurry…"

Novak jumped to his feet when he heard a distant siren, the shrillness reverberating down through the quiet woods. He told Sokolov to hold on, but the man was no longer moving. Novak ran for his truck, jumping logs and fighting through the thick underbrush. When he was nearly there, the ambulance roared by on the road to the cabin. He figured Sokolov might survive if they got him into surgery in time. He slung his backpack into the front seat, jumped in, and fired the motor. He backed up into the trees and drove hard for the highway. He swerved out onto the blacktop and floored the truck, heading north. He had to get to Petrov before the killer found those girls.

Chapter 25

Novak did not catch Petrov in time. When he reached the official border crossing, the Russian was nowhere in sight. He had used false identity papers and passports and somehow gotten past the Canadian checkpoint. By the time Novak reached Quebec City, with its great battlements and towers of gray stone where it sat on the banks of the St. Lawrence River, Petrov's GPS was moving around the city unimpeded. Novak followed the signal through the modern neighborhoods until he hit a busy thoroughfare called Rue Saint-Jean.

Petrov's Explorer finally stopped a good distance ahead of him, at what was identified as the Hilton Quebec. Novak found the hotel easily enough and pulled into the parking lot. He watched Petrov's SUV, afraid the girls might be inside the hotel. But then Novak decided that murdering two young girls inside a busy hotel was not Petrov's style. Sokolov had said they were at a convent but Novak couldn't find its name or address listed in the burner. There were lots of churches of every denomination in this city, so he started looking for a convent, but had no luck. He kept watching the Explorer, thinking Petrov was inside that hotel arranging his getaway flight to Syria and making phone calls to his Russian cronies in Quebec, trying to locate the girls.

Novak grew more nervous as the minutes ticked by. He had no weapon, and he needed one if he was going to confront Petrov. There was no way he could have gotten through Canadian customs at the border crossing without being searched, so he had wrapped his gun inside a plastic bag and slid it under the front seat of a rusted Pontiac coupe he'd noticed sitting abandoned in a weedy field a few miles south of the Canadian checkpoint. He hoped it would still be there when he got back, *if* he got back. The

Canadian officials had searched his truck thoroughly, studiously polite, but their eyes grew suspicious when they examined the contents of his backpack, especially the medical supplies and GPS trackers and his six emergency burner phones. He explained he'd gotten in the habit of carrying supplies when he was in the Navy and kept it up when he went camping and hiking. They called to check out his name, but bought his cover story well enough to let him pass into their country. They probably shouldn't have.

Sokolov had told him weapons were stashed at his safe house, and Novak had to take time to get them. He could keep an eye on Petrov's location with the GPS, but he hoped to God that the Russian did not head out to murder the girls before he got back. The Explorer hadn't moved, and he doubted that Petrov would take an Uber or call a taxi. A trained operative would not have a driver take him to an intended murder scene, especially not a man who had successfully remained on the run for years. He'd take the SUV when he located the girls, and afterward he'd wipe it clean and abandon it.

Novak did take time to call the Hilton's front desk and ask if a Joseph Lorde was registered there. He spoke to the clerk in French, a language he'd learned well from a year in his youth that he'd spent with his mother's Parisian family. The woman verified that the man had checked in several hours ago, and Novak thanked her and hung up before she could put him through to Petrov's room. He hesitated because he didn't want to lose Petrov, not in a bustling city this size. The burner Sokolov had given him had precise directions to Sokolov's weapons stash inside his safe house, which Novak found about five or six blocks from the hotel. The address was on Rue Saint-Olivier.

Despite the traffic, it didn't take him long to find it. The house looked big and old, built out of the same gray stone so prevalent around the city, and had a big round turret in the same French architecture. It looked as if it had been a grand home at one time, and sat far back off the street. There were shade trees all around it, many hugging the house. He drove up the driveway and parked near the front sidewalk. He sat there and looked around. Nothing moved inside that he could tell, and all the shutters were closed up tight. It occurred to him that Sokolov might have stowed the girls inside with an armed guard. By the time he climbed onto the porch, he dismissed the idea. He had a feeling Petrov knew about this place.

Next to the door, he found a complicated, computerized keypad and several security cameras angled down, where visitors would have to stand in order to ring the doorbell. Other cameras pointed out at the lawn and driveway. Stepan Sokolov was a careful man, but so was Petrov. He checked the GPS signal again and found the Explorer had not moved. Novak was pretty sure Petrov also might have a house or two scattered around the city. If Petrov was on the run, and he was, he would be afraid the Russian government was on to him and surveilling his properties. He wouldn't go to any of them, but he might think it safe to use Sokolov's place. Novak decided Petrov wouldn't waste the time to check it out. It would be safer for him to hole up inside a busy hotel. The Hilton was a place where he'd pass as another nondescript American tourist. Novak had holed up in hotels for the same reason. He poked in the code Sokolov had listed in the burner. Everything clicked into place, and he entered a foyer, one barely lit by dusty light flooding in through the fancy fanlight over the door. No alarms went off. He found the gun collection where he was supposed to, behind a hidden door in the dining room. It was secreted behind a magnificent floor-to-ceiling painting of the Eiffel Tower that swiveled out on a switch. The painting itself looked worthy of the Louvre. Sokolov had made some money in his time. The steel door had a lock similar to the one at the front entrance.

Novak punched in the second sequence of numbers he found in the phone and opened the door. He found a light switch and flipped it on. Then he stared around in disbelief at the sheer number and variety of weapons Sokolov had collected there. It looked like a damn post armory, including powerful sniper rifles, grenades, and even a couple of grenade launchers, as if Sokolov intended to conquer Canada by himself. Every single weapon in that room was illegal to possess anywhere in Canada and would entail a long prison sentence if he were caught. He browsed a few minutes, then chose a Kimber .45 similar to his own, a nice little Glock 19 9mm, and a Remington shotgun.

Once he was armed, Novak carried the weapons out to his truck and drove back to the Hilton. He chose a spot in the parking lot near Petrov's car. It still sat in the same place, fallen leaves scattered on the roof and hood where they'd been before, so Novak was pretty sure Petrov was inside that hotel. As soon as he got a lead on where the girls were hidden, he'd come out and take off with only murder on his mind. Novak tried again and could not find anything about a convent in the phone. He had no idea where they were. There had to be hundreds of churches and seminaries inside a city of Quebec's size, so he'd have to let Petrov do the footwork for him. If he had to guess, he would suppose that Sokolov would choose a Russian Orthodox Church, one well protected by some of Sokolov's former operatives or friends that he could trust, if he even had any friends he could count on. That's what Novak would do. If Petrov found out where they were, he'd go there, and Novak would follow him and get him before he got too close. It was a risk to sit outside and wait, but it was also risky waiting until Petrov found them. Still, it was his only choice. He was unfamiliar with this city. He had no contacts he could utilize.

Daylight waned, the sun faded away, and slowly darkness enveloped the old city. The outside lights around the hotel blinked on, and people came and went, laughing as they stared down at their tourist maps. Novak sat and waited, but he quickly grew impatient. If he was wrong, if Petrov was not inside that hotel calling his cohorts in search of his victims, Novak was making a fatal mistake. He debated going inside and finding his room number, but people were milling about everywhere, and there would be collateral damage no matter how it went down. He decided to wait until midnight before he went inside and found the Russian killer.

At half past ten o'clock, his growing fears were put to rest. Petrov appeared, walking casually out a side entrance, strode out to his car, and unlocked the driver's side door. He looked calm and controlled but had been glancing around the whole time, watching other people in the parking lot. Novak stayed low. When the Russian drove off, Novak followed at a distance. He was ready now. He had several mags of ammo in his coat pockets, and the shotgun lay on the passenger seat, well within his reach. He would take Petrov down tonight, and he hungered for a chance to do it.

Petrov turned onto the Rue Saint-Jean, and Novak came close to losing him in the busy lanes of traffic. He kept him in sight somehow, following him up Avenue de Salaberry, then took a right opposite a big park. Novak got more anxious the farther they went. He kept his speed up so he wouldn't lose him, but kept several cars between them.

Fifteen minutes later, Petrov slowed down and pulled over just past the next big intersection. Novak had pretty much lost his bearings now, but the street was called Rue Aberdeen, and he knew they weren't far off the banks of the St. Lawrence River. Petrov knew exactly where he was going, apparently familiar with the place. When he turned into the entry road of a large church complex, Novak knew he had found the girls. The sign on the front lawn had been painted over and left blank, so it probably wasn't a functioning church. Novak pulled up beside the curb but kept the car idling. Petrov was out of the car now, walking down a concrete sidewalk toward the front portico. He had put on a long tan overcoat. Behind him, Novak could see several outbuildings, cloisters, and the main church with its huge round stained-glass windows. It had to have been a former convent or seminary, definitely a church of some denomination.

Irina and Katerina were inside one of those buildings, and they would soon be dead. Either Petrov had figured out where they were, or somebody had betrayed Sokolov and informed him. When the lights flared on inside the front doors, the big round stained glass window above it glowed with a beautiful depiction of a Russian Orthodox priest at prayer. Then the light hanging over the front door came on, revealing where Petrov was standing. As the red double doors swung open, Novak knew Petrov was going to kill whoever was standing there, along with anybody else he came across inside that church. Before Novak could move, Petrov raised a weapon and shot the woman at the door, point blank in the chest. She went flying back as the retort of the gun echoed across the lawn to Novak.

Novak stamped the accelerator, made a wide turn across the street, jumped the curb, and roared up through the grass toward the front door. Petrov had already disappeared inside. Novak slammed to a stop under the portico, grabbed the shotgun, and jumped out. The woman was sprawled dead inside, her blood running in rivulets into the deep grouting of the white tiles. The nun was dressed in modern attire with only a head scarf. Novak ran from pillar to pillar, keeping them between him and the open foyer. He could not see Petrov.

The church was silent, but the tall doors to the sanctuary stood open, the lights on inside the huge interior. Rows of empty pews led up to an ornate altar. Two halls stretched out to either side of Novak, both pitch black and leading into the depths of the church complex. He stood still and listened for running footsteps, not sure if Petrov was hiding in ambush or on his way to find the girls. A second gunshot told him Petrov was down the hallway on Novak's left. He ran down it, enclosed in darkness. If he was going to die, this would be the place where he'd breathe his last. Only fitting that it was a church. Halfway to the end, he neared a lighted hallway and picked up the awful coppery smell given off by copious amounts of spilled blood.

Seconds later, he rounded a corner and nearly stepped on a second nun lying dead on the floor. Then he heard a bunch of women screaming, and fast-paced footsteps at the other end of the corridor, about thirty feet away from him. A flood of young girls rushed around the corner, shrieking when they saw his gun. They parted around him and ran screaming for the front door. The two girls were not among them. He grabbed the last woman as she ran past. "Where's Irina and Katerina? Tell me before he kills them."

She struggled and shook her head, so he repeated the question in French. Then she answered in kind, frantically trying to pull out of his grip. "Down in the chapel, through the cloisters!"

"Where's the man with the gun now?"

"Going there to get them! Let me go, let me go! He's killing everybody!"

"Get outside and call the police, tell them to get here fast."

She took off after her friends, and Novak ran down the hall from which they'd come. At the end of the corridor, he pushed outside through double doors and found himself on the open-air cloisters. He could barely see in the darkness, but some solar lights along an outdoor path revealed Petrov running toward a small chapel across a short stretch of grass. Novak vaulted the cloister wall and took off after him. He hit the doors into the chapel right after the Russian disappeared inside.

There he found Irina and Katerina, terrified and cowering behind a tall Russian Orthodox priest standing at the front of the church. He was wearing full vestments. They were right in front of the altar, while Petrov was approaching them, striding down the main aisle. His gun was beaded on the priest. Novak yelled his name, trying to draw his attention. Petrov whirled on him and opened fire. Novak dove behind a wood pew and let loose with three quick rounds. Petrov grabbed Katerina, holding the eight-year-old child in front of him for cover. Irina and the priest backed away, the former taking off toward the side door. Petrov saw her and fired. His slug hit her in the back, and she collapsed on the floor. The priest ran to help her. Petrov opened up on Novak again, dragging Katerina backwards and out a door that led to the side lawn.

Novak went after them, the .45 in hand. He went out the door low, but Petrov met him with rapid fire from where he was hidden somewhere in the darkness. When he ran, Novak picked up his position halfway back to his car. Novak fired again and missed, and Petrov turned, holding the little girl as a shield. Katerina seemed petrified, neither screaming nor struggling, just hanging there in front of her captor, her feet dangling well above the ground.

"Let her go, Petrov," Novak shouted. "You're never going to get away. The police are on their way. No reason to kill her now."

Petrov took off again, still gripping the child. Novak couldn't fire or he'd hit Katerina, so he raced after them. Petrov had entered a big garden now, one with a little prayer niche at the end. Novak followed. Then he caught sight of a second priest running toward the man with the girl. This guy had on vestments, but he also had a .357 Magnum gripped in his hand. He did not hesitate to use it. He stopped, braced, and fired at Petrov, the bullet hitting the side of his face as he looked back at Novak. Half his head simply disappeared in that instant, inside a mist of blood and brains blown apart by the direct hit. The child fell to the ground, then scrambled up in a hurry and rushed back toward Novak. She jumped into his arms hard enough to make him stagger backward. He held her close, then pushed her behind him as the priest turned and leveled his weapon on him. Novak pointed his gun at the priest's heart.

"Who are you?" the priest asked in heavily accented English. His inflection was Russian. He was one of them, all right.

"Stepan Sokolov sent me here to get these girls out before Petrov got to them."

"Are you Will Novak?"

Novak nodded, finger ready on the trigger. He didn't know who was who yet, but this guy had shot Petrov, and he hoped that made him a friend.

The Russian lowered his gun. "Yes, good, he told me of you. That you might come for the girls, if he was unable to. Is he dead?"

"He was shot, so he might be by now. Who are you?"

"His contact here. One of my colleagues must have betrayed us and told Petrov where we were. He still has some loyalty among our ranks. Stepan told us to be ready. He feared Petrov would come here to kill the girls."

Novak lowered his own gun reluctantly as the child clung to him, weeping harshly against his back . "What about Irina? Is she dead?"

"She is. I'm sorry. We were here to protect her, and we failed."

A moment later, police sirens shrilled up, far away but nearing. The priest hid his weapon under his cassock. "You can run with the child, but they will catch you before you get out of the city. You will be better served to stay and tell the authorities the truth. I believe your country will back you. I have to ask you to remain silent about us and our cell. Few people know we're here."

"What about those girls I saw? Who are they?"

"We run this place as a haven for runaways. It is our cover until we return to Russia. The girls will have already scattered back to the streets. The rest of us will return to Russia as soon as we can—our mission here is destroyed. Please do not give us away. We will never come back here, not after this."

Since the guy had just saved his life, Novak felt magnanimous. He nodded and picked up Katerina as the priest melted away into the darkness. He patted Sokolov's child's back, trying to calm her. She felt tiny and defenseless in his arms. Novak threw his weapons into some bushes and walked slowly toward the front lawn. Once he rounded the end of the cloisters, law enforcement had arrived. It looked like most of the Quebec City police force had gotten the call. They were jumping out of their patrol cars, multiple high-beamed flashlights and vehicle headlights spotlighting him where he had stopped out on the grass. They began yelling at him in French to get down on the ground. He placed Katerina on her feet, but she quickly crumpled to the grass and curled up in a fetal position. She couldn't stop crying.

Novak raised his hands high, got down on his knees, and tried to look harmless. The cops didn't buy it. They quickly surrounded him, got him on his face in the grass, and cuffed his hands tightly behind his back. Then he was jerked up by the back of his jacket and hustled away. He said nothing to them, and wouldn't, not until he found out his rights. He just hoped to hell that Canadian law gave prisoners one phone call.

Epilogue

Novak cooled his heels in an eight-by-eight jail cell for the next two weeks. He had several court appearances with harsh, severe hanging judges who looked like they wanted to knot the noose around his neck themselves. He said little, even to his assigned Canadian lawyer. He wasn't sure if he was going to get out this time, but at least Canada didn't have the death penalty. The phony priest and his Russian operatives had gotten away clean, he assumed, all of them active spies, the irony of which made him want to laugh, but his predicament was too dire.

The dead women that Petrov had murdered were as yet to be identified. Novak suspected they also had been espionage agents affiliated with the two men dressed as priests. He had his lawyer call Lori Garner at the Pentagon first thing, and he hoped she could come through for him. He wasn't counting on it, thinking she would have little clout in an international incident of this magnitude. His fingerprints had been on the guns they'd found in the bushes, but they also proved he hadn't fired the bullets that had killed anybody.

Katerina had been taken to a Quebec foster home until they could determine who she was and what to do with her. It was a big complicated mess, to be sure, and he was smack dab in the middle with no reasonable explanation of why he was in a foreign country, armed to the hilt with illegal firearms, and in possession of some unknown child. He was expecting to spend a lot of time looking through bars. He hoped Lori could pull enough strings to get him a reduced sentence, but this time, she'd have to be a political genius to do him any good.

Three days later, Lori Garner showed up in Quebec with a lawyer, the American Ambassador up from his office in Ottawa, and a whole sheaf of legal government papers explaining why Novak should be released into her custody. They walked him under guard upstairs to a small interview room. Nobody told him why, but he could tell by their faces they did not like him or his American friends. Inside that room, Lori and one harried attorney and one calm, distinguished man sat waiting at the interview table. At first Lori looked relieved to see he was still on his feet, but that was followed closely by a flush of true anger, which was not totally unexpected.

"Hi, Lori," he said, smiling at her.

She didn't return his greeting. "You're lucky you're not in some prison up at the Arctic Circle."

"But I got you, babe."

Nobody laughed.

"Sit down, Mr. Novak," she said.

Mr. Distinguished turned out to be the Canadian ambassador himself. "You're being released, Mr. Novak, but it's taken a lot of time and effort from our office. They don't want you coming back to this country ever again. You are officially banned from any Canadian territory."

"I can live with that."

He went on to explain in detail a bevy of legal maneuvers that the State Department did not like to have to utilize, especially for a U.S. citizen acting as a vigilante. He told Novak that his exemplary military service and Lori's connections with an important general who had gone to bat for him had made it possible for him to be released into American custody. Otherwise, they might not have bothered. Then he shook his head, and he and the lawyer left Novak alone in that room to face Lori's wrath.

Her harangue started out with a giant but heartfelt sigh. "I just don't know what to say to you, Novak. What do you have to say for yourself? Did you kill Petrov?"

"No, I really can't say who did. It's a matter of honor, I guess. He saved my life and Katerina's, too."

"They're going to want to know."

"I didn't see anything. When Katerina ran out to me, I picked her up and tried to get her away from him before he murdered her, too. He had already shot Irina in the back."

"Yes, I know. That poor girl never had a chance, did she?"

"No, she didn't." Novak asked the question that had been plaguing him. "Did you bring down Blackwood's network?"

For the first time, she looked pleased. "We got him dead to rights. He's sitting in federal prison right now, and all his fancy lawyers are scrambling. The news is full of damaging information coming out about him."

"I don't get much news down in my cell. Just a lot of dirty looks and awful food."

"The bust went down perfectly. We got all of them that we knew of, and the evidence we gathered will be admissible."

"So do I get out of here, or not?"

"Yes, but you're on probation up here, probably forever. By the way, Claire Morgan and Nicholas Black came to your defense as well. Apparently, Nick has a lot of pull with some important folks in Washington."

"That he does. They're good friends. They always have my back." They stared at each other for a moment. "What about you, Lori? Are you going to write me off? You don't look thrilled to be here."

"No, I am not thrilled."

"When do I get released?"

"Not until tomorrow morning. The ambassador and I will escort you onto a U.S. military jet that will fly you back to D.C."

"I've got to get my boat. It's in berth."

"Where?"

"Nantucket."

"Well, you're going to Washington first."

"You're still mad."

"Hell, yes, why wouldn't I be? But I always forgive you, don't I? Besides, I did get a promotion and a lot of prestige out of this whole thing. You'll get some glory, too, once we get you out of Canada. Their government now despises you."

Novak was hesitant to ask the next question. "What about Sokolov? Did he survive?"

"He's going to, we think, but it'll take months to get him back on his feet. Much like it did you after that gunshot blast you took in Guatemala."

"They told me his daughter, Katerina, is in foster care up here with some total strangers."

"I've already arranged for her to be transferred to foster care near her father's hospital. He's in Portland, by the way. Maybe we can drop by and say hello when I get you out of here."

"We? That mean you're okay with all this?"

"Not even close."

"How long do you intend to be mad?"

"At least until we get back home. Then I want that voyage to the Caribbean. I got a month off as a reward for my hard work. I'll decide down there if I forgive you."

"You got it. By the way, I love you for getting me out of here."

"You better love me, after all the trouble I've gone through."

They shared a glance, and then she placed her hand on top of his, which was still handcuffed to the table. He patted hers with his free one. They smiled at each other. Yeah, he loved her. Apparently, she loved him, too. Something was finally going right.

If you enjoyed *The Vanishing Angle*, be sure not to miss all of Linda Ladd's Will Novak series, including

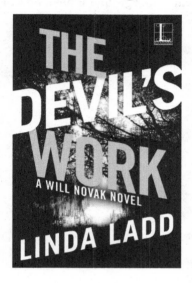

IN THE DARK
A pristine white beach near Sanibel Island, Florida, is an unlikely place for a murder, but that's where Will Novak finds himself, knee-deep in salt water trying to save a life. Maybe the frantic woman is the client he's supposed to meet. But there's no question she's got plenty of powerful enemies. And now they're after Novak, too.

IN THE DETAILS
When he meets her again, her story opens a world of nightmares: captured women, stolen children, and "adoptions" forged in blood and death. The network that tore apart her family stretches across continents and corrupts the forces that should fight against it. And its leaders will do anything to silence her.

IN THE LAST PLACE YOU LOOK
From the alligator-infested waters of the Everglades to the Central American jungle, the fight to stop a ruthless conspiracy—and to find one mother's child—will take Novak to the edge of hell itself . . .

A Lyrical Underground e-book on sale now.

Read on for a special excerpt!

Chapter 1

Off the west coast of Florida, a giant ball of flame sat atop the horizon. Blazing and brilliant, it slowly disappeared into the vast blue reaches of the Gulf of Mexico. Another magnificent Sanibel Island sunset was over, but it left a soft pink glow that colored the beaches. Will Novak was jogging along, nice and steady, heading south toward the Sanibel Lighthouse, when those faint golden spikes turned to black and a single star appeared. He liked sunsets, especially the ones out over the sea, but he was tired and ready to head back to his rental condo. The ocean winds were sweeping in, brisk and bracing, and drying his sweat-soaked skin as he ran along the hard-packed sand. It felt good to have a nice long run. He had been idle for a week, and he needed the surge of energy it gave him.

Few people were around now that the sky show was over, no doubt worn out from a day romping in sun and surf. Lights were blinking on inside the hotels and restaurants he jogged past. When it grew darker along the sand, Novak had the beach to himself, which was the way he liked it. Since he had retired from the military, he had become a loner who enjoyed peace and quiet on the few occasions he actually could get some. His lifestyle made these isolated pools of serenity rare, but now he was ready for some action. Claire Morgan Black, his PI partner, had left him an intriguing voicemail ten days ago, relating news of a case without giving him any details. So he had come to the island and checked into Ocean's Edge, waiting for Claire to make it home from Italy. While he waited, he was to watch for the arrival of a woman named Alcina Castillo and then keep a close eye on her. After that directive, Claire had pretty much ignored his texts. The mystery woman had not shown up. Will wanted the details explaining why he was hanging around that condo and doing nothing. Not that his stay in paradise was any kind of hardship. A beach bum existence was right up his alley, not exactly hell on earth by any stretch of the imagination. Sanibel Island was beautiful, and better yet, it was peaceful and quiet. Now the lights of Fort Myers Beach sparkled across the dark bay, the big luxury high-rise condos and hotels full of tourists. Restaurants over there would be packed with hungry visitors lingering over fresh seafood and imbibing fancy cocktails.

Novak usually ran at night when he was away on assignment. When he was at home in the bayous of Louisiana, he worked out at dawn, on a specific course he'd laid out to increase his speed and strengthen his endurance.

Novak was a big guy, six feet six inches, and weighed 240 pounds. His large size should have affected his ability to react to provocation, but he had worked diligently to overcome that problem and now could surprise opponents by how fast he could move. He couldn't always sustain the quickness, but usually it didn't have to last long to put another man down. It had done him well in many a barroom brawl.

Here he had no reason to tangle with anybody because he spent all day watching for the woman to appear. It was a good gig, he supposed, sitting around on the sand or in his private screened lanai, relaxing, and waiting for something to pop. No such luck thus far. In a nutshell, he was bored. All was quiet, all the time. The other guests looked to be typical tourists doing absolutely nothing unusual or criminal, just nice normal people enjoying hard-earned vacations, so good for them.

Tonight he was ready to hit the sack. He had run longer than he'd meant to, crossing the Sanibel Causeway and jogging down McGregor Boulevard on a circuitous route to Fort Myers Beach and the marina where he'd docked his sailboat. He liked to check it out every day or so. His boat, a Jeanneau Sun Odyssey 379 that he'd had factory-built to accommodate his large frame, was his prized possession. His boat was sleek and fast, a beautiful forty-footer that was comfortable when he sailed south into the Caribbean Sea. He had wanted a big bed he could actually stretch out in.

The *Sweet Sarah* was secured at a berth in the biggest marina he could find because he liked the anonymity of being lost inside a forest of masts, just in case any past enemies were still thinking of exacting payback. It happened now and then, since he had made life miserable for a lot of bad guys, both as an NYPD cop and as a Navy SEAL and now as a private investigator. For obvious reasons, he made a habit of watching his back. Things had looked good over there, his sailboat shining from the scrubbing he'd given her a few days ago and battened down tight. He would have preferred to stay aboard the boat, but Claire didn't do things on a whim. She had a good reason for him to hole up at Ocean's Edge. He just didn't know what it was.

When Claire had left the message, he had already been in Florida waters, which saved time. He'd been anchored up north at Clearwater Beach, where he had been restocking supplies after spending an enjoyable month at sea with Lori Garner. Unfortunately for him, Lori had been called to New Orleans by some family thing and had boarded a plane home in Tampa. He'd met Lori on a job that brought down a corrupt state judge in Galveston, Texas. She'd endured some bad things there, including taking a bullet, but their weeks spent out on the drink had healed that wound. It had been good for him, too.

Lori had promised to rejoin him soon, but Novak wasn't counting on it. He hoped she would. She was younger than him, and it had taken some time getting used to her slangy banter and fierce independence. She was a bit abrasive at times, but somehow that had a way of calming him down. They ended up as lovers out there alone in the vast sea, something he hadn't minded one bit. In fact, he missed her more than he thought he would.

Now he was on his own again, working a case he knew nothing about. The woman he was after was a Guatemalan national. Alcina Castillo was young, barely in her twenties, pretty, dark eyed, and dark haired. Claire was holding her cards close to the vest this time, which was unlike her. He didn't like being kept in the dark much, but maybe Claire didn't know the particulars yet. Perhaps this Alcina woman was supposed to fill them in. He wished to hell somebody would.

By the time he made it to back to the condo, the exterior night-lights lit up the place as bright as day, too bright for people trying to sleep. It was a good thing they turned them off at a reasonable hour. Looking forward to a hot shower and grabbing a bite to eat, all Novak wanted was a good night's sleep with the windows thrown wide so the sound of the pounding surf would soothe him. He was ready to get home to Bonne Terre, the old plantation he had inherited on the day he was born. There was plenty of work he could have been doing on his dilapidated mansion, instead of sitting around here and waiting for something to pop.

Dark and rolling and eternal, the ocean crashed to shore on his right. The breakers were wild and loud, pushed inland by a storm he could see out at sea. The waves curled and crested in pale ghostly lines that stretched down the beach. He slowed when he hit the condo and walked past the four buildings to the nature preserve on the far side. Everything looked peaceful. Nobody was in sight, nothing out of the ordinary, just like every other night when he'd come home from his run. He turned to face the cool ocean breeze and tasted the salt in the air as he sat on the wood bridge that led into the pitch-black, tangled preserve. He sat alone there and let his pulse slow to normal.

A wide strip of small white shells reached out in both directions on the beach. Sanibel Island was world renowned when it came to seashells; at least that's what he'd been told. Storms like the one tonight brought in treasure troves in every hue and shape and color, dredged up from their resting place on the outer shelf that protected the coast. Novak could see flashes of lightning forking down out of backlit clouds to strike the sea.

The Ocean's Edge complex still glowed under soft yellow-infused spotlights on the tan stucco walls. The condo was old but recently refurbished; he liked the 1950s feel of it and the thick walls and private porches. One could walk a matter of feet out its breezeways and wade into the shallows. It was a homey place, and employees were courteous and helpful. It hadn't taken long to figure out which residents were full-time and who was visiting for a week or two. Truth be told, he had settled in with a pair of binoculars and spied on all of his unsuspecting neighbors. Mopping sweat off his face and torso with his forearm, he relaxed there. After letting his body cool down a bit, he kicked off his Nikes and waded out into the surf. He swam about thirty yards out, well past the breakers, and then floated out there on his back, relaxing his muscles and staring at the stars as incoming waves pushed him back to shore. When his feet touched sand, he walked out and sat back down on the bridge.

Novak felt good sitting there alone. He liked the dark and the solitude, and he hadn't had enough of it for the last month. It wasn't that he hadn't enjoyed Lori's company; he had. He hoped she might be waiting at Bonne Terre when he got home. He rarely invited anybody to his plantation—never, actually. He liked her, and they fit together well. She was a former military cop and a trained Army sniper. He liked that about her, too. They understood each other and what had to be done.

When he heard a distant shout, he turned and looked up the beach. He could just barely make out three people, maybe thirty yards away. Nobody else was in sight. In the residual yellow glow that didn't quite light the sand, he could see a big guy heading out toward the water. Problem was, he was dragging what looked like a kid with him. The boy looked young, maybe twelve, maybe even younger. He was no match for the man or his long, angry strides. When the boy fell to his knees, the man just dragged him while the boy attempted to regain his feet. The other person was a woman trying her level best to stop what was going on. She looked even smaller than the kid. They had come out of the first condo building, but Novak didn't recognize them from his surveillance. What it looked like to Novak was a case of domestic violence. The woman grabbed the back of the man's shirt and dug in her heels in a fruitless effort to slow him down. That's when he stopped, spun on her, and shoved her hard enough to put her on her back in the sand.

Novak tensed up. He didn't like that. He didn't like seeing a man beat up on a woman. He didn't care who that guy was or what the problem was. It looked like he was a bully, and he looked twice the woman's size. Novak stood up and watched them. The man had on some kind of leather vest over a white T-shirt. Novak could see the big skull patch on the back of the vest. It appeared the guy might be in some kind of motorcycle gang. Although the woman looked tiny up against him, she had guts. She sprang back up, ran into the surf after the guy, and grabbed his shirt again. Novak started walking toward them. The man grabbed a fistful of the woman's hair and dragged her out deeper into the water. They were all yelling now, screaming stuff that Novak couldn't make out. Their words were flung away with the wind. Nobody inside the complex seemed to notice the altercation, but it was dark at the water's edge and the heavy surf was deafening. Whatever was going down was strictly none of Novak's business. On the other hand, that woman just might be the one he'd been waiting for. She basically fit the description, and she definitely needed help. Maybe his case had finally found him.

The trio was knee deep in the crashing waves. The man and woman were screaming at each other, and then he pushed her away and jerked the kid out deeper. The woman didn't give up. That's when the man backhanded her, knocking her backward under the water. A big wave hit them and took her bodily in toward the beach. Then the man concentrated on the kid. He held him under so long that Novak knew he meant to drown the boy. Novak took off running toward them as the kid flailed desperately but ineffectually.

The woman had fought her way back to them and was slugging the big guy in the back with one fist and trying to pull the kid's head out of the water with the other. She jumped on the bully's back, but he shrugged her off like a bothersome gnat and held the boy submerged. At that point, Novak was dead certain that man was going to drown them both. They didn't see Novak coming. That was good for Novak but bad for the big thug. Novak grabbed the guy by the back of his vest and spun him around. Novak had better luck getting the guy's attention than the woman had.

Shocked by the force of Novak's grip, the man dropped his victim in a hurry. Novak had learned a long time ago never to waste time or expend undue effort in a fistfight. If you're going to mess it up with somebody, mess it up hard and fast. He doubled his right fist and punched the guy in the nose, a hard, quick jab, the kind that put all the strength in your shoulder behind it and would send blood gushing like a geyser. Let a bully face a man bigger and stronger, a man who gave no quarter and played by no rules, and see how long he lasted. Novak's blow was brutal enough to knock the guy off his feet. He went over backward and under the water and came up choking on the blood and the briny seawater.

Novak felt the urge to hold him under the way he'd done to the boy, let him endure the kind of panic the boy had no doubt felt as his breath ran out, but decided to forgo that unless it became necessary. Sometimes a punch that brutal would end the game before it got started. Novak shoved the goon under again, and the guy floundered around a bit, perhaps drowning, but maybe not. Novak didn't really care, but he got a hold on the back of the stupid leather vest and towed the limp man back onto the beach. He dropped him on his face in the sand, where he lay hacking and strangling.

Once the guy got his breath back, he unwisely decided it would be a good idea to engage Novak. That meant he was not only a big bully but stupid, too. Novak watched him struggle to stand up and then stagger drunkenly around with his fists up like a gentleman boxer in the 1890s. He threw a punch so wild that Novak didn't have to move, but then his opponent made the mistake of grabbing Novak's arm. So Novak sent another hard jab into the guy's solar plexus. That did the trick. The guy grabbed his belly, gasping and coughing, and appeared to pass out on his back in the shallows. Novak dragged him up farther onto the sand, dropped him there, and then looked around for the woman and kid. He was pretty sure now that they were Claire's clients. He could barely see them. They were hightailing it up the deserted beach at a full run.

Novak started out after them, curious as to what the hell was going on. His gut was telling him that the woman was Alcina Castillo, so he needed to catch up with her and get her the hell out of danger. Wherever that hooligan had come from, there were bound to be others incoming and dressed just like him. They liked to travel around in packs. About ten yards up the beach, he heard them behind him. He turned around. Two guys were running straight at him. A third guy was kneeling beside their bleeding buddy. They all had on those skull vests. Novak stood his ground and waited for them to reach him. Both were bigger than the first guy, but neither had weight or height on Novak. They didn't look particularly strong or intimidating. They looked like the kind of guys who needed guns to take care of business because they couldn't fight their way out of a paper bag. They also looked like the type who would use those guns to hunt for victims in numbers, like timber wolves.

Novak was unarmed, which was unusual for him, but he'd jogged the beach every night since he'd arrived with no problems. It was a tame tourist area and not known for serious criminal activity. That was about to change, but Novak could mess it up with the best of them, and he could disarm these two kids any day of the week. His military training often came in handy. So he stood and waited for them to get close enough to put down.

They had the smarts to pull up a couple of yards away and point their Ruger semiautomatics at his bare chest. In the condo's lights, Novak ascertained that one man looked to be Hispanic, but the other one was definitely Caucasian. Both had heavy beards and long ponytails tied at the nape and more tats on their bare arms than a Folsom Prison lifer. To Novak, they looked more like frat boys at a Hells Angels party. They didn't threaten him verbally, which surprised Novak, judging from his past encounters with similar types who liked to scream out profane threats and cocky bravado.

"You got a problem?" he asked them, already on the balls of his feet and ready to move, only waiting for one of them to step in closer. These sorts always came closer so they could attempt to intimidate him. These two didn't. Instead, the short Hispanic man said, "Shut up and start walking. Down that way." He motioned toward the nature preserve with his gun.

"How about telling me why I should do that?"

The speaker wore a gang-inspired black-and-yellow bandanna tied across his forehead. He had lots of badges on his vest, mainly skulls and crossbones in various configurations to match the big one on his back. The name Mario was embroidered across the front. The other guy's said Larry. That wasn't smart at all. If they were going out to perpetrate crimes like drowning women and children, they shouldn't wear their names on their clothes. These guys were stupid, all right, but definitely members of a gang. Novak needed to know which gang it was; he'd found out the hard way that these sorts of clubs posed different threat levels.

Mario said, "Just start walking, unless you want us to end you right here."

"Maybe you should tell me where we're going?"

"You just asking for a beatdown, aren't you, dude?" That was the white guy, getting in on the fake bluster.

Novak hated it when somebody called him dude; it was just a little quirk he had. Unless it was Lori Garner, who loved to spill out all kinds of social media crap and abbreviations he'd never heard of, but he liked her and she was good looking, so she got away with it. These two didn't appeal to him. "I'm not going anywhere with you, so get the hell out of my face before I take that gun and shove it up your ass."

What that got him was Mario's gun barrel jammed up under his chin. A mistake, that was. Novak moved so fast that the younger guy was caught flat-footed. Ducking to his left, he snatched the gun out of the man's hands before he could even move, then slammed it hard against his cheekbone. He shoved him to the ground and beaded the Ruger on the other guy's face. This one was not so circumspect and pulled his trigger in panic.

Novak felt the burn of the bullet on his left biceps. It barely tagged his arm, so he ignored that and disarmed the second guy and then knocked him unconscious with a hard uppercut with the Ruger. Unfortunately, the condo lights went out about the time two more gangbangers showed up out of the dark and grabbed Novak from behind. He managed to throw one off but was now outnumbered by three. So he gave it up, stood still, and put his hands up as a gun barrel was thrust hard into his kidneys.

Lucky for him, they didn't shoot him right then and there. That was a mistake on their part. It probably meant they weren't used to murdering people in cold blood, or maybe they didn't want to do it in front of a four-building condo complex. Maybe they thought drowning was less noticeable. They started prodding him down the beach with four weapons pointed at him, front, back, and either side, boxing him in as tightly as Secret Service agents guarding a president. They stopped next to the first guy Novak had put down, who was still wallowing and moaning in the shallows.

Fingering the flesh wound on his arm, Novak decided it was nothing to worry about. He glanced at the condo complex, hoping for signs of concerned residents dialing 911, but no such luck. It was pretty much dark. Surf was too loud and the beach was too dark. Maybe he'd get lucky and some Good Samaritan hiding behind closed curtains had already summoned the cops. He listened for the shriek of sirens, but no luck there, either. He was on his own with a gang of incompetent but heavily armed little bullies. Not such good odds. Still, they had picked the wrong victim this time. He would wait until he got the chance and then take them down as best he could. He could take one of their guns easily enough, no problem. That would even things up considerably, so he said nothing and did what he was told.

This whole altercation was all about the woman and boy, no doubt about it. Both had disappeared into the darkness and hopefully headed somewhere safe. These guys were not well-trained military personnel by any stretch of the imagination, but they weren't Eagle Scouts, either. They weren't as tough as they liked to think, but they knew how to pull a trigger, had already done so, and that made them dangerous and unpredictable. He would make his move at the right time and find out how tough they really were. Fortunately, they made no move to tie him up, thinking it was over and he was afraid of them.

One particularly annoying guy kept jabbing Novak in the back with his gun barrel. They were taking him into that nature preserve, which would be a damn good place to kill him and leave his corpse to rot hidden under thick tropical undergrowth. There were plenty of beach houses and hotels all over Sanibel Island, but most places were hidden from the main roads by these kind of natural thickets, which meant lots of places to murder at will and in private. Still, once out on the street, a gang of men marching a guy at gunpoint ought to draw someone's attention sooner or later, unless they were planning a quick bullet in the head once they got him off the beach. Instead of murdering him when they should have, they walked him over the bridge and down a dark path into the preserve. Nobody said a word as the sound of the ocean subsided, muffled by thick vegetation and palms and palmettos. The night was impenetrable black, but they herded him along and seemed to know where they were going. He wondered what they were waiting for and why they hadn't brought flashlights. Nobody would ever accuse them of being geniuses. Novak strained his eyes but couldn't see his hand in front of his face. All he had to do was take one down, get his gun, and they'd all be dead in minutes. They were pathetic, really. He walked along inside their ranks and tried to remember how the path meandered from the times he'd been in there before. Once he had his bearings, he took a deep breath, poised to make his move.

High-powered beams suddenly flashed on all around them, blinding Novak and his captors. Dark figures burst out from behind the lights. Shocked, Novak didn't have time to duck down, but it didn't matter because the assault was not about him. Whoever these guys were, they were quick and efficient and knew exactly what they were doing. Within minutes, his not-so-tough captors were on the ground, bloodied up and unresponsive. Novak was the last man standing. Then he heard a woman whispering. He started to turn toward her, but something slammed hard into the back of his skull. He went down on his hands and knees and wobbled there, trying to right the tilting ground as the flashlight beams swung about and further disoriented him. He couldn't quite get his mind to work before the second blow hit him in the same place. After that, he was out for the count, unconscious well before his face hit the ground.

About the Author

Linda Ladd is the bestselling author of over a dozen novels, including the Claire Morgan series and the Will Novak novels. She makes her home in Missouri, where she lives with her husband. She loves traveling and spending time with her grandsons and granddaughter. In addition to writing, Linda enjoys target shooting and is a good markswoman with a Glock 19 similar to her fictional detectives. She loves to read, play tennis and board games, and watch fast-paced action movies. She is currently at work on her next novel. Learn more at lindaladd.com.

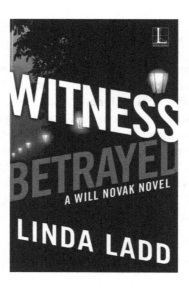

NO FRIENDS

Mardi Gras whips New Orleans' French Quarter into a whirlpool of excess, color, booze, noise, motion. So the woman in the sights of Will Novak's binoculars stands out. She's bruised, barefoot, wearing a man's raincoat. And she's looking right at him.

NO FAITH

In a moment she's fleeing into the crowd, but Novak knows she's not gone for good. When she comes back, it's with a gun to his head—and a story about crony politics, a crooked judge, a kidnapped whistleblower, and children in deadly danger. Novak can't let this one slide.

NO FURY

Through the grit of Houston's underbelly to the grime below Beverly Hills' glamour, a trickle of rot connects the powerful to the desperate and corrupts the men and women who are supposed to stand against it. Deceit is everywhere. If he's going to do right, Novak is going to have to do it alone . . .

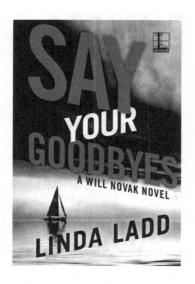

SAY YOU'RE DREAMING

When a scream wakes Will Novak in the middle of the night, at first he puts it down to the nightmares. He's alone on a sailboat in the Caribbean, miles from land. And his demons never leave him.

SAY YOUR PRAYERS

The screams are real, though, coming from another boat just a rifle's night scope away. It only takes seconds for Novak to witness one murder and stop another. But with the killer on the run and a beautiful stranger dripping on his deck, Novak has gotten himself into a new kind of deep water.

BUT DON'T SAY YOUR NAME

The young woman he saved says she doesn't know who she is. But someone does, and they're burning fuel and cash to chase Novak and his new acquaintance from one island to the next, across dangerous seas and right into the wilds of the Yucatan jungle. If either of them is going to live, Novak is going to need answers, fast—and he's guessing he won't like what he finds out . . .

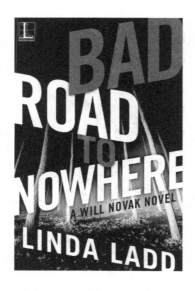

BAD MEMORIES

Not many people know their way through the bayous well enough to find Will Novak's crumbling mansion outside New Orleans. Not that Novak wants to talk to anyone. He keeps his guns close and his guard always up.

BAD SISTER

Mariah Murray is one selfish, reckless, manipulative woman, the kind Novak would never want to get tangled up with. But he can't say no to his dead wife's sister.

BAD VIBES

When Mariah tells him she wants to rescue a childhood friend, another Aussie girl gone conveniently missing in north Georgia, Novak can't turn her down. She's hiding something. But the pretty little town she's targeted screams trouble, too. Novak knows there's a trap waiting. But until he springs it, there's no telling who to trust . . .

Printed in the United States
by Baker & Taylor Publisher Services